Paper and Rags

Local author, **Morgan Wade**, brings history to life again in his second historical fiction, **'Paper & Rags'**, (released December 2019), part of a hoped for trilogy set in Kingston during the early 1800s. His first, **'Bottle and Glass'** focused on the behaviors prevalent in the 1812 community during a period of war causing great distress and deprivation. His second, **'Paper & Rags'**, illuminates not only the dissemination of news within Kingston but reveals the wide discrepancy between life lived by those with means and those without.

Local Book Clubs would do well to invite Morgan to share his experiences of discovery of the conditions of his home community during these earlier years of struggle and growth. NPY

Paper and Rags

Morgan Wade

[signature]

DEC. 2019

First Edition

Hidden Brook Press
www.HiddenBrookPress.com
writers@HiddenBrookPress.com

Paper and Rags
by Morgan Wade

Cover Design – Richard M. Grove
Layout and Design – Richard M. Grove

Typeset in Caslon OS
Printed and bound in Canada
Distributed in USA by Ingram,
          in Canada by Hidden Brook Distribution

Library and Archives Canada Cataloguing in Publication

Title: Paper and rags / Morgan Wade.
Names: Wade, Morgan, 1971- author.
Identifiers: Canadiana (print) 20190196734
          Canadiana (ebook) 20190196769
          ISBN 9781927725894 – (softcover)
          ISBN 9781927725900 – (EPUB)
          ISBN 9781927725917 – (Kindle)
Classification: LCC PS8645.A334 P37 2019 | DDC C813/.6—dc23

A news-writer is a man without virtue who writes lies at home for his own profit. To these compositions is required neither genius nor knowledge, neither industry nor sprightliness, but contempt of shame and indifference to truth are absolutely necessary...

Samuel Johnson, former news-writer

Liberty will have become extinct when an Editor of a Public Print who performs his duty with impartiality and spirit, shall cease to be regarded as an invaluable member of society.

Inscription from a silver cup presented in June 1825 to Hugh C. Thomson, Esq., editor of the Upper Canada Herald, by a group of Kingstonians calling themselves the 'Friends of Free Discussion'.

NECKCLOTHITANIA

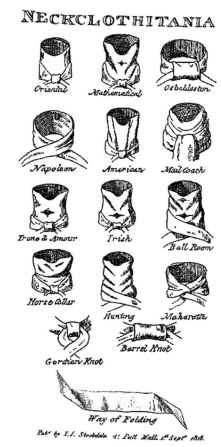

Oriental

Mathematical

Osbaldeston

Napoleon

American

Mail Coach

Trone à Amour

Irish

Ball Room

Horse Collar

Hunting

Maharatta

Barrel Knot

Gordian Knot

Way of Folding

Pub^d by I.I. Stockdale. 4: Pall Mall 1st Septr 1818.

Trone d'Amour Tie.

The *trone d'Amour* is the most austere after the Oriental Tie—It must be extremely well stiffened with starch.† It is formed by one single horizontal dent in the middle. Color, *Yeux de fille en extase*.

Irish Tie.

This one resembles in some degree the Mathematical, with, however, this difference, that the horizontal indenture is placed *below* the point of junction formed by the collateral creases, instead of being above. The color, *Cerulean Blue*.

* So called from its resemblance to the Seat of Love.

† Starch is derived from the Teutonick word, "Starc" which means "stiff."

Ball Room Tie.

The Ball Room Tie when well put on, is quite delicious — It unites the qualities of the Mathematical and Irish, having two collateral dents and two horizontal ones, the one above as in the former, the other below as in the latter — It has no knot, but is fastened as the Napoleon. This should never of course be made with colors, but with the purest and most brilliant *blanc d'innocence virginale*.

Horse Collar Tie.

The Horse Collar has become, from some unaccountable reason, very universal. I can only attribute it to the inability of its wearers to make any other. It is certainly the worst and most vulgar, and I

Illustration engraved by George Cruikshank appearing in Neckclothitania or Tietania, being an essay on Starchers, by One of the Cloth (published by J.J. Stockdale, Sept. 1st. 1818).

Rags! Rags!

Cash and the highest price paid for
CLEAN
COTTON AND LINEN

RAGS,

AT THIS OFFICE.

———

A QUANTITY OF

WRITING PAPER,

Of Quality No. 1 and No. 2,
for SALE AT THIS OFFICE

PART ONE

Chapter One
August 1817

The pit smelled of millet and blood. At the railings, men shouted profanities through a veil of dust and feathers. Below, a boy grabbed the losing bird by the hackles and flipped it into a bin.

Carmichael Jones stepped down from the tier. He shoehorned himself into the front ranks five and six deep, nudging Owen Stevens as he passed. A finger of ale sloshed from his blackjack to the tailor's sleeve.

"Packed like pilchards, ain't we?"

Receiving no answer, Carmichael looked up and down the railing.

"Forgive my sentiment but it's a tender sight. You and I standing here with our fellow citizens, tailors and ploughmen, lawyers and postmasters, all together, shoulder to shoulder. Slop sellers aside squires."

Stevens made no reply. He stared glumly into the pit.

"A great leveler," Carmichael concluded. "The cocking main."

The setters walked the perimeter of the pit, whispering encouragement into the ear holes of their champions. Each hugged their bird close with one gloved hand. From the other, they fed them a mixture of port-soaked barley. They met at the centre and brought the birds beak to beak, holding them fast to prevent broken wing joints. Catching the scent, the roosters struggled against their handlers, desperate to gore the other bird.

"Look." Carmichael pointed at the band of buff around the spangler's neck. "Reckoner wears a white cravat. He resembles your Dr. Scriven."

Stevens looked back into the saloon where Dr. Scriven sat with his copy of the Gazette, sipping porter, as far from the action as possible without being out on the street. Stevens turned back to the pit and rested his chin on the railing. Carmichael slapped his shoulder.

"What's nibbling you?" he cried. "It's the fights!"

The setters returned to their corners and released the birds for parade. Biscuit, the tavern's proprietor, made the introductions.

"Spartacus, a black clipper with white fringes, entered by Mr. McWhorter. Reckoner, a duck wing spangler, Mr. Robinson's pride."

Spartacus extended himself to full height and displayed his coal-tinted chest. He emitted a low growl. Reckoner strutted, unconcerned.

"Listen," Carmichael said. "I've something to cheer you up. You see the one that looks like Scriven, that fancy prancer?"

Stevens nodded. Carmichael looked over his shoulder and lowered his voice.

"I shouldn't tell you this," he said, lowering his tone. "That's Barney Doody's game cock. The one that was abducted. The one that's had the pips."

Stevens stared. Carmichael wondered if he'd taken his meaning.

"Spartacus," he said. "The clipper. A sure thing."

"What good is it to me?" Stevens' face reddened with resentment. "I've no stake."

"You must find one."

"Scriven won't make no more advances."

They watched as Reckoner raised his hackles and swished his tail.

"That spangler pirouettes," Carmichael said. "But, credit me, the beast is pipped from comb to spur."

"I've nothing in my pocket but thread ends."

"Payoffs this certain come but once a lifetime."

"You could lend me some."

Carmichael snorted.

"I've invested every last groat. I'd wager my mother's soul, were she here."

Stevens groaned.

"They're still at parade," Carmichael said. "Find a stake."

≈ ≈ ≈ ≈ ≈

"None of these cowards use their own name," Scriven said, from behind his copy of the Gazette. "They sign their over-long screeds Vindicator, or Joel Corn-Cob, or Timothy Peaseblossom or some such nonsense. Like the ridiculous names of those birds."

Stevens stood before the doctor, combing the fine fingers of his right hand through his side-whiskers, accentuating the sharpness of his features.

"Creedence," he said.

"This is more like it." The doctor flicked at a

column. "Notice of the next lodge meeting at Walker's. Hugh Thomson is making a presentation about paper currency. Always Hughie bloody Thomson. You'll be there of course?"

A cheer rose up from the pit. The handlers brought the two birds together, goading them until they pecked.

Stevens looked back over his shoulder. He clasped one empty hand in the other and knit them together. He swung back to Scriven.

"Creedence, they're about to get fighting again," he said.

"This might be worth a tickle," Scriven said, returning to the Gazette. "Mrs. Inchbald's Animal Magnetism was quite good last week. Not at all bad for a lady playwright."

"Creedence," Stevens said again, his voice rising in tandem with the noise escalating from the cockpit. "Could you make me another advance? A shilling or two?"

"What happened to the earlier one?"

"The Tartar wasn't t'all as advertised. Quailed like a ..."

"Quail?"

Stevens forced a smile.

"Surely these are the vagaries of sport."

"I have inside information."

Back in the pit, Biscuit called for final wagers. Stevens turned instinctively. He jammed a hand into his empty pocket, stepped toward the railings, and stopped, remembering he still hadn't a stake. He whirled back on Scriven.

"You'll want a fresh cravat," he cried, desperation ratcheting the pitch of his voice.

"I have a full complement."

"I can't lose. It's a clinch."

"Better luck next time."

"New cuffs?"

"Grover & Lewis," Scriven read from the Gazette. "Commenced the above business... three doors north of the market, at the sign of the gold watch... do work on the shortest notice... etcetera..."

"I'll pay you back this evening, with interest!"

"...in a superior style, fitted to any fashion... furnished at the shop finer than any that can be procured in town..."

Stevens brought his fist down on the table. The glass of porter wobbled, fell, and discharged its last mouthful.

Scriven let a corner of the paper drop. He met Stevens' eye.

"Does Kingston need another ha'penny tailor?" Stevens cried.

"Owen," Scriven said, his voice rich with indulgence, "have I not been your best customer?"

Stevens straightened.

"Did I not sponsor your membership at old St. John's?"

Stevens stood the porter glass upright. He mopped the ale with his sleeve.

"Did I not find you a young apprentice and seamstress?"

Stevens bowed his head.

"Perhaps," Scriven said, folding his Gazette. "I'll pay Grover & Lewis a visit and see what they have."

A great roar erupted from the pit. Stevens turned. He watched as Spartacus flew at Reckoner, leading with the twin arcs of his silver spurs. The two tangled at the wing folds, bladed feet cycling madly, beaks chiseling at the other's hackles. Bristling black and white, they whirled like tumbleweed from one corner to the other, back and forth. Dust and down flurried above their heads. The men leaned over the railings, faces contorted with vicarious fury, longing for a clear, cathartic decision.

Finally, the birds separated in a whir of plumes, tails and vanes. Already Reckoner limped. His ruffled head jigged. His dilated eyes swivelled. He panted through his gaping beak. Stevens imagined the spangler had just then discovered what he already knew, what Carmichael knew, what the savvy punters knew: his last match would be brief.

Having recovered his breath, Spartacus jumped, spread his wings, and soared high above his maimed opponent. As he alighted, he plunged one of his spurs straight through Reckoner's neck. The punters thrust their faces into the feral mist to feel the gusts of buffeted air, to taste the salty iron. They received sacraments of hot blood, flaming ellipses blotted against trembling cheeks.

Stevens could see Carmichael shouting ecstatically from the railings, his raised fist clenching a winning chit.

"I think I'll move on to the Bottle and Glass," Scriven said as he passed by Stevens, the Gazette tucked under his arm. "I told you. The fights hold no attraction for me."

Stevens shuffled to the bar and took a stool. He planted his elbow on the counter and laid his cheek in his palm. He stared back at the jubilation.

Horatio, Biscuit's own red and black Tartar, retired veteran of seventeen undefeated matches, hobbled along the bar top. He clucked and pecked from the silver chalice put out for him, sipping from his pension, a twelve-year-old French brandy. He bent his feathered head and aimed a reptilian eye at the tailor.

"Damn Scriven!" Stevens cried as the doctor disappeared out the front door. "A harpy's curse on that old, preening bird!"

"Spot of bad luck?"

The man on the next stool spoke with an Irish brogue. He pocketed his winnings into his vest and extended his hand.

"Rupert Spafford," he said.

Stevens grasped Spafford's offered hand and felt the thumb press into his first and second knuckles. A flash of understanding passed between them. Stevens dug his own thumb into Spafford's opposing knuckles. He introduced himself.

"Who was that fellow you just bade such a fond farewell?" Spafford asked.

Stevens escaped the grip. He studied Spafford's face.

"Brother Stevens," Spafford said, "I mean no harm. I'm of the opinion that a fellow should be able to level imprecations at whomever he likes, especially in the throes of a cocking main, particularly in an outpost such as this, at civilization's edge, at the very elastic tip of society's whalebones."

Spafford sprayed a handful of port-soaked millet across the bar top. Horatio nodded forward to tidy up.

"Besides," he continued, "I'm freshly arrived."

"And what brought you," Stevens asked.

"To retrieve, from the widow, what is rightfully mine. The Willowpath estate."

"One of those Spaffords."

"Nephew to the late Colonel. The same cove what had his head spun by the young, blonde dollop. Amelia, he called her."

"That all got sorted last year."

"Not to my satisfaction."

Spafford plucked a shilling from his vest, clapped it on the counter, and slid it toward Stevens.

"Perhaps you might be of assistance. Directing me to the offices of the Gazette. Introducing me to other lodge members."

Stevens regarded the slight Irishman a moment. He glanced at the shilling. He pocketed the coin.

"Could do."

"I wonder," Spafford said. "The chap that just left. Pompous and impeccably dressed. Might he be *Creedence Scriven*, physician of Bournemouth?"

"The same."

"I knew him back home. Or, knew of him. Rather notorious. Bit of a scandal."

Stevens leaned in.

"I could send home for the papers. But if you're interested now I can give you the gist. Another pint?"

Spafford ordered a pair of porters. Stevens clapped his shoulder.

"Welcome to Kingston," he said, "brother Spafford."

Chapter Two

Cranston emerged, a salver balanced on his gloved palm. Upon the tray, the latest Gazette, crisply folded. Scriven pulled the high collar of his blouse taut and wound it with a rectangle of snowy linen. He took the paper and then his seat.

"Your cravat, sir?"

Scriven crossed one knee over the other.

"A moment."

Cranston retreated to the shadow.

"It's a dreadful cabbage scrap this Gazette," Scriven said.

"Your fine columns excepted, sir."

Scriven sniffed his assent.

"By God, these so-called correspondents like the look of their own printed words."

"Sir."

"They argue who is a vile calumniator and who is merely scurrilous. They compete to see who can most elegantly and most elaborately call the other an ass."

"Indeed."

Scriven flipped the page.

He read this:

Public Service:

Your humble correspondent begs to inform subscribers of unsettling reports. Some persons of ill-repute have lately arrived in our fair town. Scoundrels known to frequent disorderly houses, to keep company with catamites. We urge inhabitants not to let the corruption of the old world infect the new. Do not be fooled by filth wrapped in fancy packaging and bow. Forthwith, we intend to obtain more information as to the identity of this villain and, when we do, we will share it with all due haste. In the meantime, be vigilant.

Watchfully,

Opprobrious

The paper fluttered. Scriven twisted his neck, looking instinctively for Cranston, to gauge his expression. The man was behind him, in the shadows, unseen. Scriven returned to the page and stared. Was that a secondary crease in the Gazette? Had it been previously read and refolded?

"Sir?"

How was it possible? How could a rumour cross an entire ocean? Surely he'd outrun it, venturing this far into the wilds of Upper Canada, to the shores of this vast, prelapsarian lake. Had it stowed away in the hold of one of the many packets crossing each week? Dormant until landfall and then communicated up the river like a pestilence?

Heat flushed Scriven's face. The ambergris paste he'd applied began to melt, making his forehead slick and shiny.

Who is Opprobrious? Coward with an overblown moniker. What does he know? What grudge does he bear?

It was a house call. That's all. The mother had come. Hadn't seen her son in weeks. The boy — a man, really — had been absent from his job at the bakery. Last seen entering the house on Windward St. where, it was said, there were peculiar happenings. Tinctures obtained. Services rendered.

Go see him, the mother had pleaded. You know him. You're a physician. Make sure he is well. Convince him to come home. That's all it was.

"Sir?"

"Mm?"

"Your cravat?"

Scriven no longer held the Gazette open. It had collapsed onto his breech fronts.

"Yes. Of course."

"May I?"

Cranston took the crumpled Gazette from Scriven's hand as he stood. He smoothed it, refolded it along the original crease, and returned it. He stepped close, his fingers at Scriven's neck. Close enough that Scriven could smell the bitter orange on his breath. As Cranston tied, Scriven studied his face. He was sure he read something different in the man's usually expressionless face. A buoyancy in the angle of the brow and the tilt at the mouth corner. Not a smirk exactly.

The cravat tied, Cranston met Scriven's eye.

Scriven flinched. He returned his attention to the paper he clutched.

"That will be all," he said.

It's nothing. A vague banter, poorly written. None have likely read it, none that matter. He would speak to the publisher, Stephen Miles, about the wisdom of unattributed slander.

He looked up, determined to present insouciance. Cranston had already receded into the shadows.

Scriven crossed to the chiffonier. He dipped the dozen teeth of the ox horn into the indigo, eased them into the thatch at the back of his head, and combed them forward until he could no longer detect a single strand of grey. He slicked the spray of hair into place with bear fat pomade, scented with sandalwood. Leaning into the mirror he dabbed the dye from his temples and the sheen of his crown, where hair no longer grew. With tweezers, he excised strays from ears, nose, and brow. He applied magistery of bismuth, filling in pits and crevices.

He gazed again. He didn't see a quacksalver, soon to be fifty, his remaining hair gathered and pushed. He didn't see Dr. Creedence Scriven in the mirror, under-engaged and indifferent physician, unacknowledged playwright and novelist, youngest son of Lord Robert Scriven. He saw Cicero in his eloquent prime, holding forth, destroying another tyrant. Or Voltaire, in the distinguished dusk of life, at the centre of his Ferney court, accepting with grace and wit the plaudits following his latest dramatic triumph.

Scriven raised a perfumed hand to the mirror.

Enough, he mouthed to his pretended audience.

He penetrated a final time, deep into the chestnut irises of the wide-eyed reflection. With his stare, he pinned the other man down, interrogating, daring him to move. He didn't trust him, despite the reflection's impeccable sense of dress.

Who are you?

He received no satisfactory reply. The fine paste he'd applied to his cheeks had left his face an empty canvas. He was now a thousand miles from Bournemouth. An ocean and half a continent between him and the unpleasantness. A new page.

Knotted and jacketed, Scriven tucked the Gazette under his arm and stepped into the glare of the street.

Chapter Three

The needle, curved from a century of use, slid past the thimble into a cushion of unprotected thumb. Lilac pulled her hand from under the hem and brought it to her lips. She licked the crimson bead from the whorl. Another one slowly formed. When it stopped expanding, she studied it. She noted its colour and sheen, glinting in the light of the dirty tallow. She studied the dawdling discharge. The pain subsided.

She jabbed the needle back in. This time, she didn't flinch. She waited for the crimson. She jabbed again. And again. An arc of new spots bubbled up. A tiny necklace of dark garnet.

Lilac had sought to escape a life of hand-gnarling, eye-dimming penury when she'd left her native Cardiff. When she'd boarded HMS Lancer, she'd expected to see the world. And the possibility of becoming... what? Bo'sun's wife? Captain's prettiest boy? She'd found only deck after deck of poxy men and sodden wood.

There had been good times: food and drink, riotous music and lusty choruses, sweaty dances. Plenty of bumbo. She could forget herself.

The men, they weren't so bad. She'd called them brothers. They tossed her a few groats, a strip of salt beef, a square of hard tack, in exchange for an impatient grappling, worrying a grimy hammock like cats trapped in burlap. Afterward, drowsy and spent, they spared her hardly a word. But they taught her how to smoke a pipe and to play cards. They kept her fed and warm.

And the rum. It also warmed.

She'd got on well with the surgeon, Carruthers. While the other wives gossiped around the scuttlebutt, she'd learned more from Carruthers than she'd ever thought possible. About setting fractures and applying compresses. About the importance of antiseptics. Carruthers had specifically sought her out for assistance in the serious cases. The amputations and the application of the dreadful lithotome. Olive, her only friend on board, had fainted seeing stones cut from a bladder. She'd needed salts herself and a bandage for her head. Lilac wasn't squeamish.

Stevens called from the showroom.

Mother Bunch! They'd almost performed a caesarean. To this day Lilac believed it would have saved the lives of both the pilot's wife and her baby. Afterall, she'd just read in the tailor's beer-dampened copy of last month's Gazette about a successful caesarean performed by a British army surgeon in Cape Town.

Stevens called again.

One of the men, Jeremy Castor, had taught her to read. He'd sat with her below decks and between drills, when he could have been snoozing or playing cards. He would break the longer words into manageable bundles, warming them with the glow of his rich, Cornish baritone, presenting each as though they were gifts. Not once had he foisted himself, despite the surreptitious glances he'd made above the hemline and below the neckline. And she'd made many affordable offers. A tanner or a half ration. It had to be something, or she'd set a dangerous precedent. Always he'd politely declined. It was not for nothing that he earned his nickname: Deacon. She remembered the heat that came from his arm, his neck, as she, sitting next to him on a coil of rope, looked over his shoulder at the open page. She remembered the smell of leather, powder, salt.

Stevens was shouting now. Lilac thrust her needle into the apple shaped pin cushion and draped the fabric over the chair. She entered the showroom sucking her thumb.

"Wadding goes in collars," Stevens said, his voice pitched high, "not your ears."

Lilac shrugged.

"Come," he said. "I need a model. You're Mrs. Herchmer's size."

She was everyone's size. Mrs. Davies. Mrs. Reynolds. Mrs. Charbonneau. Never mind that Mrs. Herchmer was shorter by a half foot and forty-five inches of hip; fat as a butcher's wife.

"Come," Stevens said again.

He curled the fingers of his diminutive hands together in front of his face as though he might groom his whiskers. His yellow nails, long enough to prise pins from hemlines, clacked together. He nodded at her shift and flicked an eyebrow.

"Off."

Lilac looked at the gown draping the dummy. She didn't move.

"Buck fitches!" Stevens cried. "As leather-headed as the boy. Off, or I scissor it."

She met his black, irisless eyes. They held a moment, narrowing, darkening further. They darted, alighting on her midriff.

He didn't frighten her. She'd dealt with men far less civilized on the Lancer. Stevens had hands as soft as sateen. She towered over him, with his rounded shoulders and tailor's hunch. She could cinch his arrow-shaped head in the crook of her arm and twist.

"Let the dummy model it," she said.

"'Tisn't the same. Little more than a barrel on a pole. I need a real doxy's figure to measure it right."

Lilac dug at her pricked thumb. She hated that word: doxy. He gave her so precious little: a corner and some sacking to sleep on, a crust of bread and a rind of cheese, a few cabbage leaves. Her shift hung from her like twill from a winterdyke. Her pittance was to be paid in kind, but that had never come. Still, Stevens was the only thing that separated her from the street. Lilac dipped at the knee, grabbed the hem and slowly, not taking her eye from Stevens, she lifted it up over her head.

"And the rest," he said, not taking his eyes from the bottom of her chemise, where it brushed the summit of her thin thighs. She wasn't wearing drawers.

"Mr. Stevens," she said. "It's a gown I'm mannequinning. Not a petticoat."

"I can't properly judge the quality of the design if underclothes create lines and distortions. You know it."

She stared, goosefleshed arms folded at her chest. Stevens held out his hand, twitching his finger against his thumb.

"Here now pussy," he said, in a singsong. "Be a good cat."

Oh, that she was a cat, with fangs and claws that she could plunge into his ferrety neck.

"You'll get some cr-eam." Stevens trilled it.

"Give it here," she said, extending her arm as though delivering a jab.

Stevens grinned and he lifted the gown from the dummy. Holding it up at the shoulders between pinched fingers, he walked it over. Lilac grabbed it with one hand, bunching it up at the waist.

"Don't wrinkle," cried Stevens.

She waited for him to turn.

"Modesty on a dox," Stevens said, fixing his gaze. "Entirely unnecessary. Like frills on underwear."

Lilac turned herself and attempted to remove her chemise with her free hand. She see-sawed it awkwardly up to her flushed neck. Just as she was able to shimmy it clear of her head, she saw across the room a pair of eyes staring back at her from the cracked door of the wardrobe. It was the boy, James, his mouth dumbly open. His younger sister sat behind him, in the dimness of the wardrobe, gnawing at a remnant of linen. Their dull expressions showed nothing, save hunger.

She jounced hurriedly into Mrs. Herchmer's gown. It fell absurdly upon her shoulders, short enough to expose her knees, wide enough that she could still feel the air swirling about her body. It domed her underfed frame like an extended parasol. She still felt naked.

"It's ridiculous," she said.

"Hardly," Stevens said, sniffing toward her, his fingernails clacking. "Very helpful. Let me take a closer look."

She stood motionless, looking at Stevens from the

side of her face, cutty-eyed. He advanced, stooped, his hands pressed together. The measuring tape draped the crook of his elbow to his pocket as though it were a tail. He was behind her. His hands were on her hips, smoothing, touching.

"Mmm," he said, his voice low and throaty, "it's a fine cut."

Lilac was aware of the boy's hot gaze. A boy of only twelve or thirteen, about the age of her younger brother Isaac back home, in Cardiff. Her face glowed scarlet.

"Mr. Stevens, please," she said, as she wriggled.

"Hold still," the tailor said. His curled hands ranged up and down her back and shoulders, vibrating her corrugated ribs. They curved back at her hips and down, below the slope of her buttocks.

"Mr. Stevens."

"Your prudery is unbecoming. Dr. Scriven recommended you as an accomplished seamstress."

Dr. Scriven. Smartly dressed. The old man she'd met at the Bottle and Glass that night, with the other men from the Lancer. He'd made the arrangement. He'd seemed kindly.

Stevens's hand traced up through the cleft back to the hips.

"Fits well?" he asked.

"No."

"Too stingy in the bust?" His grapplers slid up and cupped a breast each. She slapped them down. They returned. She gripped the index fingers and flung them away. They returned.

"Mr. Stevens."

"Pussy. What can you do? You can't sew. You can't cook."

"You give me nothing to cook."

"Can you purr?"

She said nothing.

"You didn't withhold from the men of the Lancer. I've heard it told."

The men of the Lancer provided, she thought, pressing her incisor into her tongue.

Pincers were back on her hips, patting down.

"And how is it below," the tailor asked, "a little loose?"

They scraped down the tops of her thighs stopping at the hem. They burrowed under, they scuttled bare skin. They lifted.

"Should I let it out?"

Lilac pushed at both of his forearms, but still they crept up. The hem edged higher and higher until it nearly rested on the bladed points of her hips. She felt a hooked nail lodge between her legs.

"Mr. Stevens!"

James O' Neal fell out of the wardrobe. The tailor recoiled. James lay on the floor looking up at Lilac. She tugged the skirt of the gown back toward her knees. When Stevens recovered, he picked up the nearest implement, a corn broom, and swung it wildly at the boy, catching him on the knee.

"Wretched bantling!"

James scrambled to his feet and looked to escape. As he turned, Stevens thumped him square in the back and he stumbled.

"You'll go without supper again this night, surely you will."

"Let him alone," Lilac said, "he done no harm."

"Filthy silk snatcher. Get to the storeroom and sweep the rags. Take the gutterbird with you."

The boy took his sister by the hand and led her from the wardrobe. She trailed a stretch of chewed linen behind her. Stevens hurled the broom after them as though it were a javelin, glancing it off the side of the boy's head. He closed the door and returned to Lilac.

"Coquette. Let us finish."

Stevens ducked his head under the tented expanse of the gown. The pawing continued. Lilac stared in disgust at the shape in the fabric before her; a bony, quadrupedal curve.

She'd modeled gowns for Mrs. Davies, Mrs. Reynolds, Mrs. Charbonneau, and now Mrs. Herchmer. Each time the measurements went further beyond chest, hips, and the inner seam, scrabbling fingers always extending beyond the end of the tape. What would Mrs. Kilpatrick's robe bring? Or Mrs. McWhorter's stockings?

"Present your monosyllable, you slippery bunter," Stevens muffled.

Lilac balled her fists and brought them together as hard as she could against the sides of the tailor's head. Stevens shrieked, bringing his hands to his ears. She put her hands against the bulging gown and brought her knee sharply up into his nose. He fell to the floor bawling. Lilac ripped the garment from her body, crumpled it, and threw it at the prone tailor. She replaced her chemise and shift. She selected a sturdy dress of worsted, periwinkle yarn from the rack and slipped it over her head. In the storeroom, she threw a sewing kit and her few belongings into a sack.

"I'm leaving," she said to the cowering children. "You can come."

Stevens roared from the doorway. The rag he held to his face dripped crimson.

"I took you on as a favour. Where will you go? Back to the gutter?"

Lilac lurched toward the doorway, swinging her sack.

"Would seem like Kensington."

She looked back into the gloom of the storeroom and motioned.

"Come," she said, "why starve in captivity when you can be free and starve with me?"

James O'Neal looked back blankly. Behind him his sister held her linen shred over her mouth and nose.

"He'll go nowhere," Stevens said, sullenly, pointing at James. "The bailiff will be on you if you break your indenture. You'll be a criminal, no-one else will hire you on. You too," he said advancing on Lilac with a wooden ruler.

Lilac picked up a heavy pair of scissors from a table and thrust them at Stevens.

"You're crazy!" he screamed. "Get out of here, I'll have you arrested."

"Come," she said to James. James didn't move. She edged back toward the front door, holding the scissors out before her.

"My dearest dress," Stevens said. "My best scissors. You haven't paid."

Lilac stepped into the gloaming.

"Nor have you," she cried.

Chapter Four

Jeremy Castor leapt from his bench. The fresh sheet of paper tumbled from his lap to the ground. The upset inkpot dribbled its contents over the Gazette, opened to page two.

"Carmichael Jones," said the man in tattered breeches who had just appeared, his fingers splayed over his chest. "Of the plough."

Carmichael retrieved the fallen sheet from the forest litter.

"What're you writing?" he asked.

Jeremy took the sheet from him. He looked at it, as if for the first time. The paper gleamed, a sunbeam illuminating the multitude of its constituent parts. He could see the millions of fibres, fragments of discarded clothing. Remnants of earlier generations fused into a fresh, new beginning. Infinitely empty.

"Maybe I should ask," the ploughman said, "what ain't you writing?"

At one time, when studying at Helston, perhaps to one day make deacon, Jeremy had fancied himself a writer. Nominally, he was the business manager of Willowpath Glassworks. But Bennet and his apprentices did all the glass blowing. Jeremy didn't know the difference between a blowpipe and a battledore. Amelia, young widow and heiress of Colonel Spafford, managed the books and the accounts, ordered the supplies, set the prices, and met with the customers. Jeremy was pressed into service when a man's touch was required. Useful, Amelia said, for his learning and eloquence, his ability to communicate with both the miller and the magistrate. Invaluable for his ability to write well.

Jeremy knew better. She kept him on through obligation. Because he'd freed her from the Colonel through that farce of a duel. This advertisement he was supposed to be writing was make-work.

Jeremy stood the inkpot back up. High above the orchard clearing, the first birds had begun arriving, silent and unnoticed.

"What's your business?" he asked.

Carmichael kicked at a rotting apple and its shards scattered toward Jeremy. He poked his tongue through skewed, yellow teeth.

"To see if the young widow needs ploughing," he said.

Jeremy stepped forward, formulating the flinty words that would remove the man. He stopped. The ploughman had become indistinct. He was bathed in shadow as though dusk had suddenly fallen, even though it was just past dawn. Jeremy could no longer make out the shapes of the apple trees. Carmichael looked up. Jeremy followed his wildly pointing finger. A mass of beating and buffeting wings had made the sky into a low canopy, blotting the light.

"Pigeons," Carmichael whispered.

They heard distant gun fire.

"Pigeons!" Carmichael held out his hands. "A musket. Have you a musket? Any old iron will do."

Jeremy didn't answer. He turned his face toward the feathery ceiling.

"A few years ago," Carmichael said, "that season when summer didn't come, they flew in a column a mile wide, shoulder to shoulder. Six hours full. They baffled the sun."

The distant pops increased in frequency. Carmichael bounced back and forth in front of the bench.

"A musket!"

He drew his hands roughly down the front of his cheeks, contorting his eyes.

"Shooting will never be easier. Winter's meat in an afternoon."

The ploughman stared at Jeremy, waiting for acknowledgment. None came.

Carmichael huffed from the clearing.

Jeremy stood a while longer. The imposed twilight got thicker and thicker. After a few minutes, he tucked the sheet of paper into an interior pocket. He folded his copy of the Gazette. He hadn't read it and had failed to notice this item on the back page, now made illegible by the spilled ink:

☞ Public Notice!

Inhabitants of Kingston: Let it be known that the settling of the Willowpath Estate, late of Sir Noble Spafford, has not been concluded to the satisfaction of all concerned. Colonel Spafford's loyal and loving surviving nephew, Rupert, claims a second will that is both notarized and more recent. He intends to enforce the letter of this heretofore unknown document and voyages to this town from his native Ireland, to that purpose. May any who have contesting claims be forewarned and let them prove their claim the more legitimate.

Robert McCallum,

Solicitor at Law

Jeremy turned to feel his way back to the house, ushered by the steady, unceasing whoosh of a million feathers carving the sky.

ঌ ঌ ঌ ঌ ঌ

Jeremy stopped at the top of the stairs to let the spots dissolve from his eyes. In one hand he held the sheet of paper, damp with sweat, the text of his newly written Willowpath Glassworks advertisement. With the cotton rag in his other hand he swabbed at the beads emerging from his forehead. Now, at noon, the house was stifling. The heat wave showed no signs of breaking. The year before summer had failed to arrive. This year it had returned doubled.

Millie, Jeremy's mother, the staff; they'd sought relief at the lake.

As I should have, he thought. No weather for a Cornishman.

For a moment, he couldn't remember why he'd climbed the stairs. A fly crossed the room, dipped and dove. It barely made the sill. Beyond the window, birds didn't call, leaves didn't rustle. A cicada moaned a muted song, drawn-out, twice as low and long as usual. The broad pine boards creaked beneath his feet, expanded, straining at their pegs. He could smell the last of their resins running again, an earthy musk, traces of the trees, as though they, and the rest of the materials of the house, yearned to cast off their shackles and return to the land.

Jeremy loped toward the bedroom. Usually he was self-conscious of his oversized frame, ducking lintels and clomping the floor. Not today. His animal brain was capable of only rudiments. Avoidance of pain. Attainment of desire. He moved languidly, thought-lessly, like the bluebottle butting the window. He imagined turning back, stumbling toward the lake, peeling the damp, clinging woolens from his body.

Cascading water. Just the sound of it had a cooling effect. And Lavender. Myrtle. His nostrils quickened, picking up the scents above the resin of swelling pine.

Exotic fragrances, semi-tropical, suffusing the thick air, as though from a rainforest waterfall just beyond. He advanced across the landing to the cracked door and nosed in.

"Jeremy!"

Amelia stood naked in the tub, damp and rosy, pouring water. She thrust the porcelain jug down to cover her mid-section and threw her free arm across her chest. Wisps of hair fell artlessly across her face. Floral scents puffed coolly across the room, engulfing Jeremy as they escaped out the door. He clapped his big hand over his face and backed out, pulling the door as he went.

"I'm sorry, I'm sorry."

"Jeremy!" she repeated, now laughing.

"Most sorry," he said through the door, "I didn't know...I should have knocked."

"Oh, it's fine."

"I've finished the advertisement," he said, holding the sheet up to the closed door.

"This weather is beastly, is it not?"

"'Tis."

"I think I should work the rest of the day from the clawfoot."

Jeremy dabbed the paper to his head.

"Or, perhaps, just forsake clothing altogether."

Jeremy shifted his weight and the floor groaned. He thought the blond board under his feet might buckle and pop its pegs.

"Are you still there? Jeremy?"

He cleared his throat.

"You may enter," she said.

He pushed through the door gently, taking small steps across the threshold.

"Jeremy!" she cried again, rising from the sofa, "you look awful."

She wore a flowing, diaphanous robe. The afternoon's rays penetrated the open window, framing beneath the muslin every dewy contour.

"All disheveled and red," she said. "This heat, by God. Please," she pointed at a second ewer. "The water is fresh."

Jeremy crossed the room. He put the paper down and plunged his cotton rag into the basin, dragging it around his neck and shoulders. He doused his face with the mercifully cool water and began once again to feel human.

He toweled and turned to meet Amelia. She sat on the side of the bed, one leg crossed over the other, a pale, bare arm propping her up. They stared at each other a moment, her smiling, him slightly dazed.

"So?" she said.

"So?" he replied.

"The advertisement."

"The advertisement," he repeated. "Yes, yes, of course, the advertisement. It's some hot! I'm telling you it's a miracle I managed to write anything, my mind simmering as it is, distracted, always thinking of, thinking of, well, not the topic at hand. Not glass."

"You should have gone to the lake with the others."

"Aye, I should have. But I couldn't let you stay, to work on your own."

"Of course you could have. I'd have been fine. I enjoy it."

"Yes."

"I'm finding I have a knack for this work."

"Yes, I know."

"Ledgers, accounts, numbers. Organizing, putting it all in order, making it all balance. It's surprisingly stimulating."

"Yes?"

"Very. Now, how about you read it."

"What?"

"The advertisement!"

"Goodness, yes. One moment." He retrieved the sheet from the side of the basin.

"Why don't you read it over here, so you don't have to shout."

He crossed the room to join her on the bed. The frame squeaked as he sat. A fresh cloud of moisture-laden aromatics fogged his head.

"It's lovely to have the house to ourselves for a change, isn't it?" she said, putting her hand between them, well within reach.

"Aye."

"So quiet and empty. Full of possibility."

"Aye."

They gazed at each other a moment.

"Ok, let's hear it," Amelia said, looking at the sheet.

Jeremy looked down at the dampened, crumpled paper.

"'Tis smudged. I must've sudsed it."

He scudded his sticky palm across the paper, flattening it against his thigh.

"Willowpath Glass Company..."

"A good start."

"The subscribers beg leave to acquaint their friends and the public at large that Upper Canada's first glassworks now has in stock a wide ranging inventory, which they offer wholesale and retail, at their Willowpath warehouse located up the Montreal Road on the Spafford grant, on as good a terms as can be had at any manufactory west of Montreal, with a liberal discount made for cash. Country merchants and others are requested to call."

"Runs on a bit."

"Flutes, tumblers, vases, carafes, window glass, 6x8, 7x9, 7.5x8.5, 8x10, putty and frames, at the most reasonable prices. Please inquire of this office, care of Mr. Jeremy Castor. July 1817."

Amelia extended her hand. He passed her the paper and she read over the text, tracing the lines with her slender index finger. Jeremy watched her read. His gaze traced the scented trail from the hollow of her collarbone to the fine, blond sweep that swanned behind her ear. He became fixated on this small region of her body, the open ground between her earlobe and those delicate curls. He leant in, imperceptibly, compelled to bring all five senses to bear. Closer and closer he leaned. He brought his lips to the top her neck.

"Jeremy," she said, mildly startled.

She didn't recoil. He proceeded down the slope of her neck, eyes closed, navigating now by smell and touch. The way was pliant and temperate, a welcome discovery after days of unbearable heat.

"Jeremy," Amelia said again, inclining her head now, toward him, cradling his face in the crook of her neck. She dropped the advertisement and brought her hand up to the mantel of his shoulder. Jeremy pressed his face into the valley of her reddening neck, buzzing. His kisses began to push back the hem of her gown, his lips charting the ridge of her collarbone. He planted his left hand into the mattress while his right hand found her hip.

She pushed gently at his shoulder. He pulled back, opening his eyes again, and they regarded each other. Stray curls teased her forehead. The tiniest droplets had formed on the bridge of her nose. He bent, intending to lick them, but it seemed like she might speak. She opened her mouth. Nothing emerged, only the tip of her tongue. She stopped, looking up at Jeremy, her eyes saying what her mouth could not, something unintelligible. Her lips remained parted, silent, wet.

Jeremy bent again, this time pressing his lips against hers, searching urgently for the elusive pink of her tongue, desperate to receive what it would not divulge, to decipher its secrets.

His hand was at her knee, under the muslin, coasting the outer curve of her thigh from dimple to hip. Her fingers were on the expanse of his back, running its length, pulling at the covering tunic. They shifted, and now lay across the mattress, facing each other. Amelia's robe, freed from confinement, fell open. Jeremy's hand ranged from the slope of her hip, up the other side, to the rise of her breast. Her hand covered his. He paused, holding his breath, worried he'd gone too far, bracing himself for eviction. She clutched his hand. Then, pressed it more firmly to her chest. He sighed, buried his face again in the bouquet of her exquisite neck. She was impossibly soft, and moist, and fragrant, like the coolest, darkest earth.

The thrumming was back, the insistent rush of his heartbeat, and the rhythm of their breathing, the little mewling sounds she made, like the plucking of tightly wound strings, and... was there also a knocking?

Yes, it sounded like distant, insistent knocking.

This must be what it's like, Jeremy thought in ecstatic wonderment. All five senses in harmony. Beguiling melodies conducted into rapturous symphony. The impulse to create coursing through the body. It is like music. I'm going to find out, he thrilled, I'm finally going to find out.

"Jeremy," Amelia whispered hotly. The thrumming intensified and the knocking became more insistent.

"We mustn't," she said.

The crescendo between Jeremy's ears drowned her out. He surged, determined to bring the sonata to its inevitable resolution.

"We mustn't."

Discordance. The strings followed a different signature. The knocking faded. Her small hand was at his chest now, pushing.

Was it the conductor's fault?

"Miss Barrett," a voice called, not hers, not his own.

The score didn't call for a third voice.

"Miss Barrett."

It came from the open window. They separated and Amelia smoothed her gown. She pressed her sleeve to her face, slick with perspiration.

"Are you there, Miss Barrett? Sorry to disturb."

Jeremy put his hand back on Amelia's hip.

"It's just Bennet," he said fiercely, nuzzling again. "He'll go away."

"We mustn't," she said, pushing him away again. "it wouldn't be right. I'm still meant to be grieving."

Jeremy knuckled the sweat from his eye.

"Miss Barrett? Orders are finished. But 'tis very hot by the kiln. I thought I might leave early?"

Amelia got up to answer. Jeremy grabbed her by her wrist. She looked back, severely.

"One second," she yelled toward the window.

"If I were to get pregnant," she whispered, turning back to Jeremy. "It would ruin everything. Unmarried and all."

"Then marry me."

Amelia laughed. "Weather has made you foolish."

"Seriously."

"It would be unseemly, so soon after the Colonel's death."

"I don't care."

"I'm not ready."

Jeremy stood up abruptly and started to cross the room, to tell off Bennet.

"Jeremy," Amelia said, sharply, "stop. We can't risk it. This business is very important to me. When father abandoned me to Spafford, I held no hope of happiness. But I can see it now. I can do something."

Amelia stood from the bed and adjusted her robe. With sweat stung eyes, he saw the arc of her breast. He caught a final glimpse of the peach rise of her inner thigh and, for the briefest moment, he considered hoisting her to the bed, shredding the flimsy gauze, and plunging them both back into a state of nature. But before he could complete the thought, her thigh disappeared, like the last, radiant crescent of late-summer sun. She drew the curtain of fabric at her waist and tied it with a floppy belt. Jeremy returned to the bed and sat, flushed cheek in hand, staring at his oversized feet.

"Jeremy," she said. "I can't do it without you. You are the face and body of it. Together, with Bennet, we can really succeed."

"But what am I? You handle the books, the orders, the accounts. Bennet makes the glass. What do I do?"

"You," she said. "You conduct business."

Jeremy looked away. She spied the sheet on the floor.

"You write the paper. You advertise."

He wasn't convinced.

"You're the man," she said.

Jeremy snorted.

"Patience, Jem. We are young. There will be time enough, once we are on our way."

She appeared at the window.

"Ah, there you are ma'am," Bennet called. "I hope I didn't disturb you. I was knocking downstairs..."

"It's fine," Amelia said, "Just freshening up – oh, this weather!"

40

"Yes, ma'am."

"Finished?"

"All current orders are in the annealer."

"Excellent. Close up and find somewhere cool to spend the rest of the day, if you can."

When Amelia left the window, she turned to find the room empty.

Chapter Five

On the Montreal road, kicking the dust from wheel ruts, Jeremy kept moving. He tried, and failed, to stay ahead of the mosquitoes and deerflies.

He'd arrive in Kingston later that evening and stay over. A room at Walker's. Maybe a visit to the Bottle and Glass, for dinner, refreshment, a little entertainment. Or, maybe, Mother Cook's. Why not? He remembered a girl – a woman – he'd met there once. The streets had been empty that late at night. He remembered her rough, inviting speech. He pictured again how effortlessly her blouse had fallen open, revealing... willingness.

Jeremy slapped at the deerfly chewing a divot from his neck. He pulled the collar of his tunic, damp with sweat, up and over like a cowl.

He would never betray Amelia. He was just overheated. But what sort of agreement did they have? When would the vexation end?

He shook his head. He was determined not to find trouble as he had on his first night in Kingston, with his cousin Merit and their companions, enjoying shore leave after a year at sea. His first duty was to post the advertisement. He quickened his step, rumpled paper in his fist, cicadas moaning low into his ear.

"Some urgent," a voice called from behind.

He looked around to see the ploughman in the middle of the track, waving. His square, ill-fitting tunic was unlaced at the front. His boots were so worn they resembled sandals. A ribbon of dried meat hung from his mouth, thin and serpentine. The man pointed at the paper in Jeremy's hand.

"What's it for? Message for the guv?"

Jeremy looked at the sheet. Carmichael advanced.

"Injuns? Yanks?"

"Nothing like that," Jeremy called back, folding the paper and putting it in his pocket.

"An awful hurry," the man said. "Passed right by my roadside bower, not noticing."

Jeremy stepped backward.

"'Tis too diabolical hot to be rushing anywhere," Carmichael said, strolling up. "You'd best take your time, as I do. Headed to town?"

Jeremy didn't reply.

"Capital," the man said, holding out his wineskin. "We's of the same mind, ain't we? It's town that's got the entertainments. We go together. A toast."

Seeing the bulging skin, hearing its sloshing, Jeremy realized that he had left Willowpath without refreshment. Already, a thick paste hampered his tongue. Hours of walking lay ahead.

Carmichael raised the spout to his lips, suckled it, thrust it out again.

"To the big, beautiful, wide-eyed hinds. May God grant us speed enough to catch them and bone enough to mount them."

Jeremy raised his hand in farewell.

"There's a brook not far from this place, I'll refresh myself there. I'd best be on my way. I must deliver the paper on time. Thanks just the same."

He turned and walked.

"Brook's no good," Carmichael said, matching Jeremy's pace. "Downstream from a hog farm. 'Twill make you sick."

"Excuse me, I really should be moving."

"You look pale. Need a stiffener, I warrant. Have a nip, accept my hospitality. You're a man of means, obviously, you can repay in town, buy first rounds."

Carmichael was right about the brook. Drinking from it would be a gamble.

"My grog not good enough?"

"I mean no offence," Jeremy said, breaking into a half-run. "All the same, I'll be off."

Carmichael slowed and the distance between them grew.

"I'd be with the handsome widow, 'twere me. In this heat? I wouldn't be marching all over creation. I'd be with the widow. Cooling her."

Jeremy stopped. He looked back.

Carmichael was headed the other way now, in the direction of Willowpath.

"I'd escort her to the swimming hole," he shouted over his shoulder, "shady and hidden. No need for suffocating wool and sacking there. Just a cool breeze caressing what God granted."

Jeremy pictured Amelia back at Willowpath, alone and unsuspecting.

"I'd loosen her petticoat, no charge," Carmichael continued, "invited or not."

Bennett had returned to his cottage. The rest of the staff were away.

"Come," Jeremy yelled, beckoning with a sweep of his arm. "I've changed my mind. I'll take a draught and be happy to double you up in town."

Carmichael stopped, turned, and smiled. He sauntered back. Jeremy took the offered wineskin, raised it to his mouth, and squeezed. It tasted of dried apple and smelled of turpentine. The water it brought to his welling eyes just meant further dehydration.

"A churlish scrumpy," Carmichael laughed.

They began walking toward town again. Jeremy wondered how and when he might be able to diplomatically ditch the ploughman. He stood a full head and shoulders taller. He would outwalk him. Picking up his stride, shillings shifted in the leather pouch around his neck.

"Say, that's a fine jangling you're making."

Jeremy walked faster.

"Like a sleigh horse."

Carmichael trotted alongside.

"What's the rush?"

Jeremy chopped uselessly at the air around his sweat-slicked face.

"A lather only encourages them," Carmichael puffed.

They continued, almost at a run.

"Perhaps you're perfumed, strolling out of Willowpath and all. They're drawn to sweet smellers."

Jeremy recalled Amelia's lavender and myrtle.

"A man, such as myself, used to outdoor employments, builds a natural repellent. I take care not to bathe it off too often neither, especially not these torrid months when the beasts multiply."

They slowed.

"Gadflies," Carmichael said. He spoke continuously, as someone might who'd spent too much time alone in the woods. "That's what they call them. Especially the big, pesky ones, the ones that torment the horses. Do you know why?"

Jeremy stopped.

"You know," he said. "I think I will turn back. Get some water."

Carmichael stopped a few yards ahead. He turned. He offered his wineskin.

Jeremy waved it away.

"It isn't good enough for you, is it? Some kind of elegant extract are you now, courting the widow?"

"It's not like that."

"No time for your own kind. The common man. Yes, I know who you really are. Crows of a flock."

Jeremy shook his head. *Murder*, he breathed. He started walking back the way he'd come.

"What about my show of generosity? Dismissed as easily as that? You'd double me up in town, you said. This is how nobs maintain their wealth, ain't it? Taking from them that's below, never giving, never..."

Jeremy returned, pulling the leather pouch out from under his tunic.

"Look, how about I give fair payment for that sip."

"'Twas a hearty glug."

"A sip. A noxious sip."

Carmichael feigned offense, but only briefly. He peered into the pouch as Jeremy opened it. Carmichael's eyes widened at the sight of several shillings. Jeremy pulled a tuppence from it.

"A tuppence! This is what serves as fair dealing? Won't buy a thimble full. Will barely dampen me mug."

"Console yourself that I, likewise, remain unslaked. Take it to town. I will meet you. I will buy a round there."

"Where? The Fighting Cocks?"

"If that's your preference."

Carmichael thought a moment. He examined the tuppence, judging its worth.

"I hold you to it," he said.

Carmichael disappeared around the next bend. Jeremy looked back toward Willowpath. He couldn't return now. Not with the dudgeon of his sudden exit still permeating the place. Besides, he'd already come a half-mile.

He found some shade and a tangle of wild raspberry that hadn't yet been picked clean by the birds. He waited, sucking berries, until he could be sure he'd lost the ploughman.

Chapter Six

Lamps exposed the shop front. There was a small fire, strangely superfluous in the evening's residual heat. Above the fire, hanging from a spit, two cauldrons: the first directly over the flames, simmering linseed oil, the second on the periphery, keeping coffee warm. Tobacco smoke mingled with the odours emanating from the scraps and hay and dung of the sun-roasted street. Aside from a few low dens, such as Mother Cook's or some other of the nameless shebeens in the slums of Stuartsville and Picardville, where the desperate diced and marked cards, dosing themselves with turpentine gin, only the Gazette remained open.

Scriven heard the print shop before he saw it. Spitting and cursing. Arguing. Laughing. And, as he stumbled around the corner of Store and King, the metallic clink of type.

A group of young men sprawled the verandah where it was cooler. They held clay mugs which they pointed at each other as they talked, debating Bolivar and land reform. They dressed casually; cuffs of loose linen shirts rolled up past brown forearms, trousers turned up past stockingless feet, dusty boots kicked to the corner. Collars open to the mellowing night. Not a single, stiff cravat.

Scriven recognized them; Charlie Grant, Zip MacPherson, Johnny Moore, and others; clear-eyed, fine-limbed, full of enterprise. These were the men that frequented the Headstrong Club where they would spend all night discussing the latest pamphlets, reading to each other from Voltaire, and Cobbett, and Paine. The sons of merchants, and lawyers, and clergymen. Educated men, endowed with a measure of time and energy. They read the Gazette and conducted their repartee through its Correspondents section as Castigator and Nemesis. And, Opprobrious?

"Doctor," MacPherson called out as he saw him approach.

"Please Zipporah, dispense with the 'Doctor', it's Creedence here."

MacPherson smiled, revealing a row of straight, milky teeth.

"You can call me Zip."

Scriven stood next to the knot of reclining men, one boot on the porch, the other in the dust of the street. He'd had several hours at the Bottle and Glass. Momentarily unbalanced, he clapped his hand to MacPherson's shoulder and held it there, gripping.

"You've cooked up a brew Johnny," he said, tapping his nose with the index finger of his free hand.

"Aye, 'tis so Doctor."

Scriven pulled a monogrammed handkerchief from an inside pocket and dabbed at the pearls of sweat above his brow, leaving a trace of its perfume in the lines of his forehead. He considered reminding Johnny, again, to use his given name.

"Bartlett just got in a new shipment. Arabica, from Venezuela. I baked them longer this time, before grinding. Dark as the jungle floor. The kettle is there, at the end of the spit."

Scriven inhaled deeply. Zip held his clay bowl up.

"Try it," he said.

Scriven folded his handkerchief and slipped it back into its compartment. He took the cup, sipped, closed his eyes and rolled his head.

"You're an alchemist John. You should open a shop."

"I intend to. I have my eye on the clapboard Mrs. Finkle's just built. I need only amass the capital."

"I may be able to help with that. Come by for a sherry and we'll discuss it further."

Johnny nodded his thanks.

"But, watch those flames. They had a fire here only last month."

"Be vigilant, in other words."

That phrase. Be vigilant. From Opprobrious' notice in the Gazette. Scriven was sure he detected a knowing glance. Wide smiles, teeth bared.

"Delivering a column?" Zip asked.

Scriven patted inside his jacket where he kept a single hand-written page.

"What length breeches this week?" one of the men asked as Scriven disappeared across the threshold.

His treatise wasn't about breeches. It was a comparison of the Wellington boot to its predecessor, the Hessian, discussing the triumphs and defeats of each. But he was already into the din of the printer's chapel. He couldn't correct the man without turning around and stepping back outside. Fancy packages and bows, he thought he heard one of them say. And then, once more, laughter. He kept walking.

With its scriptorium's high ceilings and tall window sashes thrown open, the chapel was a few degrees cooler than other buildings in the city, especially now that it was nearing midnight. Even so, the coffee-tinged cross breeze was not enough to fully mask the tang of perspiration and rag bale mustiness. Scriven passed the setters standing before the upper and lower type cases, arranging lines on their sticks and the man next to the low table with the handle of an ink ball in each hand. He continued toward the far end of the hall, where Stephen Miles sat perched on a high stool at a vast, angled table, pushing a line gauge over the broadsheets covering it.

"Last minute again, Creedence," Miles said, not looking up from his sheet, "we'll be up here all night and tomorrow besides."

"Do you ever leave?"

"Where would I go? Squib!"

The printer's devil with the orange goatee leapt from his rag bale. His squat legs were stained from the knees down, his arms were darkened up to his elbows, as though he'd tried to disguise himself but had run out of paint.

"Check the linseed. We can't afford another fire."

Miles held a pair of tarnished scissor spectacles, one branch of the frame held together with a length of tightly wound rag. Lamplight reflected in the lens gave his eyes an unearthly amber glow. His legs, satyr's haunches, hung only halfway down the height of the stool, crooked at the knee, tapering to compact feet. His eroded shoes were hooked behind the stool's second rung, splaying their cloven, tattered leather. He pored over the expanse of paper, marking and muttering, like a warden checking rolls. Scriven had the same sensation he always had upon entering the chapel of the Gazette; that some malevolent spirit had flipped the hot, reeking print shop, and now it sweated and pressed in a sulphurous underworld.

Squib bustled back in, a plume of smoke and rancid oil rising as he passed. Scriven watched him pass by the large, brick-coloured earthenware crock by the wall. Reminded, he walked over to it.

"I'm full of shrub. Should have attended to it earlier."

He bent down, lifted the chipped lid, and tilted it to the side. An ammonia cloud puffed from the vessel and caused him to straighten abruptly, his eyes watering. Inside the pot, the stew; two black leather bladders half-submerged in a broth of stagnant bronze.

Scriven pulled aside the curtains of his jacket and unbuttoned the front fall of his trousers. He swayed as his stream spattered into the pot.

"Tell me Stephen," he said over his shoulder, "have you gandered my manuscript."

"Manuscript? That's a grand expression for several scribbled pages."

"For someone who preaches methodistical kindness to all others, you can be particularly cruel."

"Reason in all things Creedence, that's what I live by. You'll not get greater charity from a friend than honesty. Especially when it comes to one's prose."

"Well, I admit it's a scant beginning, but there's a foundation, nay?"

"Perhaps."

"You can see where I'm headed. Are you not beguiled by my protagonist? Is he not exquisitely and heroically attired?"

"There is more to character than appearance."

"Of course, of course, but clothing signifies. *Bespoke bespeaks.*"

"Congratulations. You may have discovered yourself a title."

Scriven turned back to the wall. The torrent with which he frothed the pot continued undiminished. Miles picked up a thin sheaf of papers from one of his piles and rustled it without taking his eyes from his drafting table.

"How long have you been working on this play?" he asked.

"Three years."

"A score of smudgy pages?"

"I hardly have the time," Scriven said, his voice rising. "With my practice and the lodge, I'm uncommonly busy."

"Still pissing Creedence? Did you leave Walker any brandy? You'd do well to spend less time drinking and more time writing."

"Don't practice your method on me Miles. I'm no ploughman or convict, I have my church. Temperate in all things, including temperance."

"Sinner's logic."

Back at the drafting table, Scriven leaned in, his voice low.

"Stephen, some of the letters you've printed recently."

"Yes?"

"Some of them seem quite vague and unsubstantiated, don't they? Libelous, perhaps."

"Do you have any in mind?"

"No," Scriven said, quickly, "not necessarily."

"I aim never to censor."

"But, there are limits."

"Thomas Jefferson said where the press is free and every man able to read, all is safe."

"He also said that advertisement is the most truthful part of a newspaper."

Miles looked up from his sheets for the first time and removed his scissor spectacles.

"Creedence," he said, "you're like one of those contrivances I read about – the one Dr. Brewster invented last year – what's it called, the tube with the mirrors and the coloured beads..."

"Kaleidoscope, sir?" one of the typesetters offered.

"Yes, that's it, kaleidoscope. You're like a kaleidoscope. Pretty to look at but you never quite know what sort of picture you're going to get. There's more to you than the wrapping."

"A compliment?"

"You may take it that way."

Scriven pulled the single hand-written page from his jacket pocket and handed it to Miles.

"In the meantime," he said, "here is my column."

"Thank you," Miles said, "I'm sure it will generate many letters. Squib!"

The printer's devil had been sitting on a rag bale, swinging his feet back and forth, gnawing a patch of dried pigeon meat. He slid to the floor and stuck the pemmican behind his ear.

"The coverage is uneven. Replace the leathers."

Squib crossed the shop floor. A pair of children, James O'Neal, the tailor's apprentice, and his sister, had entered and were now loitering by the small library of books near the door. Finding a wayward capital 'Q' on the table the inker picked it up and flung it across the shop at James. The edge of the type struck the boy in the ribcage and he jumped, dropping the library book he'd been thumbing. He and his younger sister bolted from the shop.

"Let them be!" Miles cried. "Retrieve that letter and restore it to its case."

Squib sighed, found the 'Q', and put it back. He returned to the piss pot, still warm from Scriven's deposit, and plunged his hands in. He lifted the two leather bags from it and held them up, allowing the urine to cascade back. He squeezed and wrung, until they no longer dripped. They expanded gently, accordion-like, after compression. He patted the leather bags dry with a rag, inside and out, and then tucked the rag into the side of his loincloth. He stuffed both bladders with fistfuls of damp, tangled wool, impaled them with sticks, and tied them off so they resembled a pair of mummified plum puddings. The apprentice submerged the new inking balls in the vat of ink. He took the old ones from the inker, dismantled them, and tossed the leather casings into the crock. He replaced the lid, wiped his hands on the rag, took the jerky from his ear, and resumed chewing.

James and his sister returned. They shuffled in through the door sideways and they skulked back toward the books eluding, for the moment, anyone's notice. The boy found the book entitled *A Picture Book, For Little Children* and edged it out. He opened it to the middle and pointed at the picture of the peacock, decorated on either corner with four letters 'P': italic, capital, italic capital, and bold. His sister looked up and smiled.

"Now," Miles returned to his drafting table. "If you'll excuse me Creedence, I need to finish my review of Next Door Neighbours."

"You must read my play," Scriven said, "the moment I have a complete draft."

"Not something I have to worry about any time soon then."

Chapter Seven

Jeremy stepped through the front door of the Gazette, advertisement in hand. James O'Neal tucked the picture book under his arm, grabbed his sister by the hand, and sprinted toward the exit. Jeremy held the door open for them.

Miles jumped from his stool.

"They ain't free!"

Jeremy had the noise of the street in one ear and the clatter of the print shop in the other. Why was the man at the far end yelling at him?

"Thief! Don't let him go," Miles cried. "He's no subscriber. They're not library books."

The printer's devil, clutching the dripping handle of an inking ball, chased after James. Jeremy, now thinking it was Squib that had thieved, evidence in his stained hands, stuck out his arm and caught him around the neck.

Squib fell to the floor clutching his windpipe. The children evaporated into the street.

Miles stared at Jeremy.

"A syndicate?" he cried. "Is it Ikey Solomon, running a thieving ring?"

Jeremy looked down at Squib, confused.

"Stephen," Dr. Scriven said, "It's no Ikey Solomon. I think I know this man."

"Is he in league with the gutterbirds?"

"I recognize the boy, for that matter. Anyway, it's just a book."

"Six shillings a piece!"

Jeremy began to realize his mistake. His pledge to avoid trouble in town was already in doubt.

"Sir," he called, helping Squib from the floor. "My name is Jeremy Castor. I don't know Ikey Solomon. I'm unfamiliar with the flown children. My apologies. I'll fetch your book."

Jeremy burst from the Gazette's doors and he looked toward the intersection. James O'Neal and his sister, barely discernible in the moonlight, turned and scampered north. Jeremy rushed past the end of the porch and the cheering coffee drinkers. He had walked miles through the heat of the afternoon with only a sip of Carmichael's peculiar combination of flat cider and apple brandy. His head pounded. His tongue swelled. Spotting the children duck into an alley, his pace slowed. He turned right. Then left. He no longer detected their thin silhouettes at the corners. He wandered more empty streets. Almost midnight. He didn't want to return to the Gazette empty-handed. Would they take his advertisement if they thought he'd abetted a theft?

At the corner, lamplight spilled from splayed shutters, staining the middle of the next street dirty yellow. Figures reclined against the sills and steps. They drank from bowls garlanded with clouds of blue pipe smoke. The sign hanging over the door showed a rooster wearing spurs. The Fighting Cocks.

Jeremy pictured salvation in a grail of cool beer. He shook his head. Get the book, return it, post the ad, and return to Walker's for a blackjack of ale. Then, bed. He'd poke his head in, look briefly for the ploughman, and move on.

"Lor and begorrah," a woman called as he approached, "are ye as long as ye are tall?"

Jeremy crouched through the door. There were a handful of men inside the close, converted drawing room. Three sat at a table where they rolled dice and exchanged tokens. At one end of a legless divan a woman sat on a man's lap, half-resisting his groping with giggles and clouts. At the other end a body slumped over gutted cushions. A rooster strutted the bar top stopping occasionally to sip from a chalice of watered brandy.

No Carmichael. A mixture of relief and disappointment.

At the next intersection, the shadow of a boy ran past, a book in one hand, a stick of bread in the other. A smaller figure followed. Jeremy chased, passing rows of shacks and sheds, sties and coops. Endless warrens for children to hide. He rounded the corner. He rushed for the gate.

He didn't notice the cross beam until it struck his forehead. The force of it lifted him from his feet.

For several seconds, Jeremy lay concussed on the ground, half in, half out of the gate. When he came to, he put his hand to his temple, and gently probed the source of growing pain. He creaked to his feet, groaning as blood pulsated his swelling eye. The rosy veil cleared. He imagined the punishment he would inflict on the boy when he finally collared him.

"Come out," he said. "I mean no harm."

He thought they must still be nearby, cowering in a cul de sac somewhere.

"I only want the book."

He slowed.

"Come out!" he cried.

"Shush!"

The woman sitting on a crate ahead put a finger to her lips. Her frowning expression was made monstrous by the rancid lamp light. A baby writhed in the wicker basket at her feet, clenching tiny, pink fists. It had twisted its scarlet face in a squall so violent it was soundless. The woman fanned at it with a whisk.

"Quiet," she said.

Jeremy raised his hands diplomatically.

He walked on, striding past the indistinct mound that glistened in the moonlight, a thousand pale, dancing specks. He broke into a run through the cloud of flies and the eye watering stench.

"Offals," said a man nearby. Jeremy had stopped, pulling his sleeve from his face, retching. The man sat on a bale, back against the wall, one cornstalk leg crossed over the other.

"You gets used to it," he added, around the pipe in his mouth. "They should cover them with the dirt. They never do."

His companion, rooted to a second bale, puffed hard on her own pipe, half obscured by a blue-black nimbus.

"Smoke helps," she said.

A third person, wearing a tattered nightshirt several sizes too small, sat in the clay just beyond the smokers. He leaned back against a tree rising from the middle of the path. His poxy face was perfectly round with two eyes maximally distant from one another. A plug of hair sprouted from the centre of his head like greens from a parsnip. He had a stripped cob of corn in his fist, which he thrust into his grinning mouth.

For a moment Jeremy considered asking the smokers if they had seen the urchins. Then he realized he no longer cared about them or the book. He wanted only to get out of the street.

"Can you tell me how to get to Walker's Hotel from here?"

The ancient laughed until he was winded, slapping his bony thigh and stamping his foot. He puffed and drew on the clay tube of the pipe with renewed vigour.

Jeremy kept walking. Ahead, a man and a woman argued.

"Come," said the man, "give a free one."

"No," the woman pushed him away.

"Greedy slut," the man growled, returning to clinch. "You know you want it. You give it away free t'others."

"No," she said, pushing away again. "I don't."

"Come along," he said, twisting her arm up behind her back. "Christ's pants, you're thin! I bet I have a vittle I can give you, a bone you can gnaw."

"A shilling or nowt."

"A shilling? What flattery! Nothing worse than a prideful whore. Not worth a tuppence. I've a mind to take it and all. Cut you down a notch."

Jeremy grabbed the man by the shoulder.

"I'll give it to you," he said.

"Leave off," the man started, turning to thrust his chin at Jeremy. "Find your own."

Jeremy looked down into the florid face of the ploughman.

"Oh," Carmichael said, "you. Chouser and cheat."

He peered up at the crust of blood darkening Jeremy's brow.

"What mischief have you got up to?"

Jeremy didn't reply.

"You owe me a round," Carmichael continued. "Proper. Waited for you at Fighting Cocks 'til they threw me out. A chipped tuppence gets you a swig, that's all. Sour beer. And, as you can see, won't even meet a bunter's asking price."

Carmichael glanced at the spot where he knew the coin pouch resided.

"Did I not give you succour out on the Montreal Road? What of man's humanity to man? Let's have a polished shilling and we'll call it square."

Blood throbbed behind Jeremy's eye.

"Well," Carmichael said, unnerved by Jeremy's manner, "at least let me alone with the whore."

The woman turned, her raised hand balled into a fist. Jeremy saw her for the first time.

"Lilac?"

Lilac neared. She studied his face.

"Deacon!" she cried. She threw her arms around him and kissed his cheek.

"What's this?" Carmichael pulled them apart. "Jumping the queue?"

Jeremy turned on Carmichael. He grabbed his tunic with both hands, tearing the leather thongs that knit the front. He brought his face close to Carmichael's. The blood at his temple glistened.

"Be gone," he said.

Carmichael raised his hands. Jeremy released him. The ploughman retreated, muttering down the laneway.

"Come into some light," Lilac said, after the shadows had swallowed Carmichael. "Let me get a better look."

She tugged Jeremy back to the hovel where the ancients smoked their pipes. She bent him down to the paltry flame of the betty lamp.

"Light ain't free," the old man said.

Lilac held Jeremy's face in her hands.

"Jeremy," she said. "It is you. Dear old deacon. You're bleeding!"

"At least pass us some tobacco," the old man said, "or penny for a crust."

"Black bread," chanted his overgrown son, pounding his thigh with the denuded corn cob, "black bread!"

Lilac took Jeremy by the thumb and led him away, deeper into the Stuartville slum.

"Come," she said. "I'll mend you."

She led him another hundred yards. The structures and signs of settlement thinned. They passed a pair of cows propped together flank to flank, snoozing, and just beyond them a lean-to on the edge of a pasture. Lilac lifted a plank of wood from a notch in the makeshift frame and pulled the unhinged door aside. Jeremy ducked his head and they stepped in. She dragged the door across and barred it.

Inside was marginally less pungent than the street. Traces of dung, mildew, and unwashed linen evoked in Jeremy the sleeping quarters of the Lancer, scores of men sleeping in their sweat-damp work clothes, night after night, separated only by the slight canvas of their hammocks. He wondered how many of those same men had found their way to this shack by the glebe.

A single tallow stuck into the top of a crate shed a brassy globe of light, revealing the interior: an envelope of soiled sailcloth on the floor, straw sprouting from each end, covered with a patched square of wool, and, incongruously, a periwinkle dress of the finest, worsted yarn hanging from a cross beam.

In a jumble of hay next to the candle, a knob of bread in one hand, the *Picture Book, For Little Children* in the other, sat James O'Neal.

Jeremy stared at the child a moment, blinking to make sure it was the right boy and the right book.

He lunged, kicking dirt from the floor to the mattress. He crossed the room in two strides. James scrambled from his reclined position, struggling to find purchase in the loose hay. He'd barely found his feet before Jeremy seized him, snatching the book from his hand.

Jeremy cinched the boy's collar around his slender neck.

"A devilish headache you've caused," he cried.

"Jeremy," Lilac stepped between Jeremy and the boy. "What is wrong with you?"

"You've a filcher stowed away. Probably here to do a job."

"James?" Lilac scoffed. "And what do I have to steal?"

Jeremy scanned the room. There was little he would touch, let alone steal. Lilac pursed her lips and blew out derisively.

"Let him go," she said.

James peered back at Jeremy, his eyes bulging. Jeremy let go and the boy fell to the floor. He rejoined his sobbing sister, clinging to Lilac's skirt.

"I'll keep the book," Jeremy said.

"I know him Jeremy," Lilac said. "He's my friend. Apprentice to the tailor. He and his sister come here when Stevens plumps him with his broomstick and worse. I let them stay if they want."

Jeremy continued to eye the boy.

And, sometimes I read to them. The deacon I know would do the same.

Jeremy shifted his weight and looked at the book in his hand. It was open to a page near the front. The illustration showed a quartet of young women wearing jewelry and fine gowns. They sat in a room chatting. *Nice folks*, read the caption. He flipped the page. A woodsman bending down to a boy at the side of the road. *Do be kind to the poor boy.* Again, a young girl in a yard, a woman standing over her, scolding. *Old folks should never forget they were once young.* He closed the book. He looked up to see the two children on either side of Lilac, her hands stilling their trembling.

"You're right," he said, finally, letting his arms drop to his sides. "It's been a difficult evening. I'm sorry James," he held the book out to him, "please, take it. I'll settle the bill with Stephen Miles."

James reached out, tentatively, and snatched it.

"But no more stealing. You're fortunate it's me and not a shoulder clapper."

James nodded.

"Sit down," Lilac said, taking Jeremy by the hand. "Let me look at you."

She led him to the mattress, next to the candle, and pushed on his hip until he sat. He shut his eyes tight imagining the assortment of lice and bed bug. Lilac picked up the candle and brought it to his face.

"Odds blut and nails," she said. "'Tis a proper wound and all. Don't move."

She stood again and went to a corner of the shack where she lifted an oilcloth from a small chest. She opened it with a key and pulled out a shallow cylindrical tin filled with amber wax. It had five lengths of stiff, stubby fabric set into it at intervals, so that it resembled an oversized sand dollar.

"My cook stove," she said.

"Bee's wax?" Jeremy asked.

"Of course."

"Don't burn it on my account. Save it."

"Nonsense. How will I boil the water otherwise?"

"Water." Jeremy nearly croaked the word. "May I have some, Lil?"

"I must boil it. Sit back. Let me work."

She lit the five wicks from the tallow candle already burning, put the disc down and folded a metal apparatus over it. On this scaffolding, an inch from the five flames, she placed a tin pot. And into the pot, a measure of water poured from a skin hanging from a nail. From the chest she pulled a curved sewing needle and a length of linen. She threaded the needle and added them both to the pot.

"A queer broth," Jeremy said.

Lilac pulled a rag hanging from a stretch of twine.

"For the stitching Jem," she said. "Carruthers taught me it, aboard the Lancer. The old crocus said that Galen boiled his instruments before scalpeling gladiators. Carruthers claimed the top survival rate in the RN."

She doused the rag in water from the skin.

"Also for the tea," she said, dabbing at the dried blood at Jeremy's hairline. "Aristotle had Alexander boil water for his soldiers to drink."

Lilac wiped the cloth along the fissure at Jeremy's temple causing fresh pain to slash across his face.

"You're very well read for a whore," he said through gritted teeth.

Lilac let her hand drop to her side. Jeremy blinked the tears from his eyes until the pain subsided and he could see the expression on her darkened face. The men of the Lancer had abided by the fiction that Lilac was Finn Davies' wife, though they were never truly married. Davies was more of a sponsor than a mate and aboard ship she was not exclusive. Jeremy understood she was sensitive about her place, but seeing her in the street, fending off a customer...

"Lilac," he said, extending one hand to her and the other to his forehead, "This thump. I misspoke. I meant only I'd forgotten how much you loved to read."

Lilac went back to the dried blood.

"Why are you here at all?" Jeremy asked. "I thought you were working with a tailor yourself, as seamstress."

"Didn't work out," she said, busily, as James O'Neal looked up from his picture book.

"It was the tailor that Dr. Scriven referred, wasn't it?"

"Dr. Scriven is a decent man."

"I saw him earlier tonight, briefly, at the Gazette. Surely mending gowns would…"

"It didn't work out."

Jeremy watched Lilac apply more water to the rag and wring it out over a wooden chamber pot in a corner of the shack. She twisted her stick fingers around the rag.

"What of husband Finn?" he asked.

Lilac clucked and returned with the freshened rag.

"You missed it all, feathered up with your young lady at Willowpath."

Jeremy blushed. For a moment he wondered about inviting Lilac back to Willowpath. Surely there was something she could do there to earn her keep, assist at the glassworks, keep house. He imagined Amelia's reaction.

"Gone," she continued. "Stokes gathered them all up, Finn, Neven, and all the rest of my lovely brothers. Sailing for Caracas or Port of Spain or some other godforsaken place."

She looked around the close confines of the shack, appraising her surroundings. She laughed.

"Read to them a minute, will you?"

"What?"

"Read to them. Like you used to read to me aboard the Lancer. While I prepare the dressing."

"Tea first?"

Lilac nodded. She pinched dried leaves from a pouch and sprinkled them into a mug. She poured some of the hot water from the tin pot into the mug and handed it to him. It had a metallic taste and a whiff of sulphur, but it rinsed the paste from his mouth.

James looked at Jeremy. Jeremy looked at James.

"Go on," she said. "you'll neither of you bite."

Jeremy patted the edge of the sailcloth on either side of him. James hesitated. Finally, having the words of his new book read out outweighed his fear and mistrust. He got up from the crate.

"Take the candle," Lilac said.

James pried the candle from the crate top and stepped to the mattress with the book. Jeremy held out his hand.

"It's ok," he said, "I'll take good care."

James passed the book to Jeremy. He remained standing.

"A picture book, for little children," Jeremy read the title page. "Now, you aren't so little any more are you? No matter."

He opened it to the first page.

"A walk in the garden."

Jeremy read slowly and deliberately, tracing each word with his finger. Then he studied the picture and described the strolling couple. James continued to stand.

"Strawberries grow on little vines. My, those are some juicy looking berries, aren't they? Wish we had a bowl of them to share right now."

By the second page, James' sister had left the crate and sat next to Jeremy on his left.

"What troubles the old woman? She looks cross doesn't she? Maybe she's just hungry."

The girl nodded.

"We cannot see ourselves in this glass. 'Tis a beautiful mirror and I wager it is dear, don't you? Have you ever seen yourself in a mirror?" he asked, looking down at the girl. She shook her head.

"Let me be your mirror. Look into my eyes. You have...James, could I trouble you to bring the light near so I can reflect your sister?"

James inched forward. He held the candle closer, bending at the waist so his feet still had jump.

"Thank you. Let's start at the top, shall we? Hair. You have a captivating head of auburn curls, full and wild like a privet hedge. A high forehead reflecting candlelight through smudges of dust, signifying your natural cleverness and wit. Eyes of freckled hazel, ever widening, indicating the triumph of curiosity over fear. Pale, pinch-able cheeks, soft and globular, like a pair of expensive silk cushions scattered with rose petals. And a silent, diminutive mouth, smiling now, though not often enough, teeth interspersed with a series of charming gaps."

Jeremy tapped the girl's knee.

"Looking glass," he said. "Can you see yourself?"

She nodded and smiled and leaned further in. She put her hand on his lap.

The next illustration showed a woman seated with several children around her. The caption read: Children obey your mother.

"Children, be good to your friend Lilac," Jeremy read out loud.

"It says that?" James said, sitting down next to Jeremy, on the right. He held the candle directly over the book. "It says Lilac?"

Jeremy looked up. Lilac had turned and was watching them.

"What?" he asked. He was fully illuminated by the candle, a child on either side.

"Deacon. 'Tis really you."

Then she frowned.

"What is it?"

"Blood. You've got more of it down your chest. Loosen your tunic."

Jeremy handed the picture book to James.

"Children, I'm sorry, give us some space. I need to stitch Mr. Castor's wound, make him better. He'll read to you afterward."

James and his sister got up from the mattress and went back to their crates. Lilac pulled the collar of his shirt to the side and examined his chest.

"It's fine. Forehead blood, not another laceration. I'll wash it in a moment, after I've stitched."

With tweezers she plucked the threaded needle from the pot, waved it, then held the end of the needle gingerly between thumb and forefinger. Even in the close, warm air of the lean to, it steamed with heat. She knelt and blew out the beeswax cooker. Holding the needle aloft in her right hand, Lilac picked up a tuft of muslin, stained red, with her left. She brought it to Jeremy and patted it against the top of the gash.

Jeremy lurched. Pain shot from hairline to brow, flashing white behind his eyes. It was as though Lilac had re-incised his temple with a hot knife. James and his sister, alarmed at his sudden cursing, made ready to bolt.

"This might hurt," she said, a trifle late.

"I can confirm it does," he said.

Wetness trickled down the side of his face. It smelled of sour wine. He stuck his tongue out and sampled.

"That's some hospitality. You might have offered me a cup for the pain, rather than pouring it over my head."

She began stitching. The pain of the muslin compress lingered as the needle and thread passed through the two sides of the rift.

"Tastes a poor vintage anyway."

"Vinegar. I treat the wound per Celsus – De Medicina. Vinegar sponge flushes it out."

Jeremy shifted.

"Don't fidget," she said. "What happened to our brave, royal marine? Have you gone soft?"

"Ex-marine. Failed marine."

"Oh yes. Glass magnate now. And what brought you into Stuartsville?"

Jeremy didn't answer. He detected Lilac's gentle facetiousness and he wondered again. Who is this Jeremy Castor? Manager of the Willowpath Glassworks. He couldn't say it to himself and make it sound convincing.

Jeremy gritted his teeth and clenched his eyes as the needle passed through a final time. Lilac tied it off and leant down, close to his face, to bite the end. He could smell perspiration and her natural scent, a sort of essence of dried grass, but also clove and bergamot. The combination blotted out the unpleasantness of the shack and street.

"Done," Lilac said, straightening again.

She scrutinized his face, appraising her work.

"The shirt," she said, "let me mop away the blood."

He grabbed the shirt bottom and raised it over his head, jostling the leather pouch that still hung around his neck.

"Oh my," she said. "You are well breeched. There are only two reasons why a swish such as yourself would come to Stuartsville."

She straddled his thigh and swabbed his chest, stroking in lazy, sensual circles, from shoulder to neck to sternum to rib. The slight palm of her hand was firm and warm.

"One," she continued, "for cheap drinks at odd hours."

Lilac gazed into Jeremy's eyes as she slid further up his thigh to get the damp muslin up the side of his neck.

"Or two, for...oh, Jeremy. Really?"

"No," he protested, "I chased the children. That is all."

"Don't you have your hands full with your frolicsome doe in the country? What's her name, Laurel? Lily?"

"Amelia. We haven't..."

Lilac widened her eyes.

"We aren't..."

She took Jeremy's prominent chin in both hands and swung his face back to hers.

"I mean, I've never..."

"You've never?"

He shook his head slightly.

"James," she said, "leave us now. Mr. Castor and I have some things to discuss in private. Just as I did with Mr. Braithwaite and Mr. Harris. Remember? Come back in the time it takes to darn a sock. Knock first."

James closed his book and put it on the crate. He removed the bar from the door, slid it across the dirt floor, stepped outside with his sister, and replaced the door.

"I will show you," Lilac said to Jeremy. "It's a simple function. Nothing could be more natural."

He remembered Amelia standing in the bath, dewy and supple, all contour and crescent, free of sharp, straight lines. He cast his eye briefly over Lilac, noting the lines of her ribs showing through her threadbare shift, her spiky elbows, the prominent eye sockets sunk into her angular face.

"I want nothing in return," she said. "It would be my pleasure."

"I've missed you Lilac," Jeremy said finally. "You're a good friend, the only one that remains from the Lancer."

He opened his purse and pulled all the coin from it, putting a few shillings back. It was too late to wake Walker now anyway. It was warm enough to get a few hours of sleep in the park. He wasn't sure how he'd pay for the Gazette advertisement. Or the stolen book. He'd think of something. Tomorrow.

"Lilac," he said, putting the coins into her hand. "Take this, please."

She frowned.

"I said I want nothing in return."

"Nor do I."

"I don't want charity."

"Please. One friend to another. Buy yourself some bread. Some meat and vegetables. For the children too."

Her pointed chin dimpled.

"This is fine, isn't it? A customer paying for nothing and a whore giving it away."

She looked like she might start to cry.

The door of the shack clattered aside.

"I told you to knock!" Lilac shouted.

James pushed his face into the opening. His eyes were wide and darting, his mouth open, no sound coming out. Seeing him, Lilac forgot her anger and sadness.

"Jeremy! You must leave. Immediately!"

She stood up from his lap and pulled at his arm. When he protested, she slapped him.

"Go!" she screamed. "Go now. Run and don't look back."

He stood and he held out his hand, intending to pass her the coins. She cuffed his wrist and coins went everywhere. She stuffed his bloodied shirt into the empty hand.

"There isn't time. Get out! Follow James."

She shouldered and kicked and punched and he was out the door. James and his sister vanished into the darkness. Jeremy followed.

კ კ კ კ კ

"Did you see him?"

Carmichael Jones stood with the bailiff at the edge of the pasture.

"Saw him earlier. A tall one."

"Left in a hurry too. Barely had time to fasten his trousers."

"Could you catch him? In this murk?"

"Never mind him. He's gone. Let's pay our respects."

The bailiff ducked his head through the doorway, poking his bullseye lamp ahead of him. He saw Lilac sitting on the dirt floor, hair disheveled, shift slightly torn. She was picking up coins.

"Heavens," clucked the bailiff, "quite a windfall. Quite unambiguous."

"You have it wrong, sir," Lilac said, biting her lip.

She saw Carmichael's round face poke in.

"You!" she cried.

"You acquainted with this woman," the bailiff asked Carmichael.

"Never seen her before," the ploughman said, "'cept for tonight, soliciting Jack O' Legs out in the street. Appalling."

Chapter Eight

Jeremy backtracked through the fence holes and culverts. Even at this late hour, people were out in the street, young and old, attempting to stay cool. He found no trace of James and his sister.

He neared the print shop. He heard shouting.

"You wanna play mister?"

"Mister molly, he likes games I think."

"Wants to play cock-a-roosty, don't he?"

"Toad in the hole, ain't that right."

"Not so. I know his game."

"What is it, Sweeney?"

"A round of back gammon is what he craves, I wager figs to farthings."

"Most amusing." A man's voice, forced low and even. "Make way now. I'm homeward."

"Pa said beware of fancy packages. Skink told him. Skink can read. 'Twas in the paper."

"This here mister molly is fancy as they come. Look at that sash."

"Made of angel hide and fairy dust."

"Such a pretty bow."

"Let me by now." Desperation crept into the man's quavering tone.

"He doesn't seem to want to play after all."

"How about tossing us a bean then? A shilling in lieu."

"I haven't any coins just now. I'm homeward."

"He'll have to play then, won't he Sweeney?"

"Yes. He will."

"Come over, red rover."

Jeremy approached. He found the man surrounded by a ring of seven boys and girls of various age. Jeremy nudged aside a boy who couldn't have been older than six.

"That's enough now," he said. "You've enjoyed your japes. Bedtime."

The children jeered.

Even in the murk, Jeremy recognized, by his Augustus sweep and immaculate cravat, the man in the middle.

"Doctor!" he said.

Scriven looked back at him blankly.

"Take my arm," Jeremy said.

Scriven hooked his wrist into Jeremy's offered elbow. Jeremy began to lead them out of the laneway and toward the print shop. The oldest boy, the one called Sweeney, rushed to that side of the ring.

"A king's picture to pass," he said.

Jeremy lent forward until his face was inches from the boy's. Sweeney glanced at the jagged line of stitching.

"I'm a royal marine," Jeremy said. "I've just killed a deserter. Flayed him alive with a dull scissor. Don't want to do it again. But I will."

Jeremy and Scriven passed through the ring, rounded the corner, and continued to the front porch of the Gazette. Behind them, the children debated the truth of Jeremy's claim.

As they neared the print shop, Scriven pulled his arm from Jeremy's.

"A clever tactic," Scriven said. "I was about to get stern with them myself. Just as you happened along."

Jeremy nodded.

"I'd had rather a lot of the shrub at Bottle and Glass earlier. Not quite myself. If I'd had my walking stick, I'd have given them a good thrashing. Wretched bantlings."

"Yes."

"I'm in your debt. Stop by the porch lantern a moment."

They stood in front of the print shop. The coffee drinkers had snuffed their fire and they had moved on. The linseed oil continued to simmer. Inside, the printer and his devils toiled. Light from a stained-glass window distorted Scriven's face, making it all at once wan and livid, sallow and flushed.

"What happened to you?" he cried, getting a good look at Jeremy for the first time. "That cleft in your head. You look all in pieces."

Jeremy recalled the sordid absurdity of his first couple of hours in town. Where was Lilac? Was she in trouble? He regretted leaving her. But she had insisted, hadn't she? She wouldn't permit him to stay. He wondered how much he should say to Dr. Scriven. It was he who had placed Lilac with Stevens, the tailor, in the first place.

"Robbed?" Scriven asked.

"Not exactly."

Scriven inclined his head, puzzled, urging more detail.

"I'd rather not say," Jeremy said.

"Bend down a minute."

Jeremy bowed at the waist.

"First rate needlework," Scriven said. "Who did you engage for patching at such a ghastly hour?"

In the dim light, Jeremy could see the melted powder on Scriven's pitted face, streaked with perspiration. His breath smelled bitterly of tobacco and brandy. Sandalwood residues had soured, no longer capable of masking the day's fermentations.

"A friend."

Scriven studied him, intrigued by the air of mystery and the hint of transgression.

"I'm meant to be in town on business," Jeremy continued, "to buy an advertisement at the Gazette, nothing else."

"Jeremy Castor, isn't it? Your cousin, Merit Davey, used to be a regular at the Headstrong Club."

"Yes sir."

"Creedence, call me Creedence. I saw you here earlier this evening."

"Yes, I'm sorry, I don't have the book."

"What book?"

"The children's book stolen from the Gazette. I let the boy right out the door. Unintentionally of course. Mr. Miles thinks me a thief."

"Never mind that."

"I intended to reimburse him. I know as well as anyone what a rare and dear thing, a book. But, I've no money now."

"But you weren't robbed."

Jeremy shook his head.

"Well, that doesn't matter. I settled it with Stephen. It's square and level."

"You did? Then it is I who is in your debt."

Scriven studied him a moment.

"Where will you stay?"

It was a warm night. Jeremy wondered if he could sleep in the park.

"Come home with me," Scriven said.

"Oh," Jeremy raised his hand in protest. "You are most kind."

Scriven rehooked his arm around Jeremy's elbow. He steered him toward his rooms at William Street.

"That's a devilish knock you've had. You need rest. I'll give you a proper examination."

"It isn't necessary."

Scriven patted the top of Jeremy's hand and gave it a gentle squeeze.

"You'll listen to me. I'm a doctor."

Chapter Nine

Scriven pressed his ear against the door to Cranston's quarters. He heard only snoring. He went to his own bedroom, splashed water on his face, changed his shirt, and applied another combful of pomade. Crisp and creased, he returned to the parlour. He poured two glasses of Croft's and brought one to Jeremy.

"I want to show you something," he said.

Scriven picked up a framed painting that had been leaning against the wall.

"I had Mr. Wentworth paint it today, at the Bottle and Glass."

Scriven regarded his portrait again, as if for the first time. It was exactly as he had pictured; the strong insightful brow, the distant gaze casting out from clear, blue eyes, ruddied cheeks accentuating the black curls swept forward, framing his face, the bright patina on the forehead, suggesting wit and intelligence. Each fold and dimple of his cravat faithfully reproduced. It was a harmonious blend of the Prince Regent and Beau Brummell, on their most glorious day.

He held it up against the wall, above the drinks trolley.

"Perhaps here?"

Jeremy nodded.

"Over the mantle might be best," Scriven said, crossing the room with the canvas.

"Help me with this will you Castor," he said, inclining his head toward the jumble of instruments obscuring the mantle. "Move them aside, make a little room."

Jeremy lifted an open, half-empty box, arranged the loose scalpels and hammers back into their green velvet grooves, carefully closed it, and stacked it at the end of the mantel. He picked up the flaking pestle and replaced it into its chipped mortar. He slid the collection of cupping jars down as far as he dared, so they crowded the apothecary cabinet and set the bronze scales seesawing. He put the two mottled trepanning drills on top of the cabinet, sneezing at the dust.

"Thank you and gesundheit," Scriven said, as he propped his portrait on the newly cleared space. "You should see a doctor."

"Do you have many patients?" Jeremy asked.

"Enough," Scriven stepped back to view the painting in the proper light. "Too many, to be frank. They aren't what they used to be. You're familiar with windy hypochondriacal melancholy?"

Jeremy shook his head. Scriven picked up a tubed device from the mantle and spanked his hand with its tarnished spout.

"That's my typical diagnosis. Vehement griping, fulsome belching, rumbling flatulence. The usual complaint of the harried wife, which is to say half the adult population. She desires rest. A reason to lie down.

Tobacco enema is what I generally prescribe."

Jeremy declined to take a closer look.

"I'm the one that could use a rest," the doctor continued, gesturing that they should return to the armchairs. "Between the club, my good works with the Lodge, my column in the Gazette, my prose and dramatical writing, it's difficult to find time for my practice. And, there is the time required to dress. Brummel recommends no less than five hours preparation each day. Kingston is hardly Grosvenor Square, but we must keep up standards, mustn't we?"

"I suppose we must."

"I should take on an apprentice, like Stevens, my tailor," Scriven said. "I could finish my play while I live off the avails of another."

"You know, those apprentices, the children, the ones that stole the book, they aren't so bad. Not thieves really, just unfortunate."

"Quite right. They need guidance, education, and some warm food. Those feral creatures tonight. Something must be done. In fact, I'll raise it at the lodge. I've proposed the founding of a school for the orphaned and indigent. We must push it forward."

"I actually read to them awhile, this evening, the boy and his sister. The boy's master is a bit of a sadist, apparently. His seamstress, a friend of mine, has run off. I fear she may be in some trouble."

Scriven got up, shaking his head.

"A master should look after his apprentice's needs. To do otherwise is just bad business."

He fetched the Croft's and refilled their sherry tumblers.

"Speaking of business, how fares the glass trade?" he asked.

"Ours is a fledging works," Jeremy said. "Most glass, like paper and other commodities, is imported. It's been difficult for us to get a toehold. That's why advertising is so important."

"Stephen Miles is a friend and I am his best contributor and benefactor. Stick with me. We'll get your announcement posted. How are you dealing with the contested will?"

"Contested will?"

"The notice," Scriven said. "In the Gazette."

When Jeremy still didn't show comprehension, Scriven brought him the copy of the Gazette, and opened it to the section. Jeremy read it and blanched.

"Not to worry," Scriven said jovially. "Likely just a crank. A false report designed to extort money. I've seen other notices like that in the paper that gave me a fright. Nothing will come of it, I'm sure. Have you engaged legal counsel?"

"No," Jeremy said, exasperated, "this is the first I've read it."

"Mr. Calhoun is a capable prattlebird. And, a fellow lodge member."

Scriven clapped his hand on Jeremy's shoulder.

"Have you ever considered the craft?"

Jeremy looked back blankly.

"Freemasonry," Scriven said. "You could come to the lodge with me tomorrow, as my guest. No better entrée into society. No sturdier lever acting upon the machinery of commerce."

"I've never met a freemason before."

"Worth a thousand notices in the Gazette," Scriven continued. "Might be just the thing to boost the fortunes of the glassworks. Miss Amelia would surely appreciate it."

"If you think I would be welcome."

"The lodge could use more upstanding young men such as yourself. Men given to good works."

"Thank you, sir, I shall consider it."

Scriven regarded Jeremy as he nursed his sherry.

"I'm grateful for your chivalry this evening."

"Pleased to be of service."

They sipped in silence, smiling, nodding.

"Let me take another look at your wound," Scriven said, finally.

Scriven retrieved a foot stool and placed it in front of Jeremy. He picked up a small tin from the bureau and removed the lid. He stood on the stool and he examined Jeremy's forehead, peering at the gash that was already beginning to crust at the edges. There was minimal inflammation and no discharge. He poked at the stitches.

"This really is first rate work."

He took a dollop of emollient from the tin with his index finger and he proceeded to rub it around the reddened flesh. He stood very close, emanating sherry and freshly applied sandalwood. Jeremy remained motionless. Scriven dabbed, his breath on Jeremy's ear, his chest pressing against Jeremy's shoulder. For a moment, he lost himself in his task and the rising warmth.

The uncommon heat of this long summer's day had made time malleable and stretched. It seemed like it might never end. Beyond the meager lights of the tavern stoops and the print shop lay the empty endlessness of the woods, dark and cathedral-like. Silent pines and maples standing aloof, indifferent to the struggles of people making their way on the shore of the lake. A few years before, Scriven had arrived at this distant outpost, alone, hoping to embroider a new pattern. An outline traced on a blank page that he could fill in. He had his acquaintances at the Bottle and Glass. His brothers at the lodge. There was Cranston. A hint of colour. But it was neither rich nor deep. He longed for something else.

At this late hour, Opprobrious' letter seemed like yesterday's news.

Scriven leant to the side, made unsteady by the evening's refreshment. The stool tipped and he lost his balance. Jeremy lunged and caught him. For a moment, they were frozen, Jeremy cradling Scriven in his arm, eye to eye, as though in the middle of an intimate, intricate dance.

It was just an instant that Scriven moved his hand up Jeremy's back. Just a moment that he lent forward. Quite as quickly Jeremy backed away, confused.

Scriven searched Jeremy's eyes, fearing anger. Or worse, disgust. There was neither. Still, they communicated much. Rejection. But also, kindness.

Scriven straightened and took a step back. He adjusted his frock coat.

"Apologies, Mr. Castor," he said, with an excess of

cheer, "my sense of balance is far from peerless at the best of times. Thank you for saving me from embarrassment."

He put his hand on Jeremy's upper arm and gestured toward the drinks trolley.

"A night cap? I can tell you about the lodge. We can plot a strategy to sell your glass."

"It's been a long day," Jeremy said. "I think, if you don't mind, I might turn in."

"Yes," Scriven said, tonelessly, "quite right."

❧ ❧ ❧ ❧ ❧

The morning might have been awkward. Cranston moved about the dining room with an air of barely concealed flippancy; the way he slid the scones from tray to platter a trifle more abruptly than usual, the thunk of the creamer as he set it down, the pots of preserves clinking as they were introduced to the table.

"Just as Mr. Castor stepped into the Gazette, the little cherub nabbed the book and dashed!"

Scriven boomed his report over the jangle of the cutlery and the shriek of the kettle.

"Conscientious as he is, Mr. Castor chased the boy, clear into Stuartsville and, on his return, helped me sweep the riff raff from the front of the print shop. Poor fellow was mugged it seems, his purse snatched, his head gashed — you take your chances in that part of town, that time of night. Naturally, I invited him to stay the night."

He stopped. He didn't owe Cranston explanation. The man was his servant after all. Besides, he'd brought drinking companions home from the tavern on several occasions. Still, he felt relief when Cranston had finished laying out breakfast and had left the dining room.

Scriven gestured to the spread. Jeremy smiled, helping himself to a glass of cider, and then another, and a cup of coffee with cream. He sliced a scone and pasted it with butter and jelly.

Once more, the doctor felt gratitude. Jeremy showed real appreciation, behaving as though the night before was the figment of an overheated imagination. The events were discussed no further. Scriven told him more about old, Ancient St. John's, Number Three, about some of the brothers, and who might be best to approach concerning the purchase of glass. He urged him to consider joining and he explained some of the ritual, without giving anything away that was truly sacred. Jeremy asked him about his play and, unlike so many others, he seemed to be genuinely interested. He talked about his own desire to write poetry and prose. They discovered a mutual admiration for Cowper and Coleridge. Jeremy even began to talk about his concern for the glassworks and his uncertainty about his place in it. He mentioned Amelia. He hesitated. Scriven could tell the young man wanted to say more. He wanted to unburden himself. He'd taken Scriven into his confidence. In this outpost brimming with flinty churls and grizzled tars here was a young man with a measure of refinement. A friend.

Chapter Ten

At Walker's hotel they ascended the stairs to the second floor and walked in silence down the corridor. With the brass handle of his cane Scriven struck three distinct raps against the last door on the left. As its interior shutter slid across, the Judas window in the centre of the door glowed amber, like a single, beastly eye. It darkened again. The Tyler stared out. He rapped back, three distinct times.

"Brother, how do Masons meet?" he asked from behind the door.

"On the level," Scriven replied, winking up at Jeremy.

Scriven adored being a Mason; being part of something exalted and greater than himself. He reveled in the symbolism and the ritual and the camaraderie. The sense of belonging. It pleased him to bring another young man into the fold.

The door opened. Behind, they could see James McTaggart, in a leather apron, his hand resting on the hilt of a scimitar.

"Brother," McTaggart said, "from whence do you come?"

"From the west and traveling to the east," Scriven replied.

"Why? What do you most desire?"

"Light," Scriven replied, "we search for more light."

"Welcome brothers," McTaggart said. He took several steps back, allowing the men to enter the vestibule before bolting the door behind them. Taking McTaggart's extended right hand, Scriven pressed his thumb nail into the joint between the first and second fingers. McTaggart returned the grip.

"Jeremy Castor, a prospective Brother and, tonight, my guest."

McTaggart retrieved a leather smock from a hook and handed it to him.

Satisfied that Scriven had his apron tied and entirely visible, and that Jeremy was not wearing a hat or anything similarly offensive, McTaggart delivered three deliberate raps against the interior door. Talking within broke off and three raps answered. The door opened a crack.

"Junior Deacon," McTaggart whispered. "Scriven and Scriven's guest, Mr. Jeremy Castor."

The door closed again. A moment later, it re-opened.

The Master, sitting at the east end of the hall, flanked on either side by the senior deacon and chaplain, motioned them in. The assembly, cloaked in the shadows cast by lamps arrayed along the walls, watched as they crossed the hall. The faces of their fellows were obscured by the partial light. But they felt the heat of their stares; it was warm on Scriven's skin, life-affirming, like an ancient sun-god's blessing.

Could any of these be Opprobrious?

Yellow light flickered against their gleaming, receding foreheads; not enough to fully illuminate faces. Some elders bent forward, hands cupped to their ears, better to hear the festival chairman who now took the floor. With their long, white beards, made misshapen and monstrous by the gloom, they resembled supplicating magi. A penumbra of candlelight marked the sharp instruments placed atop the altar, as though awaiting sacrifice. Scriven could imagine he participated in some ancient, Mithraist ceremony; a cavern far below ground hidden away from common society, reserved for senators, and centurions, burly and hard, browned by long campaigns into Parthia and the Eastern beyond. Swirls of frankincense and myrrh snaked up from censers, heightened senses, and expanded notions of possibility. They might, for a rapturous moment, become connected; to each other, to a higher power.

None of these could have written the letter. He couldn't credit it.

Scriven looked to the east, where the treasurer and secretary sat, and between them, in the raised, upholstered chair, this year's Worshipful Master, Hugh Thomson.

"Brother Scriven," Thomson said with a beneficent half-smile, "who is our guest?"

"Worshipful," Scriven replied, bowing slightly, "Mr. Jeremy Castor, late of His Majesty's Navy, now proprietor of Kingston's first glassworks. A prospective candidate for entered apprentice Mason."

"Brother Scriven, you are well aware it is customary to petition the Lodge first before admitting a candidate to proceedings."

"Worshipful. I thought Mr. Castor might be allowed to witness a meeting that he might better appreciate the eminence of the Lodge before officially putting forth his candidature."

Thomson leaned over to confer with the Senior Deacon. He whispered to the Secretary and the Treasurer.

"Welcome Mr. Castor."

Inside the lodge, all brothers are considered equal and, as a man, the Worshipful Master is only the first among these equals. Even so, for the duration of his term, the chosen brother represents the entire glory and light of the Master of the lodge; he demands, and receives, the full respect of his fraternity. Scriven accepted this article of Masonic propriety as surely as he did the number and extent of creases in the perfect cravat. Even so, acceptance made it no easier for him to reconcile Hugh Thomson, hatter, purveyor of rorams and beaver bonnets, with grand exalted Master, rightful wearer of the lambskin apron and the jewelled Master's medallion.

Thomson ran a tolerable hattery. His stock, made on premises with local beaver and muskrat, wouldn't be out of place in a shop window on the Strand. Even better, from time to time he imported the latest fashions from Europe. Just last month Scriven himself had purchased a John Bull made in London at Cecil House, from the glossiest hatter's plush.

Still. Scriven couldn't forget that, on the outside, Thomson took his orders. Outside the lodge, the man was just a hatter.

Worshipful looked back from the Master's chair

serenely, like there was nothing more natural that a hatter should be crowned king. With two hands above his head, he steadied his Master's topper, a towering, velvet empire with brass circlet he had introduced as a further symbol of Masterful authority. With his outsized stem and elevated position he loomed over the rest of the assembly.

"Right Worshipfuls, Worshipfuls, Wardens and Brethren."

Thomson addressed them now in the stentorian voice he used in meetings, as though he projected to an amphitheatre of thousands, not a close conference room of forty. It was a grave offense to disclose any lodge business outside of its tyled walls, but surely Walker's guests one floor below and even the strollers out on Store Street could hear Thomson now.

"Paper," Thomson said. He held up above his head between the thumb and forefinger of his two hands a piece that looked to be about as big as a quarter-page of the Gazette.

"What we have here today, is the first prototype of a Bank of Upper Canada note."

He handed the note to the junior warden who circulated it through the room. He went on to give a report on the proposed Bank and the confusing state of currency in the province with crowns, guineas, silver dollars, York ratings, and Halifax ratings. A provincial standard, Thomson argued, in which the bank can print the money and better control monetary policy would be a boon to all those men of enterprise in Kingston and throughout Upper Canada.

The brethren applauded.

Hugh Thomson. Always Hughie bloody Thomson.

The Senior Deacon stood and read last minutes, speaking of plans for the upcoming St. John the Evangelist festival, the proposed foundation of a Lancasterian school, and a list of prospective new members. Then, he opened the floor to general business.

"Brother...?" Senior Deacon asked a man who had stood in the North.

"Spafford."

The dust of Walker's old hall rose and fell in the shafts of lantern light, as though in suspension. Jeremy breathed in violently at the utterance of the name Spafford, lodging a fleck in the back of his throat. He tried, in vain, to muffle his spluttering.

"Rupert Spafford of Lodge 223 Meathfield," continued the man in the North, louder now, to be heard over Jeremy's coughing. "Nephew to Colonel Noble Spafford, one of your own, recently deceased."

"Ah yes," Thomson said, "Noble. We are sorry for your loss brother Spafford."

"I thank ye for that."

"What brings you across the water?"

"I am here on legal business, Worshipful. To settle my late uncle's estate."

"Was it not settled?" Thomson asked, turning to the secretary. "Didn't Brother Douglas handle that case last fall?"

"Not to my satisfaction," Spafford replied, before the secretary had a chance. "I am currently seeking good legal counsel. If, after the meeting, any brother might recommend to me an advocate both reliable and discreet, I'd be much obliged. I have the pleasure of enjoying Brother Walker's hospitality right here in his fine hotel."

Jeremy's fit intensified. Scriven leaned into him.

"What is wrong with you?" he asked.

"Spafford," was Jeremy's strangled, whispered reply. "Come to reclaim the glassworks."

"We welcome you to Ancient St. John's Lodge, Number Three, of Ancient, Free, and Accepted Mr. Spafford, and to Kingston."

Spafford bowed and took his seat.

"Mr. Castor," Thomson said, annoyed. "Are you unwell? We all could use a drink, of course. But perhaps you most urgently? There on the table is some watered wine."

Jeremy bowed and crossed the floor sheepishly to pour himself a windpipe-cleansing cup.

"How do mason's part," Thomson asked the Master Warden.

"On the square," came the reply.

"Please inform the Tyler we now intend to close the lodge. So mote it be."

Chapter Eleven

Amelia crossed her leg and adjusted the hem of her robe so that it extended all the way to the crest of her bare, lifted instep. Despite the perspiration that gathered at the hollow of her throat and trickled uncomfortably down her breastbone, she wound the silk scarf around her neck once more to suppress any hint of décolletage. Still, Pastor Charles Ainsworth, of the King's Mills Methodists, would not meet her eye. His gaze roved over her shoulder to the curvaceous apples, straining their spreading boughs to nearly touch those that had fallen. It followed the pairs of chasing squirrels, looping the trunks. And it went beyond their bench at the edge of the thicket, to the rows of corn, standing erect, bending slightly beneath the breeze. His attention settled on every facet of creation, from greatest to least. Everywhere, everything, except Amelia.

"My," Ainsworth said, revolving the brim of his felt hat through clenched fingers, "it's another scorcher, isn't it?"

"Yes," she said, "that's why I thought the orchard might be more pleasant. I hope it meets your needs?"

"The Lord has seen fit to test us, I think, to see how we behave in heat."

The pastor's eyes darted from the corn tassels to Amelia's lashes, scanning for signs of affront.

"In the heat," he corrected himself quickly. "The heat. Pardon."

His eyes were back in the trees, embracing the pink, hanging fruits.

"Shall we discuss your vision for the new apse window," Amelia said, clamping her hand over her well-clad knee. "A blue background with a gold cross? Our Bennet is a superb craftsman. He'll be able to devise something both handsome and tasteful."

"Shouldn't we wait for Mr. Castor?"

"He's yet to return from Kingston, I'm afraid. I'm not sure what must be keeping him. In the meantime," she said, leaning forward conspiratorially, "you have me."

"Oh, I see. Maybe I should go and return another time?"

"I assure you that I can be just as helpful as Mr. Castor."

"Perhaps I should meet with this Mr. Bennet?"

Amelia pictured herself leading timid, god-fearing Ainsworth across the yard into the sooted brick cavern of the glassworks to introduce him to her glassblower, Bennet, with his raggedy, scarecrow frame, his rotted jack-o-lantern face, his stump-toothed grin, bellowing a hellish furnace.

"If you were able to give me the dimensions of the window and the precise design," she said. "I could make some calculations and arrive at an approximate price."

Ainsworth pinned his knees together, folding his hat in half between.

"Oh heavens," he said, "I wouldn't dream of coarsening you with business matters. Though I do appreciate your company while I wait."

"I don't find it vulgar. Not at all. I find it stimulating."

"Stimulating? Surely not. Not the appropriate activity for a young lady, I shouldn't think."

Amelia wanted to snatch the hat from his fiddling fingers and put her dainty foot through it. She wanted a word or two with Jeremy also, who'd been due home late morning, but still hadn't arrived. It was well past noon.

"Be that as it may," she said, inhaling deeply, "I am here and perfectly capable. Mr. Castor must be held up in town. You don't want to have wasted your trip."

"What if he disagrees tomorrow with what you guarantee today?"

She wanted to say that Mr. Castor wouldn't dare. He was merely the face. But, she reminded herself, there was nothing mere about it. Presentation was everything.

"He appoints me as his proxy in these rare situations when he is indisposed. In the most unlikely event that he should see things differently, we would send notice to you immediately. I'm intimately acquainted with all aspects of the business."

Ainsworth looked past her ear at the bumblebee tipped into a purple aster, wobbling at its petals as though intoxicated.

"Intimately?"

"Oh, Mr. Ainsworth! Sweet Mary's wig!"

The pastor looked stricken. He leapt from the bench.

"There he is," he cried, already on the run back toward the house. "Mr. Castor! Over here!"

Jeremy didn't look like the same man who had left Willowpath a day earlier. His sweat-slicked hair hung over one side of his face, pasted over his ear like a leather cap. His face was darkened by the chin strap of his rudimentary beard and he had ashy circles around his eyes. He paced before the back door of the house, shouting, Amelia! Amelia!

Ainsworth accosted him with hand extended. Jeremy swung round wide-eyed.

"Mr. Castor?" the pastor said, less certainly, withdrawing his hand.

"Who are you? Amelia!"

She had arrived shortly behind. She steered Ainsworth out of the way.

"Mr. Castor, this is Charles Ainsworth," she said. "Pastor with the King's Mills Methodist Church. You were to meet today, regarding the apse window. We met with him once before, at the church, a week ago."

Jeremy's directed his filmy eyes at Amelia, then to Ainsworth, then back to Amelia. As soon as the meeting at the Number Three lodge had let out, he had given his regrets to Scriven and he had rushed up the Montreal road as fast as he could. He had left before the post-meeting luncheon. Again, he'd forgotten to take refreshment. Blood pulsed behind his eye. He felt like his head might cleave at the point of the wound, the hammering was so great.

"News," he managed. His mouth opened. It snapped shut. Open. Shut. A netted fish. He collapsed.

"Oh my," Ainsworth said. "Perhaps I should come another time."

"Jeremy!" Amelia cried, crouching at his side. Nearing, she noticed the gash along his hairline. "He's been hurt."

She cradled his head in her lap and fanned him with her hands. She looked up at the parson, not knowing what to do. Ainsworth stood before her, tearing at his felt hat, desperate to keep his eyes on the heavy, nodding sunflower or the fat rose hips, anywhere but down her gauzy dress, the front of which had opened as her scarf fell away.

Jeremy regained consciousness almost immediately, overheated blood flowing back to his head without having to traverse upwards the length of his towering body.

"My apologies, Mr. Ainsworth," he said, his eyes clearing. "I've been to town."

"I see, I see," the pastor said, as though that might explain it all.

"Little parched, is all," Jeremy said. "This heat."

"I'm glad to see you feeling a little better."

"Jeremy!" Alice had emerged from the house and now knelt beside her son, pushing the damp hair from his eyes. "What's happened?"

And Millie, Amelia's mother, and Mrs. Simkins, and the other help, and before long Bennet arrived to crane his pumpkin head over the crowd.

"I'll come another time," the parson said, not thinking anyone heard him. He replaced his hat and set out down the lane for the Montreal road.

"Thank you for coming," Amelia called after him, "hope to see you again."

He pivoted, gave a little wave, and carried on. She watched him disappear down the lane.

"We've lost the patronage of the Methodists, I fear."

"Amelia." Millie said. "There are more important things."

"Sorry," Jeremy said, looking at Amelia. "I will go to see him at King's Mills."

"When you've fully recovered."

"I'm fine," Jeremy said, between deep draughts of the water Mrs. Simkins had fetched.

"We should call for a doctor," Alice said, "Dr. Scriven."

"No!" Jeremy cried, sloshing the cup of water. "A little parched, is all," he added, seeing the alarm in their faces. "Just need a little rest."

"And this?" Alice said, pointing at the tidy line of thread crosshatching his hairline.

Later, Jeremy would wonder how much to tell.

After a bucket-full of fresh water and a lunch of bread, butter, and molasses, he'd snoozed a while in the shade of the willows. Renewed, he joined Amelia outside for a supper of cold trout, new potatoes with dill mayonnaise, tomato slices drenched in oil and vinegar. Jeremy pushed a forkful of the coral flesh into his mouth and chewed thoughtfully. He pushed another forkful in directly behind, before he'd swallowed the first. Amelia had yet to take up a utensil.

"Well?" she asked, her head tilted to the right, a finger stroking her sharpened eyebrow.

Jeremy made a noise through a mouthful of potato.

Her head flopped sharply to the left and her brow knitted. He stopped chewing, studied her a moment, and swallowed noisily. He drank from his mug of cider.

"Why don't you start with that," she said, pointing at the stitching.

Jeremy eyed her. He wondered whether he should reserve sympathy potential for last.

He told her about the stolen book, his chase through Stuartsville, his collision with the beam, his confrontation with Carmichael.

"Interestingly," he said, stuffing in another forkful of tomato, "it was the same fellow I had met along the way."

Amelia frowned.

He chewed. "A ploughman."

Amelia massaged her brow as though she had a sudden headache.

"I'd forgotten to bring any drink with me, and he offered. I promised to pay him back in town. I couldn't part ways without returning the favour."

"Name?"

"Carmichael. Carmichael Jones."

"Jeremy!" Amelia's face contorted and she thumped the table, causing her pewter mug to topple to the grass.

"Steady," Jeremy said, looking regretfully at the cider returning to the soil.

"That's the man who ruined my father."

"I couldn't refuse him, he, he..." Jeremy didn't want to say that unless he'd diverted him, Carmichael showed every intention of showing up at Willowpath.

"I was thirsty," he said. "I'm sorry. He tried to lead

me to some vandemonian slum, the only ale house open at that hour, but I refused him."

"You went to Stuartsville? With Carmichael Jones?"

"Not with him. I found him there."

"Never," she said, the tablecloth balled up in her small fists, "promise me you will never deal with that wretch again."

Jeremy held his hands up, the fork and knife dripping oil.

"I promise."

"You should know better than to loiter around Stuartsville late at night."

"Well," he said, "there were the children, also. Won't you eat something?"

Amelia stared.

"Urchins," he continued, "I helped them cadge a book. Inadvertently, mind. I chased them through the slums to get it back. These tomatoes are delightful."

Her frown deepened.

"What else?" she asked, waving him on. Now that he had begun to spill the tap opened fully.

"I'm to become a mason."

"Indeed?"

"Yes, of the free and accepted masons. That's why I'm late. I went to an introductory meeting. I'm to be an entered apprentice. Dr. Scriven, himself a Master third degree, impressed upon me that there being no better emollient for the calloused world of business."

"He did."

"Aye, he did. He agreed to sponsor my candidacy."

"That's so?"

"'Tis," he said. "I did it for you Amelia. For the glassworks. For us."

He waited. She said nothing.

"Please, try the trout," he said. "For Mrs. Simkin's sake, she made it especially. The mayonnaise is sublime."

She made no move toward the silverware.

"I'll still be able to act as an agent for the works. The connections I'll make will be invaluable."

She stared at the fallen pewter, nudging it with her toe.

"I'll be in town more often, though. I'm sorry to say, we'll see a little less of each other, but I suppose that is the price that must be paid for securing more business."

He wished she would say something.

"I do hope our reunions will be made that much sweeter."

Her gaze, like Ainsworth's earlier, was now in the orchard, where a thin tabby called Lancelot scattered the shrilling squirrels.

"So," he continued, when he could no longer bear the silence. He'd placed his knife and fork at three o'clock and pushed his empty plate into the centre of the table. "I'm to take my test Thursday of next month, at The Ancient St. John's Lodge."

"Number Three," she said.

"You know it?" he said, leaning forward, relieved to hear her speak again.

"Yes, of course. The Colonel Spafford, my late husband; he was a member, Third Grade Sachem, or whatever it is. He was often there. Told me next to nothing about it."

"Spafford!" Jeremy repeated. "Spafford! I almost forgot. That is why I rushed up here in the first place, taking no food or water. I have news to tell."

"What? What is it?"

"There was a Spafford. Another Spafford. At the meeting."

"Another Spafford?"

"Yes, a nephew. Rupert. Fresh from Ireland. With a claim. Said the settling of his late uncle's estate wasn't to his satisfaction, or some such rot."

Amelia turned to face him again, with such directness and heat he looked away.

"It shouldn't be anything," he asked, "should it? It was settled, by that Douglas fellow. The solicitor. Wasn't it?"

"You took this long to tell me," she said.

"I intended to tell you first thing. I keeled over and then forgot. The trip was so eventful, there was a lot to tell. But, I'm sure it's fine. Douglas settled it."

For an eternity, they were quiet. Their own silence amplified the clamour of the cicadas and crickets. Jeremy felt light-headed again and still hungry. The breeze had died away. Under the late summer sun at the top of its arc and the proximity of Amelia's hot glare, he sweltered, as though caught beneath a giant magnifying glass. He looked across at Amelia's untouched plate, longing to swat away the bluebottles traipsing the shining fillet, wishing he could ask if she was done and could he finish it.

"What about the advertisement," she asked, finally, her eyes flashing.

"The advertisement?"

"You submitted the advertisement, at least?"

His failing expression was answer enough. She snatched her plate, clapped it over his, and took them both up. She strode across the lawn toward the kitchen side door of the house, her left thumb lodged in congealing mayonnaise. Halfway, with her free hand, she picked up the glistening trout from the plate and she flung it into the orchard.

It landed at Lancelot's brindled feet.

Chapter Twelve

Fish bones, head and tail attached, slapped wetly against the transverse of the pillory. The carcass slid down the crossbeam and rested against the back of Lilac's head. She nodded and shook but managed only to entwine it further. Tines of bone combed into the crown of her matted hair. Her hands moved as though they were disembodied and unaware of their arms, outstretched on either side of the pillory's frame. Her birdlike fingers fluttered and clutched from their holes.

Sweeney wiped fish slime from his hands by rubbing them up and down his trousers. He brought them behind his back and posed like an artist, admiring his work, appraising the justness of his aim, exhorting his younger associates to share in his laughter. James O'Neal emerged from behind one of the market stalls and flung himself at the bigger boy, bringing him to the ground. He flailed at the boy's chest with his fists. Younger boys and girls gathered and cheered. James' sister remained at the corner of the stall, her face half-obscured by the linen remnant she chewed.

The supervising constable stepped across and pulled James off the boy by his collar, tearing it.

"Is this how young gentlemen behave?" the constable asked, jerking both boys by their elbows.

Jeremy took the opportunity of the distraction to edge toward the pillory. He'd been lingering on the edge of the market, not wanting to get too close. He was there to meet with Dr. Scriven and a couple of his fellow brothers. After lunch at Old King's Head they were to go over the procedure, to learn the lines, to prepare for his initiation. He'd gone ahead with the enterprise, despite Amelia's skeptical silence, assuring her that nothing would go wrong this time, that membership in the lodge would lead to a dozen more contracts that year. He hadn't told her about Lilac. There'd been no good way of mentioning it. Maybe it was best left unsaid. It had been a shock, stumbling upon Lilac in the square, the rough wood of the stocks clamping her neck. He had to speak to her. To give comfort. To apologize.

Few people seemed to be taking any notice of the ruckus. They carried on with their haggling and gossiping. Gone were the days when a villain in the stocks caused the market to swell. The idle and bored and vicious reserved their rotting vegetables for livestock. Nowadays, the spectacle was purely for children.

Jeremy crept closer.

"I'll have you up before the magistrate for causing a public disturbance."

The constable kicked Sweeney hard in his trouser seat.

"Clear out," he said.

Jeremy stood next to the stained, stinking pillory. He was close enough to hear Lilac's sniffling. Close enough to see the spittle glossing her ringlets. He leaned in.

"I'm so sorry," he whispered. "I didn't know."

"Deacon," she heaved, without looking up.

"Is it because of me?"

"Get away."

"Because of the other night?"

"It will be you digging rotten egg from your earholes," the constable was saying to James O'Neal, as he led him back toward the pillory by his ear, twisting at the cartilage like it was a troublesome hasp.

"I'll help you," Jeremy said, fiercely. "I promise. Only a half hour and all will be right."

He pinched the fish tail between his thumb and forefinger, intending to extricate it.

"Hello," said the constable, booming, back at the platform. Jeremy dropped his hand and pressed it to his side as he did when drilled on board the Lancer.

"Acquainted?" the constable asked.

Jeremy turned. He shook his head.

"Best move along then."

Jeremy nodded and turned to go.

"He knows her," a voice called.

Carmichael Jones stood up from the nearby fencepost against which he'd been resting. He wiped at his chin with his handkerchief.

"In fact," Carmichael said, advancing, "this is the cove who availed her services."

The constable turned back to Jeremy.

"That true?"

Jeremy continued backing away. What scandal if the manager of Willowpath Glassworks was found consorting with a prostitute in the pillory? He glanced around. Still, no-one in the market had taken any notice.

"I seen him." Carmichael said.

The constable lifted Lilac's chin, pinching her neck painfully against the cuff of wood.

"Know this man?"

Strands of damp hair clung to her face, covering her flooded eyes.

"No," she said.

"I seen him leave her shanty," Carmichael continued, "half-clothed, panting like a goat."

"Mr. Castor!"

Dr. Scriven approached, a cane in one hand, a fresh Gazette in the other. Stevens and Coulson followed.

"Excuse me," Jeremy said to the constable, over his shoulder, as he crossed to meet Scriven. In his haste, he swung his long legs a little further than intended and kicked one of the cages littering the market edge. The rooster inside blared angrily, which spurred the next rooster, and the next. Outrage cascaded across the cages and the square erupted in fury.

"Well done, Castor," Scriven shouted. "Come away from this racket."

Carmichael badgered the constable, insisting it was Jeremy who had solicited Lilac's services the night she was arrested.

"He appears to be an associate of Dr. Scriven," the constable said, uninterested in pursuing the matter further. "If the doctor vouches for him, that's fair enough. Move along now Carmichael. Stay out of trouble."

The constable stood and glared until Carmichael left, reluctantly. He sat James with him on the platform behind the pillory.

"Do you know that woman?" Scriven shouted, puzzled, pulling Jeremy away.

Jeremy nodded. When they were clear of the poultry sellers and could make themselves heard, Scriven introduced him to fellow lodge members Stevens, his tailor, and Coulson the lawyer.

"It's appalling," Scriven said, gesturing toward the pillory. "The colonies always cling longer to the perversities of the mother country don't they? Westminster as much as banned this particular humiliation, not a few months ago. Here, the mob isn't quite ready to let go, the opportunity to reduce one of their own. Who is the poor, unfortunate woman?"

Jeremy looked at him. He wanted to tell him it was his friend, Lilac, and that she had been mistreated at the hand of Stevens. But he couldn't bring himself to do it. Not here, in the street, having just met these two men, fellows meant to help him get his lodge membership.

"Has its place," Stevens said, shrugging. "How else to deal with a common doxy? Shame for shame."

The tailor found a wayward button in his pocket and he pulled it out. He took a few steps toward the pillory.

"Such disregard. Willing to sell themselves. A half hour in the stocks is just the cost of doing business."

He flicked the button at Lilac's head.

"Doxies! Common as fleas and just as filthy."

Lilac raised her head.

"I am not a doxy," she said.

"Owen!" Scriven cried, recognizing Lilac now. "That's your seamstress. Is it not? What's her name?"

Stevens took another step, scrutinizing.

"So it is. Lilac."

"Owen," Scriven said, turning on the tailor. "What's the meaning of this?"

Stevens stared at Lilac.

"I told you she was willful," he said.

"I recommended this young lady to you."

"I told you she was wild and unable to take instruction."

"You agreed to take her on as your assistant and charge."

"She run off, ain't she?"

"You have a responsibility to her."

"A thief and all."

"Owen. What sort of example are you setting for our new initiate? Remember your Preston. 'To relieve the distressed is a duty incumbent on all men, but particularly on Freemasons. To soothe the unhappy, to sympathise with their misfortunes, to compassionate their miseries, and to restore their troubled minds, is the great aim we have in view.'"

Stevens scraped the mire from the bottom of his shoe against the stipes of the pillory. It fell near Lilac's bare foot.

"Once a doxy, always a doxy," he said.

Lilac tagged his shoulder with spit. Stevens raised the back of his hand like he might cuff her.

"Steady, Mr. Stevens."

The constable drew up from his seat at the back of the platform.

"You may throw the blackened fruit, the stinking straw, the mucky clumps, as custom allows. You mustn't strike the prisoner."

Free of the constable's hand on his shoulder, James O'Neal stood up.

"Owen," Scriven cried again. "Your apprentice. The boy I found for you."

Master and apprentice beheld each other. James bolted from the platform and scattered up a side street, his sister following far behind.

"This is most disappointing," Scriven said. "That boy shouldn't be loitering around the market. As his master you should be attending to every level of his education, not just vocational, but social and moral as well. And to see your seamstress here, so indelicately, what impression must that make?"

Stevens stared, his hand still raised, his glossy eyes reflecting everything: Scriven's purple face, the twinkling market, the pillory's cruciform shadow.

"Find him," Scriven said.

"What of lunch?" Stevens asked. "It was mutton at King's Head, I thought."

"Get your boy," Scriven said, "and feed him. With bread. Gentle instruction. Kindness most of all."

Stevens turned, with petulance, and shuffled down the street in the direction that James and his sister had fled.

Scriven held out the bundled Gazette. He regarded it a moment before handing it to Jeremy. He stepped closer to Lilac. He waved away the constable, indicating he meant no harm. The constable retreated to his bench.

"Quiet, child," he said as he removed the dross from her hair and stroked her trembling cheek.

He extricated the fish bone gently from the tangles and dropped it to the ground. He swept away the flies. He took his handkerchief from his pocket and he wiped the coppery string of tobacco juice from the frame of the pillory and the nape of her neck.

"You're a sturdy weave, aren't you?"

He folded the soiled handkerchief and put it back in his pocket. He began to release his buff cravat from its tightly controlled mathematical. When it was completely unraveled, he dabbed her face with it. It's residue of neroli and ambergris masked for a moment the reeking street. He draped the creamy silk over her head like a shroud. It shielded her from sun, biting insects, censorious looks. He held his hand out to Jeremy. Jeremy passed him the Gazette. Scriven unfolded it and lay it down over the filth beneath her feet.

"Aren't you afraid to know me?" she asked, her voice a low whisper.

"On the contrary. After all, we all make mistakes, isn't that right Castor?"

Jeremy stepped across.

"Yes, we do," he said. "I'm so sorry Lil'."

"I apologize on behalf of Owen," Scriven said. "It's disgraceful what he said. I'll talk to him. I'll have you reinstated."

"No!"

Scriven stepped back. He ducked his head and peered beneath the tented cravat and saw wounded misgiving on Lilac's face.

"We'll find us both another tailor," he said.

Lilac's gaze dropped back to the straw and mire.

"We'll get you stitching again."

Jeremy ran his fingers along the fissure at his temple, measuring the rate of renewal, as he'd done habitually twenty times a day since Lilac had stitched him up a week earlier. It was healing admirably, in short order and without complication. There was every indication that any scar would fade to nothing. He traced the waning ridges of tight, perfectly symmetrical cross hatches with his index finger.

Expert stitching.

"She can work for you!" Jeremy shouted.

Scriven stared.

"She did this," Jeremy continued, pointing to his head. "Remember? In your drawing room you remarked on what fine work it was."

Jeremy lifted his hair from his forehead and Scriven examined the scabbing more closely.

"That's her? There is almost no trace."

Jeremy nodded. Scriven continued to examine.

"Well, I'm not sure," he said finally, coughing. He eyed the Gazette now smutted with mucky footprints. "I'm not sure I need an assistant just now. It's a small circle of patients."

"But, you do. The other afternoon, before the Mason's meeting, you said an apprentice is what you needed most," Jeremy insisted.

"Did I?"

"Very busy you said, need a rest, an assistant to help with your practice, so you can devote time to more important endeavours, play-writing and such."

Scriven tugged at his lapels and fingered his cufflinks. Above the general din of the square, barkers bellowed their claims about Bateman's Pectoral Drops, Gilson's Female Pills, and the miraculous Paregoric Elixir.

Scriven turned back and called across the platform. "Constable?"

"Sir?"

"What becomes of Miss Lilac?"

"A month in jail."

Scriven tossed the constable a shining guinea.

"Please make sure she is well taken care of in the meantime."

He grabbed two fingers from Lilac's trapped left hand and waggled them.

"You're hired," he said, "we'll call on you in a month. It's perfect timing. Mr. Castor, your first good deed as a free and accepted Mason."

Chapter Thirteen
September 1817

The tavern's noise was muted and distant. A bittered sling had been put down. Jeremy's eyes had still not adjusted to the dim light of the Bottle and Glass. Images of the ceremony at Walker's continued to swirl his brain.

Minutes earlier, he'd been standing in the middle of the Masonic hall, wearing only a loincloth around his middle and a linen rag over his eyes. A spot of blood pearled at his left breast where it had been punctured by a compass point.

"From whence have you come?" the Master had asked.

"From the west and traveling to the east."

"Why do you leave the west and travel to the east?"

"In search of light."

"Brethren, stretch forth your hands and assist in bringing this newly made brother from darkness to light."

The great hall filled with the noise of shifting chairs and scuffing boots. Members circled, clapping and stomping. There was the crack of hands and the clinking of metal. It became perceptibly warmer. Perspiration gathered at Jeremy's hairline and trickled down his neck and jaw. Hot fumes singed his nostrils and made him light-headed. His breath grew shallower. Unconsciously, he tightened his fists. His ears pricked, involuntarily. Boot heels thunderous. Hard palms percussive. The chanting began. It lunged. Soft, then louder.

"Brother, to you the secrets of Masonry are about to be unveiled, and a brighter sun never shone lustre on your eyes. What do you most desire?"

"Light."

And, he'd got it.

"God said let there be light, and there was light."

The junior released the blindfold and let it fall.

Jeremy opened his eyes to a bank of flaming beeswax. He fell to his knees, blind again.

"Congratulations."

The inflected voice brought Jeremy back to the Bottle and Glass. His eyes began to adjust.

"Rupert Spafford," the man said.

He was slight, almost elfin, his marble-like skin pale to the point of translucence. A forelock of black, glossy hair fell across his face. With his tawny cravat, ruffled shirt, and hessian boots, he could have passed for Scriven's protégé.

He extended his fine-boned hand. Jeremy took it and engulfed it in his own. Spafford dug his thumb into Jeremy's forefinger executing the newly acquired secret handshake.

"From what I've seen so far," he said, "you've joined a damn fine lodge. May I?"

Jeremy nodded and kicked out a chair. Spafford

bowed, sat, and slid the chair closer. He sipped from his own bittered sling.

"I understand you are involved with the Willowpath Glassworks," he said.

"I am," Jeremy said.

"Business manager?"

"Yes."

"Have you met McCallum?" Spafford asked, hooking a thumb back toward a man behind him.

"No."

"One of your lodge fellows and the best lawyer in the district, I'm told."

Jeremy exchanged a Masonic handshake with the man who'd dragged over a nearby chair.

"I've come a long way," Spafford continued.

"Yes?"

"Ballivor. Ireland. Do you know why I'm here?"

"Yes, I heard you speak at the last meeting. You are contesting the will and rightful ownership of the Spafford grant."

"That's it exactly. Number Three is fortunate to have you. Sharp. Proper Masonic material."

It sounded facetious, but Jeremy couldn't be sure.

"At any rate, we're brothers now. You should know my intentions. Nothing adversarial, not t'all. Two wills. That's the walnut. I knew uncle Noble was dotty. Never the same after the Siege of Roses, mother says. But two wills? And a wife fifty years his junior, give or take. But maybe it was her that spun his head sponge, what?"

"Mr. Spafford..."

"Come along, old boy. Just brothers sharing a drink after lodge. We can speak plainly here, surely."

"I don't think it's appropriate..."

"Amelia she's called, Amelia Spafford, yes, your boss?"

"Boss? Well, I..."

"The widow. Her name on this other, ostensible will. You're her employee, technically speaking."

"Yes."

"Try that bittered sling, before it loses its cool."

Jeremy nodded, but didn't sip.

"I must admit," Spafford continued, "I'd despaired of finding a decent cocktail in the colonies. Consider my fears allayed."

"Amelia," Jeremy started, "that is to say, Mrs. Spafford, has retained my services to help manage her estate and the operations of the glassworks."

"Yes, of course, that's what I'm saying. Whether the estate is hers, in the eyes of the law, well that's what I've come all this way to settle. But I say this as a friend," Spafford paused and put his hand on Jeremy's forearm, "and as a brother. I'm certain we can come to some amicable solution, satisfactory to all involved."

Spafford raised his glass, almost empty, and waited. Jeremy picked up his own, untouched, and raised the lip of the glass, so it kissed Spafford's, briefly. Spafford downed the final mouthful and rapped the table with the heavy bottomed glass.

"Your round?" he asked.

"You know," Jeremy said, "we have engaged a lawyer too. Calhoun. Also of this lodge."

"I'm aware."

"If I'd known we'd be discussing the matter of the will..."

"Matter of the wills. Plural."

"I'd have made sure Mr. Calhoun was here."

"Oh, 'tis fine. This is just getting acquainted. Purely informal. And toasting your initiation into the order. Anyway, Calhoun will be along presently."

Jeremy had brought the glass to his lips but lowered it again.

"We've been in touch with Mr. Calhoun, of course," Spafford continued. "It's all arranged. Besides, we couldn't have any serious discussions without Miss Amelia."

"Oh, it's a long way from Willowpath," Jeremy said with confidence. "I come into town and conduct business on behalf of the estate, on her behalf. She doesn't enjoy the journey, the dust, the deer flies, the drunks... "

The front door of the Bottle and Glass clattered. Calhoun stepped in. He moved to the side. Amelia followed, wearing a lavender gown and a feathery muslin scarf draping her shoulders, obscuring her neckline. She stood in the foyer a moment, her eyes adjusting.

"Apologies, old boy," Spafford said to Jeremy, waving his hand up by his brow, his eyes not straying from the foyer. "Distracted. Please, continue."

"Amelia!" Jeremy called, his tone louder and more startled than he intended. Amelia turned her head, smiled, and putting her hand on Calhoun's elbow, moved toward the table.

"I hired a coach and sent Calhoun to fetch her," Spafford said.

They stood as Amelia approached. Jeremy felt any

remaining sense of control ebb away. He moved to intercept her, toppling a chair as he did.

"Amelia," he said, offering his own arm. Calhoun moved on toward the bar.

"What are you doing here?"

"I was invited," she said.

"But you hate the journey into town."

"I'm here," she said, her voice lowered, "to save Willowpath."

"But, Calhoun. And, me as well. We're getting to the bottom of it."

"I've come to see for myself," she said, with a forced whisper, "to get to know him, take him into my confidence."

"But I've just been meeting with the fellow."

"How did the mysteries go?" she asked, changing the subject abruptly. "Are you part of the club now?"

"Initiation," Spafford said, as he edged in, pipping Jeremy. "It's a lodge, not a club."

Amelia bowed her head slightly.

"He did well. Number Three's newest Entered Apprentice."

"Mr. Spafford," she replied.

"Mrs. Spafford," the Irishman said as he took her hand in his and, bending at the waist, kissed the top of it.

"I was just telling your business manager, Mr. Castor here," he continued, not releasing her hand, not taking his eyes from hers, "how Ireland's tipples can't hold a candle to those I've had the good fortune to sample so far in your town. And knowing Erin as I do — a more bibulous land you will not find — that's saying something. Now I have proof positive the comparison holds favourably to her women also."

"Flannelmouth!" Amelia said, laughing. "You speak like a man who desires something."

"That so?"

"I've heard such men speak before."

"Amelia," Jeremy said. "This really isn't the place to discuss legal matters."

He took her free hand and led her back toward the end of the table so she stood between the two men, one hand held by each. Jeremy sat her in his chair and Spafford retook his own.

"You're absolutely right, Mr. Castor," Spafford said to Jeremy, who remained standing, there now being nowhere for him to sit.

"This is nothing but a getting acquainted," Spafford continued, sweeping his hand toward McCallum and Calhoun. "We'll let these capable men sort out the rest. Please, won't you be seated?"

While Jeremy hunted another chair from the far end of the tavern, Spafford turned to Amelia.

"I trust you had a pleasant ride?"

"Yes, thank you. Smoothest carriage I've ever stepped into. I wouldn't have guessed the Montreal Road could be made tolerable."

Spafford clapped.

"Tell me, are the dishes here as good as the cordials?"

"They do a passable mutton crock," McCallum said, "and the soda bread is decent."

"Excellent. Luncheon is on me."

Jeremy shoehorned a footstool on Amelia's left,

between her and Scriven, and sat, a head lower than everyone else.

"To Mr. Castor, our newly initiated brother."

Wooden bowls were passed around and then the thick hunks of bread. Jeremy listened as Spafford told Amelia about his home back in Ballivor: the country fête, the horse races he, with his jockey's frame, regularly won, the hunting in the deer park, the picnics beneath the giant oak. Jeremy watched the Irishman, hating his chirpy talk, his bright eyes, the way his manicured hands waggled as he spoke. At the climax of Spafford's story about how, as a boy, an angry cob swan had chased him from the pond to the barn and how the eggs he'd pilfered had smashed in his pockets when he'd unsuccessfully vaulted the dry stone wall, Amelia laughed, and her fingers brushed his forearm.

Jeremy wondered if he should challenge Spafford to a duel, as he had his uncle a year before. He'd defended Amelia's honour and well-being on that occasion too. But on what grounds? For being overly pleasant and charming? For being an accomplished raconteur? Jeremy wanted to demand satisfaction for any one of these offences but knew they wouldn't stand. For someone who'd sailed thousands of miles to wrest an estate from the hands of a young widow, Spafford was uncommonly good and generous company. Knowing Amelia's trusting nature, Jeremy believed she'd been completely disarmed. He considered it his duty to separate them at the earliest opportunity.

"Mrs. Spafford," he blurted, interrupting the Irishman's story about how he'd won a fortune at the baccarat table run by Ballivor's parish priest. "Perhaps I should escort you back to Willowpath now? We can better discuss these matters there with Mr. Calhoun's counsel."

"Why, I've just arrived Mr. Castor," Amelia replied, flopping her hand to her chest, amazed. "I haven't finished my julep. Besides, I'm enjoying the conversation. It does the soul good to get out of the house and be with people."

"It won't do Castor," Dr. Scriven said from Jeremy's left. "I need you to come with me, to help me find my apprentice."

Jeremy glared at him, reddening.

"Yes," Scriven said, "you must take me to her today. Your first good deed as a Mason."

"Fine," Amelia said, indifferently. "Anyway, I'd quite hoped to spend some time in town, I so rarely get to do so. Perhaps look in at Thomson's to see what's new."

"I could accompany you," Spafford said, "I've nothing to do this afternoon. Perhaps you'd do me the honour of showing me around?"

"Yes, of course," Amelia said.

"And," Dr. Scriven said, prising Jeremy's clenched fingers from the edge of the table. "We need to meet with the school fund-raising committee later this evening. I want to introduce you to the chairwoman of the Female Benevolent Society. She's coming by my office this afternoon. We can talk about the proposed school."

"But it will be too late to escort Amelia back to Willowpath."

"Possibly I'll take a room at Walker's. Make a night of it," Amelia said.

"You know I've never been to Willowpath?" Spafford said.

"Not once?"

Spafford shook his head.

"Uncle never thought fit to invite me. A churlish coot, your late husband. I mean no offence."

Amelia smiled her silent agreement.

"You must come visit," she said, ignoring Jeremy's stricken face. "Without delay."

"How about today? I'll hire another carriage. After a tour of town and the shops, if Mr. Castor is still indisposed, I humbly offer to escort you back to the country. Mr. Calhoun and Mr. McCallum can follow behind in the second carriage and wrangle, while you tell me all about uncle, Willowpath, everything."

"Today?" Amelia said, meeting Jeremy's glower with semaphored eyelashes. "Yes, why not. It won't be enough time for Mrs. Simkins to prepare a proper spread, but with what we have I'm sure she can put together a cold supper that will suffice."

Spafford waved such concern away.

"We'll eat in town," he said. "In fact, we could leave now."

"Now?" Jeremy shouted. Amelia met his questioning with a flash of anger.

"Certainly, Mr. Castor," she said, "I see no reason to delay."

She stood and Spafford pulled out her chair. Jeremy got to his feet as well, as if he would join them.

"We'll meet you back at Willowpath," she said.

"A pleasure," Spafford said, extending his hand. Jeremy clasped it and dug his thumb into the man's knuckle so hard it threatened separation.

"Bloody huffle!" Spafford cried as he pulled his hand from the vise. The Masons looked up from their mugs.

"A grip like a terrier," Spafford said with a forced laugh, rubbing his finger.

Jeremy turned to Amelia, his hand extended.

"Careful Mrs. Spafford," Spafford said, "lest he shatter it."

She laughed and tossed her head back, jouncing the ringlets framing her shining face. Spafford put his hand on her upper arm. Jeremy watched as the two Spaffords strolled to the door and out on the street.

Dr. Scriven drained his cup and clapped his hands together.

"It's settled. Let's go Castor, plenty to do."

Jeremy turned and regarded Scriven, studying his gleaming boots, tight trousers, crisp shirt, and cream cravat. He stood close enough he could see the verge of plucked eyebrow and detect the scented pomade in the forward sweep of hair.

"You don't understand," he said. "I should accompany them."

Dr. Scriven put his hand at Jeremy's back, guiding him out of the Bottle and Glass. At the foyer, Jeremy stopped and looked back. McCallum pulled a sheaf of papers from his satchel and pointed at something halfway down the first page. Calhoun looked over his shoulder and nodded.

"Nonsense," Scriven said, "I know well enough."

He pushed Jeremy through the door.

"Put your faith in Calhoun, he'll sort it. You're a Mason now. This is how it's done."

Chapter Fourteen

Jeremy retraced his steps. He and Scriven navigated the abattoir's stinking heaps, the smouldering dung fires, the hag, and her parsnip-headed son. Jeremy worried unnecessarily about the doctor's finer nature. Scriven strode the wagon paths as though they were high streets.

They found Lilac in the shanty at the pasture's edge. She brightened instantly, her smile a puffy scarlet. In her protruding eyes, thinning hair, and flaking skin Scriven saw early onset scurvy, the result of thirty days bread ends and slumgullion.

Lilac gathered her few belongings into a sack. They followed her from the hut to the street. She produced a key and padlocked the door.

"My dear," Scriven said. "Whatever for?"

"You never know," she said.

"You're coming with me. You needn't trouble yourself with this place a moment longer."

She handed him the key.

"Hold it."

Scriven narrowed his eyes. He took the key and put it in the short, inner pocket of his waistcoat.

ॐ ॐ ॐ ॐ ॐ

"Creedence," Jeremy said. "I really must get back to Willowpath. This Spafford is no better than the last. I worry Amelia is too trusting. I should be there."

"Nonsense. Calhoun is with them. He'll make sure he stays on the level. Take a pipeful."

Reluctantly, Jeremy sat back in his armchair. He tamped an imported burley blend into the bowl of a pipe and lit it. He and Scriven charted Lilac's progress around the parlour.

She started with Scriven's portrait, newly hung over the mantelpiece. She leant in, examining the brush strokes around the neck and chin, marveling at the perfect folds and shadows of the cravat. Then, the array of diverse instruments jumbled beneath like an abandoned game of spillikins. She looked back at Scriven. He nodded, giving her leave to explore. She poked at the tarnished scalpels and bent hammers. With one of the scalpels she flipped open the lid of the nearby wooden box. Additional implements sprawled the green velvet grooves of its interior. It also contained a misplaced dessert fork, fruit flan residue glazing its tines. And a spent pipe, spilling its ash.

Lilac let the box lid drop and stepped to the barrister's bookcase. A worn and well-thumbed copy of Dr. Johnson's dictionary sat on top. Inside, a profusion of gilt-edged books stood at attention. She opened one of the glass doors, removed a volume, and opened. The blue leather of its cover squeaked.

"Dr. Buchan's Domestic Medicine," she cried, swinging back to face Scriven and Jeremy.

"Old Carruthers had just obtained a copy when I left the Lancer."

She fanned its pages.

"In great condition too. Like it's never been cracked."

"I consult it from time to time, whenever necessary, young lady. I'm thoroughly familiar with Buchan."

Lilac continued the room's perimeter, stopping at the apothecary cabinet. She peered into a jar containing a score of leeches, half-submerged in a grey puddle at the bottom. When she tapped the glass, none moved. She ran an index finger over the flaking ceramic of the pestle and the divot in the mortar. She held the cupping jars up to the light of the window, peering through the layer of dust and water stains. With a scalpel, she tipped the upper pan of the scales, scraping its encroaching verdigris.

"Well, young lady," Scriven said. "Your diagnosis?"

Lilac dropped the scalpel to the pan.

"Appalling," she said, beaming.

Scriven yanked the pipe from his slackened lip.

"Very sad trim," she continued. "Infirm, I'd say."

Scriven pointed the pipe stem at her.

"And you'd do well to quit your puffing," she continued before he could speak, "that's a toxic soot you draught into your lungs."

"Look here…"

"Would you wrap your face around a chimney flue?"

Scriven looked down at the smouldering bowl.

"I thought not," she said.

"I prescribe tobacco to all my clients," Scriven said, astonished. "As salubrious as brandy dram in the morning and toddy at night. Aromatics keep noxious vapours at bay."

Scriven looked over at Jeremy who'd just pulled again on his own pipe.

"Don't they?" Scriven continued. "It's known."

Jeremy turned to Lilac and back to Scriven, nodding and exhaling.

"I'll defer to you professionals, but I've always found a pipeful a most pleasant balm."

Lilac put her hands on the protruding ridges of her hips and tilted her head.

Scriven harrumphed. "I recommend a regular course of tobacco enemas to all my patients with the windy hypochondriacal melancholy."

"You might reconsider," she said.

"I say, Castor," Scriven said, turning back to Jeremy. He put his pipe down in a saucer on the side table. "You might have mentioned her impertinence."

"It was for her pluck that I recommended her to you," Jeremy said, enjoying Scriven's agitation. "And her skill with a needle."

"For what duration do you prescribe these enemas?" Lilac asked.

"Ongoing," he said, unable to mask his petulance.

"None fully cured?"

"Not yet."

"There might be indication enough."

"Young lady..."

"You know, of course, windy hypochondriacal melancholy involves a sizeable mental component."

"Yes, naturally."

"What does that suggest?"

Scriven stood from his chair.

"What does it suggest?"

His shouting bounced from the drawing room walls.

"What does it suggest?"

Jeremy put his pipe down, stood from his chair, and raised his hands between them, worried she'd gone too far.

"Yes," she said, her tone patient, "I think we can conclude that physical treatment, such as tobacco enema, is largely superfluous."

"Physician," he cried, spitting the word from his mouth.

Lilac frowned, not understanding.

"Heal thyself!"

Lilac crossed her arms across her chest. Her smile faded for the first time since arriving.

"What do you mean?"

"Look at you," Scriven said, extending his palm toward her. "A bag of bones. Hips as sharp as ploughshares. You could punch leather with those elbows. And that sacking you're wearing. Nothing could be less flattering. Not to mention the vermin and disease that must infest it."

Lilac averted her gaze, around the parlour to the scattered plasters and misplaced trepanning drills. Jeremy and Scriven exchanged a glance. They weren't sure whether Lilac might bolt. Or cry. Or worse.

"Now Lil'," Jeremy said, his hands raised again. "Easy does it. The doctor only returns what you've dished out. You are a bit pungent."

"Eat something," Scriven continued. "Take a bath."

Lilac dashed the length of the Persian rug toward

him. Scriven shrank, half expecting raking nails and thrust knees. She embraced him.

"I love it," she cried.

"You do?"

"Aye," she said, her smile returning. "Clearly, I'm needed."

"Well, that's fine," Scriven said, "I suppose."

Lilac skipped between the armchairs and squeezed Jeremy's neck.

"Thank you, Deacon," she said.

"I had little to do with it," he said.

"'Twas your recommendation," she said, poking his chest. "Your recommendation."

"I've had Mrs. Grady put together the spare room for you," Scriven continued. "and I've taken the liberty of picking out some appropriate outfits. I trust that's not too presumptuous. If you're going to be my nurse, you'll need to look the part."

Lilac nodded.

"Mrs. Grady has drawn a hot tubful. Leave those rags next to the stove. She'll burn them."

"I can get the tarnish off those scale pans in no time," Lilac said. "If you have some natron."

"I'm sure we have natron," he said, peering at the confusion of phials in the apothecary cabinet.

"And lemons."

"I'll have Mrs. Grady find you lemons, lots of lemons, for the scales, and yourself. A squeeze or two in your tea. Just the tonic."

Lilac clinched Scriven again.

"Thank you," she said. "I'll make them gleam."

"I implore you," Scriven said, plucking her thin arms from his shoulders. "Take a bath."

෩ ෩ ෩ ෩ ෩

For the third time, Jeremy told Scriven and Lilac that he should be going, that he had to return to Amelia and help her negotiate with the newest Spafford. Just as he stood from his chair, shortly after 3pm, Lenore Stokes arrived.

"Jeremy," she cried, extending her arms.

"Mrs. Stokes!"

"You know each other?" Scriven said. "I forget, this is no metropolis."

"Mr. Castor billeted with us a few months last year," she said as she reached up and Jeremy bent to kiss her cheek. "One of Perry's young marines."

"Perhaps I shouldn't be surprised to see him here with you," she continued, turning to greet Scriven.

"What do you mean?" Scriven asked, a trifle defensively.

"Such a talent with a needle. 'Twould give your tailor pause."

Scriven turned. Jeremy's cheeks began to colour.

"Oh yes," Lenore said, "you didn't know? A marvel."

She put her hand on Jeremy's upper arm.

"Do you know," she said to Jeremy, confidentially, "Creedence has a fine eye for fabric? Ostensibly, he's my doctor, but mostly I value him for his flair. None other in town can keep me abreast of what women, en vogue, are wearing in Mayfair and Les Tuileries."

Scriven bowed deeply. Lenore released Jeremy's arm and slapped it.

"I'm rather disappointed in you, Mr. Castor."

"Ma'am?"

"You'd promised to teach me to knit. One lesson and then you're off to Willowpath with the young Spafford widow. Didn't I warn you about Canadian girls?"

"I'd be happy to resume the lessons any time," Jeremy said.

"I still haven't finished the scarf. It looks atrocious; more rag doll than muffler."

"He'd better be ready to teach," Scriven said. "I'm hoping he'll be our prospective schoolmaster."

Lenore clapped.

"Jeremy is the young gentleman you've been telling me about?"

"Yes," Scriven said, "you'll have plenty of time for knitting instruction and what else."

"Splendid!"

"First, your check up."

"My fettle couldn't be finer. You know I'm here for the fashion. And the gossip. And the sherry."

"We'll have tea and get re-acquainted in a moment. Let's make it official. Step into my office."

"Schoolmaster?" Jeremy called after the two as they entered Scriven's office. "I didn't agree to become a schoolmaster. I run a glass works."

Scriven looked back at him from the door with a half-smile that suggested he was being humoured. Jeremy recalled the recent scene at the Bottle and Glass with Amelia and Rupert.

"Creedence," he said, "I really must return to Willowpath. I have much to do. I must help Amelia."

"Oh, please do stay a while longer Jeremy," Lenore said, poking her head back out. "It's been so long since we've seen each other. We won't be long inside, I'm hale as heather. It would be lovely to be catch up."

Jeremy met Lenore's warm gaze. He recalled their time spent together the year before, when Major Stokes, her husband and his superior, was away, long winter nights spent beside the fire, glasses of sherry, knitting and stitching, and sometimes reading to each other from Coleridge, Burns, and Blake.

He returned her smile.

Chapter Fifteen

Having had a hot, leisurely bath and a bowlful of Mrs. Grady's cabbage and beef, Lilac already looked less a patient and more a nurse. She'd found the jar of natron and with a quantity of cider vinegar had burnished the scale pans until each reflected like looking glass. She'd collected all the scalpels and hammers and scissors and forceps, arranged them in a pile on the desk in Scriven's office, and had begun to clean each with a fresh rag before returning them to their proper velvet groove.

"Oh, pardon me," she said, standing from her seat. She threw the remaining implements into the case. "I'll finish in the other room."

"No, no," Scriven said. "If you're to be my acolyte, you'll need to start training right away. Miss Lilac Evans...please meet Mrs. Lenore Stokes, wife of Major Peregrine Stokes, of her Majesty's Royal."

"Yes," Lilac said, taking Lenore's hand, "I know of Mrs. Stokes and her husband. I met the Major aboard the Lancer."

Scriven huffed. "It's impossible to introduce anyone to anyone in this wretched place."

"Knew him intimately," Lilac continued.

"Really?" Lenore said, stretching the word.

"Certainly did. Applied plasters to his neck and chest and..."

"I see."

"A more decent and honourable bloke, you'll not find. Not that I need tell you that, missus. Always treated me fairly, despite my station. He needn't have talked to me at all, but he did."

"Did he?"

"Always had a kind word for you Mrs. Stokes. Mentioned you often. Faithful as an albatross, the Major, which is more than I can say..."

"Miss Evans, please," Scriven said, leading Lenore to the chaise lounge next to his desk. "A little patter is helpful, makes the patient feel at their ease. Too much does more harm than good. You know the credo?"

"Primum, non nocere."

Scriven swung back toward Lilac surprised at her use of Latin. He let Lenore drop the final inches to the cushion.

"First," Lilac said, "do no harm."

"Yes, " Scriven said, "that's correct. Well done. Now, continue your work with the instruments. If I require any assistance, I'll let you know. Watch and listen."

Scriven took Lenore gently by the shoulder and eased her back into a reclined position on the chaise lounge, putting a cushion behind her head. He brought a stool around and sat at her knees, extending them. He unlinked her crossed ankles and turned to face her, his hand firmly on her left shin.

"Now, Mrs. Stokes," he said, "did you receive your..."

He paused.

"Oh Creedence."

"Your flowers. Did you receive your flowers this month?"

"Must we?" Lenore put the back of her hand over her face.

"Of course. Mrs. Stokes. We must."

He raised his voice to make sure Lilac would hear.

"I apprenticed under Dr. Alexander Duncan of Croydon."

"I know."

"I spent a year at The Royal College in Warwick Lane."

"I know."

"What honour would I do their instruction if I was anything less than thorough in my examination? What sort of example would I set to my own young apprentice?"

Lenore nodded.

"As your physician and your friend, I must ask these questions. We've discussed this before. You are entering a particularly fraught time of life. A woman of a certain age must begin her preparations."

"Creedence!"

Startled, Scriven removed his hand from Lenore's shin. He glanced at his new apprentice. Lilac studied the lancet she polished.

"I'm not a relic," Lenore continued, her voice rising.

"Irritability," Scriven said. "One of the chief symptoms. A sign of hystericism."

"Please." Lenore pulled back the gauze of her gown where his hand had been.

"Mrs. Stokes. We must look at this through a scientific lens. I fear that your womb must be wandering. It may be pushing up into your chest. That might explain the rashes you've been presenting on your..."

"Creedence!"

"Increased sensitivity, easily agitated," he said, ticking a mental checklist.

Scriven leant forward and put the back of his hand against her forehead.

"Mm-hmm," he said.

"What?"

"Hot. Flushed. You're the colour of a first-rate claret."

"Of course I am," she said, "thanks to you."

"It isn't pleasant, but we must face it. Women of a certain age..."

"I spoke to Hugh Thomson this morning."

Scriven paused. Hugh Thomson could not be escaped.

"He said you had a copy of the latest Hemming designs from Cecil House."

"Women of a certain age must curtail the activities of their youth. Coffee and sherry. Theatre and dances. Gallopades with young officers. It all amounts to overstimulation."

"Tell me about the beaver bonnets. Are they any lighter this year? I must replace mine before autumn."

"Humours backing up. The bile. The phlegm. It lodges in the organs and glands, in the breasts and armpits. Causes all manner of disease."

"Did you see the adorable poke bonnets Thomson has got in? The ones with the ruffled brims?"

"Mrs. Stokes."

Lenore sighed. "Yes, Dr. Scriven?"

"Did you receive your flowers this month?"

"Oh Creedence," she said, letting her chin fall to her chest. "No."

"And neither the month before."

"No."

"That's what I feared."

"It doesn't necessarily mean a thing," she said. "It's happened before. It happened when I was twenty."

"Yes, but we both know why. The opposite reason."

"Peregrine will be home soon, he must be. All will return to normal."

"Lenore," Scriven said, his fine, manicured fingers at her shin again, smoothing the silk. "As your long-time friend and confidante, listen to me."

Scriven caressed her ankle until she raised her chin again and met his gaze.

"Don't torment yourself," he said. "You know, I've come to terms myself."

"Yes? What about?"

"In all likelihood I'll never sire any children," he said, his voice lowered.

"Of course you won't!" Lenore cried. "You don't want any!"

Scriven looked over at Lilac again, to gauge her reaction. She polished as if alone.

"Major Stokes may be in Venezuela for years to come," he continued. "You must brace yourself for that possibility."

Lenore met Scriven's expression of sympathy, but her face was blank.

"No," she said, raising her chin. "You're right."

"Better. Now. I could prescribe a course of leeches," he said.

"I don't think so."

"Applied to the vulvular dominion."

"No!"

"As you wish," Scriven said. "I should say, you are far from a model patient today, my apprentice's first. Still, instructive," he turned to Lilac, who looked up from the mallet she buffed, "presenting with these symptoms of hystericism. Agitation. Contrariness. See how they must be met with a calm, authoritative deportment. Bedside manner: more important than any miracle tonic. We can't impose prudence, we can only advise and..."

With his hand still on her shin, Scriven moved Lenore's left leg gently out from the right.

"...alleviate symptoms."

His hand found the hem of her gown and ducked under. It crept the bare length of her calf to her knee before she caught it with her own two hands and trapped it between her thighs.

"Creedence, what are you doing?"

"Palpating," he replied, straightening, his terseness pitched higher. "Naturally. Loosing the paroxysm. Alleviating."

"Now?" Her bloodless hand was over his, bunching the fabric of the gown.

"Yes now. As always."

"With her? In the room?"

"And why not? Many physicians these days recommend a chaperone, a female, to verify nothing untoward."

Lenore half-laughed, half-snorted.

"Creedence, I've never feared anything untoward from you. It's why I've never requested a chaperone. It's why I come regularly."

"Miss Evans, my nurse, would make a fine overseer."

"Next time," Lenore said, giving his hand a squeeze through the muslin. He withdrew it.

"Hmph. A most perfunctory check-up."

"I told you. My fettle couldn't be finer. You know I'm really here for the fashion. Can we pour the sherry now?"

Scriven's face lengthened. After a few moments he stood up, crossed the room and plunged his hands into a bowl of scented water. He plucked a towel from the stack.

"I'll go arrange the glasses while you re-assemble."

Lenore sat up from the chaise lounge as Scriven exited.

"Thank you," she said, to the back of the door.

෧ ෧ ෧ ෧ ෧

Lenore patted and plumped her gown and crossed the room to look at herself in the glass. Dismayed at the redness in her cheeks and collarbone, she dipped into the bowl and splashed at her face. She pinched a fresh towel and pressed it to her forehead. Inhaling deeply, she looked in the glass again. She sighed and her shoulders sagged. The splotches hadn't faded.

"Mrs. Stokes?"

Lilac continued burnishing as she spoke.

"Mm? Oh, pardon me," she said, straightening. "I think of him like a brother, but he does wind me up sometimes."

"He's a decent man," Lilac said.

"You know, he means well. He's no Hippocrates, though physician enough."

Lilac made a sound through her nose, as though trying to clear it.

"It's true," Lenore continued, "that he's more often interested in the threads covering the body than what's underneath. Still, I think you'll do well to apprentice under him."

Lilac reiterated her snuffle.

"He seems kind," she managed to say.

"I'm sure there is much to learn," Lenore said, her voice rising to a question.

"Indeed, there is."

The women fell silent. Lenore returned to the lined face in the looking glass.

"The womb doesn't wander," Lilac said.

"I beg your pardon," Lenore said.

"The womb doesn't wander. It's been thousands of years since anyone took the idea seriously."

"That so?"

"Yes ma'am. May I speak freely?"

"Why stop now?"

"I've lived... that is, circumstances have required me to..."

"Yes?"

"I have experience..."

Lilac paused as she considered how to most delicately explain her resumé.

"Let's just say I'm intimately acquainted with the human body, both male and female."

"Not something to bruit about, perhaps."

"Perhaps not. But I apprenticed under Dr. Carruthers on HMS Lancer. We cared for over one hundred men and women, suffering from every possible ailment, in every condition. We very nearly performed the Empire's first successful caesarean birth."

"I'm not sure what that is."

"A foetus that cannot egress in the traditional way, through the birth canal, is extricated from the womb via an incision in the mother's abdomen."

"Oh my. You don't talk like any ordinary, unfortunate woman."

"I'm not." Lilac picked up the next tarnished scalpel.

"Evidently."

"I learned much from Carruthers. And the Deacon, who taught me to read."

"The Deacon?"

"Mr. Castor, in the next room. Jeremy."

"Oh yes, our young corporal. He has an instinct for teaching, hasn't he?"

"Mrs. Stokes, does it feel like your womb has ever wandered?"

Lenore put her hands on her abdomen, framing her belly with outstretched fingers.

"There are remedies," Lilac continued, "feverfew, amaranth. Used judiciously, your flux can be regulated, returned to normal."

Lenore frowned as she peered at the triangle her hands made.

"Of course," Lilac said, slotting home the shining scalpel, "if you'll pardon my indelicacy, Major Stokes is in Venezuela indefinitely, isn't he? Perhaps this is all magpie chatter."

Lenore looked up. She opened her mouth as if to speak. The Major home or gone, she wanted to say; it made no difference. Her best friend Eliza, the brewer's wife, gave birth to a fifth child this spring. Lenore had no reserve of forced excitement left, to coo and fuss over Eliza's newest baby. She felt nauseous just imagining Eliza's fat, glowing face and its benign expressions of pity at Lenore's own childlessness. She knew having a child made no guarantee of happiness and purpose. But not having one meant undeniable absence. Who was Lenore Stokes? The Major's wife. Nothing more.

She slapped her belly with the flat of her hand. It made a hollow sound. It was echoed by a tapping at the door.

"Sherry has been poured," Scriven said, from the other side. "Are you ready, Mrs. Stokes?"

"Julienne Blouin of Brittany had a daughter at 52," Lilac said.

"French women," Lenore said, curling her lip.

"Mr. Castor is eager to speak to you about plans for the new school," Scriven continued, shouting through the door. "But we mustn't detain him – he must leave soon."

Lenore met Lilac's gaze.

"Coming," she said.

Chapter Sixteen

Coppery light shafted through the front window of Stoke cottage. Lenore opened the rosewood armoire, retrieved two crystal schooners and a bottle of Amontillado. She'd placed them on the table before Jeremy had doffed his cap.

"Mrs. Stokes," he said, raising his hands. "I'm not sure. Maybe I've had enough. I really should get back to Willowpath."

"Don't say that Jeremy," she said, sounding genuinely hurt. "Don't say Mrs. Stokes. It makes me sound so old. I married young, you know. I'm only a handful of years older than you."

Jeremy smiled and nodded.

"Thank you for walking me home."

Lenore filled each of the schooners.

"One more can't hurt, I suppose," he said.

Her face brightened and she handed one to him.

"It can't. We have so much catching up to do. How long has it been?"

Jeremy looked to the ceiling.

"Over a year, I believe."

"Shame! That's how you repay our hospitality? Not visiting once in all that time? It's like a mausoleum here with Peregrine away in Granada or Colombia or torrid wherever. He has his marines. Whose company he prefers, let's face it."

Jeremy began to explain, how he had been busy at Willowpath, helping to launch the glassworks, how he rarely went to town.

"I'm teasing," she said, touching his forearm.

Earlier glasses of sherry filtered the length of Jeremy's body, making his steps deliberate as he followed Lenore into the sitting room. He plodded behind, transfixed by the pleats of her gown swishing behind her as she walked. He admired her graceful step, marveling that, with so much lateral movement, still she glided forward. Her youthful appearance and lissome carriage belied her age, which he knew enough never to ask.

"Hungry?" she asked. "Abby could put a plate together."

Jeremy shook his head. Lenore gestured with the fine fingers of her outstretched hand and he dropped into the offered armchair. She placed her glass on the side table and floated into the chair opposite, plumping the gossamer of her skirt over her crossed knee. From the other side table, she retrieved a confusion of wool and needles and cradled it in her lap.

The ball of yarn fell to the floor and rolled. Jeremy stopped it with his foot, retrieved it, and let it fall into her open hands. A twisted loop hung to the floor, tracing the outline of her shin. Jeremy followed it down and glimpsed the perfect triangle of her ankle pointing back up the full, smooth slope of her bare calf.

A shame, he thought; this warm, generous woman

spending so much time alone. Like the sherry; complex, beguiling, full-bodied. Distilled sunshine. But, kept in a dark, private cellar.

"Oh Jeremy." Lenore looked down at the same wayward thread, laughing, "why so sad? It's only a scarf. Or, the notion of a scarf."

Jeremy pinched the paired strands and held them out. She took them and her fingertips brushed his. He sank back into his armchair. He brought his glass to his lips and took a long draught.

"I really should get back," he said. "Before it's too late."

"What could possibly be so urgent?"

Jeremy thought back to lunch at the Bottle and Glass. He pictured Spafford and Amelia dining at Walker's or the Black Bull. Spafford handing her a third julep, and then a fourth, whispering in her ear. Her laughing, an unrestrained warble he'd never even heard before, let alone elicited. Her ringlets caroming about her face as she threw back her head. As he'd left, he'd seen Spafford touch her shoulder.

"The Canadian girl," Lenore said, a thin smile at the corner of her mouth. "I warned you."

"It's a business matter," Jeremy said. "A legal matter. She's..., we're..., in danger of losing the glass factory. I should be there to advise."

"Bottles and glass?" Lenore said, laughing. "What do you know about bottles and glass?"

Jeremy was about to explain how he had learned quite a lot about the process from Bennet and that his job wasn't to manufacture the glass anyway, it was to supervise…, or rather to manage…, that is, to promote…

He stared down at his hands, one folded into the other.

"Forgive me," Lenore said, "I didn't intend to sneer. My God, I'm the last one who should cast aspersions on a person's usefulness. I have one role, barely-fulfilled."

She gestured around the empty, noiseless cottage.

"But I can't accomplish that simple thing. How can I?"

They regarded each other for a few moments.

"Lamb," Lenore said finally, leaning forward in her chair, "I mean only that I'm not sure you're the entrepreneurial type. You're too thoughtful, and patient, and kind."

Jeremy frowned.

"Not ruthless enough," she said. "'Tisn't a defect. Not at all. I suspect you are better suited to the pedagogic life. Now," she looked back at the jumble of yarn, "if you can teach me how to make sense of this, you'll have proved your mettle as Kingston's newest and best schoolmaster."

Jeremy stood and stepped across. She looked up, pushing the curls from her forehead. Late afternoon sun spilled through the window, bathing the side of her face, bronzing the angle of her cheekbone. The slight creases around her mouth and eyes dissolved beneath the pressure of her smile. Wafts of jasmine reached his nose and filled his head. The affect was one of warm invitation.

He shouldn't have been there. What of Lenore's husband, Jeremy's one-time commanding officer, Major Peregrine Stokes? Fighting for liberty in Venezuela.

What might he think? Besides, Jeremy had pledged himself to Amelia, hadn't he? He couldn't betray her. But, what sort of agreement did they truly have? They'd never made any explicit vows. Amelia, it seemed, thought more of Willowpath than anything else. And, she'd made clear her determination to postpone any romantic attachment until she was ready. When would that be? She'd only kept Jeremy on because he'd saved her from the old Colonel. At this very moment, she was probably in some dim corner effervescing under the influence of his nephew's ribald stories and witty asides. To attain his confidence, she'd said. An unsettlingly convincing act.

Lenore's loneliness was tangible. Jeremy valued her friendship and felt like he owed her the same. She'd comforted him through dark times and he desired to give her comfort in return. He could provide affection without being untoward, couldn't he?

He looked down past the fine peak of Lenore's chin, along the burnished elegance of her throat and neck, and beyond, to regions indistinct and finally, to the entanglement in her lap.

"It's to be a scarf?" he asked.

She nodded.

"Not a tea cozy?"

She shook her head.

"Draught excluder?"

She shook her head again, ringlets swinging.

Jeremy descended to one knee and bent before her. He brought his hands over her thighs to take up the wool-sheathed needles. The backs of his fingers grazed the thin muslin of her skirt. He didn't notice her slight shiver. He stared down at the mess of yarn, trying to find the leading thread and the key to how it could be unraveled. He stretched and twisted and separated. He shifted the needles and then put them back the way they were. Finally, with both hands he extended the pile back out over her lap, beneath her bright gaze.

"A trivet," he said. "As is."

"As is?" she cried, clutching at his thumbs. "A trivet? You promised a scarf."

"Lenore," he said. "It's summer."

"Nearing autumn. You admit defeat already? "

He looked at the tangle. Jasmine continued to rise from the pale blue of her exposed inner wrists. He looked up at her. Her face suspended over him, framed by the playful Apollo's knots. Her features seemed to become rounder and softer.

"Am I unteachable?" she asked.

"Let's start again," he said.

She released his thumbs and clapped. He withdrew the needles and began to disengage the wool.

"Now," he said with mock seriousness, as he unraveled, "I expect you to be a better student."

"Yes sir."

"Attentive."

"Of course."

"Obedient."

"Yes," she said, a half-octave lower.

He took the strand and wound it around one of the needles and started the first dozen stitches. He put the yarn ball in her right hand and the needle with the stitches in her left. Gently, he folded her slender fingers around its shaft, positioning her thumb and forefinger. His hand lingered over hers. He'd forgotten how cool and soft and delicate they were.

Jeremy paused. He really shouldn't.

Lenore tapped his hand with one of the needles.

"You promised," she breathed.

Jeremy returned to the needles, her silky fingers, the burgeoning row. He covered her hands in his. Together they stitched and purled and before long they had produced a durable foundation.

They had thirty rows completed before Abby entered with a platter.

"Thank you Abby, you can return home now," Lenore said.

"Aye miss. You're sure you don't want me to..."

"No, that's all, thank you. Have a good evening."

"You're sure, miss? You might want some tea made."

Lenore bunched the yarn in her fist. Jeremy looked to the window. He got to his feet.

"Perhaps I should also go," he said.

This was the intrusion that might break the spell.

"Not on my account," Abby said, gauging Lenore's expression. She crossed the room to the front door. "Supper's there. I'm just leaving."

Abby hefted two bags over her shoulder, chopped the latch with the calloused edge of her free hand, and stepped out. From the front step she swung the door shut and, with a furtive look, re-latched it.

"Jeremy," Lenore clutched his knee. "It's late. You shouldn't walk the roads now."

Jeremy put his hand over hers. He looked back out

the window and caught a glimpse of Abby, lingering beyond the shrub. He met her gaze. She turned and was gone.

"At least stay for supper," Lenore said, gesturing toward the platter on the table. "You haven't eaten all afternoon. You must be hungry. I know I am."

Jeremy looked into her upturned eyes. They were a lustrous copper. He flipped his hand over and, when she put hers in his, he encased it within the shelter of his fingers. She got to her feet and allowed herself to be led to the table. They sat and she poured two glasses of claret from the ewer, passing one across. She watched, delighted, as Jeremy transferred to his earthenware plate two thick slices of butter-painted bread and a panoply of apples, carrots, fish and cheese. She watched and waited, as though she would get more enjoyment from spectating. Finally, she took a bread end and a smattering of the rest.

Jeremy chewed and nodded. She smiled, pushing at a piece of fish with her fork.

"I suppose I was hungry, after all," he said, finally. He rubbed the napkin across his mouth and paused to take a draught from his goblet.

"Oh," she said, "let me show you." Lenore left the table and returned with a book. She placed it down next to Jeremy's plate. He looked at the title: *A Picture Book, For Little Children*.

"I know it," he said.

"Any child can be taught to read." Lenore retook her seat. "I firmly believe it. Even the poorest behaved. The adorable scenes keep their interest."

Jeremy licked the butter from his thumb and opened

the book. Lenore studied Jeremy; he studied the book. He took another bite of bread. He resembled to her a lunching schoolboy, instantly absorbed.

"I can't tell you," she said, "how lovely it is to share a meal at this table with a proper human being for a change."

Jeremy leafed through the primer.

"Not Eliza," she continued, "kind friend though she is. Not Abby, dear God, my servant. Not some phantasm, which is what I'm usually reduced to."

Jeremy ushered in another mouthful.

"You know," she continued, "I've sometimes considered..."

Lenore stared at her plate, hardly touched. Jeremy looked up from the book. She shook her head, her smile fading.

"It's the sherry," she said. She brought a hand to her face and shaded her glinting eyes. "Forgive me. I've become maudlin."

Jeremy stretched his hand across the table.

"Please," he said.

"No, it's too ridiculous. You'll think I'm more pathetic than you already do."

"Lenore, I'll never think you pathetic."

She made a doubtful sound.

"You've been so good to me," he said, "like a mother."

She groaned. "Don't say that. So unkind."

"I'm sorry. It's true. When they executed Augustus. When they caught my cousin Merit. When I got that awful letter. You took up my burden. Let me take up yours."

She dropped her hand from her dampened eyes.

"When I was a young girl..." she began, hesitantly. Jeremy enveloped her hand in his.

"My father," she continued, "was a lieutenant in the Royal Navy. He was away most of the time. I barely recall him."

With her free hand she pointed, without looking, to a small sketch on the wall by the armoire.

"A blister, as you can see for yourself. Without that painting I don't think I'd even remember what he looked like."

"Mother..." Lenore paused to remove a fragment of apple pith from the tip of her tongue, "I didn't see much of her either. Mother enjoyed society. Young officers. Gin and lemon. Dancing. Children in the parlour annoyed her only slightly less than deer in the rose garden. Needless to say, I have no siblings. I'm quite sure I wasn't intended."

"Lenore."

Her gesturing had skittered a fork to the floor. Jeremy motioned to pick it up.

"Leave it," she said. "It's fine. I'm fine. We must be stoical, mustn't we?"

Jeremy nodded.

"I had a governess. Sissy. I called her Sissy; I think her name was Sibyl. A boundless mulatta from Trinidad. She always wore these bright, flowery kerchiefs on her head. Black, curly hair burst out of them. For many years, my only companion. Until, one day, she brought along a friend. Big and colourful like Sissy. Soft and huggable like Sissy. Made up of many different strands."

Confusion descended Jeremy's face.

"A doll," Lenore said, "a doll. Sissy had asked my mother if she could keep all the yarn ends from all her mending projects. With the leftovers she knitted a huge doll of a hundred different shades and textures. I called her Poly. She had silk remnants for hair, chaff for stuffing, and bright, brass buttons for eyes. Her mouth was stitched into a permanent smile. And, unlike Sissy, she never went away."

Jeremy wanted to ask what became of Sissy, but Lenore continued.

"Mother used to say I should practice my repartee with Poly – polish the flummeries I would one day use to snare a husband away from the other girls. I practiced. Poly and I were inseparable. What good did it do? I have a husband, yes. I share him with the doñas and señoritas of Venezuela."

"He would never."

"You're right. A more honourable man you'll never find. What use is it to me?"

"Lenore."

"Poly listened with such interest to everything I had to say, laughed at my every childish joke. I loved her. I spent countless pleasant hours with her, serving her pretend tea, putting her down for naps, reading to her. I imagined that I might one day have a whole brood of wooly headed progeny, flesh and blood, that I could call my own, that wouldn't give me a moment's peace, that would stuff my life from stem to stern. But listen..."

Lenore cupped a hand to her ear.

"...nothing."

"Where is Poly now? Can I see her?"

"I lost her on a move from Southhampton to Port Royal. Father said he'd buy another."

Jeremy ran a finger gently down the fine ridge of bone from her wrist to her knuckle. It was quiet except for muted shouting from distant Store Street.

"Sometimes I've thought," she continued, "I'll learn how to knit. I'll make another Poly, to give to my own child."

Jeremy got to his feet. He took both of her hands in his and lifted until she too was standing. He embraced her, encompassing her. The noise outside seemed to get closer, louder.

"Aren't you sorry?" Lenore muffled into his chest. "You shouldn't have encouraged me. Now you think I'm daft, as well as old."

"I think neither," Jeremy said.

Jeremy ran his hand slowly from her shoulders to the valley of her lower back. He massaged and caressed. His big palms glided the gossamer up and down, feeling the sighs as they escaped through her ribs. She kissed murmurs into his chest as though they were being exorcised. Their vibrations entered through his breastbone and reverberated his own ribcage. He put his face to her hair, breathed in the jasmine, kissed the top of her head. His breathing quickened, in time with hers. Tremors pulsed the length of his body.

He thought he heard a jangling at the door.

He pulled away. Lenore looked up, confused.

"Did you hear that?" he asked.

She shook her head.

"I thought I heard..."

He cocked an ear down the hall.

"...keys."

Like Major Stokes, come home. He listened again. Nothing.

"At the door."

She pursed her lips and they stared at each other as they listened. And listened. And heard nothing.

She gripped the first two fingers of his right hand. He didn't clasp back.

Didn't he have an understanding with Amelia? He shouldn't be here.

"You were right," he said. He leant down and kissed her crinkling forehead. "Too much sherry. And, it's late."

"You're going to leave?" she asked.

"Early in the morning. I must get to Willowpath first thing."

"Of course."

"But it's too late for travel now. May I stay the night?"

"I'll prepare a bed."

Jeremy clasped her elbow as she turned.

"Lenore," he said. "I will come to visit more often. I promise."

"Of course."

Chapter Seventeen

Amelia stood with her back to the staircase. Her hip nuzzled the arc of the flared bannister. In one hand she held a lamp. In the other, a new poke bonnet.

Spafford stood facing, one foot on the step, one on the floor. He gazed up at her, squinting through the halo of light, eyes tilted up from the lace of her neckline. If it had been Jeremy standing there, she reckoned, they would have stood eye to eye.

"End of the tour?" Spafford asked, sliding his hand up the rail.

"For tonight."

"No presentation of the lady's antechamber?"

"Far too late."

"I'd like to see the cushion upon which my most fortunate uncle last laid his blessed, grey head."

"I'm still grieving the Colonel."

"As am I."

"It wouldn't be seen as proper."

"I desire only to pay my last respects."

"What would the others say?"

"They'd praise the hostess' unrivalled hospitality, I would hope."

"You'd be optimistic, then."

"What choice, an Irishman?"

Spafford stepped up onto the other end of the first tread and ran his hand over the newel knob. For a moment, they were nearly level. Amelia took another step backwards and up, holding the lamp between them.

"Mrs. Simkins has prepared a very comfortable room for you."

"And where does Mr. Castor sleep, when he stays?"

"My business manager has a room upstairs."

"Cozy."

"Mr. Castor is thoroughly professional."

Amelia remembered the last time Jeremy had been in her bedroom; the humid grappling, the bewildering heat.

"A perfect gentleman," she added.

"I wouldn't doubt it. And, you're in mourning, after all."

"Yes."

"Am I to sleep down here with the prattlebirds, McCallum and Calhoun? With the helps?"

"It's a most handsome room, fitted with the late Colonel's souvenirs and trophies. He often slept there."

"He had occasional night terrors," she added, in response to Spafford's quizzical look.

"Dearest aunt."

Amelia wrinkled her nose. She took another step back. Spafford matched it.

"What of family? Your very own nephew."

"In law," she said.

"And it is a legal matter I'm here to resolve."

"We can continue that project in the sobriety of morning."

"Not being blood relatives raises other interesting opportunities."

"I had a delightful time in town. I adore this charming bonnet. I shall wear it tomorrow when I tour you around the rest of Willowpath and the glassworks."

Amelia brought the hat to her face. She stifled a contrived yawn.

"Heavens," she said. "Excuse me Mr. Spafford, Morpheus beckons."

"Morpheus. Uncle. This Castor, perhaps. You fly to them. Everyone but me."

"Mr. Spafford."

Spafford reached across and stroked her forearm.

"None of them are here tonight. You might get lonely. You might want a tuck in."

"Mrs. Simkins!"

Amelia knew the woman stood somewhere in the shadows, within shouting distance.

"Yes Mrs. Spafford," Simkins replied, materializing at the foot of the stairs.

"Please show Mr. Spafford his room. It is well past time for us to turn in."

"Yes ma'am. This way please, Mr. Spafford."

Simkins stood at the foot of the stair and waited. The lamp she held emphasized the features of her unsmiling face.

"Remarkable," Spafford said. "You must be some kind of sorceress to conjure a domestic just like that."

෨ ෨ ෨ ෨ ෨

Amelia lay awake even as the gibbous moon began its descent. She extended her limbs in four directions, spanning the rifts and undulations of the mattress. The bed sheet twisted around her calf and thigh and torso, wreckage of her repeated attempts at sleep.

It wasn't long ago, at the height of the heat wave, Jeremy Castor sat on that same chaff and ruffled those same sheets. She hadn't minded. There was a certain appeal to his mountainous presence, his uncomplicated face, his graceless movements, his earnest attempts to please. As clear as a freshet.

He'd been a loyal friend. He'd come to her defence on several occasions, even when it meant danger to himself. When he'd found trouble, admissions of guilt tumbled right out of him. When it came to the glass factory and conducting business, he was no Cartwright. Still he was competent and trustworthy. Solid. Everything a mother might recommend to her young daughter.

Entirely unlike Rupert Spafford.

She'd had a lovely day. It couldn't be denied. It had been over a year since the elder Spafford's death and she'd affected to be in mourning ever since. She'd only rarely been to town or out in society. She'd concentrated on the glass factory, doing everything she could to make it successful. What a pleasant change it had been to stroll the entire length of Front Street, down by the water, to Mississauga Point and back up King and Store streets. In a lavender gown no less, free, finally, of dowdy, detested black. How satisfying it had been to take the younger Spafford's worldly arm when the sidewalk's boards were missing, broken, or loose.

He embroidered the most tempting blarney. While Jeremy often had to be drawn out, there was no stopping Spafford, even on their first day of meeting. All along the promenade he spun his tales of County Meath, the old country, the continent. He'd told of lavish suppers with the port-swilling, card-playing bishop. He'd described, lovingly, getting thrown by this or that spirited filly, or riding a golden mare to a fifty-guinea purse. He'd chuckled, remembering his fly-fishing expedition along the Kells Blackwater with Coleridge and Wordsworth, partaking of their opium, listening to their ecstatic declamations echo across the heath.

"Were they good?" she'd asked.

"Perfect gibberish," he'd replied.

Ostensibly, Amelia gave him a short tour of Kingston. Spafford showed her the world. On his arm, she felt, for once, fully connected to that exotic, alluring realm of the squirearchy, with their exceptional ways and singular mores. As she dipped deeper into the crook of his elbow and nodded demurely when he doffed his empire hat to Reverend Stuart and Mrs. Kirkpatrick and Mr. Hagerman, Amelia felt less a share-cropper's daughter and more an elegant extract.

Amelia kicked her legs until she'd unraveled the bedsheets from her body. She twisted from the bed and got to her feet, hopping until her cotton shift fell back. Then she stopped and crouched, arms extended, remembering that Spafford had the room directly below hers. She paused and listened. Nothing. With one tiny step after another, on the balls of her feet, she traversed the squeaking pine until she arrived at the window. She eased open the shutters.

Juno continued her inexorable descent, draped now and then in a flimsy rag of cloud. Her luminescence ebbed and flowed, rarely illuminating, unnoticed by the sleepers below. Amelia could just make out the low brick rectangle of the kiln. She imagined the interior animated with blue-orange flame. She pictured Bennet, the pock-faced, wispy-haired genius, tending the fires, bellowing, extracting beauty and grace from its sweltering depths.

Calhoun had said that if Rupert Spafford's will took precedence, the entire estate, including the glass factory, would likely be his to dispose of. What would he do? Dismantle and sell probably, Calhoun had replied, as speculators do.

What of Bennet? He'd be in his one room cottage now, asleep, resting his pumpkin head on a pallet of straw, dreaming of the next exquisite phial he'd coax from the inferno. Would he go back to boiling scum?

"My redeemer," Bennet had said to her once when she'd come by to oversee the operation. "You can't know the depth of my gratitude. 'Tis what I'm meant to do. I'd sooner throw myself into the kiln than give it up again."

And what of the two young apprentices they'd taken on, Asa and Frederick, the former an orphan and the latter with six siblings and a mother dying slowly of swamp fever? What of Mrs. Simkins and the other domestics? Jeremy and his mother? Her own mother? Herself?

Amelia's gaze drifted back toward the declining moon. From her vantage point, it seemed to linger over the north, brooding over the stubby acreage her father had attempted to tame, and the lake beyond that. Poor Dorephus, printer's son. What did he know about harrowing and crop rotation? Stubbornness was the only strength he had. Almost as intractable as the land he had scratched.

If Amelia wasn't still so infuriated, she might feel some sympathy. She'd begged him not to go ahead with the work bee. She'd pleaded with him to dismiss the worst element, the men already drunk at midday, the ribald chorus propped by their axe handles, the men fondling her with their red, wolfish eyes. He'd been bewitched by the promise of surplus harvests and a new barn. A vision reduced to choler and ash. They might have survived even that. They might have carried on. Instead, Dorephus settled his debt and gave her away, offering her no part in the decision.

And what if Dorephus had succeeded? What if the work bee hadn't ended in flames? Amelia would still be living in that infernal barn, with its perforated roof and its animal residue. A life of hard labour trapped within a corral of burdock and pigweed.

She would never suffer that again. She would choose.

Her year spent as the scandalously young wife of Colonel Noble Spafford had been distasteful at times, even grotesque. But it had also involved long hours of leisure, of losing herself in Willowpath's extensive library, of champagne and quail's eggs, of goose down ticking, and cool, crisp linens free from unwanted guest; flea, bed bug – the Colonel himself. The year following had been even better, securing her and her mother a life of comfort, establishing the glass factory as a going concern, discovering her own latent abilities. Her mind blazed with ideas. She could succeed, she knew it.

Whistling broke Amelia from her reverie. She listened. It got louder. She recognized it – an old folk tune. In fact, she'd heard it the day of the work bee. One of the brutes, probably that Carmichael Jones, had sung it. O'Reilly's Daughter. An Irish folk tune. The whistling stopped and a cloud of blue smoke floated from the window below, past her face, redolent of brandy and spice. The whistler began to sing now, lilting:

> As I was settin' by the fire
> Tellin' lies and drinkin' porter
> Suddenly a thought came to mind...
> I'd never shagged O'Reilly's daughter

Amelia crashed the shutters closed. She strode back to her bed, not worrying this time about the creaking floorboards. She leapt back to the mattress, pulled the pillow corners over her ears, and stared at the ceiling's confusion of stucco.

Dorephus sowed all of this, she thought.

I shall reap it.

Chapter Eighteen

Jeremy lay on his side, hands folded beneath his head. A breeze ruffled the muslin draping the window sash, carrying with it a hint of cooler temperatures. It soothed his fevered skin and the dull ache at his temples. He digested the day's events into rapidly dissolving bites until they began to fade away. He drifted. And drifted.

He heard the barest sweep against the floor. Tiptoed feet jittered a crescent around the end of the bed and then stopped. The mattress padding rustled as the interloper slunk into the sliver of bed in front of him. The sheet lifted and a body pressed backwards. It brought with it a familiar fragrance. His left arm was jerked from its prayer position and pulled across, as though it was another blanket. The body shimmied until every dorsal contour fitted into each cleft and rise of his tucked front.

Wide awake now, Jeremy resolved to lie perfectly still. He would provide this woman, his fond friend, with human warmth. He would be her cover, her comforter. Nothing more, nothing less. Slack, like a quilt, he would regain sleep.

He tried unsuccessfully to banish disturbing thoughts: Major Stokes returning unexpectedly early from Gran Colombia, full of brio, having won the war and made lieutenant colonel, bursting through the door, anticipating warm reunion with his adoring, pining wife, finding her, instead, nearly naked in the grip of a feckless shirker, late of his own platoon, and running them both through with his new ceremonial sabre.

Delicate fingers guided his own. They overlay and encouraged. Jeremy shifted; his every retreat met with a corresponding backward wiggle.

Or, somehow worse: Major Stokes, broken and maimed, the conviction of his wife's eternal fidelity a pole star guiding him home across the thousands of miles, her virtue granting him strength to endure endless gales, and fevers, and privateers. Damaged Major Stokes finally hobbling through the door, the sight of Jeremy groping his willing wife the last image his jaundiced eyes would see as he crumples to the floor, his heart disintegrating, unable to withstand this final outrage.

Before long, Jeremy's buttocks hung over the other edge of the bed. He inched forward. His skin tingled with the pressure exerted by the other body.

In the brief intervals in which Jeremy was able to keep an imaginary Stokes from the verandah, it was Amelia breaking down the door with her dainty foot, skewering him with her many expressions of disgust. He went over every sentence construction, plumbing the most subtle phrasing, searching for those felicitous words that would soften her. Was what he'd done so awful? It was just a tender embrace. A shoulder offered to a friend in need. They weren't exclusive, were they? There was no understanding, was there?

Chapter Nineteen

Amelia emerged mid-morning, beckoned only by the breakfast bell and her mother's laughter tinkling up the staircase. She arrived at the table to see Millie sitting next to Rupert Spafford, her right hand on his shoulder, her left covering her nose and mouth, ineffectually stifling sporadic whoops. Spafford neared the climax of another story about Meath's sybaritic bishop.

"So bish' dips his cup into the aspersorium," Spafford continued, winking at Amelia as she entered, "you know that silver chalice they use for baptisms and such?"

Millie nodded, barely able to contain herself.

"He tips it back and drains the entire thing. I says 'Bish! You're drinking holy water now?' Bishop stares. He hiccups. He says, 'Heavens no! It isn't wholly water Rupert. In fact, 'tis mostly rum.'"

A moment of silence followed as Millie gaped at Spafford, her mouth frozen in an anticipatory rictus.

"Wholly water," Spafford said, enunciating the 'wh', "isn't wholly water."

Millie roared. She slapped the table and the flask standing next to her teacup toppled. Amber fluid dribbled from its open neck. Spafford righted it and replaced the stopper.

"This young Mr. Spafford is too much," Millie said.

"Entirely," Amelia said.

Millie leaned in conspiratorially. Brandy fumes wafted ahead of her words.

"So charming," she said, "And the stories."

"Good morning Mrs. Spafford," Rupert chirped, "you slept well?"

"Passably," Amelia replied.

She looked across at Alice Castor, Jeremy's mother, the only other diner at the table. Alice had finished her breakfast. She hadn't yet looked up from her knitting and the snicking, tsking needles.

"I'm afraid we've already had our breakfasts and you've missed our earlier toasts," Spafford said.

He picked up the flask and leant across.

"Still, there might be just enough left here to enliven your tea."

Amelia covered her cup.

"We like a tot first thing in the morning, for health of course, but an entire flask?"

"Special occasion. It's not every day I get to visit the lovely ladies of Willowpath."

Millie cooed. Mrs. Simkins brought Amelia a plate of cold ham and congealed eggs. She added hot water to the tea. No-one spoke as Amelia sawed at the bread. Spafford trickled the last of the flask into Millie's cup and then his own. He picked up the tea pot and began to pour. As he did, he whistled a low tune.

O'Reilly's Daughter.

"Mr. Spafford," Amelia said, more stridently than she intended, startling her mother.

"Change of heart?" he asked, pushing his teacup toward her. "You can have mine."

"It's impolite to whistle at the table."

"Oh sweetheart," Millie said, "it's just a bit of music."

"Mother, please."

All were quiet again. Spafford drained his cup and brought it down on the table. He pushed his chair back.

"McCallum and Calhoun breakfasted early," he said, patting his stomach. "They've continued their informal meeting. I've requested that they break shortly so we can meet with each individually and privately to get their assessments."

"Good," Amelia said, using a berm of bread to dam the yolk spilling from her egg.

"I thought after lunch you could complete my tour of the grounds and the rest of Willowpath."

"Delighted."

"And then I will return to Kingston with McCallum."

"Ideal," Amelia said, not looking up from her busy fork and knife.

"Then," he said, standing from his chair, tipping an imaginary hat to the seated women, "If you'll excuse me, I'll go and change into my day clothes. À bientôt."

"How continental," Millie said as Spafford left the dining room.

"Moonie," she continued, slapping her daughter's thigh. "Why so unfriendly? Where are your manners? Mr. Spafford's traveled all the way from Ireland, honouring his uncle's memory. You're as chilly as a jellied eel."

"Mother please. Don't preach what you don't understand. And," Amelia looked pointedly at Millie's teacup, "you promised."

"Oh Amelia, don't. You're too young to be a scold. 'Twas just a little drop. I was being a good host. It wouldn't hurt you to..."

Millie noted her daughter's reproving look and paused.

"I didn't sleep very well last night for some reason," she continued, yawning. "I think I'll go upstairs and have a lie down."

"Good idea," Amelia said as her mother stood and shuffled out.

"Seems queer," Alice said, looking up from her knitting and speaking for the first time, "rival claimants to an inheritance, promenading the town, dining together, communing late into the night, breakfasting with one another."

"It's an unusual situation Mrs. Castor, I grant you," Amelia said.

She brought another forkful of egg to her mouth.

"It's nothing Mrs. Castor," Spafford said, ducking his head back into the dining room. "Nothing but a getting acquainted. We'll leave the wrangling to the professionals and keep it civil."

He fastened a cream cravat around his neck.

"We're family after all," he continued as he looped and tightened.

"Oh." He stopped; his fingers gathered around his windpipe.

"Well, you aren't, are you, Mrs. Castor?" He looked at Alice meaningfully. "Not family?"

Alice met his grinning eyes. She considered a response, glanced at Amelia, then returned to her knitting.

そ そ そ そ そ

Calhoun didn't have a lot to report. He and McCallum had talked a lot of precedent. McCallum had brought with him reams of judgments on similar, previous cases. They had discussed some of the most salient. McCallum was a thorough and proficient lawyer, Calhoun said. He'd worked cases at the same law office in Montreal where Calhoun had articled.

"A good man," Calhoun said, "I learned a lot from him."

"Yes," Amelia said, "but can we trust him?"

Calhoun looked shocked, almost a little hurt.

"Mrs. Spafford. Mr. McCallum is senior deacon at Ancient St. John's, Number Three. I assure you, he's a decent man."

"Fine, fine."

"Your claim is all in good order and will stand on its own. Provided everything you've told me is correct and there isn't anything you've left out."

"There isn't anything."

"Good. But, as I've mentioned before, much hinges on which will was notarized most recently and takes precedence. And then, the contents of that succeeding will."

"That hasn't been determined yet? Have you seen the other will?"

"No, I haven't, it is currently in a safe in Montreal."

Amelia frowned.

"Mr. Spafford was unwilling to transport it to Kingston without first being sure of its safety. And necessity. McCallum has briefed me on its contents.

"And?"

"I'm afraid there isn't any mention of a Mrs. Amelia Spafford, only a Mr. Rupert Spafford."

"And, do you have a sense of what Mr. Spafford would do with Willowpath and all of its effects if he were to win?"

"Well, he is Irish gentry. Mr. McCallum has given every indication Mr. Spafford will want to settle his affairs here and return to his more substantial estate in Meath."

Amelia became quiet and thoughtful. For a moment, thistled images of her life before moving to Willowpath tumbled through her mind. She saw herself in the centre of a barn-like prison, staring forlornly through the burdock and pigweed, never fully able to remove the stink of animal residue from her calloused, sunburned skin.

"That's all then, Mr. Calhoun, thank you," she said, finally. "Please let me know the minute you've had access to the second will."

Chapter Twenty

Amelia sat in the same shady alcove where, weeks earlier, she had entertained Pastor Charles Ainsworth, of the King's Mills Methodists. Then, she could not get the Pastor to meet her eye. Now, it was she who looked away, avoiding Rupert Spafford's conspicuous appraisal.

"Voluptous," Spafford said as he helped Amelia into her chair and took his own.

"Charming, and comely, and ample," he added, leaning forward in his seat.

Amelia turned back and stared.

"I beg your pardon."

"Willowpath," Spafford said, waving his arms at the orchard and back towards the house. "It's lovely. Everything I imagined and more. Thank you for such a warm and generous introduction."

Amelia crossed her leg and watched a butterfly zig through the mauve of a flowering sage bush. As it capered from cup to cup, she wondered idly whether it was a monarch or a viceroy. She tried to remember again which was more toxic.

"Amelia," Spafford said, "may I call you Amelia?"

"Yes, of course."

"Amelia, I think the gallopade began brightly, but I may have missed a step."

"I'm not sure what you mean, Mr. Spafford."

"Rupert, please. Surely we've spent enough time together by now. I'd like to think we had a fine time in town yesterday."

"We did. I hope I properly conveyed my appreciation."

"I say again, this is only a getting acquainted. I mean you no harm, none of you here at Willowpath. I'm grateful for your hospitality and I've thoroughly enjoyed my stay."

"I'm relieved to hear it."

"You understand, this matter of wills, it's only business. We can leave it to the counsellors."

"So you keep saying."

"It's my fond hope that this business doesn't get in the way of our close familial relations."

Amelia noted again Rupert's flawless, ivory complexion and his green, smirking eyes. She admired the natural ringlets of glossy black that fell to his shoulders. And the two elfin rosettes that coloured his cheeks when he got excited. His cream cravat was expertly knotted, tied, naturally, into an Irish. His shirt spouted a magnificent cascade of ruffles and his knee length Hessian boots reflected light like a shiny new guinea. Amelia prided herself on sizing someone up accurately quite apart from their wardrobe. Even so, there was no denying the overall impression. Quite different from the one elicited by Jeremy's homespun, hand-mended togs.

Amelia glimpsed a fork of lightning over Rupert's shoulder. She heard a distant grumbling. She sighed. There had been many thunderstorms as summer came reluctantly to an end. Thrilling. But also, noisy and disruptive. Hours of humid tension and then, deluge.

"Rupert."

"Should we move indoors?"

"No, it's miles off. May I ask you a question?"

Rupert's smile widened. He leaned forward.

"If your will succeeds, what do you plan for Willowpath?"

"Naturally, I must do what sound business practice dictates."

Amelia fell silent. She stared deeper into the orchard and studied the garden shed that stood twenty yards away. Some of its boards had warped and were curling away from the frame. Several cedar shakes had fallen from its roof. It was in bad need of paint.

"Let's not discuss it any further. I can see that it upsets you. Should we seek shelter?"

"We have time."

Rupert moved his fine-boned hand across the latticework of the table so that it almost touched the edge nearest Amelia.

"If only," he said.

"Yes?"

His outstretched fingers took a few deep bows.

"If only there was some other way of resolving this whole affair. Without the messy legal proceedings. Without the expense of these black boxes, McCallum and Calhoun."

"I agree."

"I can understand why you would be so attached." Rupert looked up at the towering cumulonimbus framing the main house. "So winsome– I can see why you would become so committed."

"I've grown to love it."

"I've fallen in love in just a day. If it were offered to me, I'd dedicate my life too."

"Rupert, if your will succeeds..."

"Yes?"

"Well, couldn't you just move here, and everything could continue on as it is?"

Rupert withdrew his hand and sat straight up in his chair.

"Rain," he said. "I felt a drop of rain."

"Couldn't you?"

"But what would I do? What would I be? Nephew Rupert, permanent lodger, perpetual layabout?"

"Lord of the manor. I ask only one thing, that you permit me to continue running the glass factory."

"Run the glass factory? You're a rare orchid, Mrs. Spafford. And what about mountain man Castor?"

Amelia said nothing. She wiped the droplets from her cheeks and brow.

"If only you really were Mrs. Spafford," Rupert said.

"I am."

"And I was really Mr. Spafford."

"You are."

The rain increased. Rupert tried to tuck his cravat further into the collar of his shirt, to protect it.

"Rupert!" Amelia cried, Rupert's intimation dawning.

He returned an expression of startled innocence.

"What of the propriety?" she asked, her horror feigned. "A woman marrying her own nephew-in-law."

"And what of the propriety of a woman marrying a man fifty years her senior?"

She glared. Rivulets coursed from her hair into the hollow of her collarbone, collected and spilled down the vee of her neckline. The buff gauze of her gown clung to her body. It was quickly becoming sheer.

"Come," she said, grabbing his hand. "The house is too far. We'll run for the shed."

They ran deeper into the orchard, hand in hand. The sky opened. They skidded and slipped. Rupert once caught Amelia around the shoulders to prevent a fall. She once caught him around the waist. Despite herself, she found herself laughing.

By the time they reached the shed, the sky was dark. Amelia forced the door open. They jumped in. The rain was so thick beyond the open shutter of the single window they could not see back to the house. It drummed against the thin cedar roof with increasing urgency, vibrating the fine mist inside. They heard nothing over the din.

Rupert unraveled his cravat and unbuttoned his shirt to the bottom of its ruffles, just below his breastbone, revealing an arrow of glossy black hair on his chest. He handed the length of silk to Amelia. She looked back at him, still fizzing with laughter. He mimed dabbing at his face and neck. She held the cravat up to her nose. It smelled of sandalwood and heather and smoke. She patted her forehead and cheeks, sponging the water from her eyes and brows. She ran it around her shoulders and neck and beneath the hem of her gown. It made little difference.

She held the cravat out again, shrugging. Rupert took it and traced a circle in the air with his elegant finger. She turned. He folded the cravat into a trim square and caressed the tops of her shoulders with it. He traced the translucent stretch of skin behind her ear. He combed the damp strands of her hair up between his fingers and patted at the back of her neck. The cravat glided with short hops the extent of her lower back until it was saturated and useless. He gave it a gentle squeeze.

Amelia turned again. She pulled her clinging gown away from her body, laughing again at the tingling sensation. The storm surge had abated into a milder, steadier rhythm. They could speak again without raising their voices.

"I detest the thought," Rupert said, handing the cravat back to her, "that you might have the wrong impression of the Spaffords. That you might think we are all the same."

"What do you mean?"

"My uncle and I were very close. We corresponded regularly."

"Yes?"

"Uncle was a crosspatch, as you know. He complained of everything."

Amelia nodded.

"His war wounds. His ailments."

She smoothed the water from the sharp end of her eyebrow.

"His dissatisfactions. His shortcomings."

Her smile faded.

"Obligations unmet. Biblical. Conjugal. Legal."

She let the sodden cravat unfurl from her hand.

"His inability to fulfill that single most important matrimonial duty," he continued.

Amelia's mind swirled. She couldn't speak.

"But we Spaffords aren't all the same," Rupert said. "I would consummate. You can bet on that."

The impertinence stunned. Amelia imagined a handful of cards held up in front of Rupert's merry face. There was the bishop of Meath, standing over his shoulder, winking and gloating, poking out his port-purpled tongue. She wanted to ram both her hands into Rupert's dripping chest, push him back through the door, and out into the rain. She wanted to shove so hard he reeled backwards, up the St. Lawrence, across the ocean, back to the bog from which he'd emerged.

She rewound the cravat tightly around her hand, wrenching water from it. As her eye wandered the interior of the shed, she noted the jumble of rakes, hoes, and spades in the corner. The strangest thoughts occurred:

Must ask Nat to tidy and oil the tools.

He should add fresh sorghum to those corn brooms worn to the stitching.

Over Rupert's shoulder, she spied a scythe hooked to the wall. Rust speckled the great crescent moon of its blade.

Needs honing, but still.

It reaps.

Amelia advanced on Rupert. She pulled open his shirt front. She thrust the cravat behind it and began to sponge away the dampness, starting just above his heart.

Chapter Twenty-One

A ridge of black cloud to the north-west pushed hot, humid air down the Montreal Road. The southern sun was now high in the sky and a line of sweat trickled down Jeremy's back, from his neck to the tops of his trousers. The whirr of late season cicadas harmonized with the rush of blood in his ears, exacerbating his headache. The paste in his mouth had a strange metallic taste. No amount of rubbing could remove the grit from his reddened eyes.

He stopped under the shade of an elm where the Loughborough Road intersects, near the crucifixion scene; a thick beam of cedar standing twenty feet tall with another beam lap-jointed against it. He opened the flask that Lenore had packed for him and sucked at the cold tea inside. He opened the clean, linen rag and plucked out a jammy biscuit.

Jeremy recalled her, puttering in the kitchen, as he lay in bed, half awake. The smell of biscuits browning. A familiar folk tune whistled over the clank of crockery and the shrill of a kettle.

At breakfast, she'd looked about ten years younger, her cup held between pink fingertips, her lips pursed as she blew gently across its surface. Girlish almost; like she had just assembled a toy tea service and Jeremy himself consisted of wool and brass. He recalled her warmth the night before, the way her body fit so perfectly, nestled into his own. With supreme effort, he'd managed self-restraint, but now, alone and weary on the isolated road; regret.

He lay back on a cradle of moss at the foot of the crucifix, next to the devotional items. He meant to close his eyes only a spell to ease their irritation. He meant just a minute or two.

Lightning concussed Jeremy out of his fathomless sleep with such violence that he was unable to breathe. He ran circles around the base of the crucifix unsure which direction to take. Ozone filled the clearing.

He stopped. He could no longer hear cicadas. Or crickets. Or grackles. Nothing.

He looked up. The top of the crucifix was splintered. Was it always? He looked down at his unclenched fist. Sticky. Congealed red from palm to wrist; remains of a crushed biscuit.

The sky opened. Sovereign-sized drops struck his face and neck. Again, lightning cracked. Thirty yards distant. He bolted, sliding the sopping moss. He scrambled; smearing his trousers, twisting his ankle, tearing his tunic. He hobbled into the thicket and crawled beneath deadfall. Rain fell with such intensity he couldn't see beyond his outstretched hand. It lashed the ground like grape shot. It threw spongy humus up from the forest floor. He closed his eyes and plugged his ears. Was it a punishment?

The rain tapered, adrenaline ebbed, and Jeremy became drowsy. He drifted. When the rain finally stopped, he rolled out from under the rotted trunk. He shuffled back into the clearing. He sat on a stump.

A post-chaise entered the far end, heading south. A man leaned out the back. He had black, curly hair, skin as fair as freshly laundered linen. A coral cravat puffed at his neck.

Jeremy got to his feet. The man barked at his driver. The post-chaise slowed.

"Hallo old chap," Rupert Spafford called, waving a mauve swatch. "Coincidence, what? Helluva storm. Were you caught out?"

Jeremy raised his hand. It still showed smears of red and black.

"Heavens," Spafford said. He looked Jeremy up and down as the post-chaise neared and then passed. "You're a patched knee. Rough night?"

Jeremy said nothing.

"Not me," Spafford continued, pushing his head out the window. He drew air deeply into his lungs and stretched his arms. "Slept like a sultan. Country air does me a world of good, it seems. Puts me in touch with my more primitive nature."

"And Willowpath," he shouted, craning his neck. "'Charming, and comely, and ample,' that's what I said. What I still say. I look forward to seeing more of her."

Spafford slapped the side of the cabriolet.

"You should get yourself one of these," he cried, "gets you in and out quickly. No fuss."

The post-chaise exited the clearing and disappeared.

Jeremy stared. He clapped his hands together to knock them free of crumbs, and mud, and jelly. He plunged them into a rain-filled rut and wiped them on his tunic. Inside the linen rag he found a porridge of liquefied biscuit. He flung the bundle to the foot of the crucifix, where it landed next to the other votive offerings.

He continued north.

❧ ❧ ❧ ❧ ❧

Nat sat out front of Willowpath, oiling a scythe. A riotous clamour erupted among the crows. The boy glanced up and noticed Jeremy limping from the woods. He put his rag next to the whetstone, lowered the scythe, and went inside.

Jeremy was twenty yards from the door when it re-opened. Amelia appeared beneath the lintel. She watched as Jeremy neared. Her eye roved from his dragged foot, mud-caked trousers, torn jersey, wild hair, spattered face. Her expression steadily darkened. He stopped a few paces from her, rehearsing the lines he had laboured over for hours the night before.

She made a noise. A caustic blend of disappointment, exasperation, and regret. She turned sharply on her heel and disappeared into the house.

"Amelia?"

Jeremy kicked his muddy boots next to the ornamental scraper. He rolled his rain-heavy socks from his feet, threw them on the boots, and limped through the door.

"Amelia?" he called again.

He ascended the stairs, calling her name, his voice

rising. No-one. He came to the door of her room and found it locked. He knocked. No answer. He knocked again. He called her name. No answer. He pounded the door with the side of his fist. Amelia, he shouted. Why wouldn't she answer? Could she have possibly heard of his liaison with Lenore?

The door opened. Amelia stood with one hand on her hip, the other on the doorknob. Despite the stuffiness of the room, she was wrapped in layers of muslin, a shawl about her shoulders, and a scarf around her neck. The air was stale as though the window hadn't been opened for a few days. So different from the gusts of lavender and myrtle that had greeted him when he burst in on her a month earlier. She appraised him again, wrinkling her nose at his grime streaked face.

"Amelia," he said. "I came as fast as I could."

She tilted her head.

"I helped Dr. Scriven locate his apprentice and with the planning of the new school. We discussed strategies for increasing business. It took longer than I'd hoped."

She made no answer.

"He's a respected, well-connected man, I think he can help us. What did Calhoun have to report?"

He wished she would say something. Something pleasant, something spiteful. Anything.

"I passed Spafford on the road."

He looked around the landing, looking for some clues of Spafford having been there, a trail of spores that had been left behind. He fought the urge to demand details.

"He seemed very pleased with himself."

"Jeremy," she said, finally. "I was given to Colonel Spafford when I was sixteen. A child really. I've never felt so helpless about the fate of my life. About what I am to be. I don't mean to ever feel that way again."

"Yes, but..."

She raised her hand.

"Before anything else," she said, "I'll do what is necessary to retain Willowpath."

She closed the door.

"Amelia," he said, "I got caught in a storm."

He listened. He sensed her standing just on the other side.

"I nearly got struck by lightning," he added.

Her voice came through the door, quieter and softer now.

"Jeremy, know that I'm fond of you. I mean you no harm. You saved my life and released me. You are always welcome here."

"What? What are you saying?"

"I'll do what is necessary."

He heard her footsteps fade away from the door.

"Amelia."

A hand on his elbow stopped him from knocking a fourth time.

"Son," Alice frowned at his bare feet and torn clothing. "Are you unwell?"

"Mother? I'm fine, I'm fine. I want to speak to Amelia."

"I think she wants to be alone, just now. There've been queer happenings. It'd been better that you'd been here."

Jeremy let his hand drop.

"Come," she said, "have an early supper. You need a rest, I warrant."

Jeremy followed Alice to the kitchen. She asked Mrs. Simkins to heat some soup.

While Jeremy ate quietly, he wondered at Amelia's petulance. What happened here while he was gone? He felt a warmth rise to his face. This was no way to be treated. Was he or was he not the manager of the Willowpath Glassworks? At the very least, this was a question that needed answering. He resolved to confront Amelia that night and demand answers. He would brook no evasion.

Jeremy finished the first bowl of soup, and a second, and a thick wedge of bread. Together with a warm bath, he found himself restored and utterly exhausted. He told Alice that he would go to his room and put his head down for a nap. He asked that she wake him for supper so he could speak with Amelia, refreshed and renewed.

When Jeremy woke the next morning, well after breakfast, Amelia had departed.

Chapter Twenty-Two

For two days Jeremy waited at Willowpath. He asked everyone.

Bennet, the glassblower, shaking his pumpkin head, wringing his hands: Almost out of orders, Mr. Castor. What then?

Millie, Amelia's mother: A willful girl, always has been. She means well. I'm sure she'll work something out with the new Mr. Spafford. Charming young man, just delightful.

Alice, his mother: I don't trust him. You shouldn't neither. Mouth full of flannel.

Simpkins, head of house: Lovely mistress. Hope she isn't in danger. No-one tells me anything.

Joseph and Sarah, groundskeeper and his wife: You seen her Sarah, didn't you? She don't look so happy. Ain't that right Sarah?

Nat, groundkeeper's son: Cab come at dawn. She and Calhoun gets in. Headed south.

On the third day, tired of waiting, he made the long walk back into Kingston. He asked at all the likeliest establishments.

Calhoun's office: Closed.

Walker's Hotel: Mrs. Spafford has not checked in and has made no reservation, though we look forward to her next visit.

Thomson's: Madame has not been seen since last week, when the Irish gentleman purchased for her a poke bonnet in the latest style. If you see her, please let her know the Cecil House shawls have arrived.

The Gazette: Amelia Spafford. Amelia Spafford. Sounds familiar, but..., haven't seen her. Don't recall any of our correspondents reporting on Mrs. Spafford neither. Would you like to take out a missing person notice?

That left Bottle and Glass, the last place in town she'd been seen.

"Another?" Poncet asked.

Jeremy nodded. The taverner poured a third.

"Brother Castor." Dr. Scriven sat down at a stool to his right. He extended his hand. Jeremy gripped it. They dug their thumbs into opposing finger joints. "A pleasure to see you in town again so soon."

Jeremy stared at the foam at the top of the porter, disintegrating. Scriven put a hand on his thigh.

"What troubles you brother?"

Jeremy eyed Scriven wearily. The doctor thrust his ambergris'd face in at him. His eyes, blue as French toile, shone with eagerness to fulfill his Masonic oath.

Jeremy considered him. It was Scriven that had distracted him with the Masonic rites, the rescuing of Lilac, the matter of the new school...

"This inheritance business?"

...that bumbler lawyer, just because he's a brother.

"I'm telling you, leave it to Calhoun. He's a professional."

"Amelia's disappeared," Jeremy said. He took a deep pull from his mug.

"That so? Are you certain you want to find her?"

Jeremy frowned. Did he?

He conjured an image of Amelia, as she was that day in August, when he interrupted her bath, rosy, glistening, cheerful. He'd asked her to marry him that afternoon. She hadn't taken it seriously. And, perhaps she'd been right. Maybe he'd been heat-addled, as she'd said. Since he'd challenged the Colonel to a duel, to defend her safety and honour, he'd assumed that they were fated to be together, forever. It occurred to him he'd never really considered whether that's what he wanted. Or, wondered if it's what she wanted. It had just seemed like the next thing to do. What else?

"Not to worry," Scriven said, sensing his unease. "We'll find her."

Scriven leaned in.

"Where are you staying? Walker's? Have you supped?"

Jeremy put his hand on his chest. He felt for the single shilling left in his purse.

"Come," Scriven said, dropping a guinea on the bar. "Let's dine at the Black Bull. Stay the night with me. Lilac will be happy to see you again. We'll get to the bottom of this. Tomorrow."

❧ ❧ ❧ ❧ ❧

When they arrived at his rooms, the door to Scriven's office was shut. Scriven turned the knob and pushed it open. Jeremy followed.

They discovered a woman bent forward over the back rest of the chaise lounge, dun-coloured pantaloons at her ankles, skirts pulled over her waist to her shoulders. A livid, eggplant-tinted carbuncle seethed from the centre of one of the woman's bare buttocks. Lilac advanced on it with a spring-loaded lancet in one hand and a pewter bleeding bowl in the other.

A muffled voice came from the upholstery.

"Is that you, doctor?"

"Ah yes, it is me."

"Doctor," Lilac said, dropping the lancet. She straightened. "My apologies. Mrs. Abernethy came by. She has this complaint."

"I can't sit. I can't stand. I can barely lie down," Mrs. Abernethy added.

"I see," the doctor said, "I see."

But I wish I hadn't, he thought, as he averted his gaze to the cabinet and admired how Lilac had arranged the instruments behind its glass doors, grouped according to disorder and application.

"I admitted Mrs. Abernethy, anticipating you'd be back soon. Such discomfort. I offered to examine her. A carbuncle."

"I noticed."

"Isn't the first I've seen," Lilac continued. "Seen 'em all the time at sea. Old Carruthers let me handle them. I thought I should avoid delay and get started. Put Mrs. Abernethy at her ease."

"Yes, yes, of course."

"Hello Deacon," Lilac called happily, now noticing Jeremy behind the doctor.

"Deacon?" Mrs. Abernethy asked into the sofa.

Scriven gestured Jeremy from the office doorway back out into the sitting room. Jeremy backed away with a little wave.

"Doctor. Not to worry Mrs. Abernethy," Lilac said, "I misspoke. Doctor, I meant to say."

"Is your apprentice qualified Dr. Scriven?"

"Quite so, quite so. Trained her myself. Carry on Miss Evans."

"Thank you doctor," Lilac said, beaming. She retrieved the lancet from the floor and submerged the business end into a bowl of vinegar.

"Now please hold steady Mrs. Abernethy. Deep breaths. Almost done. This will hurt a little, but will bring great relief, I promise. Big girl now."

Scriven backed into the next room and shut the door as Mrs. Abernethy erupted. He went to the liquor cabinet and poured two sherries. He handed one to Jeremy.

"She's a revelation, Castor," he said. "That's not the first patient she's seen. She's handled at least a half dozen and they've all left satisfied, promising to pay promptly and to come back again. Most remarkable, she seems to actually enjoy it, draining pustules, extracting bile, changing bandages."

Jeremy took a seat.

"With me overseeing her development, she could become first-rate. I don't want to go so far as to say she has the makings of a physician. Medical practitioner might be a better term. Remarkable isn't it?"

Jeremy looked around. Every surface was clean and bare. All instruments were stowed. Scales gleamed.

"To be perfectly honest," Scriven said, guiding the words to Jeremy with the back of his hand, "I'm happy to let her do it. I don't go in much for boil lancing, and bleeding, and the rest. Pedestrian. If I can impart my expertise to her, use her as my proxy, another instrument in my steady, experienced hand, there is no reason not to. If it brings her some peculiar satisfaction? All the better."

"You've done her a good turn," Jeremy said. "I've never seen her happier."

"It isn't completely selfless. With the time she's freed up, I've been able to write three new pages. I've told you about my play, haven't I Castor?"

Jeremy nodded.

"It's the story of a prodigal son. Must leave home, it's not clear why, but it's an injustice. He has impeccable taste. He's misunderstood. Unlike his fellows, he recognizes that money without a guiding principle, without wisdom..., it's just so much printed paper. Still. He wonders what he shall be. You're an avid reader, aren't you? I think it might resonate. Perhaps I could read you some, get your literary opinion."

"Dr. Scriven," Jeremy said, "I really need to find Amelia and Calhoun. I need to find out what is happening."

"It's nearly supper time. There's nothing to do until tomorrow. We will seek out Calhoun tomorrow, I promise. I know his haunts. In the meantime, we dine at The Black Bull. We'll plumb the depths of my little tragedy over champagne and pork pie. Let me find the manuscript."

Scriven left for the bedroom. Mrs. Abernethy emerged from the examination room, walking slowly, her legs stiff. Jeremy got to his feet.

"You're not Dr. Scriven," she said, her face reddening. "Where's Dr. Scriven?"

Lilac followed close behind, guiding her toward the front door.

"This is our next patient Mrs. Abernethy," she said, "Mr. Jeremy Castor. Now," she held the door open, "be sure to get lots of rest, change the plaster each morning."

She handed Mrs. Abernethy a small amethyst ampoule.

"Take a drop or two of this with your tea, for the pain and to help you sleep. Any trouble, don't hesitate to pay us another visit. We can come to you. Best not to sit down for a few days."

Mrs. Abernethy nodded and, at the threshold, paused to look back for Dr. Scriven.

"Must have just stepped out, missus. I'll be sure to inform him of our success."

Mrs. Abernethy nodded again and stepped gingerly out into the street. Lilac shut the door behind her. She dashed across the parlour and threw her arms around Jeremy's neck. She kissed his chest.

"Deacon!" she cried. "I can do this, I can really do it. I set a fibula yesterday. I extracted an abscessed molar the day before. And I have you to thank."

"You deserve it, Lil'. And you're a boon to Dr. Scriven, he just told me so."

The front door opened again. Lilac released Jeremy and stepped back. They looked toward the door.

Lenore Stokes stepped in.

"Jeremy," she said. "I didn't expect..."

Scriven emerged from his bedroom, a sheaf of papers in his hand.

"Lenore," he said, "exquisite timing. Would you like to join Castor and me for dinner at the Black Bull."

"Thank you Creedence. I'm actually here to see your nurse."

"Miss Evans?" Scriven turned to Lilac.

"Yes."

"Whatever for? Has anything changed? Are you unwell?"

"I'm fine Creedence, thank you."

"I'm as well versed on female concerns as any," Scriven said.

"I know."

"No matter," he said, shrugging. "Castor and I are off to The Black Bull. Perhaps we'll see you on our return?"

"Perhaps."

Jeremy followed Scriven toward the door. He stopped to kiss Lenore's cheek.

"It's good to see you again, Mrs. Stokes."

"And you. Were you able to bring your business to a satisfying conclusion?"

Jeremy met her warm gaze. He was gripped with a sudden desire to leave with her instead of Scriven, to Stoke Cottage, and to unburden himself to her.

"Not yet."

"Will we be able to meet again to discuss the new school? I'd like to get your opinions on curriculum."

"Soon, I hope."

"Please stop by Stoke cottage any time, you are always welcome."

"Let's go Castor," Scriven called from the front step. "Before Chestnut runs out of pies."

Chapter Twenty-Three

Jeremy nestled further into the chair's accommodating arms. He brought the mug to his face. Steamy tendrils carried the aroma of Venezuelan beans, roasted overnight, ground that morning, steeped just moments before, fertile with condensed energy. He tested the mug's lip with his own. Still too hot. He balanced it on the overstuffed arm of the chair and with his free hand he opened the morning's Gazette. He reflected how few pleasures there are in life that rival a freshly brewed cup of coffee, a crisp, uncreased broadsheet, and a spare moment in which to enjoy them.

Scriven's not so bad, he thought. *He means to help. There is no doubt of that.*

The doctor had already been out that morning, before Jeremy had awoken. He'd inquired after Mrs. Spafford at the Lodge. He'd dropped by John Moore's and he'd asked the young men of the Headstrong Club if they had seen her, or Calhoun, or McCallum. He'd purchased a pouch of Moore's finest Arabica granulate. He'd visited Stephen Miles at his Gazette offices and he'd questioned the printer, Squib, and the inkers.

Miles had said, as he usually did, "I'm very busy Creedence."

When Scriven had pressed, Miles had said, "Yes, familiar name. Can't you see that I'm in the middle of printing? Mr. Castor was in yesterday asking after her too. Wait. I remember. We received a note from her lawyer, Calhoun, for inclusion in this next issue of the Gazette. No. I don't have time to find it and tell you. Do I resemble a town crier?"

Miles had waved his black-streaked hands.

"I print paper for a living. Read the Gazette when it comes out."

Scriven had learned that Calhoun's messenger had come from the King's Arms out of town on the Kingston Road. He had paid Squib a farthing to deliver a copy of the paper when it was printed. He had returned to his rooms with the coffee, had explained to Jeremy that he had information about Calhoun's whereabouts, and had left again to hire a carriage that could take them to the King's Arms. Twenty minutes later, just as Mrs. Grady brought coffee, Squib had delivered a warm copy of the Gazette.

Jeremy scanned the front page. He learned of Jethro Jackson's missing red cow, and Major Glegg's strayed white pointer, MacDonell's lost gold seal, and George Blake's mislaid twenty-pound note. His eye roved the advertisements for cheap woolen goods, spruce beer, broadcloths, yellow soap, snuff, and bombazine. He read, twice, the poem in the upper right, Thomas Moore's Last Rose of Summer, enjoying its cadence without absorbing its meaning.

And then this:

☞ NOTICE!

Rupert Spafford, of County Meath, Ireland, begs leave of subscribers to announce his intended marriage to Mrs. Amelia Spafford, née Barrett, at St. George's Church, the fifth day of January 1818, Rev. Official Stuart presiding. Mr. and Mrs. Spafford hope all friends and family will be able to join us on this joyous day.

Jeremy's index finger had been hooked lightly around the mug's handle. When his arm jerked involuntarily toward his chest, the mug came with it, part of the way. The liquid inside, hot and black, tipped to his lap like pitch from a rampart. He leapt from the chair. The mug cartwheeled and smashed next to the disheveled Gazette.

Lilac burst from the study door.

"Jeremy," she said, in a strained whisper. She glanced at the mess at his feet. "What are you doing?"

Jeremy didn't look up from the remainder of coffee darkening the Gazette's crumpled masthead.

"I'm treating Mrs. Kirkpatrick in there," Lilac continued, hushed. "Nervous melancholia. As you might have guessed, sharp noises aren't helpful."

Jeremy glared, plucked up the sopping paper, and bolted from the room.

Chapter Twenty-Four

Lenore stood from her seat at the kitchen table.

"What a charming surprise! I didn't expect to see you again so soon."

She smoothed the hem of her thin cotton shift to just above her knees and swept a hand across the wide triangle of her neckline.

"In fact, I didn't expect anyone, as you can see. I'm still in my chemise."

Jeremy said nothing. He stood rooted to the threshold. The damp Gazette was bunched in his fist like a great, grey bloom.

"Sweetheart," Lenore said, now realizing his distress. "What is it?"

She crossed the room, spotting the tar-coloured ellipse on the thigh of his trouser leg.

"Abby, you may go."

"But missus."

Lenore narrowed her eyes. Abby exited, pulling the door closed behind her. Lenore barred it.

"Jeremy," Lenore said, her hand now on his arm, caressing. "Tell me. Let me help."

He thrust out the thistle of paper. She took it delicately between her thumbs and forefingers. She peered at the smudged text.

"Oh dear. Major Glegg has lost his white pointer again." she said.

He shook his head.

"Jethro Jackson's missing red cow?"

He shook his head with violence.

"What then? What is it?"

Jeremy grabbed the paper and jabbed his finger at the notice, nearly skewering it.

She read. She sighed.

"I warned you."

He moaned.

"Come, you smell like a Turkish cafe. You'll want to wash."

Lenore led him in, pulling at his elbow, and sat him on a chair. She prattled as she filled the kettle and stoked the stove, hoping that a shower of light talk might help to rinse away the sadness: better to know now rather than later, you can't quarrel with what's not meant to be, you're both still young, you'll collect another butterfly, lovelier and brighter. Who knows, maybe she'll tire of that Spafford as quickly as she tired of the last one.

Jeremy's shoulders slumped.

"Come," Lenore said as she pulled him from the chair, "take them off."

She mistook his expression for shyness.

"I've told you," she said, "I've seen it all before. If we've had one young marine billeting at Stoke cottage, we've had a hundred. You'll not shock me."

He loosened the drawstring of his trousers and let them drop.

"Jeremy!" she cried.

An oval of scarlet ran from the bottom of his drawers to the top of his knee.

"You're scalded."

He looked down and flinched when touched.

"I have something for it. It will ease the pain and prevent scarring."

Lenore hurried, pouring several buckets of water from the cistern into the hip bath in her bedroom, followed by the water from the kettle. She led Jeremy in, had him remove his tunic and drawers, and directed him to sit, leaning forward. She sponged his back and neck and scraped them with a block of yellow soap that smelled of oatmeal. She dipped the sponge into a separate pail of cool water and squeezed it over his reddened thigh.

"Finish up," she said, handing him the sponge and the soap.

She pulled a towel from the top of a dresser and put it next to the bath.

"Dry off and I'll be back with the balm."

Lenore returned, a few minutes later, with an earthenware bowl in her hand. Jeremy stood dripping, next to the bath, the towel around his waist.

She arranged the pillows against the frame of her bed so they made a bolster.

"Lay on the bed."

He sat on the mattress, keeping the towel in place. He lifted his feet and swiveled to rest his back against the cushions. Gently, she pushed his knee outward. She plunged two fingers into the bowl and scooped out a measure of salve. She daubed it on, lightly at first, then with increasing firmness. Her delicate fingers, curved slightly at the ends, drifted and slid, stroking from knee to towel and back. The salve began to melt, absorbed by his overheated skin. His thigh became glossy and slick.

Lenore leaned in and her hair fell forward. Her ringlets parted, revealing a creamy stretch of neck inches from Jeremy's confounded face. As she massaged, her nightshirt swept and swayed.

She thrust her fingers once more into the bowl.

His towel shifted.

She made a dainty noise of surprise.

He pressed his face to her neck.

She quavered.

Without taking his eyes from hers, Jeremy took the bowl from her outstretched hand, two of his own fingers accidentally dipping deep into the liniment. He put it down on what he thought was the edge of the bed. It toppled and smashed.

He pressed his lips against hers.

She cinched him in her arms, smearing the dollop of cream into his back.

He engulfed her, his own salve-laden hand searching and caressing.

"I've never...," he said, pulling back one last time.

"Teacher," she said. "You'll learn."

❧ ❧ ❧ ❧ ❧

Blood rushed and thrummed Jeremy's head. It kept time with the insistent thump of his heart, the rhythm of their breathing, Lenore's tremolo. Major Glegg, Jethro

Jackson, Rupert Spafford, Amelia, Willowpath; all evaporated. Music returned.

It was symphonic. Every movement. From the opening, impetuous sonata, to the slow tenderness of the adagio, to the quickened ardour of the scherzo. As they built to a final, frantic rondo, Jeremy was amazed to hear a novel composition performed in his head, budding with exquisite, unheard harmonies. For one breathless moment he felt he could recreate himself, and anything he conceived, sui generis.

Then, the sweet afterglow of the coda.

Chapter Twenty-Five

The day following his discovery of the Spafford wedding announcement Jeremy took a room at Walker's Hotel. He'd left Lenore Stokes' cottage just before sunup and for a few hours, with his wool cap pulled low, he'd skulked the waterfront, before arriving at Walker's later that morning. Once inside the room, the door latched shut, he threw himself into the bed's cool, clean linen and slept until early afternoon, woken only by the charwoman rapping the door. After a meal of cold meats, relishes, and bread, he spent time in the lounge, his head bowed behind the back issues of the various news sheets Walker kept arrayed across the low tables; enticements to the prominent men of business and politics frequenting his hotel. Fearing another nasty shock, he assiduously avoided the local Gazette and perused instead a month-old copy of the Canadian Courant, a few remaining pages of the Niagara Spectator, and a crumpled Boston Daily Advertiser. He attempted escape into the complaints and calamities of distant unknowns. He didn't know what else to do.

His thoughts returned to the sickening jolt of the wedding announcement. Not only had Amelia rejected him, claiming she wasn't ready, she'd accepted the oily Irishman's proposal having known him only a few days. He recounted their last conversation, outside her room at Willowpath. This is what she'd meant? Learning the truth in the paper had been one of the worst moments he'd ever experienced.

And then, the wondrousness of what followed, the most euphoric night of his life. Memories of Lenore's chestnut curls, the coppery light of her eyes, the consolation of her pliant kiss, the impossible silkiness of her inner thigh... he wanted nothing more than to return to Stoke Cottage immediately. But it was impossible. Not with Abby lurking. And, Major Stokes around every corner. He cared for Lenore, now more than ever. He deplored the idea of making her life precarious.

His mind reeled.

As supper approached, two men joined him in the lounge, introducing themselves as a forwarder from Montreal and a bookseller from Albany.

"I'm not saying it hasn't changed," the forwarder said, apparently continuing an earlier conversation, gesturing with his pipe stem at a headline on the front page of the Gazette. "It has. How could it not?"

Jeremy folded the Advertiser and exchanged it for a year-old London Morning Herald. He nodded and presented a grim smile as if to say, 'Quite so', before spreading the paper in front of him. He pictured Amelia and Spafford, sitting at the Willowpath dining table, going over invitation lists.

"Quartermaster says there's less than two thousand

in the garrison today," the man continued. "'Twas double that just two years ago. He suspects it will be down to a thousand six months hence. I delivered them five shipments of trousers and stockings last year. This year? Nothing."

The bookseller in his homespun jacket nodded vehemently.

"My agent in Adolphustown is a Friend," the forwarder said, inclining conspiratorially from his armchair, "say, neither of you are Quakers are you?"

The bookseller shook his head with a laugh. Jeremy cleared his throat.

"So, I say to my Quaker agent," the forwarder continued, "it's all well and good to love thine enemy and to conscientiously object but, damn it, war is damned good business. None better grease for gearwheels of the modern economy. Damned good business!"

Jeremy raised the palisade of his paper an inch higher. He revisited images of Lenore, her hand on his bicep, her head on his chest, his nostrils full of the jasmine rising from her Apollo's knots.

"What'd the Quaker say?" the bookseller asked, grinning.

"What could he say? Struck dumb. Listen. An army needs kitting out. Soldiering puts regular shillings in a young man's pocket. Gives him an occupation. He needs merchandise on which to spend it. A new chapeau. The latest cravat. Some sort of reward to make all the sweat and blood sacrifice worthwhile. To give him the sense he's amounting to something. "

"The soldier may want to improve himself," said the bookseller, with an excess of congeniality, "and spend that extra shilling on a library subscription."

"Them's that remain," the forwarder straightened his torso to glance over the top of Jeremy's Herald, "you can see them down at the waterfront, scrounging and begging, a tanner here and there for a mug of lees at the Pig and Whistle or some other grubby shop."

"Many of them that's leaving are officers," the bookseller added, "them's that do the reading."

"Take a decommissioned officer then. Maybe he's got a land grant. But will he cultivate it? No. Doesn't know the first thing. Just wants to sell. Best of luck, bigwig! Nowadays, you couldn't trade a cup of warm tea for an acre of this here granite and bramble. If they would lift the ban on immigration. This is what I rave about. Ship some proper Scots and Yorkshiremen in. Set them loose on the muskeg. Then you'd see a blossoming."

"Americans too," the bookseller added, "My brother-in-law Silas had an agreement to buy a hundred acres near Ernestown from a captain of the 41st. Fallen on hard times, the fella was. 'Twas giving it away. They wouldn't let him in."

The forwarder appraised the bookseller from the corner of his eye, through a sphere of pipe smoke slowly disintegrating.

"They can hardly be blamed, can they?" he said. "Just two years ago they was lobbing great chunks of lead at each other. Having beat Brother Jonathan back from the front gate, waving about his bayonet and flintlock, now they're going to admit him through the back door armed with rake and hoe?"

The bookseller's expression darkened.

"Silas means only to make good."

"I ain't saying it's right. But a man of business must face reality if he's to succeed. I ain't too worried. They'll let 'em in eventually. They'll have to. They're desperate not to cede another inch to those southerners and republicans. They want to develop the province. Requires new blood. In the meantime, folks'll still want their silks and satins, cambrics and cassimeres."

They were quiet a moment. Jeremy had given no more than the barest murmur to anything the men had said. He'd hoped they might give up. The silence that now descended on the lounge suggested it was being considered. His thoughts returned to Amelia, her bath towel slipping from her shoulders. But it was Rupert's fine-boned fingers that helped the towel on its way. And then, his hand slick with liniment, tracing the rise of Lenore's hip. He wanted to drop the broadsheet, jump through the bay window, and sprint back to Stoke Cottage.

"So, fella," the bookseller said at last. "What line you in?"

Jeremy lowered the leading edge of the Herald. He met the man's eye. He paused.

What line was he in?

He might have said, "I'm in glass". But in what sense was that any longer true? Surely the Spafford wedding announcement had put an end to that. And anyway, had he ever really been in glass? He'd often wondered at the tenuousness of his position at the glass factory. He'd hardly been indispensable. He wasn't involved in the manufacture of the stuff. Despite his nominal position as the figurehead of Willowpath Glassworks, he knew very little about it.

What would his standing be now? He imagined that this worldly young Mr. Spafford must already be resident at Willowpath. With all his experience within circles of powerful and influential men – maybe he even knew these brash merchants discussing matters of importance in the lounge – Mr. Spafford was probably just what the glass manufactory required. What it didn't need was a failed deacon with no connections and no prospects.

"Between engagements," Jeremy said, before re-raising the Herald's masthead.

The forwarder acknowledged Jeremy with an 'mm-hmm' tinged with disappointment and then sucked loudly at his pipe.

Jeremy continued to wonder.

Deacon? The notion belonged to a faraway place and time. So much had changed. The soul saving business in this town, as in his hometown of Porthleven, seemed a closed shop. He wouldn't know where to start. Truthfully, his heart wasn't really in it.

Royal marine? Discharged, without honour. Rather, just this side of dishonour. Despite the lure of regular pay, there was no going back down that path. He'd shown no real aptitude and besides, as he'd just heard, all over the empire British arms were receding.

Teacher? It seemed to be where the tide pushed him.

But even this lacked plausibility. They had yet to find a location for the school. They'd yet to secure the funds. An initial list of subscribers had been published in the Gazette but it was Jeremy's understanding that even if all of these pledges were honoured they may still not be enough. He could put his name forward as Lenore and Scriven had urged him to do. The full committee of the Kingston Compassionate Society would interview candidates. Why had he entertained it? To please Lenore. To have an excuse to spend time with her.

A thought occurred with sudden, almost violent strength:

I don't like children.

The Herald wilted.

Runny noses, filthy faces, peculiar smells. What does one say to them?

A civic minded thing to do, Scriven had said, won't take up too much time, could be done in addition to your present duties selling glass.

A part time employment then.

Jeremy's face blanched. Another thought jarred: Scriven had expounded Masonic devotion to service. He had never mentioned prospective salary. He'd never mentioned wages at all. Was he to be a volunteer?

Jeremy regarded the two men across from him: the meaty forwarder with the rosy, globular head, jutting cravat, gold watch chain, the angular bookseller with the sculpted jaw whiskers and tortoiseshell pince-nez. Cosmopolitan men, he imagined, equally at home on Charles Street, Wall Street, Regent Street.

Teacher? What stock would such men put in the

position of teacher? It carried a whiff of desperation. Worse; defeat.

"I see here," the bookseller said, finally, "they're putting on Heir at Law this evening at the Bottle and Glass, a half dollar for the pit. Wonder if they have any tickets left."

"Last time I was through," the forwarder replied, "I had a well-trimmed venison joint there. Serving girl wasn't half saucy either, truth told."

"I hear their porter has proper backbone."

"It does indeed." The forwarder angled out of his armchair again, warming to the new topic. "Say, I find myself suddenly peckish."

"Dinner and a show?"

"Unquestionably."

"Want to come along, fella?"

Jeremy's paper palisade collapsed.

"Me? Oh, thanks awfully. I'm afraid I couldn't."

The men waited.

"Ah yes, I'm meeting someone."

The bookseller nodded without conviction.

"Shortly," Jeremy added.

"Well, you'll know where we'll be," the forwarder said. "There are few perquisites available to hard working commercial men but, wolfing and gorging away from home must be near top of the list. I, for one, aim to take full advantage. Ta-ra."

Jeremy waited a few minutes until he could be sure that the two men had left the hotel and he could return surreptitiously to his room. He resolved not to return to the lounge for the remainder of his stay.

Who was this Jeremy Castor?

Man of means, replete with prospects, favoured suitor of the widow Spafford. An exhausting pretense. He had a vague but unshakeable sense that, behind his back, people snickered. Even strangers. Albany booksellers. Forwarders from Montreal.

Maybe he should return to Willowpath. He couldn't stay at Walker's forever. When in town on business for the glass factory, when meeting an important potential client, a Cartwright or a quartermaster, Jeremy would stay a night at Walker's Hotel to project an air of prosperity. Two, at most. If ever he had to stay longer, he might take a room somewhere less expensive, The King's Arms or The Black Bull. In either case, it was Willowpath Glassworks that paid the bill. He should confront Amelia. Meet the truth of the situation head on. But he couldn't bear it. He felt paralyzed. It took great effort to speak more than a few words, to request a wash basin of the charwoman, to obtain his room key from the front desk. He strove to avoid everyone.

Everyone, except Lenore.

A few hours after sundown, when he could count on Abby having already left Stoke cottage, Jeremy, with his cloth cap again pulled down low over his eyes, slipped out the side entrance of Walker's hotel and, by a roundabout way of Kingston's darkest paths and laneways, arrived at the cottage. He crouched in the shadows of a nearby cedar grove until he was certain not a soul breathed, and he lowered himself down through the cellar door that had been left unlocked. He removed his boots, felt his way up the skewed, unhewn stairs, eased the latch, nudged the door, and crept the hall to the parlour.

There he found Lenore alone, sitting before a pair of crystal schooners, a newly uncorked Amontillado, and an entanglement of the finest Merino.

Chapter Twenty-Six

An hour before sunrise Jeremy retraced his steps, back through the side entrance of Walker's. He sidled past Antoine, Walker's discreet Maître d'hôtel, with a nod and finger raised to the brim of his tilted cap. He went straight to bed and slept until roused once more by the charwoman's knocking. Avoiding the lounge, he picked up a small bundle of food, an apple, a heel of bread, a rind of cheese, and he walked toward the outskirts of town, to the lakeshore, to find a lonely thicket unlikely to be disturbed. He passed the hours looking out across the grey, tumultuous water until the sun began to dip and the light fade. Then he began the walk back into town by which time it would be dark enough that he could return to Stoke cottage.

Jeremy repeated this routine, mechanically, for a week. It was far from unpleasant. Days were spent in an underworld of unfeeling, drowsy limbo and nights in an alternate universe of euphoric stimulation and heightened sensuality. He was unwilling to contemplate what must be done. An acceptable alternative hadn't occurred.

On the tenth day a letter addressed to him arrived at Walker's, from Alice.

My Dearest Son,

Where have you gone?

I hope this letter finds you at last, healthy of body and sound of mind. No-one seems to know where you've disappeared. Bennet suggested you might be at Walker's Hotel.

I remain here at Willowpath, a slipped stitch amid the sash. Miss Amelia is ever gracious, claiming I may stay as long as I wish. Master Spafford, the wolf cub, between licking his lips, says the same. I keep my head down and mind my own. But 'tis devilish uncomfortable.

You daft sprat! Where are you?

Did Paris and Menelaus greet each other on either side of Helen, with arms outstretched, to say, 'No, please, you take her.' 'No, no, please, you go ahead.'

Indeed not. War commenced without delay.

When his palace at Ithaca burst to overflowing with foreign suitors did Odysseus shrug his shoulders and spend the rest of his life floating aimlessly around the Med?

No. He fought like a Spartan for the next ten years to get home, slew the cheeky colts loafing about his hearth, and claimed what was rightfully his.

Dozens he had to contend with. You have but one, Jeremy. An insincere wisp of peat smoke you could clear with a wave of your hand. You don't have to outwit Cyclops or outswim a whirlpool to gain the honour. It is not mine to say so, of course, but I don't think she is seduced.

She is a cipher. Pure Penelope.

Return to Willowpath Jeremy.

Bend your bow.

Your very own Alice,
Ever-loving mother and castaway.

Jeremy's first thought: the Trojan War didn't turn out so well in the end, did it? Certainly not for slain Achilles, nor slaughtered Paris, nor his father Priam, nor Cassandra raped at the altar, nor for the rest of Troy razed to the ground, nor for Ajax and countless other Greeks who never made it home, nor for Agamemnon, Odysseus, and others for whom consequences came later. He could have also pointed out that Odysseus spent eight of those ten wandering years dallying with older, more experienced women such as Circe and Calypso.

He was in no mood to quibble, but he did feel a moment of remorse. In the Charybdis of these first few days of learning of the Spafford wedding engagement Jeremy had forgotten about his mother entirely. She might as well have been back in Cornwall he'd spared her so little thought. He shouldn't leave her stranded.

He wasn't ready to face the reality of Willowpath. Content with the knowledge that Alice was healthy and safe, Jeremy folded the letter and stuffed it into a pocket. He slipped out the side entrance of Walker's and made his nightly pilgrimage to the Stokes grotto.

On the eleventh day at Walker's Jeremy found a salver on his pillow and a neatly folded sheet of paper on top of that. He picked it up and opened it.

It read:

Dear Mr. Jeremy Castor,

For hostelry services provided – private room and board – for the period September 14th to September 21st, 1817, inclusive.... 10 dollars.

It has been our esteemed pleasure and honour to host you. Please meet with our Monsieur Antoine in order to settle your account and arrange for extended terms if required.

We hope your stay has been an agreeable one.
Sincerely,

Robert Walker
Proprietor, Walker Hotel

Jeremy peered into the bottom of his leather coin pouch. One guinea, six shillings, two tanners, five thruppence, one ha'penny.

He shook the pouch. Recounted. He cinched the pouch and raised his face to the timbered ceiling, eyes shut tight. The few coins he had, representing all the money he had in the world, weren't enough to pay his debt to Walker. Not by half.

It required additional stealth to slip out the side entrance that night undetected. When he returned the next morning, it was with an additional two guineas in his pouch, extra funds pressed upon him by Lenore, who insisted that he take it and arrange for an extension of his accommodations. He'd suggested he could arrange a loan with Dr. Scriven. She wouldn't hear of it.

He met with Antoine, settled his account, and paid for an additional day and night, leaving him eleven shillings and change.

Later, nibbling the bread, butter, and cheese brought to him in his room at his request and skimming through the latest Gazette that had been delivered at the same time, he read this headline:

Extract from the Caracas Gazettes of the 7th and 14th August, Venezuela

He scanned the article. It proceeded to give an account of a pitched battle that had taken place between the Royalist forces in El Sombrero against a force of Republican insurgents led by Simon Bolivar and "an itinerant band with the title of invincible" led by Scottish freebooter Sir Gregor MacGregor, self-styled general-in-chief. The article claimed that the fighting was fierce and rebel losses heavy. Sir Gregor himself was found amongst the dead. A detachment of the invincibles managed to escape, however. The desperate group fought their way across the Savannah and melted back into the jungle. They were led, it is believed, by an ex-marine of the British Royal Navy - Major Peregrine Stokes.

Jeremy folded the paper on his lap. He looked around his modest room at Walker's with its four poster bed, chaff mattress, and crisp, clean linen sheets, the wash basin with clear water and cream, cotton towel, the rosewood wardrobe with spotlessly mirrored doors, the writing desk with ink pot, fat bees wax candle, the black walnut trencher board laden with fresh butter, warm bread, sharp cheese.

He imagined Stokes, his former superior, bunkered in a fetid swamp, assailed by ticks and tsetse flies, breaking his teeth on the hard tack of his dwindling rations, wondering whether to risk washing down the biscuit with the turbid, green water, all the while calming the skittish young men remaining under his charge, just as he had Jeremy aboard the Lancer. Perhaps, when he had made sure the perimeter was secure, and a detail had been put on crocodile watch, and the men had eaten something and they had found water that could be stomached, and the injured had been tended to the extent the situation would allow, he might incline his broad back against the trunk of a tree, take a sheet of paper from his pack, and write a letter home to his loyal, waiting wife Lenore, whose dutiful stoking of the hearth fire had given him the strength to persevere through these last few months of unheard hardship and privation.

Jeremy put the Gazette down on the bed spread and moved to the writing desk. He began his own letter.

Dearest Lenore,

Will you forgive me?

I have behaved in a manner too beastly to recount. Last week's shock announcement left me unmoored and, by turns, selfish and mean. In my time of need I took advantage of your good nature and graciousness and for that I will be forever ashamed.

I don't deserve your friendship. I wonder whether you will continue to offer it.

You understand that the present arrangement could not continue indefinitely, as much as I wish it with the entirety of my body and soul. You know it but are too kind and generous to say otherwise. It would not be fair to you. It would not treat well enough of those it might affect most but who are too far away to protest. I would rather boil my head than have any part in sullying the sanctity of your good name and reputation, so richly deserved. I've been the worst kind of fool. My most recent behaviour notwithstanding, I desire only to redeem myself and become champion of your life and virtue. To that object I give my solemn pledge.

I will put all my energies into making the school a great success and I will savour every moment we are able to spend together in that capacity. And I will repay every tuppence of your generous loan.

Thank you for all that you have done on my behalf.

Jeremy laid the quill he had borrowed from Antoine into the narrow trough of the writing box. He dusted a measure of fine pounce over the still damp words, gently vibrated the sheet of paper, and then tipped it, allowing the excess powdered bone to fall to the floor. Once the ink was dry, he folded the letter and sealed it with melted beeswax from the lit candle on the writing desk.

He returned to Stoke cottage, taking the usual murky route. He placed the letter on the front step, knocked loudly, and retreated to the cedar grove. After a few moments the front door unlatched. Lenore's puzzled expression emerged from within, accentuated by the light emanating from the lamp she held in her hand, looking left and then right, unable to discern anything in the dark. Finally, she looked down and, seeing the letter, she picked it up, withdrew into the cottage, and re-latched the door.

Jeremy remained, crouching among the cedars. He shivered. A new sharpness in the air suggested the coming end of summer. He stared at the yellow glow of the cottage's front window. Inside, Jeremy imagined, the air would be laden with the fumes of Amontillado, jasmine, and lanolin. The coppery sheen of Lenore's loosened Apollo knots would be reflected by the extra warmth provided by an additional Argand lamp, reserved for special occasions. These same lamps would dust gold over sleek shoulders, smooth arms, and flushed neck made bare by the now discarded pelisse of green, opaque silk. Light would penetrate her muslin shift, tracing the magical contours beneath.

Light, Jeremy thought to himself, recalling his initiation into the Freemasons.

What do you most desire? the Worshipful Master had asked. Light.

Jeremy pictured Lenore, alone in the parlour, reading the letter. The luster of her smile which had brightened Stoke cottage these last seven nights now dimmed. The music of her laughter, the easy grace of her movements, stilled.

Inside, a robe had been put on over cool, white shoulders and pulled tight around the waist. Wool had been put away, essential oils stoppered, Amontillado corked.

Jeremy stood. He took a step toward the front door of the cottage. Suddenly breathless, he realized the depth of his feeling.

One lamp was extinguished.

He took another step forward. And then another. He was almost at the flagstones.

The second lamp guttered. Darkness descended on the cottage.

Jeremy had added a postscript to his letter:

P.S. I know you will take the greatest care of this letter, for everyone's sake. Yours most of all.

Reply came in the puff of smoke and ash exhaled from the chimney. Blackened letter fragments, some with edges still glowing crimson, emerged from the flue and floated lazily to the ground, falling like infernal snow.

Chapter Twenty-Seven
October 1817

Amelia moved fitfully about the room, stretching, then stooping, insinuating herself into Jeremy's line of sight as he packed his few belongings into a trunk. She never could catch his eye. Alice continued to drift in and out of the room, adding her own belongings to the trunk with little sighs and sidelong glances, trailing her climate of silent reproach.

Amelia remembered how not long ago, in another of these upstairs rooms, Jeremy had averted his gaze under very different circumstances. It hadn't been difficult to get his attention then.

"We won the King's Mills Methodists contract," she said, making a show of straightening a pillow on the bed near where Jeremy collected and stacked his copies of Cowper and Thomas Paine.

"Yes," she continued with a hint of laughter, hoping to lighten the mood. "Pastor Ainsworth returned last week. For a calmer visit. He met with..."

Jeremy raised his head. He nearly looked her way but corrected himself and glanced out the window.

"Well," she continued, "he didn't have to meet with just me this time, anyway. The wicked temptress."

Jeremy didn't reply.

"Bennet joined us too," she added. "Still. Pastor asked after you."

"Mm," Jeremy said as he stuffed a pair of tunics into one of the sacks.

She longed to rush across the room, hold his face in her hands, and force him to look into her eyes. What choice did I have, she would cry, what else could I have done? I'm sorry. Don't leave.

"Joseph and Nat finished building the new paddock," she said, straightening a watercolour near the dresser Jeremy was emptying. "They did a wonderful job. You really should see it."

"Mm."

Jeremy pulled the strings of the haversack together. He closed the lid of the trunk and slid it toward the door. He put the haversack over one shoulder and picked up a second one, already packed, and slung that over the other shoulder.

"Jeremy," Amelia said, taking the other end of the trunk, ostensibly to help. "You needn't leave. You could stay on as general manager of business."

Jeremy stopped and put the trunk down. He turned and looked at her for the first time, his mouth hiked into a sour grin.

"Were just starting to get somewhere," she continued, putting the other end down, "we'll need your..."

She paused. She looked for the diplomatic word. Jeremy snorted. He picked up the end of the trunk again.

"Acumen," she said. "Your acumen. Your easy facility with people."

"Amelia," he said. "You needn't spare my feelings. You've made your choice. I respect it."

"It's not like that," she whispered, "I'm very sorry I didn't tell you. That you had to read it in the Gazette. I wish we could have talked. You were sleeping when I left."

Jeremy softened. He put the trunk down.

"Everything happened so quickly," she continued, her voice low. "It seemed the only way. I care for you very much."

He faced her.

"Be careful Amelia. I don't trust him any more than the last Spafford."

She smiled sadly.

"If, like the last one," he said, "you ever need me to challenge him to a duel, don't hesitate to drop your handkerchief. Please."

She crossed the floor, entwined her arm around his and tugged gently until he bent at the waist. She kissed his cheek.

"You know me," she said, letting him go. "Tough as burdock. But I will always accept your chivalry. I hope you will come to visit us often. I know Bennet, and Mrs. Simkins, and Nat, they'll all want to see you. They'll miss you."

"As often as I can," Jeremy said, picking up the trunk end.

"I'll miss you."

Jeremy met her gaze.

"Couldn't you stay?" she whispered.

Wistfulness in his eyes held the answer.

"Mister Castor has the right idea," Rupert Spafford said, from outside the door. He'd appeared suddenly at the top of the stairs across the landing, noiseless in a pair of the late colonel's tatty slippers. He stood with one hand tucked in the recesses of his silk robe and another wrapped around a mug of steeped chicory. He'd been at Willowpath only a few days, but he gave the impression of someone who'd been installed with the hearth.

"Other concerns in town, isn't it?"

Spafford paused to take a demonstrative slurp.

"Not for our Mister Castor a life of quiet domesticity."

"I can take it from here," Jeremy said, dragging the trunk to the top of the stairs.

Amelia retreated to her room. She closed the door.

"Can I help?" Spafford asked, his smile as broad as a Dublin sunrise. His left hand was full of hot chicory, the other remained pocketed.

"I can take it from here," Jeremy repeated.

He negotiated the trunk down the stairs, buffeting first this side, then that, twice nearly missing a step, steadying himself with an elbow, finally driving the corner of the trunk into the bannister end, where it flared. Jeremy let one end of the trunk down to the floor with a thump and leaned it on edge while he caught his breath and examined the six-inch gouge.

"Don't mind that," Spafford said, all treacle and cream. "Joseph will put it right in a thrice."

Jeremy huffed, picked up the lower end of the trunk,

and lugged it to the threshold. On the fourth attempt with a flapping elbow he managed to unlatch the door and push it open with his forehead.

"I say," Spafford said, descending the final steps. "Do you intend to wrestle it all the way back to town?"

Jeremy stopped at the threshold, panting. Again, he put the trunk end down. His tunic beneath the two haversacks stuck to his sweat-dampened back. He turned to Alice. She gazed back expectantly. In his pique and determination to rescue her from Willowpath he hadn't thought much about the return. He hadn't factored in the trunk. He'd forgotten Alice's advanced years and abbreviated stride. If it had been just himself, he would have walked.

Could he engage Joseph and his son Nat to hitch up one of the horses to a wagon and drive them back into town? Jeremy looked back up the stairs toward Amelia's room. He couldn't now ascend those stairs and request the services of her servant and his son.

Spafford ran a finger over the new groove in the bannister's arc. Fresh colour rose in Jeremy's already flushed face.

"I've an idea," Spafford said, "why don't you take the post-chaise? I'll have my driver take you."

Jeremy glanced out the open door. He patted the few shillings in his pocket. He could walk the few miles down the path to the neighbouring farm and hire one of the Dalgleish boys to drive them back in one of their wagons. It would be uncomfortable. It would take many hours to arrange. It might mean they would have to stay another night. His fist clenched around a coin.

"Mr. Castor!" Spafford said, laughing, misinterpreting Jeremy's pocket rummaging. "Gratis, of course. Brother to brother."

Jeremy turned back to see Spafford holding out his free hand with thumb raised ready to dig into its opposite, freemason-wise. Jeremy stooped, picked up the trunk with a grunt and began see-sawing it through the door's opening, scraping his knuckles against the rough jamb. He would drag it back to town. Alice could ride atop.

"Dearest chap," Spafford said.

"Jeremy," Alice called. He turned back. She hadn't budged from the threshold. At first, his expression was severe, full of hurt and irritation and defiance. It fell under the heat of her glare. Finally, Jeremy let the trunk drop to the front step and the two haversacks slid from his sagging shoulders. He left the porch in search of Bennet, Mrs. Simkins, and the others, to give his farewells. Spafford's man readied the buggy.

∾ ∾ ∾ ∾ ∾

Under different circumstances Jeremy would have readily agreed that Spafford's post-chaise was a far superior way to get from Willowpath to Kingston through overgrown briary, over corrugated ruts, across jolting corduroy. The bench still launched them into the air at regular intervals. But well-cushioned landings were made altogether more pleasant - almost entertaining if one was in the right frame of mind - by the ingenious system of springs and stays beneath them. As it was, Jeremy felt compelled to mumble a noncommittal mm-hmm to every one of Alice's sunny, almost girlish, outbursts: isn't this lovely? Dúw, what a lark! Oooh that was a bouncy one!

Fortunately, the cab was also considerably faster than the usual poky wagon and so it was a shorter span of time he had to feign interest. By the time they were tired of even this mode of relative comfort, they were nearly there.

"You received my letter, obviously," Alice said, after a prolonged silence.

Jeremy nodded. She studied him a while as he stared out the window. Percussion of the wheels against the furrows of the road made the only sound. And crows, laughing.

"Pilchard," she said finally, dispelling the returned silence. "Choughs will recite sonnets. Herring will waltz. Before Jeremy Castor condescends to take advice from his old mabmik."

Jeremy tilted his head closer to the window of the post-chaise.

"It would take only a shred of spriggan," she added. "Like Paris."

Jeremy sighed and rehearsed his various lethal retorts about the Trojan War.

"Alice," was all he said.

"It's just us now," she said quickly, encouraged by the word she'd elicited. "You know that my annuity is modest. It won't get us very far. I can take on some sewing, I suppose. Some knitting. But my eyesight, you know."

Jeremy didn't reply."

"Did you get my letter?"

"Alice!"

He couldn't tell whether she was nagging or had just forgotten his earlier answer. He'd noticed she'd been repeating herself lately, misremembering names, forgetting her purpose minutes after setting out.

About a mile from the crucifixion scene that marked the intersection of Montreal and Loughborough roads the post-chaise passed a rare section of cleared land. Its confines rippled a swath of yellow.

"Couldn't you farm?" she asked, as Jeremy looked out over the wheat stalks.

"You're a big strapper. It seems to be what the lads do over here. Get themselves a square of this here wilderness, knock down some trees, make the potash, grow the barley, corn, and wheat."

She was right. That is what they did. He knew Lieutenant Coulson and LeSaux, the bosun's mate, and others who he'd served with on the Lancer, who'd done exactly that. But as retired officers they were granted hundreds of acres each from the crown. They surely had a comfortable pension besides. More than enough to make a go. If Jeremy was to pick up the axe and hoe, he would have to purchase the land on a seven-year mortgage, assuming he could find a willing lender. He would also have to get all his equipment and seed on credit. He'd probably owe more than twenty-five pounds a year before first muddying a ploughshare. Even Willowpath last year, with its many acres of cleared land, had an annual crop revenue of only twenty pounds.

What did he know about farming? There were only

three typical occupations for men from his part of Cornwall: fishing, mining, soldiering. For his part, Jeremy had worked on the wharves helping with the catch and to store the equipment. In the meantime, he'd been studying at Helston to be a deacon. He didn't know a sickle from a dibber from a flail.

"Maybe you could hire yourself out as a farmhand first," Alice said, as if reading his thoughts. "Learn the trade. Put together some capital."

The cab neared the crossroads and they could see the thick, twenty-foot beams of cedar with the coils of rough hemp and giant wreath of briars; the crucifix erected by the King's Mill Methodists. Noise preceded the circle of scythed sedges. Two families were spread out at the foot of the crucifix. As they entered the clearing a woman came up to the side of the post-chaise waving a piece of sharpened iron.

"Perfectly good bill hook," she shouted. "One shilling."

The postilion clucked the horses and the post-chaise accelerated.

The woman trotted along, clearing thin strands from her dampened face. She gestured over to the foot of the crucifix where the rest of her people camped amid devotional offerings and a collection of various agricultural implements. A boy pulled a dog's tail. A second woman swung a broom at the boy. Her shrieking, the barking, the child's wailing, the cries coming from a nearby bassinet; desperation filled the clearing. A man with a stringy beard slouched against a stump, cradling an earthenware jug against his forearm. To his right, a motionless body. He lifted the jug to his lips, drank deeply, and passed it to a man on his left, stripped to the waist. Their black, stony eyes followed the post-chaise as it clattered by.

"Ten pence. A tanner. We shan't refuse a reasonable offer," the woman cried as she tried to keep up with the post-chaise, waving her arm back to the clearing. "A fine assortment of hoes and rakes and saws. 'Twill cost you treble in town."

They were one hundred yards back into the woods, the woman returned to the clearing before the carriage slowed and the postilion called back from the saddle.

"Wheat miners," he said. "Sorry for that. Not made their last notice, I 'spect. Ain't looking like they brought in no harvest neither."

The driver swiveled and attended to the horses. For the next league, they rode in silence.

"I'm going to be a teacher," Jeremy said, finally. "That is how I will make a living and support us both. Dr. Scriven has inquired of a room we may rent. Clean and decent."

They approached Kingston and encountered more signs of civilization: occasional shanties and log structures, out-buildings, a herd of cows lying down. The post-chaise had to slow frequently to avoid trampling the geese and chickens, mongrels and swine, shrieking and squawking and snarling across their path.

Jeremy peered out the window as they passed through the glebe on the edge of town. He recognized the shack where Lilac had taken him months earlier. It was still barred, just as they had left it, deemed unworthy of break-in even by the destitute. Jeremy remembered the sordidness of that evening and looked over at Alice, imagining that somehow, she knew. She stared out the other window, unfazed.

The post-chaise came to a stop. A cow stood lengthways in the middle of the lane. The postilion hurled imprecations and brought the horses close. The cow went on chewing, unperturbed. Finally, the postilion descended from his horse brandishing a crop.

Children assailed the post-chaise from all sides. Grime-streaked and bramble-headed, they scaled the running board and hung from the carriage rack. They pounded the lacquered walls and pressed their sodden faces against the windows Jeremy and Alice had just shut and latched.

"Oh my!" cried one. "Sween, take a look. Will you just?"

"'Tis quite the gingerbread cage," said Sweeney, running a grey, inch-long fingernail along the post-chaise's trim of gold paint, "for a pair o' pigeons."

"Spare us a bean," said a third, peering in.

"Not your typical swells, is they?"

"A tanner then?"

"A thruppence?"

Sweeney pressed his mottled face against the thin glass of Jeremy's window, contorting his features into a wet, flat-faced sneer. His yellowed eye pivoted.

"Who's the petticoat," he asked.

"Duchess of York," the first laughed. "Must be."

"And the Duke?" Sweeney said. "Never. Too young."

"Ain't proper, is it?"

"That your mopsey?" Sweeney asked, his eye returning to Jeremy. The window bowed behind the slope of his forehead. "A bit ripe, ain't she?"

Jeremy looked across at his mother, mortified.

"What sort of parents?" she was saying. "Where are they? To just let them run wild."

"Charivareeee!" the second cried as she began to thump the side of the post-chaise. All the others clinging to the sides, it was impossible to tell how many, began to wail charivareeee and pound the walls as if it was a giant kettle drum.

"Toss us a spangle," Sweeney said. "We'll end our rough music."

The glass bent further as he pressed his face harder against it. Any minute he would fall into Jeremy's lap in a cascade of shards and splinters.

When the sharp crack struck, Jeremy jumped, fully expecting the urchin to tumble in. Sweeney's face shattered instead, dark lines of shock and pain spidering his expression. A slash of red from his split ear spattered the window as though flicked from a paintbrush.

"Oy!" the postilion shouted, re-coiling his whip. He re-mounted the left-hand horse. "Off my buggy!"

He struck the flanks of each horse with the whip's crop. The post-chaise jerked forward and jettisoned some of its boarders as it shot past the irate short horn. Sweeney crouched in the dust and howled at the sky, pressing together his newly cloven ear with both hands. The post-chaise plowed through new waves of poultry, parting the sea-foam sprays of feathers, listing to port where a few remaining moppets clung to its side. The driver turned and applied the whip until the cab was free. As the lane receded in the back window, they turned a corner. The chants and jeers ebbed. Finally, even Sweeney's shrill bawling trickled to nothing.

They watched the squalor of Stuartsville roll by from their respective windows.

Unaware he'd spoken out loud, the realization tumbled from Jeremy's mouth.

"These will be my students."

Chapter Twenty-Eight

Jeremy shifted. He stretched his neck left, right. He jutted his chin.

"Quite alright Mr. Castor?"

"Please Mr. Hagerman. Go on."

Jeremy maintained eye contact with the chairman, struggling to follow. His borrowed Hessian boots were a size too small on all sides. Fitted leather trousers prevented him from crossing his leg. The latest pearl cravat, newly purchased from Thomson, prodigiously starched and tied snugly into an Oriental, flattened his carotid and abraded his neck.

Jeremy hadn't eaten anything substantial since yesterday lunch time, just before he spent his last shillings at Thomson's. He and Alice subsisted on her meagre pension and the few pence they picked up for mending work. There had been little margin for extras, such as fresh meat. Dr. Scriven had insisted that Jeremy wear appropriate attire to the interview instead of his usual relaxed pantaloons and homespun, open-necked shirt. He, like others of his wealth and station, had no conception of the daily dilemmas facing the lower classes. In Jeremy's case, the choice had been between a quadrangle of linen and a wedge of venison pie.

Accepting Scriven's insistence on the former, Jeremy denied himself the latter.

Vapours gusted the corridor from Walker's kitchen and drifted in to fill the close meeting room: duck fat sizzling, potatoes roasting, gravy reducing. Jeremy jerked his head and over-corrected, head rolling the other way, until he thrust it again turtle-wise, up and out of the tight cylinder of the Oriental. He forced his eyes back on the chairman. Christopher Hagerman continued to address Jeremy and his fellow committee members on the aims of the new Lancasterian school. He described, with disgust, the moral failings of each of the previous instructors.

"Izzy Maunder."

Hagerman had the fingers of his one hand splayed, the other enumerating. He stood next to Jeremy, towering over him.

"Imbecile," Hagerman continued. "Claimed to have studied at St. Swindon's Academy. We caught him teaching the children that a syllable makes a delicious dessert and that lake trout are highly prized for their thick pelts of fur. No brighter than a doorstop. An illiterate. St. Swindon's? No such school. More fool us."

Jeremy managed a furtive glance at Lenore, sitting at the end of the panel. He hadn't seen her since he'd watched her pick up his letter up from the front of Stoke Cottage. She studied something on the opposite wall, her eyes tracing the paper's intricate arabesque. Not once had she looked his way.

He traced the elegant line of her jaw to the curve of her chin. In profile, Apollo's knots at her temple, the semi-circle of her cheek cool and pale like porcelain, she seemed a finely carved cameo. Hot memories of the evenings spent at Stoke Cottage licked his brain, replacing, for a moment, the stomach pangs. He was overcome with a desire to return to her bed, to once more lose himself in the haze of jasmine, sherry, and the urgent warmth of her body.

Lenore, he willed. Look at me.

"Sam Courson." Hagerman tugged at another finger. "Tethered Harold to the latch of the door and left him to mind the children while he went off to the White Bear to drink his wages. Harold is a Scotch terrier."

Jeremy heard the distant clatter of crockery. It reminded him of the narcoleptic mornings; Lenore heating a kettle in the next room, him shifting languorously beneath the sheets, exhausted yet renewed, basking in the lingering fragrance and warmth of their latest tryst.

Hagerman pinched a third finger.

"There was Mal Phelan, the defrocked priest. He had a penchant for... Well, the less said about Phelan, the better. It's been a long, ignoble parade of incompetents and idlers. Why, in no small part, that our attempts at a free school have failed thus far. We are determined to make sure we have the right candidate this time."

Keep good eye contact. Integral to a successful interview, Scriven had insisted. Jeremy twisted up to Hagerman, now looming to his left. The sharp fold of the Oriental pressed into his throat impeded his strangled *yes sir*.

Hagerman strolled back to his seat but didn't take it. He pulled a gleaming sovereign from an interior pocket and flipped it several times, getting up steam for his final summation.

"Now, you understand these are not the children of officers or justices or vicars. They're the offspring of devoted skulkers and lame fiddlers. The sorts of kinchin tasked with begging by those that spawned them to settle a publican's debt."

"Christopher," Lenore said, finally, her voice lowered.

Jeremy's head turned at the sound of her talking. Still, she would not catch his eye. Her pique served to make his hunger greater.

Look at me.

"Pardon," Hagerman said, as though withdrawing a question in court. "You don't see them like I do. You don't daily contend with the wicked, wheedling reprobates."

"Redeemable souls, every one, under the eyes of God," Lenore continued, her tone lower still. "Which is why it is so important our new school is a success."

"Quite so," Hagerman said. "Each of these, unlike their degenerate kin, can be made a respectable, productive member of society. With the correct measure of discipline and domestication and..."

Hagerman paused, searching for *le mot juste.*

"Schooling," Lenore said.

Jeremy loved how she'd said it. Her insistence on compassion. Her capacity for forgiveness.

"Yes, schooling. Look here Castor," Hagerman

continued, rapping the sovereign against the table, "I'm no agricultural man. But it seems to me if we're to survive and thrive here in this wilderness we need to take it by the scruff of the neck, bend it over our collective knee, and thrash it into submission. That is, cultivate it. Clear the deadwood, break the ground, and improve the soil so that it is tall, fruitful stalks that sprout up. Pull the noxious weeds that leach out all that is good."

Hagerman paused again to gauge Jeremy's expression.

"Neither am I a literary man, of course. I hope I haven't asked too much of the metaphor."

"No sir."

Jeremy wondered whether he should qualify that he was simply agreeing with Hagerman's take on the promise of education, not his lack of literary guile.

Hagerman ploughed on.

"They'll never be our next generation of counsellors and magistrates, of course. But, it's as Mrs. Stokes says. They could be made perfectly acceptable footmen, tanners, and seamstresses."

"A bit more specific than my point," Lenore said.

"Yes, yes, of course."

Jeremy decided that he would write another letter to Lenore. He would take back what he'd written earlier. He would propose that they send a note to Major Stokes in Venezuela, informing him of what had unexpectedly transpired, and request that he grant Lenore a divorce. If he should refuse, Jeremy would gladly accept a duel. Hunger, and restricted blood flow, had made him light-headed.

Hagerman ventured back out from behind his chair toward Jeremy, again as though he was approaching the accused.

He clutched Jeremy's shoulder. Jeremy, jarred from his daydreaming, started.

"Steady on Castor."

Hagerman grabbed Jeremy's bicep.

"Stand up," he said.

Jeremy did. They stood eye to eye. Spots appeared in front of Jeremy's eyes and he felt his knee buckle. His feet ached, toes triangled at the boot ends.

"You've got one thing going for you," Hagerman said. He gaveled his fist into Jeremy's chest. "You're a proper monolith. If you use your size to your advantage you should keep the buggers at bay."

"Now," Hagerman said, returning to the committee, "I understand that you attended school at St. Michael's in Helston."

"Yes sir."

"And that you went on to study under the curate at St. Michael's for a time, perhaps to train for a deaconship."

Jeremy nodded. He swayed.

"Please," Hagerman said, pointing the sovereign at the chair, "take your seat. Now, we've been able to determine that St. Michael's does exist and there is in fact a school. But we have no proof that you actually studied there. We have no references from any such curate."

Jeremy angled back into his chair with as much grace as his leather breeches would allow, dropping the last several inches with a thump. Out of necessity, he left the long timbers of his legs outstretched. Blood began to flow back into his unclenched feet.

"No sir," he said.

"But you are fortunate enough to have two members of our committee that have put your name forward and are willing to speak on your behalf."

Lenore still had not acknowledged him.

"Dr. Scriven," Hagerman said. "Would you like to say a few words?"

"Yes, of course, thank you Mr. Hagerman." Scriven got to his feet. He tugged down the hem of his frock coat and adjusted his immaculate buff cravat. "I do most certainly vouch for Mr. Jeremy Castor. I've come to know this young man well in recent months and I must say I've met few others who more closely embody the principles and deeds of old Ancient Number Three. To mean well and to do well. He wishes, as we all do, to provide the children with knowledge. With light. We've had many discussions and I know that he is well-versed in the classics as well as contemporary writers, he has a good command of the King's English. I've heard from independent and trustworthy sources that he, without any expectation of reward, has taught many, young and old, how to read. In my judgment, a natural born teacher."

"Very good, thank you Dr. Scriven. And you, Mrs. Stokes?"

Lenore continued to trace the wallpaper design with her eyes.

"Mrs. Stokes?"

"Mm?"

"I beg your pardon, Mrs. Stokes. Do you, as I've been led to believe, vouch for this Mr. Jeremy Castor sitting before us?"

Lenore swung back around to the committee. She managed to face Hagerman without glancing at Jeremy, as though the lone chair was empty. Jeremy's stomach constricted further. Might she disavow him? What other occupation might he take up to avoid starvation for both himself and Alice? Bone picker? Scum boiler?

"Mrs. Stokes?"

"Hmmm," she said, as though considering the matter for the first time.

"Le-nore," Dr. Scriven said, with scolding emphasis. She whipped round, her ringlets swinging. Scriven met her petulance with an expression of puzzlement.

"Yes," she said.

Scriven looked up at Hagerman. Hagerman turned back to Lenore.

"You vouch for Mr. Castor?" he asked.

"Yes, of course."

Jeremy emitted a peep of relief. For a moment, all faced him. Including Lenore.

His eyes met hers. Through flashing pupil and widening iris, he attempted to signal his new resolve: the letter to the Major, his acceptance of a duel, his profession of love. Her lashes fluttered before she looked away. She'd understood. She'd reciprocated. He was sure of it.

"Would you like to say a few words?" Hagerman asked Lenore.

"I concur with Dr. Scriven," she said with a careless wave of a hand.

"Well, that's fine," Hagerman said, unconvinced. "I suppose if there are no more declarations or questions we can adjourn. After a break for lunch we will discuss whether we should recommend Mr. Castor to Schoolmaster for the final decision. Walker informs me that it is beef broil today. Mr. Castor, any final remarks?"

Jeremy stood and faced the panel, hands clasped before him, head bent.

"May I stay for lunch?"

Chapter Twenty-Nine

Home District Grammar School took up College Square, just north of St. James' Cathedral, an oasis of calm and good order amid the outlying filth of little York. Jeremy was at the closed classroom door just as the clock in the common room announced eight. Inside he could hear children reciting. A poem?

"Grant us thy salvation," he heard them say.

Schoolmaster's voice: "O Lord, save the King."

"And mercifully hear us when we call upon thee," the children replied.

Morning prayer. Jeremy waited for a pause.

"Endue thy Ministers with righteousness."

"And make thy chosen people joyful."

He knocked lightly. The recitation stopped. Then recommenced. He waited. He knocked again, with more insistence, in another moment of silence. Voices hushed. Then, they started again.

"Halt gentlemen."

The recitation stopped a final time.

"Come in."

Jeremy opened the door and eased his face past the threshold.

"Ah. Mr. Castor. Please. All the way in."

He stepped into the room. Sixteen boys sat on benches behind tilted desks in two rows. Schoolmaster stood at the other end of the room.

"We begin instruction promptly at the strike of eight Mr. Castor," Schoolmaster said, "but I expect the boys to be at their desks, sitting quietly attentive by a quarter of, so we may commence morning prayer without delay."

Jeremy reddened.

"Please introduce yourself to the rest of the boys, Mr. Castor."

Jeremy studied Schoolmaster's expression, looking for some hint of joviality. Finding none, he turned to face the students. He began to explain how he had travelled from Kingston where he now lives with his mother, Alice, but that he was raised in Porthleven, in Cornwall...

"That will do, Mr. Castor. Eyes front."

The students turned their faces to the large easel standing behind Schoolmaster.

"Please take your seat."

Schoolmaster gestured towards a chair that sat along the far wall, beneath a pair of windows, adjacent to the two rows of benches and his own desk at the front of the room. Jeremy strode across the room and folded himself on to the seat made for a boy. Just the sharp point of his buttocks made contact, his knees splayed to the side. Not one of the sixteen boys let their eyes stray from Schoolmaster and the front of the class. Even so, Jeremy detected traces of amusement. He sat as straight as possible, bringing himself level with the boys on their higher bench. He nodded at them with a prim smile and projected an air of confidence, as if to say: All as planned. I'm at the Schoolmaster's right hand, his assistant and your tutor. I'm aware the chair is tiny. It's so I can better understand the pedagogical experience.

On his own against the far wall, without a desk in front, his knees at his ears, a sharp chill descended from the windows and down his back. He fought the rising qualm: he took up the customary position of the outcast. The dunce.

They completed the morning prayer.

"Your pledge," Schoolmaster demanded.

"On my honour," the class chanted, "I promise that I will do my best, to do my duty to God and to the King, to help other people, and to stay true to my country."

Schoolmaster picked up a book and a glowing Argand lamp from his desk.

"This morning we shall review our geography. Who will read today?"

Schoolmaster strolled along the first bench.

"Philips?"

"Yes, Schoolmaster."

Schoolmaster placed the book and the lamp in front of the boy named Philips who looked like he might be seven or eight.

"From the beginning please Mr. Philips."

The boy began to read, enunciating every word.

"The British Empire consists of the islands of Great Britain, Ireland, and other smaller islands; of extensive colonies in North America, in the West-Indies, in Africa, and in the East Indies; and of the fortresses of Gibraltar and Malta, in the Mediterranean. By means of its powerful and unequalled navy, the British

Government is enabled to extend its authority over all seas; and Britannia is justly said to be Mistress of the Ocean, and Queen of the Isles."

"Is it meant literally Mr. Cudmore? In what sense is Britannia mistress of the Ocean?"

"In a poetic sense, sir?"

"Have strength in your convictions, Mr. Cudmore."

"In a poetic sense, sir."

"Thank you, Mr. Cudmore. Mr. Philips, please continue from number seven."

"The island of Great Britain includes three distinct divisions and ancient kingdoms..."

"What are they Mr. Hunter?"

"England, Wales, and Scotland."

For forty more minutes the boys read aloud from the geography textbook, passing it along the bench when instructed by Schoolmaster. Jeremy listened intently, impressed at the easy knowledge displayed by the boys. He'd also become aware of something else: the pressure building behind the front fall of his trousers. He'd been in such haste to get dressed and downstairs to breakfast he'd forgotten to use the chamber pot. Several extra cups of tea, taken for their early morning invigoration, had by now coursed their way through his system and had worked their magic. The question and answer of Goldsmith's Easy Grammar of Geography receded into the background as he began to plot his strategy for this newly urgent problem.

"Turn to chapter twelve if you will Mr. Cudmore. Begin at four hundred forty-four."

"The immense territories of North America, still

connected with Great Britain, extend east and west from Newfoundland and Nova Scotia, to the great lakes;"

"From the North pole to which line of latitude? Someone we haven't called on yet."

Schoolmaster strolled to the far end of the bench.

"Mr. Castor?"

Jeremy started from his chair. He hadn't expected to answer questions.

"Ah," he said. "Ah. Ah. Ah."

"Mr. Brown?"

"Forty-five degrees, sir," Brown replied, without hesitation.

"Continue please Mr. Philips. From forty-seven."

"Canada. This immense country was originally colonized by France, but conquered by General Wolfe, in seventeen fifty-nine. Since then, it has been possessed by England; yet the majority of its inhabitants still speak the French language, cherish French customs, and profess the Roman Catholic religion."

"What are Canada's five main hospitable tracts? Mr. Castor."

Jeremy shimmied. His left leg palsied.

"Me sir?"

"Please."

"Of course." Jeremy lobbed another forced smile at the benches. "There are Upper and Lower Canada naturally."

"Naturally."

"And Nova Scotia, of course."

"Yes."

"Let's see. New Cornwall? Middle Canada?"

A snicker came from one of the benches.

"Mr. Chandler?"

"Newfoundland and New Brunswick."

"What are the three inhospitable tracts Mr. Castor?"

"Inhospitable? Oh, yes, of course, uninhabitable."

"No, not uninhabitable. Lest we forget the Esquimaux living north of Hudson's Bay. Inhospitable."

"Ah," Jeremy said, his knee bouncing. "Ah. Ah. His Majesty's Regent's land?"

"Little conviction there, Mr. Castor. Mr. Mason?"

"Labrador and New South Wales, sir."

"Number four hundred fifty Mr. Philips, please."

"The houses are built chiefly of timber. The winters are exceedingly severe, the snow lying for many months on the ground, and the St. Lawrence being closed with ice, although the centre of the country is in the latitude of Devonshire. The exports from the Canadas are furs and skins in great abundance..."

"Name the other four primary exports. Mister..."

Jeremy raised his hand.

"Mr. Castor."

"Sir. May I be excused?"

A boy in the front row guffawed.

"Silence Jarvis. Mr. Castor, would you like to answer the question first? The four primary exports."

"Ah. Exports. Of course. Cod?"

"Fish, yes."

"Wheat?"

"Grain, yes."

"Po..po..potatoes?"

"No."

"Beer?"

"No."

"Whisky?"

"No."

"Glass."

"No."

"Paper."

"No."

"Furs!"

"We covered that."

The same boy snickered again.

"Jarvis! Perhaps you would like to answer?"

"Yes sir. Hemp and potash."

"Well done Jarvis. Continue reading from four hundred fifty-two."

Four hundred fifty-two concerned the Great Lakes and their vast quantities of water. Cold, flowing water. Billions of gallons of it. Lake Superior fifteen thousand acres in circumference, full of water. Lake Ontario covering over two million acres of wet, dripping water. And then, the colossal falls at Niagara.

Water. Water. Water.

"The quantity of water which falls per minute, is six hundred seventy thousand tons," Jarvis was reading. "Just below the great pitch, the water and foam may be seen puffed up in large spherical figures."

Jeremy prayed he would soon move to the next topic.

"They burst at the top and project a column of the spray to a prodigious height, and then subside and are succeeded by others which burst in a like manner."

"Mr. Schoolmaster, sir," Jeremy said, his hand still raised. "I really must..."

"Yes, go ahead. Gentlemen, your slates. Jarvis, another stick in the stove, if you please."

The students stood and crossed the floor. Jeremy rolled from the tiny chair, deked the smirking Jarvis, and exited. As he bolted for his room and blessed relief, he was sure he heard laughter, boyish and otherwise.

When he returned the class had moved on to long division. Schoolmaster paused from the problem he was writing on the large slate at the front. Sixteen pairs of eyes followed Jeremy as he tip-toed the pine beams, stealthy, despite the already disrupted class. They watched as he origamied himself back into the chair.

He wasn't asked any division problems. Later, in the geometry lesson, he was asked how to solve for the area of a parallelogram. Jarvis corrected him, breaking the shape into one rectangle and two triangles. They broke for lunch. Schoolmaster left for his study. The children talked amongst themselves. Jeremy sat alone.

After lunch, Bible study. Jeremy ventured that the belt in the armor of God represents peace. Jarvis reminded him that it is truth. He guessed that the passage was from Corinthians I 12:8. Jarvis declared Ephesians 6:14. Jeremy translated the line Una Salus Victis Nullam Sperare Salutem from Virgil's Aeneid as "one false deed undoes a lifetime of good intentions." Jarvis translated it more accurately as "the only hope for the doomed, is no hope at all," and Jeremy at once had a renewed appreciation for the Roman poet.

Spelling the word charlatan correctly had been Jeremy's only success before they adjourned for the day.

Each day and night of the week unfolded in the same way. Class during the day. Supper alone at night. In the evenings, Schoolmaster went off to meet with his associates in the Executive Council or the Loyal and Patriotic Society of Upper Canada. The only words Jeremy had exchanged with him since he'd arrived were faulty answers to quizzes. Each day Schoolmaster called on him less and less, as though he'd already made up his mind. Jeremy shuddered to think of what Schoolmaster would write back to Macaulay and Hagerman.

At the end of Thursday's lesson, Schoolmaster warned the boys that they would be covering the great poets the following afternoon. Jeremy borrowed copies of Milton, Dryden, Coleridge, and other collected works from the shelf in the common room. He spent the evening reading and memorizing. He crammed.

At breakfast, Jeremy ate an extra bowl of porridge, twice as many sausages and, when he thought no-one was looking, he smuggled four boiled eggs into the recesses of his coat. Insurance against future hunger.

It was well after lunch break and Schoolmaster had not once turned to Jeremy for an answer. He hadn't asked him about Donne, or Pope, or Ben Jonson. Instead, he'd asked Mason to put into his own words *Whan that Aprill, with his shoures soote and The droghte of March hath perced to the roote.* He'd called on Cudmore to scan Shakespearean sonnet twenty-nine, Coleridge's favourite. Tests that Jeremy could have met successfully, had he been asked.

"One last, Mr. Jarvis. Be so good as to recite for us Coleridge's The Good, Great Man."

Jarvis stood from his bench. He started:

How seldom, friend, a good great man inherits

He faltered. He looked to the ceiling.
"Pass Mr. Jarvis your reader please, Mr. Philips."
Philips slid the book down the desk in front of Jarvis.
Jarvis continued haltingly, reading from the open page:

Honour or wealth with all his worth and pains
It sounds like stories from the land of spirits
If any man obtain that which he merits
Or any merit that which he obtains.

Jeremy rolled from his sitting position. He stamped to his feet and the pine boards resonated. He stepped up onto the chair, boot ends extending past the edge of the seat. He balanced like a bronze upon a pedestal.

For shame, dear friend, renounce this canting strain!

Jeremy projected with all the flourish he could muster, gesturing toward Jarvis.

What would'st thou have a good great man obtain?
Place? titles? salary? a gilded chain?
Or throne of corses which his sword had slain?
Greatness and goodness are not means, but ends!
Hath he not always treasures, always friends,

He rang out like a klaxon.

The good great man? three treasures, love, and light,
And calm thoughts, regular as infant's breath:
And three firm friends, more sure than day and night,
Himself, his maker, and the angel death!

Jeremy stepped down. He retook his miniature seat.

At first, shock. No-one at Home District Grammar School ever spoke without invitation. There had been tales of it happening before. Years ago.

Then, admiration. An entirely new universe of possibility opened up.

And finally, curiosity.

All eyes were on Schoolmaster. What would the response be? What could it be? The fact that it was so long in coming suggested for the briefest, most awful moment that perhaps Schoolmaster himself wasn't sure, making anticipation ever more dreadful. And, delicious.

It was quiet save for a senile, winter fly butting half-heartedly into the window directly above Jeremy's head. His heart pounded. He looked over at Jarvis. The boy's expression had changed, conveying something closer to esteem.

"That will be all for today gentlemen," Schoolmaster said at last, in his usual measured tone. "Mr. Castor, you may stay behind."

His inflection, the burr bleeding through, left no doubt as to whether the offer was truly optional.

Boys rose from the benches, replaced the slates, collected their hats and mitts, and filed from the classroom. The smirk had returned to Jarvis' face.

Schoolmaster remained at his desk, organizing papers, straightening books. When the voices of the last boys could be heard calling and laughing outside and beyond the front steps, he stood.

"Will you join me in my study, Mr. Castor?"

Jeremy sat in one of the two green leather armchairs. Directly across from him the fireplace radiated a sweet, maple haze. For the first time in a week, since he'd arrived, he was truly warm. He ignored the crackling that came from the quartet of boiled eggs stowed in the inner pocket of his coat, pressed between his ribs and the wingback.

Schoolmaster had taken the other armchair, sitting with a stack of letters. As Jeremy watched, he opened each of the sealed letters in a silent, unhurried manner. His eyes, puffy and unlined at the orbits as though unaccustomed to laughter, scanned each letter in turn. The greased dome of his head resembled a beaver's arched back. There was no suggestion of Schoolmaster's hair ever having been swept forward in the style of a Brutus or a Titus. His coat was well-tailored and undertaker black. Beneath, a simple white linen shirt. No frippery. No cravat.

The study smelled of vinegar. The only ornamentation: a portrait of Charles Manners-Sutton, Archbishop of Canterbury and a Constable-style watercolour of Windsor Castle and environs. No more than a handful of books clustered the centre of an otherwise empty bookshelf: The King James, of course, the Common Book of Prayer, a volume by Edmund Burke, The Canterbury Tales, Macbeth and The Tempest, Hume's The History of England. Even the fledgling subscription library at the Gazette could boast more. On the desk: an ink pot, a collection of quills in an earthenware jar, a silver pen knife, a bone paper knife, and two symmetrical stacks of paper.

Behind Schoolmaster, a cane hung from a hook. Next to it, a perforated paddle. Next to the paddle, a coiled horsewhip.

"Never used them," Schoolmaster had said with a diminished Scottish burr. "Not once. It is a deficient educator that relies on physical punishments."

He had, overall, an air of studied suppression.

"The threat of violence is not without its uses, of course."

For a moment Jeremy fantasized about pulling the horse whip from the wall and thrashing him with it. Jeremy couldn't have possibly known the answers to all the questions he'd been asked. He hadn't been asked the questions he knew the answers to. He'd had no other opportunity to prove his worth.

I'm as intelligent and knowledgeable as any of those children, aren't I? More so. I'm not asking to be made lieutenant-governor. Why couldn't I be a teacher? A measly teacher.

"Brandy, Mr. Castor?"

Jeremy looked back, too surprised to answer.

"Isn't a quiz," Schoolmaster said, hinting at a laugh. "End of the week. Well deserved, don't you think?"

Jeremy nodded.

Schoolmaster stood before him, offering a half-full snifter.

Jeremy glanced at him. Then back at the fire. Was it to be a St. John's Blessing? A final aperitif shared between executioner and condemned? He thanked Schoolmaster, taking up the crystal. He held it to his nose, letting its fumes tickle his nostrils. He did not drink. He would not toast his own downfall.

Jeremy felt a bead of sweat form above his breastbone beneath the four layers of wool, carapace of every article of clothing he'd brought. In wintry York, as in Kingston, one was either too cold or too hot.

"That was a fine oration," Schoolmaster said finally, before emitting a sound that echoed a chuckle. Jeremy hadn't once detected the notion of a smile through the entire span of five days.

"A most gratifying expression on Jarvis' face."

Schoolmaster picked up the andiron, poked the fire, and made the chuckling sound again.

"They likely all think I'm in here caning you six of the best. A hulk such as you. Won't hurt my reputation any."

Jeremy gripped his glass more tightly. His forehead became shiny.

"Truly. A fine oration. I never tire of hearing Coleridge and you declaim it very well. Jarvis and the others, they repeat it by rote. Sometimes. If they can get that right. But there is no life, no comprehension. Not like your impassioned address. You are clearly a man of good breeding, of civilized comportment. A sensitive soul."

"Thank you, sir."

"These are good boys though, full of promise. Well behaved. The future backbone. Not the sort they hope to civilize at this proposed Lancasterian school."

Schoolmaster became quiet again. Jeremy simmered.

"I'm recommending that the Schoolmaster post go to

Mr. Hamilton, an old acquaintance from Aberdeen. I've already sent for him from Montreal."

Jeremy gripped his still unsipped snifter and nearly snapped cup from stem.

"May have been a sensitive soul at one time too."

Schoolmaster stared into the fire.

"If he was, I don't remember it. He'll brook no dissent. Tough as a buzzard."

Jeremy imagined snatching the andiron from Schoolmaster's hand and wrapping it scarf-like around the older man's neck. Schoolmaster looked over at Jeremy for the first time. He extended his glass and offered it to clink.

"I will, of course, recommend you wholeheartedly as Hamilton's apprentice and assistant. I'll write you a letter to take back that Hagerman will be well satisfied with."

Jeremy stared.

"Congratulations, Mr. Castor. Welcome to the profession."

"Thank you, sir."

Jeremy rang his glass against Schoolmaster's. He took a deep draught.

"The newest recruit to our distinguished and most exclusive fraternal order of Praeceptors. Fiat Lux. Let there be light."

Jeremy laughed. From relief. He'd passed. He would have a paying job. He and Alice would not starve.

"Amused?"

"No sir."

Schoolmaster looked at him skeptically.

"Docendo discimus. Are you familiar?"

Jeremy shook his head.

"By teaching, we learn. Seneca the Younger."

"Oh yes, of course."

"You have much to learn."

"Yes sir."

"Look here Castor, you're a good lad, I can tell. Of the correct church. Civilized. Loyal. Our little colony needs men like you. Let me give you a little advice. Rev Stuart said much the same to me many years ago. I pass it on. If you're going to make your way here, and I understand you have little in the way of other prospects..."

Jeremy flushed, conceding the point.

"...you could do worse than applying yourself to the education project. You must take the long view. It is the teacher that shapes the next generation. It is the teacher that molds the minds and characters of future magnates and magistrates. I've been patient, my pupils have got forward, some into the House. I shall have more in my power. In this fledgling Arcadia, teaching is the most essential form of husbandry. You take my meaning?"

"Yes sir."

Schoolmaster lunged with the andiron and staggered a smouldering maple wedge. Its embers scattered.

"Do you know how I got my start?"

"No sir."

"Cornwall in 1803. Not your Cornwall. A grubby knot of shacks and outbuildings at river's edge, upstream from Kingston. A society of thistle growers and shoat breeders. None literary minded. None with true religious feeling. Thronged with Methodists and Lutherans prone to sudden inspirations and revelations. Overrun with Americans. Eight years I was in that spiritual desert, honing my craft, coaxing wheat stalks from stony ground. I instructed scions. I made a name. Now I am a member of the Executive Council. And, if all goes well, soon to be a member of the Legislative Council. And one day, Lord willing, bishop."

Schoolmaster quaffed the remainder of his brandy.

Jeremy put a hand into his coat. His fingers ran absently over the fractured surfaces of hard-boiled eggs.

"You have a gift for oration, Mr. Castor, I heard it today. You could follow the trail I've blazed. And, I could use another lieutenant in Kingston."

Schoolmaster pointed to the puffy, unlined orbit beneath his sharpened brow.

"Another waking eye added to my ever-watchful Argus."

Schoolmaster turned and the men regarded each other. Jeremy was unsure how to respond. Five minutes earlier he had been reconciling himself to a lifetime boiling scum. The conversation had taken an unexpected turn.

"A second brandy, Castor?" Schoolmaster said, finally.

"Yes sir, thank you."

Chapter Thirty

The clack of single pick horseshoes and the constant shush of the coach's runners were the only sounds. The sun peeked hesitantly over the horizon, lending pale yellow streaks to the morning's continuum of grey, a lethargic attempt to disperse the fog.

Jeremy shivered and pulled his allotted buffalo robe closer to his chin. They'd picked up a passenger on the other side of Cobourg. A Scot. Every second traveler was a Scot. Jammed to the joists with sporrans and kilts in this part of the province. The passenger introduced himself, his accent smoothed a little by his obvious education, as Robert Gourlay. Jeremy sipped applejack from the offered flask, thanked Gourlay, and passed it back. He offered him a hard-boiled egg but Gourlay refused it.

The coach slowed as it once more turned inland and detoured around a group improving the trail. A score of men swung pickaxes at field stones pulled from the track. As the coach slid silently by, Jeremy looked out the window. Amongst the men, he saw boys, not much larger than the picks they struggled with. Boys the same age as Cudmore, Mason, and Jarvis. One boy, standing amid the slush, wore rope sandals on his raw, red feet.

"Disgrace, ain't it," Gourlay tutted. "Pauper's children. Wouldn't see that back in Fife. That's convict's work, no task for innocents. Should be in school."

Jeremy nodded and turned his attention back to peeling his egg.

๛ ๛ ๛ ๛ ๛

Jeremy returned to Kingston in the New Year. After unpacking and visiting with Alice, he went straight to Mr. Hagerman's office with the stack of letters. Hagerman read them and told Jeremy that the new Compassionate Society Lancasterian School had already been in session a week, initiated by the newly arrived Mr. Hamilton and that Jeremy should report to him the following morning. He would receive a salary of forty pounds a year. Half the headmaster's salary. It was hardly a princely sum. A carter might make more. Still, might be enough.

Jeremy approached the front door of the two-story frame building that the Compassionate Society had leased for the purposes of the school. He listened. It was as quiet as the Home District Grammar School back in muddy York. He knocked. He waited. He heard boots scuff across the floor. A boy of about nine or ten opened the door, his damp face a sickly yellow-grey. He wore a man's sweater, more hole than wool and he had a foot-long piece of wood shackled to his ankles.

"Headmaster says come in," the boy said, before he vacuumed a cable of snot back into his head. He shuffled backwards and continued an awkward circuit around the perimeter of the classroom, each step circumscribed by the block of wood between his feet.

Jeremy crossed the threshold. He toed gingerly past the collection of frayed caps, patchy coats, unraveled scarves, eroding galoshes. The classroom was quiet save for the unsteady clomp of the boy's march. About twenty boys sat at benches before tilted desks. Some wrote at slates with chalk. James O'Neal, Lilac's friend and the tailor's apprentice, was one of them. Three boys craned their necks through pillories, two halves of a log hollowed out in the middle. They sat rigidly, facing the front, keeping the lumber balanced on their shoulders. Near the ceiling, a small wooden cage hung from a hoop of iron fastened to a cross beam. A rope tied to a hook near the Headmaster's desk secured it. Jeremy looked more closely. The cage contained a boy with a cloven ear.

Sweeney stared back at Jeremy cutty-eyed.

The Headmaster stood next to the desk, beneath the cage. He wore black breeches, black frock coat, and black leather slippers. His cheeks were hollow and his thinning ginger hair radiated backward. He said something to Jeremy in a nearly impenetrable brogue. The only word Jeremy managed to identify was his own surname.

"I am," he said, hoping he'd answered correctly.

He made out "Hamilton" and possibly "Aberdeen" from the second volley.

"Pleased to meet you, sir," Jeremy said, bowing slightly.

"Order", "early", "establish", and "discipline" was all that he could glean from what came next.

Hamilton continued. Jeremy nodded. Twice he gambled and shook his head at what sounded admonition-like. Hamilton's voice began to rise in volume and pitch, making decryption even less possible. The headmaster gestured with increasing wildness. He pointed at the staircase. He shouted. He stabbed a finger at the ceiling.

Finally, meaning dawned.

"My class?" Jeremy asked, aping Hamilton's hand movements.

"Aye!" Hamilton cried with relief.

"Upstairs?"

"Aye!"

"Yes, of course, I understand."

Jeremy bowed apologetically and began his retreat.

"....simple.....?"

It sounded like a question. Jeremy shook his head and walked on.

"....quine....and abecedarians...."

He crossed to the stairs. As he climbed, Hamilton continued his harangue. Jeremy detected "wee", "worst", and what sounded an awful lot like "doom". With each step, his progress up the stairs slowed. If shackled and pilloried boys were downstairs and Sweeney snarled in his cage, what awaited him inside the door at the top of the stairs? The truly feral? Quine? Abecedarians?

Jeremy crossed the landing at the top of the stairs. He put an ear to the door. Nothing. He put his hand on the latch. He opened. He stepped in sideways, leading with his left leg as though he might bound away with his right if necessary.

Fourteen students stared back at him, their faces framed with slack ringlets and makeshift braids. Fourteen poorly mended, homespun frocks concealed fourteen pairs of tattered, wool stockings. At one end, Jeremy recognized James O'Neal's sister, the little one with the hedge of hair, gnawing on her ever-present triangle of linen. At the other end, the eldest stood from the bench.

"Good morning Mr. Castor sir," she said, "My name is Placidia Sykes, your monitor-general. All slates are clean and in their proper places. All girls are present and accounted for."

Chapter Thirty-One
January 5th, 1818

Reverend Stuart drew a lungful through his nostrils and shuttered his eyes. The shine from two candles on either side of the pulpit flickered in the expanse of his towering forehead.

"Dearly beloved," he rumbled. "Good news."

His eyelids tightened and his voice softened.

"Surely that was the thought of anyone who opened their copy of the Gazette two months ago and read the simple engagement notice on the front page. Good news. That these two God-fearing youngsters, Mr. and Mrs. Spafford, could have another chance at love and happiness and fulfilling God's plan."

The first several pews of St. George's listened, rapt.

Further back, parishioners looked over their shoulders. They clucked at the mother who was unable or disinclined to soothe her baby. They sighed at the fitful, kicking youngsters who beat out a march against the seats in front. They shook their heads at the catarrh sufferer who really should have stayed home.

ৡ ৡ ৡ ৡ ৡ

Creedence Scriven sat in his customary seat, on the aisle three rows from the back. He met the gazes of those turned in their seats and affected a sympathetic frown. The indigo arc of his hair betrayed not a single grey. He brought his hand up and fondled the flawless Oriental Cranston had constructed from the silk at his neck. Traces of sandalwood clung to his fingers and brought with them a shiver of pleasure. Surveying the nave, he noted how his splendour was reflected back and he congratulated himself. Everywhere he looked he saw his own benign influence.

There was old Mrs. Wotherspoon, whom he'd given extra laudanum free of charge, well after the agony of her kidney stone had passed. And there was the widow Abernethy whose husband was killed the year before at the battle of Plattsburgh. Her baby had contracted the puerperal fever two days later. Lilac, under Scriven's supervision, had performed venesection and applied leeches. He'd prescribed a generous course of calomel mercury and syrup of ipecac for purging. And when, to his delight and surprise the whippet recovered, he'd waived his usual fee.

Lenore Stokes, too, seemed completely revitalized. Her melancholia had completely abated. Scriven couldn't remember hearing the light tinkle of her laugh, untinged with sarcasm, as often as he had these last few weeks. She'd seemed to have shed ten years. Of course, he couldn't deny the influence of his new protégé.

The revelatory Miss Lilac Evans. Scriven's paid accounts had doubled since her arrival, proportionate to the increase in his spare time for the club, the lodge, and his literary pursuits.

He craned his neck slightly to see McCallum and Calhoun sitting together near the back. They chatted, amiably and confidentially, the satisfied expressions on their faces signifying their convictions of a job well done.

Owen Stevens. He sat with the young lad, James O'Neal. And the boy's sister, shyly gnawing at a piece of rag. Scriven smiled to see his tailor reconciled with his apprentice. Perhaps he would pay him a visit soon, end his embargo, and order a new waist coat.

At the altar, Amelia and Rupert Spafford. It may not have been Jeremy Castor's preferred outcome, he seemed to despise Spafford, but they certainly were well matched. Spafford would provide his new bride the gift of old-world sophistication and entrée into society. Amelia, spirited filly, would retain Willowpath, and the glass factory she cherished. Besides, Spafford was a freemason, someone to be trusted implicitly.

Anyway, it was just as well that Castor hadn't been netted. He'd be in town all the time now and he would have more to spend at the club and at the lodge. Scriven had come to treasure his company. Despite his initial disappointment, Castor seemed to be taking Amelia's rejection surprisingly well. He'd seemed uncommonly engaged in the founding of the new school. He asked continually after Lenore, wanting to confer with her about the school. She was always unaccountably indisposed, but that never stopped him asking. It all went to prove that a man needs a project, a purpose, needs to be kept busy. He needs an outlet for his creative impulse. A busy Castor makes a model Mason.

Who better than myself, Scriven wondered, exemplifies the Masonic dictum: if we sow well, we reap well.

Best of all: no more letters in the Gazette from Opprobrious. It had been a one-off. Most likely, it had nothing to do with Scriven at all.

As he continued to survey the nave and found himself at the centre of countless good works, he went so far as to think it was the best possible thing; this enforced exile of his. Let Geoffrey, father's favourite, manage the estate. One can re-invent himself, after all. The sordid scene in the old country left behind. Re-written. He had his annuity. He had his practice and renewed reputation. It can all be made clean, pressed, and starched.

❧ ❧ ❧ ❧ ❧

Reverend Stuart continued, his eyelids clamped shut, as if only one voice vibrated his cranial dome.

"Last Sunday," Stuart said, "a darling boy asked me, how old is the bible? Where did it come from? How do we know it's true?"

A mutt, her yellow fur dotted with mange, nosed through the jarred front door.

"Darling boy. We know, of course, that God's word was first delivered unto Moses on Mount Sinai. God wrote those commandments himself, into stone. Moses, and the other prophets, recorded the truth so it could be handed down to future generations, such as our own."

The mutt made herself low, shimmying beneath pews, snaking between ankles, sniffing for possible scraps.

"A single Torah required one hundred and fifty feet of continuous sheepskin. An entire flock." Stuart's voice swooped again. "The merest error, a Tav instead of a Tet, or the scribe's thumbprint in tar and honey, they would destroy the panel, and the panels around it, and start again. Their reproduction was always faithful and true."

Mr. Staunton's spaniel, Wellesley, had been snoozing peaceably at his master's feet. The street-ripened scent of the scavenging bitch reached his nostrils and Wellesley began to bark. Mrs. Abernethy's startled baby squalled. Parishioners' heads swiveled to take in the fresh distraction.

ഌ ഌ ഌ ഌ ഌ

Scriven tugged at the ends of his Oriental, making sure they were crisp and even. He pulled at the bottom hem of his jacket to prevent the collar riding up. He returned Mrs. Wotherspoon's knowing smile. Admiration of his attire and deportment from the feminine portion of St. George's was usual; it was expected. The contemporary female was attuned to these sorts of things. As Kingston's best dressed man, it was too easy. It was the gaze from his peers and the younger men, the Loyalist scions, the captain's sons that he most coveted.

Scriven caught Hugh Thomson's eye. What did he have to offer young Thomson? Hughie, as the younger lodge brothers called him, dressed nearly as well as himself. His cravat was tied with an American, yes, but what exquisite ivory silk. Frock coat and trousers fit admirably. Thick hair was pushed forward into a diadem Augustus himself would have relished. No indigo required, of course. He looked so comfortable with his arm draped over the back of the pew, one leg crossed casually over the other. He had that easy way of someone whose local history spanned generations. If he heard once more how Hughie's father had built this very church...

Scriven touched a finger to his brow. Thomson smiled and turned back to whisper to Charlie Grant, Zip MacPherson, and the other members of the Headstrong Club with whom he sat. Probably they whispered about Hughie's latest contribution to the Gazette, some witty letter or poem. They all wrote letters to the Gazette.

❧ ❧ ❧ ❧ ❧

"You are my flock," Stuart wavered, now aware of the disruption. He brought his eyebrow down like the platen of a press, vised shut as though his temples ached.

"And, in a sense, the truth is written in each of us. Imprinted onto our very limbs and sinews."

Wellesley pulled away from Mr. Staunton who, like his dog, had found in Stuart's sermon an opportunity to rest his eyes. The leash snapped from Staunton's slack hand.

"The apostles bore witness to Jesus' miracle and, like Paul, preached the gospel." Stuart's voice built in volume and pitch like a great storm coming in off the lake. "They spread the good news near and far. It was written down and translated, into Greek, Latin, and ultimately, English, first by Wycliffe, and later Tyndale."

The uninvited dog fled before Wellesley's slobbering pursuit, lapping the church's perimeter.

"Through the press, Gutenberg said, God will spread His Word. A spring of pure truth shall flow from it."

Despite the protestations of their parents, children clapped and grabbed at the dog's tails as they raced by. The Cochrane and Andrews infants began to cry.

Stuart let his head drop and closed the King James with a thunderous clap.

"So you see, darling boy, an unbroken chain, the word of God, from Mount Sinai to our own St. George's."

He thrust his chin over the pulpit and winched his vocal cords to their highest possible pitch.

"John 8:32," Stuart said, his voice scything through the nave. "Ye shall know the truth, and the truth shall make you free."

And now, for the first time since Stuart embarked on this last portion of his sermon, he opened his eyes, each of them lustrous and round, like the opposite ends of a spyglass. He finally noticed the dog chase and sighed, his vigour dissipated.

       ~o ~o ~o ~o ~o

Across the nave, as Stuart continued his liturgy, Lenore Stokes leaned in toward Lilac Evans.

"It worked!" she whispered.

"What?"

"Your prescription of feverfew and amaranth. Your regimen. It worked."

Lilac frowned. Lenore framed her fingers in a triangle over the midsection of her gown.

"Julienne Blouin of Brittany," Lenore whispered. "Remember? A daughter at 52."

"But the Major..."

Lenore held a finger to her lip. Lilac nodded and returned her eyes to front but couldn't resist stealing a glance at the silk straining at Lenore's midriff.

"You must come and see me at the doctor's office."

❧ ❧ ❧ ❧ ❧

Amelia stole a quick glance into the congregation to see Jeremy, sitting with his mother, Alice. He wasn't paying attention. He was looking across the nave, toward where Lenore and Lilac sat. Alice returned a slight, angled smile which in a moment somehow managed to convey a multitude of contradictory meanings, some less generous than others.

"If any of you can show just cause," Reverend Stuart was saying, "why they may not lawfully be married, speak now; or else for ever hold your peace."

Amelia looked away from Alice and Jeremy and back into Spafford's glassy black eyes. Her own eyes began to well and Spafford assumed they were tears of joy.

Stuart bade Spafford and Amelia to repeat their vows.

ও ও ও ও ও

Five rows from the back, McCallum whispered at Calhoun.

"There isn't one."

"One what?"

"A second will."

"I beg your pardon?"

"No second will. No fortune. No peerage. Just discovered."

"But the estate..."

"Fortunately," McCallum interrupted, nodding toward the altar as Spafford leaned in to kiss his bride, "the tale ends happily."

The two men shook hands, each pressing the top of his thumb in between the other's first and second knuckle.

ও ও ও ও ও

"I pronounce," Stuart continued, the rings having been exchanged, "that they be man and wife together..."

For a moment, Stuart lost his place. His attention was drawn to the aisle to the narthex, just before the door to the street. Wellesley had caught the mutt. With his jaw clamped on her neck, the spaniel mounted her.

Stuart concluded with a hasty Amen.

PART TWO

Chapter Thirty-Two

Lenore lay on the chaise-lounge in Dr. Scriven's office, her arms and legs draped langorously along its length. Her left hand fanned out over her belly. She gazed up at the string of small, painted paper lanterns hanging from the ceiling, the only remaining Christmas ornaments. The room's single smudged window admitted a few rays of weak, winter light. Still, despite a post-holiday layer of dust, the pastel coloured globes brightened the room. Lenore imagined what it would be like to see the lanterns at night with their babyish candles lit. She pictured them through a child's eyes.

Dr. Scriven sat in the adjoining room at his writing desk. He, too, stared at the ceiling. And the walls. He missed the baubles and wreaths and streamers that used to adorn them, the trimmings Lilac had insisted upon. It hadn't been difficult for her to convince him of their necessity. He had funded the entire decoration effort. He declared the office "delightfully festive and charmingly gay" when she'd finished.

Scriven forced himself back to the next perfectly unblemished page of his masterwork, *Bespoke Bespeaks*. He struggled to ignore the mocking inner voice. He banished, for the hundredth time, the recurring image of a sherry schooner freshly poured.

In the next room Lilac attended to Lenore. Though she continued to depend upon Scriven for gossip and matters of the cloth, Lenore had made it clear that she preferred meeting with his assistant when it came to receiving medical advice. It was how it went with most of his patients now, particularly the females and the children, which made up most of his clientele. They had come to rely on Lilac's unfailing insights and intuitions and, truth be told, her more womanly bedside manner. As apprentice to Dr. Alexander Duncan of Croydon and attendee of the Royal College at Warwick Lane, Scriven acknowledged his demeanour could be brusque. He was a professional, after all. No matter. His instruction gave her facility. If his patients preferred to hear his counsel and his prescriptions through the softer, Welsh lilt of his apprentice, so much the better. Medicine had never been his true calling. Calliope was his muse; writing his vocation.

He stared hard at the empty paper expanse. He kept his ear cocked in the direction of the door of the examination room, waiting for the telltale clink of the iron latch. When Lilac emerged with Lenore he could justifiably break from his labours for a measure of sherry and a friendly chat.

❧ ❧ ❧ ❧ ❧

Inside the exam room, Lilac advanced upon her patient. She brandished an instrument, a wooden cylinder with a brass suction cup on the end. It looked like a disfigured trumpet. Lenore recoiled from her position of repose and brought her knees up tightly to her chest. Her child-like expression contorted.

"What is it?" she asked.

"A stethoscope."

Lenore retained her defensive posture.

"A listening device," Lilac continued, patiently. "A little like an ear horn."

Lenore's expression didn't change.

"I had the doctor order us one. It's very useful. I put this end up to my ear like so. And the other end..."

"I think not," Lenore said, both hands barricading her belly.

"Mrs. Stokes. Used externally. Just for listening."

Lilac pointed at Lenore's chest.

"I can hear your heart and its pulse..."

Lilac lowered her finger until it aimed at Lenore's midsection.

"...and other burblings..."

Lenore relaxed slightly, bringing her knees back down from her chest.

"...that indicate health and well-being."

Lenore studied Lilac's face.

"That's fine, then," Lenore said finally, unclenching and stretching out once more on the chaise-lounge.

Lilac cautiously placed the bell of the stethoscope on Lenore's chest. She put her ear to the end of the hollow, wooden cylinder. She listened and counted to herself.

"Good. Good," she said.

Then, not taking her eyes from Lenore's, she carefully moved the trumpet bell directly over Lenore's navel. She listened. She removed the stethoscope, stepped away, and sat in a chair.

Lenore's eyes followed her. She waited.

"Well? You heard something?"

Lilac nodded.

"Movement?"

"Perhaps. A second beat. Maybe."

"I don't need to hear," Lenore said, triumphantly, "I know. I just know."

"A quickening?"

"Yes," Lenore sat up. "At least, I think so."

She noticed Lilac's expression and her smile dimmed.

"I don't understand why you are so glum. Your treatment worked Doctor. I will recommend you to all my friends."

"I didn't expect such immediate results."

Lenore caressed her belly.

"Nor I."

"The Major. He is still in Venezuela?"

"I believe he is."

Lilac looked away. It was her turn to regard the dormant Christmas lights.

"It wouldn't have mattered if he was here or not. I'd never been the problem. Of that I am sure."

"It would be impertinent of me to ask..."

"Then don't."

"But, Mrs. Stokes..."

"This should be a happy occasion."

"Yes, it should."

"A Christmas gift."

"Received immaculately, as per the season."

Lenore shifted. She frowned.

"Miss Evans, you forget yourself."

"I beg your pardon, Mrs. Stokes. Perhaps I should retrieve the Doctor."

"No."

"He will want to examine you. He will want to discuss your options and advise."

"No," Lenore repeated, softer now, "I'd very much appreciate keeping this between ourselves."

The two women regarded each other.

"Please," Lenore said, finally. "In your confidence, as a physician. As my physician."

Lilac looked away from Lenore and down at the stethoscope in her hands. She twirled it and peered down into the flared end of the bell, imagining the sounds it channeled, real and imagined, led to some unseen future.

In the next room a door was unlatched and noisily shut. Another man's voice could be heard, greeting Scriven. They heard the doctor's eager, almost relieved, reply. It was a familiar voice. Animated and cheerful. They listened as Scriven pushed back on his chair, rose from his desk, shoved the chair back in, and crossed the floor to the liquor cabinet. They heard the clinking of sherry schooners and the brittle ting of the decanter's glass stopper. Scriven asked questions. The man replied, speaking in an unmistakably Cornish accent about lessons, alphabets, and slates.

Lilac regarded Lenore. She had receded into the chaise-lounge, studiously avoiding Lilac's renewed gaze. Lilac remembered the last time Lenore and Jeremy had been in the office together, several months back, when Lilac had first prescribed to her the amaranth and feverfew. She recalled how Lenore's voice had changed. It had become more animated, more tuneful. She remembered how Lenore's gloved fingers had clutched at Jeremy's arm when she spoke to him. They had spoken of her work with the school committee. They had discussed his role as prospective headmaster. They had planned their meetings.

Lenore shifted her attention from the office door, to the grey window, and back to the delicate, paper globes. The hand that had caressed her belly was now brought up to her face which, unlike the lanterns, began to glow.

"The Deacon," Lilac said, in what sounded like an accusation.

Lenore didn't correct her.

"It is the Deacon?"

Lenore rolled to the side and hid her face behind her shoulder.

"Mrs. Stokes."

Still no reply.

"Does he know?"

Nothing.

Lilac got up from her chair. She crossed the office to a bureau and began opening its drawers. She pulled a variety of stoppered bottles from them, examined their labels, and returned them.

"What are you doing?" Lenore asked.

"I'm looking for my ergot. My pennyroyal."

"Why?"

"Abortifacients."

"What is that? What is an abortifacient?"

"A compound designed to induce miscarriage."

Lilac was all business now and spoke as if nothing could be more obvious. She held a green glass bottle to the dim light of the window, examining the dessicated herb within.

"Miscarriage?"

"Yes, of course. It must be initiated immediately."

Lenore sat up. She smoothed the crumpled, muslin layers of her gown so that they lay taut upon her lap. She balled one hand into the clasp of the other.

"There will be no miscarriage," she said.

"Mrs. Stokes..."

"It will not happen."

"It must."

"And by no means will it be induced."

"What can be done? Consider the scandal. The Major a thousand miles away."

"I'll be travelling to New Haven. To stay with my sister who lives there."

Lenore now faced Lilac directly, her look pointed.

"On the advice of my physician who, for my persistent case of the blue devils, which lately has been so pronounced, has prescribed time away, to the south where it is warmer and free of snow. Proximity to the ozone of the sea. Winter tonic."

"New Haven?"

"Yes."

"So far away."

"'An extended visit."

"But what if Jeremy should learn the truth? What if anyone should learn the truth? 'Twould be a mighty scandal. None would understand. He would get run out on a rail."

Lenore's tone became ferocious.

"None shall learn the truth," she said, leaning forward, her eyes blazing. "I am trusting you on this account."

Before Lilac could give it any thought and before she could continue to make her argument for pennyroyal, there was a knock on the door.

"Yes?" the women said in overly loud unison.

"Lenore, it's Creedence. May I come in?"

Lenore looked at Lilac.

"Dr. Scriven, the patient," Lilac piped, "is presently indisposed."

Lenore nodded her gratitude.

"Oh. Ah. I see," came the reply from the other side of the door. "Is she alright?"

"Yes, Doctor, 'tis a female complaint."

"Ah, yes, of course. Could you let her know that Mr. Jeremy Castor has come by for a visit? He has just completed his first week at the school and is eager to visit and give a report. I've suggested we repair to Walker's for a proper debrief. He is very keen to pay his regards to Mrs. Stokes. Would she like to emerge and say hello?"

"She is quite indisposed and in a state of undress at the moment, doctor."

"Perhaps she could meet us at Walker's after her examination for an aperitif?"

"She indicates to me that she will indeed endeavour to do just that."

"Splendid! Please let her know we will await her arrival with great anticipation."

"Yes doctor, of course."

They waited, breathless, until the door to the street re-latched and they could hear boot heels on the board walk outside.

"Thank you, Miss Evans," Lenore said, rising and crossing to fetch her cape. "I greatly appreciate your discretion in this matter. I owe you a debt. If it weren't for you, none of us would be in this joyous predicament."

Chapter Thirty-Three
June, 1818

Jeremy knocked on the front door of Stoke Cottage. He waited. He stepped to the right, put a hand over his brow, and peered through the slight gap between the shutters. Nothing could be seen through the gloom.

Over the last few months, as the snow had receded and crocuses had first raised their lavender heads, Jeremy had come by the cottage often. Ever since Lenore had abruptly disappeared, leaving vague explanations with Lilac and Scriven that she'd gone for an extended stay with her sister in New Haven, Jeremy had drifted by, looking for some sign of activity, some indication that she had returned. Some days he would have a feeling and he would knock. Most times he would linger a while by the cedar grove before moving on. Buttercups had shone yellow. Trilliums had turned out as finely white as any of Scriven's cravats. Always the cottage was shuttered and dark.

"The blue devils," Scriven had said when Jeremy had asked if he knew where she'd gone. "Hypochondriacal melancholy. Lenore has been susceptible every year since she moved here. Over-long winters, of course. And it can't be easy with Peregrine half a globe away.

Now, I've prescribed the tobacco enema. She flatly refuses. It's fine. Miss Evans has the right idea. Time with family. A little sun. Some coastal ozone."

Jeremy knocked once more. He craned his neck, so his ear nearly touched the door. He heard nothing. He turned and started back down the path. He had reached the cedars when he heard the door open behind him. He swung back. Abigail's face emerged from the cracked doorway. She had her hair in a kerchief and an assortment of rags tucked into the strings of her apron. In her hand she held the tail of a mouse whose head and torso were flattened between two blocks of wood.

"Oh, ah, I beg your pardon," Jeremy said. "I wondered," Jeremy said, "if your mistress, Mrs. Stokes, might be in? There are... some matters. Matters regarding the Lancasterian school. I wanted to bring them to her attention."

"She ain't here. Just me. Cleaning."

"Do you know when she might return?"

"She ain't here. Gone to stay with her sister in New Haven."

"Yes, yes, I understand. I just wondered if you knew when she might return."

"Don't know. New Haven."

"Right, I thought she might be back."

"I'm to clean once a week..."

Abigail reduced the crack in the door to a sliver.

"...and to not let anyone in."

She closed the door and barred it from the inside.

❧ ❧ ❧ ❧ ❧

Jeremy returned from Moore's coffee house holding a handle-less pot between two swatches. He placed the pot on the ground, retrieved his key, unlatched the front door, and then the interior door. He carried the pot inside and re-latched both doors. He poured tea into a pair of clay mugs and brought one to Alice. She sat in a chair by the window with the shutters open. An occasional breeze brought the usual street essences: horse dung, rotted hay, bedpan leavings. But today, something else: traces of lilac.

Dr. Scriven had invited him to the theatre that Saturday afternoon to see the comedy Who Wants A Guinea. "No children allowed," Scriven had added as incentive. "For you, a true holiday. I'll pay."

He'd politely declined. He didn't want to be beholden. But he'd agreed to go hear Robert Gourlay speak at Old Sam's when he arrived.

Jeremy took Alice's hand from her lap where it had been feeling out a shirt collar's stitching. He guided it to the mug's ribbed curve and wrapped her trembling fingers around it. They steadied, warmth radiating from the clay, soothing rheumatoid joints. Next, he unwrapped the bundle sitting atop the mantle. He pulled out one of the two currant buns remaining from yesterday's half dozen, placed it on a square snipped out of the Gazette, and brought it to Alice. With her free hand, she adjusted the cracked frame of her glasses, the ones salvaged from Dr. Scriven's office that had helped at first but now made no difference. He removed the last bun, shook wayward currants from the paper folds, and tipped them into his mouth. Crunching them released their lively essence, an even mix of sweetness and a cleansing, acidic burn.

Jeremy picked up a half-finished stocking from the side table, the first of a pair that would clothe the feet of James O'Neal's sister. He had yet to coax from her a given name. James, on account of her muteness, called her Gabby. He didn't know her true name. James said his mother had only ever called her "sister".

Jeremy had taught the abecedarians the alphabet. He had taught them the simplest of sums. He'd showed them how to sew and knit. The day he conducted James O'Neal's sister through ten stitches without a drop, he'd leapt to his feet. He'd clapped. He'd danced an improvised gallopade that was frantic and ungainly. It had prompted Mr. Hamilton to rush up the stairs to Jeremy's classroom, paddle in hand. From James O'Neal's sister it had elicited a smile, which was enough. Since then, on most school mornings, she brought him remnants of yarn discarded by her caretaker, Owen Stevens, the tailor.

Teaching had gone relatively well. Of course, there was the day when Beatrice McCann had brought a caged squirrel into the classroom and had liberated it in the middle of reading lessons. A chorus of fourteen girls shrieking in unison had caused Mr. Hamilton to sprint up the stairs again, spouting his barely intelligible exclamations, demanding to know the fire's location. Then, just two days later, a proper fire. Georgia Walsh, with the reading candle, had set alight Beatrice's unflattering doodle. An adjacent stack of paper erupted into flames. Once more, the shrieking crescendoed. Once more, Mr. Hamilton blustered up the stairs, a whirlwind of Aberdonian dander. This time he had been gratified to find an actual conflagration, smothered in a timely manner with a cloak and snow scraped from the window sashes. Apart from these and other more minor mishaps, order was kept, and students took instruction. They progressed. The Lancasterian method, with older students mentoring the younger, worked well with the offspring of canters and costermongers. Placidia Sykes, a scullion's daughter, proved to be a most effective head monitor, capable, if entirely unlikely, of transcending her fate.

Jeremy made the pleasant discovery that he didn't despise the little bantlings after all. He had a natural way. Hagerman was satisfied. The committee was pleased. Jeremy had even received a congratulatory note from Schoolmaster in May with a hint that, in the event of Mr. Hamilton moving to a new assignment in the autumn, Jeremy might be promoted to the Headmastership, with commensurate pay rise. Perhaps, Schoolmaster wrote, he would recommend Jeremy for the school committee.

Jeremy added twenty more stitches, the needles making their comforting, metronomic snick, before he stopped to take another mouthful of tea. He sighed. He looked around the small room: the frayed curtains, the bare, whitewashed walls, the wardrobe, its few shirts and breeches exposed by the missing door, the soap shard next to the chipped basin, the scraped, unfinished floors, the hearth empty of wood, free of ash, the stain colonizing the ceiling plaster nearest the infiltrated chimney. He nibbled at the dry shell of the bun. He sipped. He took a deep breath and let it escape slowly from his lungs. Forty pounds a year combined with Alice's small pension barely knit together body and soul. It wasn't much. It was enough. It kept most of the rain from their heads. Some folks, the families of some of the children he taught, had it much worse. At the end of each month, Jeremy was able to stow away a few coins – insurance against future calamity or, perhaps, when he was feeling expansive, the foundation of a move to something better. A fund from which to repay Lenore.

The children had returned to their farms and sculleries and mill floors for the summer. Jeremy once again had full days to himself. He spent his time reading and walking and thinking. He managed to pick up some part time work helping Stephen Miles in the print shop at the Gazette. The rest of the time he spent knitting, incorporating all the many yarn ends brought to him over the last months by James O'Neal's sister. He also found a use for the spool of silk remnants she had surprised him with on one occasion. One day he walked up the Montreal Road, to the outskirts where the hayfields began. He returned with a bag of chaff slung over his shoulder. He cut four buttons from his Navy fearnought and rubbed them with a measure of natron obtained from Lilac's apothecary until they gleamed. He rummaged through Alice's sewing kit and found a length of pearl white linen that would do perfectly.

"What are you up to?" Alice asked, turning her face in the direction of his puttering.

"Knitting."

"I haven't lost my hearing."

"Nor your powers of speech."

"If anything, my ability to hear is stronger now that my eyes have dimmed."

"I've heard that can happen," Jeremy whispered.

"Pilchard! I can hear you."

"Then it's true!"

"A knitter of sound mind doesn't make such a racket. What's all this scuffing and scratching and tiptoeing about."

"I've a project."

"Clearly. What is it?"

A gift for Lenore. He sighed a third time. Alice slapped her empty mug against the sill.

"More of a breeze coming from your direction," she said, "than through this here window. What's wrong with you?"

Jeremy didn't respond. He recounted his thoughts, wondering what was wrong with him.

"It's her, isn't it?"

His pulse quickened.

"I don't blame ye. A young man in his prime. Dashing. A steady employment and a shilling or two in your pocket."

"Ma."

"She's a cipher Jem, I told you."

"Ma?"

"Always kind to me. And obviously still overly fond of you. You should march back up to Willowpath this afternoon. Reclaim your Penelope."

"Willowpath? Amelia's married, Ma!"

A veil of confusion descended Alice's face.

"To that Irish bloke, Rupert Spafford. She's done with me."

"Spafford's dead."

"His nephew! Rupert, nephew of the Colonel."

"You needn't shout. I guess you hardly want to be cooped up here with yer sightless old mam, pouring weak tea, gnawing day-olds, making stale conversation."

"Ma."

"When you ran off last time..."

"Merit and I were pressed. We didn't..."

"I had no idea where you had fled to. Samarkand, for all I knew."

"They broke my nose."

"In your letters, when you bothered to write any..."

"Captain Rowton withheld them."

"It wasn't until a year later they came."

"I posted them from here, when we were finally ashore."

"You wrote that you wanted to come home. A kettle of hot bohea on the old stove."

"I did, Ma, I do. This is lovely."

"To be together. To knit."

"I'll stop sighing."

Chapter Thirty-Four

Cacophony within Old Sam's pulsed the windows and flooded the transom. Pipe exhaust and ale fumes gusted through the opening past the man at the door. Beyond him a full house sat at tables, tipping tankards and lighting bowls, shouting and laughing.

"Castor!"

Dr. Scriven appeared behind the man at the door. In each fist he held a pair of wooden mugs on his way from bar to table.

"Where've you been? He's just finished his address. Let him in. Let him in."

The man pushed the door wider and moved to one side. Jeremy stepped into the foyer of Old Sam's.

"Come on Castor, I'll introduce you. Interesting fellow. Has some schemes to lift our province from the grip of these damned blue devils."

Jeremy followed Scriven into the miasma. Edging past knots of men gathered in threes and fours, jesting and roaring, they reached an oval table inundated with wooden mugs, leather blackjacks, trencher boards of black bread and cheese and smoked sausage. A dozen clay pipes, some spent, some newly tamped, lay among the sheaves of paper, pamphlets, and books. Around the oval Jeremy recognized other members of the Headstrong Club and fellow Freemasons, young men with whom Scriven liked to surround himself: Charlie Grant, Zip MacPherson, Johnny Moore and others. Owen Stevens moped nearby. Hugh Thomson, leaned ardently forward at one end of the oval, asking Robert Gourlay, their guest speaker, to elucidate on his idea of full employment.

"Mr. Gourlay, Mr. Gourlay," Dr. Scriven shouted as he slammed the mugs down, one in front of the Scot. "I'd like you to meet Mr. Jeremy Castor, our town's newest pedagogue. You must reiterate your thoughts on education."

"We've met," Gourlay said, as he stood and extended his wiry hand. He looked up at Jeremy. "You don't forget a fellow of Castor's dimensions. Please, take a seat."

"Already met?" Scriven cried. "This is the minutest colony in all of this vast empire, is it not?"

"We shared a stage from Cobourg to Ernesttown last winter. You remember Mr. Castor?"

"I do, sir."

"A most welcome companion. We had ourselves some enlightening chats. Also, witnessed some altogether unpleasant scenes."

Jeremy remembered the children, barefoot in the snow, breaking rocks with mason's mauls they could hardly lift. Since he'd joined the ranks of the working poor, an educator no less, he'd been following Gourlay's regular letters, reprinted in the Gazette. He was sympathetic to his decrying of Toryism. His calls for social and economic justice had resonated.

"It's a marvelous thing this Lancasterian school you've founded. I find it perfectly scandalous that no provision has been made by law for free schools in this province. One cannot sustain a functioning democracy and a prosperous country if the people are kept ignorant."

"I agree entirely," Jeremy said.

"Though, let us also be candid. Some would prefer to keep them stupid."

"Schoolmaster has a remedy for that," Thomson said on Gourlay's left, eager to recapture his attention.

"Schoolmaster?"

"Schoolmaster. Of the Home District Grammar School."

"Oh yes! The arrogant priest! A monstrous little fool of a parson – rogue is nearer the truth."

Nervous laughter stuttered round the table. Half of the men had spent portions of their youth under Schoolmaster's instruction, either in a classroom or tutored at home. The other half wished they had, proof of their family's standing. They eyed each other furtively over the tankards they chortled into, seeking the unspoken and collective understanding that if they all laughed together at this audacity no single one of them could be held responsible. Thomson grinned, fully aware of the contents of the pot he'd stirred. Gourlay's recent letter exchanges with Schoolmaster were well known and avidly followed in the Gazette, an entertaining respite from the long, dark winter. Or, as the duels were known among the wags of the Headstrong Club: epistles at dawn.

"If it weren't for my wife's uncle," Gourlay continued, "asking him to come to serve as tutor for a prominent family, he'd be back in the heather, wiping young Aberdonian noses."

His vehemence approached a boil. His brogue became rampant as he continued; fricatives crunched, r's stretched and rolled to an extent that the words they led faltered and dissolved. He drained a third of his blackjack at a go, perhaps to soothe his frayed glottis. He grabbed Jeremy's wrist as he spoke. The whites of his unblinking eyes glowed hot around the flat black of his irises. Jeremy politely ignored the wet flecks launched from his quavering bottom lip.

"And what of Castigator? Or Nemesis? Opprobrious? Surely men of great conviction. Have they no courage? Must they hide behind pseudonyms?"

"Cowardly," Scriven said.

"Perhaps they fear not getting printed?" Jeremy asked.

"It's been no impediment to me," Gourlay said, rounding on him. "Your weekly has been most accommodating. Mark me, if you wish to effect change as you say you do, it's not soil you need beneath your fingernails, it's the ink of the press."

Gourlay drank what was left in his blackjack. He clapped both hands down on the table and rose abruptly.

"Speaking of which," he continued, "could one of you fine gentlemen direct me to the offices of the Gazette?"

Gourlay picked a topper from the table and pulled it

hard over his head with both hands. Though the band strained at his prominent forehead, he forced it down until the brim met his ears and bent them forward.

"I forget where it is from here," he said. "I've an important notice for Miles' next edition."

Gourlay took the beaver felt from his head, turned it once, and crammed it back down.

"The younger Hagerman holds hostage knowledge of the district, of the needs and aspirations of its people."

Gourlay pulled hard again on the brim of the topper, his caliper-like fingers white with strain. The seams in the beaver felt looked like they might split.

"When confronted, the uncouth fellow spewed blasphemies at me with a tinker's eloquence."

Gourlay see-sawed the abused hat from one side of his head to the other.

"The third brother Hagerman," Gourlay gave the brim a quarter turn, "is a convicted forger, many years a guest of the State prison, now hanged. The public has a right to know."

Gourlay lopped the hat from his head as though it was the dome of a hard-boiled egg. He clapped it back on the table. His prominent forehead shone with a scarlet halo where it had contended with the brim. He planted both sets of bloodless knuckles on the table, one on an ale-stained pamphlet, the other in a pile of spent tobacco. He leaned in. He was close enough that the young men could smell the rot coming from a vexatious molar.

"Who can direct me?" he breathed.

"Dr. Scriven and I can escort you to the Gazette and

get your notice printed," Jeremy said. "The doctor is on excellent terms with Miles."

Gourlay gathered up his books, papers, and pamphlets and stuff them into a leather satchel. In moments, he was at the foyer.

"Mr. Gourlay," Jeremy cried after him. "Your hat."

"No," Gourlay called back over his shoulder, "this one's mine, here on the hook."

Gourlay plucked a beaver felt from a rack near the door, flipped it on his head without adjustment, and gusted out. Jeremy lifted the other, battered topper from the table.

Stevens ripped it from his hands.

"Mine."

"Don't sulk Stevens," Scriven said, "take it to Thomson. He'll hammer out the dents."

Scriven and Castor fetched their own hats, exited Old Sam's, and attempted to reel in Gourlay. Stevens followed at a discreet distance.

☙ ☙ ☙ ☙ ☙

Inside the print shop, Stephen Miles sat on his high stool, examining the proofs.

"Mr. Miles," Gourlay said. "I have an article that may be of interest to you."

Miles continued to guide the gauge along the line.

"It will surely be of interest to your subscribers," Gourlay added.

Miles replaced the scissor spectacles with a magnifying glass and bent closer to the broadsheet.

"It involves nefariousness and disgrace amongst the brothers Hagerman."

Miles flicked a wayward fiber from the bottom of a long "S".

"Mr. Miles," Gourlay persisted, approaching the vast, angled table. "The public deserves to know."

Miles looked up. He returned the scissor spectacles to his face. The glass flickered with the light of the lamps and reflected back Gourlay's eyes of glistening black and white.

"Is it scurrilous?" Miles asked.

"Nay, not scurrilous."

"Is it scabrous?"

"Nay, 'tis the truth."

Miles returned to his proofing.

"It's been reported to me that the third Hagerman brother who had once been confined for forgery in Montreal but then escaped justice in Canada has since been convicted and hanged in the United States, also for the crime of forgery."

Miles licked an inky fore finger, pinched the corner of the broadsheet, and turned it.

"You value truth," Gourlay said, "and the spreading of that truth."

"Aye. I also value freedom. Neither with the king, nor the people, but with both."

"Mr. Miles, you are a man of the Method."

"I am."

"Then, of course, you are familiar with the proverb about pride and destruction."

"Yes," Miles looked up from his paper. He brought the spectacles to his face and met Gourlay's glare. "And, haughty spirit, also. You wish to cast a mote from your brother's eye, do you?"

"No truth should be concealed," Gourlay replied, "which could humble the pride of the Hagermans."

The front doors of the Gazette clattered open. Daniel Hagerman entered, followed by his brother Christopher. If they had looked, the men inside might have glimpsed Owen Stevens, skulking near the simmering linseed, keen to witness the scene to come. He had his apprentice, James O'Neal, with him.

"Ah," Gourlay said, "the brothers Hagerman. In this town, I suppose, a private conversation cannot be had."

The Hagermans advanced on the high angled table. Each held a cane of blackthorn. The typesetters put their partially loaded line sticks down gingerly, careful not to disturb the texts they'd already set. They picked up empty ones. Squib pulled the sharpened rods from the leather casing of the inking balls and held them, dripping black, in front of his squat, bare chest.

"Castor!" Christopher Hagerman cried. "Scriven! Why are you here?"

"Squib," Miles called, "please move the lamps away from the printing stock and snuff the linseed fire."

"Mr. Hagerman," Scriven said, his tone conciliatory, "we mean you no harm. We'd gone to hear Mr. Gourlay speak at Old Sam's. Afterwards, he'd requested that we guide him to the Gazette."

"Mr. Miles," Hagerman said, ignoring Scriven and advancing on Miles. "You must not print this man's wicked slander."

"We needn't another conflagration."

"Do not submit to it!"

"Is it true?" Miles asked.

"Of course it's true," Gourlay answered. "I have done this third brother Hagerman a great service. If he's alive he should thank me for openly declaring what has been said of him that he might at once put an end to a story so discreditable, by publishing the truth or making his appearance."

"Mr. Miles!" Daniel continued, gesturing at his brother, "we have a mother! And sisters! Think of how their feelings might be injured!"

"I also have a mother and sisters," Gourlay said, unmoved. "And a wife and child to whom my character is very dear. Every species of slander against my character has been admitted into this paper often at your behest, Mr. Hagerman. Since these falsehoods have been published, and might go home to England, our dear printer must not now flinch from doing his duty in publishing the truth."

Miles stowed some of the sharper bodkins, sheep's feet, and ink slices lying about.

Christopher cut the air with his blackthorn. A stream of obscenities frothed from his mouth. Gourlay stood unflinching, his hands planted on the backs of his hips, his front fall thrust forward, the suggestion of a smile forming around his gnashing teeth.

"Mr. Hagerman!" Miles cried. "Cursing within the confines of the printer's chapel is strictly forbidden. It ought never to happen. When it does, as it does with depressing frequency, it's a penny in the Wayzgooze pig."

A type setter, who had earlier made penance for his joke about the undertaker's daughter, lifted the clay pig and shook it. Daniel walked over, pulled a tuppence from his coin purse, and dropped it in.

Spittle flew from the spike of Christopher's tongue as he continued to hurl his imprecations. He waved his blackthorn vaguely around Gourlay's head and shoulders.

Daniel inserted another tuppence into the terracotta.

"This," Gourlay said to Jeremy, well pleased, "is tinker's eloquence."

"Mr. Hagerman," Jeremy said. "I understand the delicacy of your situation. But I don't think you can threaten the freedom of the press in this manner. It's as Mr. Gourlay says, he merely passes on the report so that your brother has an opportunity to easily refute it."

"I'd expected more of you," Hagerman said. "Given the favour you've been shown."

Daniel put his hat on a table and tucked his blackthorn under his arm. He took a deep breath. He folded one hand in the other and bent lightly at the waist.

"Mr. Gourlay," he said, his tone conversational now, "let me entreat you, in mildness, to withdraw your publication."

"Sir," Gourlay said, "since you entreat me in mildness, I shall make you this offer – insert in this day's newspaper an apology for your letter to me, which appeared in the last Gazette, and, the article that you complain of shall be instantly withdrawn."

"Great God's bollocks!" Christopher cried.

"Penny in the pig!"

Christopher hammered his cane against the old pine boards of the press shop floor and the chapel reverberated like the inside of a drum. He brought the cane back up to his left shoulder and sawed it back and forth.

"I'd rather cut off my own arm," he cried before spewing another flood of toxic language. He filled the chapel with phrases like whore-pipe whistler, mimping bum-fiddler, and puckled crowdy swiller, many of which Jeremy had never heard before.

Daniel had an entire shilling in the terracotta before Miles opened his mouth.

"Get out," the printer said evenly, meeting Christopher's glare.

Christopher held his gaze. None moved. Christopher glanced first at Jeremy. Then Scriven. Finally, Daniel. For a moment, it looked like the brothers Hagerman might topple the type cases. Daniel closed his purse. He crossed the chapel floor, took his brother by the shoulder, and steered him toward the door. On the way out, their walking sticks rattled against table legs and cabinet corners.

"Mr. Printer, I expect an invitation to Wayzgooze with the funds I've helped raise," Gourlay said, a moment after the doors had closed. He pushed a single page across the surface of Miles' table until it covered the line gauge.

"My letter. I've never met a pair of blackguards more deserving."

He tamped the letter down with a forefinger as though he was driving a stake through it.

"Humble their pride with truth."

Gourlay hummed A Man's a Man For A' That as he stepped through the chapel doors.

Scriven motioned to Jeremy that they should follow. Miles called them back.

"Creedence!"

They stopped at the threshold. They looked back at the printer and his glowing, bespectacled face.

"He that saith he is in the light, and hateth his brother, is in darkness even until now."

"Yes," Scriven said, "I suppose. But still. Light will be shed. And papers sold."

Chapter Thirty-Five

A knock at the door avoided the need to explain to Alice, for a fifth time, Amelia's wedding to Rupert Spafford and all the events surrounding it, before and after. At the threshold, a trotter handed Jeremy a letter. It bore the Schoolmaster's seal. News of a promotion? Inside, Jeremy used a paper knife to open its sealed envelope.

> My dear Mr. Castor
> It has been brought to my attention that you have had dealings with a Mr. Robert Gourlay of Fifeshire.

"What is it, Jeremy?"

> I want you to understand that he has done a good deal of mischief in the province by his seditious publications exciting discontent amongst the people. I, of course, saw through him at once. I opposed him with my usual vigour and, as I'm sure you're aware, the press has groaned with his abuse of me.

"Who was at the door?"

> Don't be fooled. A character like Mr Gourlay in a quiet colony like this where there has been little or no spirit of inquiry and very little knowledge can do much harm and, notwithstanding the check he has received, he has already done great mischief.

"Was it the foot post?"

> All my pupils, including you Mr. Castor, are now leading characters in many parts of the Province. They have opposed him sternly — as I expect you will, as well.
> I am, as ever, your humble Servant in the Cause of Education

"Did you get a letter from Willowpath?"

"Alice."

"Did the widow Spafford invite you back?"

"Alice!"

"Where were you just now?"

"I had to help my friend with a few things."

"I'm not sure I like this Dr. Scriven."

"He's a decent man. He means well."

"I'm not sure I trust him."

"I also picked up the latest Gazette."

"Pah! The man who reads nothing at all is better educated than the man who reads nothing but newspapers. I read that somewhere."

Alice pulled the cracked glasses from her face. Jeremy held her hand. He guided it to the fluted edge of the small fish and potato pie he'd brought her.

"Most likely you read it in a newspaper."

He took the lit, half-burned candle from the sill and brought it to a side table next to the chair with the torn red velvet. He took the Gazette out from under his arm, sat, crossed his leg, and unfolded it.

He was unsettled by the letter from Schoolmaster. But also offended. He hadn't pledged allegiance to him or his project. He hadn't agreed to do whatever he commanded, whenever he commanded it. Besides, much of what Gourlay had to say made sense to him, especially in his penurious position. He would abide by his own conscience, come what may.

"Did you take the candle?"

"I'd like to read."

"Newspaper?"

"Yes."

"Why do you want to stupefy yourself?"

"It keeps me up to date."

"Those poor children. Their beloved teacher: paper-addled."

Jeremy scanned the first page house to let notices, dreaming of one-day living in a two-story, multi-roomed residence, with a study for quiet reading, maximally distant from the room where Alice would sit, knitting.

"I wasn't finished with the candle."

"But Alice, you can't see."

"Yes," she replied, her voice rich with umbrage, "Jeremy, but I can feel."

"Anyway, I'm not sure it's wise for you to light a candle next to the curtains, without being able to see what you're doing."

"I can sense it."

"Plus, they're dear."

"You burn them happily enough."

"I'm reading. Eat your pie before it gets cold."

Alice bit into one end of the pie and began to chew, murmuring noises of pleasure as she did. Jeremy began to read.

He read through Robert Gourlay's latest letter in which he relayed what he knew about the capture and hanging of the third Hagerman. He shuddered to learn of Henry Corl running off with the wife of Charles Witherey after "cruelly beating his aged mother" and hoped he would be brought to justice. He pitied poor Mr. McDallogh, whose wife Bridget had run away, again, this time to take up with Tim Ghigon, the lame fiddler that was put in the stocks last Easter for stealing Barney Doody's game cock.

And then this:

TAKE NOTICE

The subscriber respectfully informs the general Kingston public that an infant, weeks old, was left in a wicker bassinet on the front step of Stoke Cottage early Wednesday morning. Mrs. Lenore Stokes, lately returned from New Haven, Connecticut, has sheltered and fed the newborn these past two days and nights. It remains with her and is otherwise healthy. Mrs. Stokes has hired a wet nurse for the baby's welfare. She urges the misguided parents to contact her without delay. As soon as rightful parentage can be proved before a magistrate, said infant will be returned forthwith, without charge.

Jeremy was glad, on this occasion, not to have hot coffee balanced on his lap.

Chapter Thirty-Six

The front door of Stoke Cottage opened.

"I wondered," Jeremy said, "if your mistress, Mrs. Stokes might be in?"

Abigail eyed him. She peered at the burlap sack in his fist. A baby's cry squalled from somewhere over her shoulder in an interior room.

"She is."

"I'm Mr. Castor, the new abecedarian."

"I know who you are."

"I'd like to speak to her if I could."

Abigail remained motionless.

"With regard to the Lancasterian school. I have something for her. Something school-related."

Lenore's voice came from inside. The baby's crying abated.

"The teacher bloke ma'am," Abigail shouted over her shoulder, "the one I told you came by while you were away."

"Jeremy?"

Lenore was now at the threshold, over Abby's shoulder. It had been months since Jeremy had seen her last. Her eyes were slightly puffy and red but, when they caught the light, they retained their coppery twinkle. The Apollo's knots that framed her wan face were slackened, but they held traces of their former spring. Jeremy was relieved to see that, unlike their last meeting, she seemed pleased to see him.

"Mrs. Stokes," Jeremy bowed his head slightly. "I've brought something for the baby."

Jeremy lifted the sack.

"A small gift."

"How thoughtful, Mr. Castor," Lenore said, over Abigail's shoulder. "Not so small from the looks of it."

"It's a trifle."

"Do come in," she said, "Abigail, let him in. Come and say hello."

Abigail stepped to one side and Jeremy entered. Lenore led him to the parlour and gestured to an armchair. Jeremy sat on the edge of the armchair, burlap on his knee.

"Mrs. Langley is just feeding baby. She gets so fussy if mealtime is just a little late."

Jeremy nodded.

"Some tea, Mr. Castor? Abigail made a pot not long ago."

"Lovely."

Lenore stepped into the kitchen, poured a cup and added a drop of milk, exactly as he took it. She lowered the cup and saucer to him. A hint of jasmine evanesced from the pale blue of her inner wrist. Jeremy took the saucer in the mitt of his left hand and steadied the jittery cup. He followed her bare arm up to her shoulder and finally her curl-fringed face. On the cooking stove, a spoon clanged against a saucepan.

Lenore took a seat in the armchair opposite Jeremy, re-arranging the silk of her gown over the bare calf and foot of her crossed leg.

"Now, what have you brought us?"

Jeremy clattered his saucer to the side table and a measure of tea crested the lip of the cup. He began to open the neck of the burlap sack.

"Perhaps," she said, "we should wait for baby?"

"Yes, of course."

In the kitchen, Abigail quartered a capon with a cleaver.

"Do you know her name?"

"I don't," Lenore replied, in a tone that seemed to suggest she was happy with the fact. "She arrived on my doorstep with only the bassinet and the piece of linen she was swaddled in. I'm not sure she has a name. For now, we call her 'baby'."

"No-one has come forward?"

Lenore shook her head.

"What will you do?"

"I'm not certain. She's a cherub. For now, it is enough that she is safe and happy. We must give it time. For all we know, the mother may be alone and in desperate straits, afraid to take responsibility."

Jeremy nodded thoughtfully.

"You are doing well?" he asked. "Your sojourn was salutary?"

"Most! There is something about the ocean, isn't there? Those regenerative breezes. Coming in off the surf, pregnant with that distinctive, seaside scent. The meditative nature of the waves, the immensity of the tides, so regular, so eternal. Very meditative, very life-giving. I am reborn."

"I'm very glad to hear it." Jeremy looked at Lenore meaningfully. "I know Dr. Scriven was concerned for you."

"Dear Creedence. He and his assistant gave me a full checkup and pronounced me healthy as hollyhocks."

"He's grateful to have you back in town. He missed you immensely."

"And I missed him."

Abigail struck a lid against a stockpot so that it chimed like a cymbal.

"But what of your news?" Lenore cried, clapping her hands together. "How fares our little academy?"

Jeremy told her about the incomprehensible Mr. Hamilton and, to her delight, described some of his many outbursts throughout the term. Her expression turned serious when he told her about Sweeney, caged and suspended from the ceiling.

"There is such a thing as too much discipline," she said with feeling. "I fear Mr. Hamilton may drift into the realm of abuse. You needn't be a devotee of Rousseau to reject the view that children are born beastly. Don't you agree?"

Jeremy nodded his agreement, but inwardly he reckoned there might be one or two exceptions.

"It's time," Lenore continued, "we pass up such Puritanical notions, along with witch burnings and bans on the theatre. I must bring this up at committee."

Jeremy went on to tell her about Beatrice McCann's squirrel and Georgia Walsh's arson, and how grateful he was to his first lieutenant, Placidia Sykes, who kept the ship fighting trim and in good order. He told her about James O'Neal's sister and how she'd learned to write and that he was sure she wasn't mute, though he'd yet to coax a word from her. At the Lancasterian School they were making progress.

In the kitchen, a kettle had been whistling upwards of a minute. Lenore frowned in that general direction but relaxed when finally, it was removed from the heat.

Lenore showed interest in the school news and told Jeremy eagerly about the baby left on her step. It was a significant improvement from how she'd behaved at the committee meeting when she showed every sign of denying his existence. Now, at least, she met his gaze, returned a smile, and conversed easily. Still, Jeremy longed for the immediacy they had shared through that one bronzed, autumn week, when it seemed no space remained between them, when they had, in a very real sense, merged. The polite way they conversed now over sips of tea, the formality of their speech, the 'Mr. Castors', the 'Mrs. Stokes'; it was a mild form of torture. He hoped that the chill was due mostly to Abigail's presence in the adjacent room, performing her one-woman culinary fife and drum.

Mrs. Langley emerged from the bedroom with a bundle in the crook of her elbow.

"All done, ma'am. Fed and belched."

"Wonderful! I'd like to show baby to Mr. Castor."

Mrs. Langley crossed the room to Lenore.

"Perhaps," Lenore said to Jeremy, "you would like to hold her?"

"Oh. Ah. Hmm."

Jeremy shifted in his seat and clutched his knees.

"Don't be silly, she's not a porcupine. It's very simple."

Lenore motioned to Mrs. Langley to take the bundle to Jeremy.

"To the gentleman?" the woman asked, doubtfully. "Is it wise, ma'am?"

"Yes, it's fine, just for a moment."

"All right then," Jeremy said, seeing it was of some importance. "A moment or two shan't hurt, perhaps."

"Hold your arms like this," Lenore said, miming, "like a cradle."

He followed her actions, turning his forearm inward at an angle against his chest.

"That's it," she said. "Now support her head with your free hand as Mrs. Langley instructs."

Baby nestled into the nook formed between Jeremy's great arm and his chest. He took care to cushion her head. She burbled. A faint thermal rose from the whorl of hair at the top of her head. He breathed in a scent of milk and newness. A tiny pink hand emerged from the folds of linen. It gripped his shirt.

"Instant rapport!" Lenore said. "You hold her a while. She's taken to you."

Jeremy smiled, looking down at baby, not wanting to disturb her with his voice.

"Shall we see what you've brought?"

Jeremy nodded. Lenore retrieved the sack at his feet and brought it back to her chair. She thrust her hand into it. It felt of wool.

"More yarn? I thought you'd given up trying to teach me, hopeless student as I am. Is it a do-it-yourself?"

She pulled the mass of wool free of the burlap sack and placed it on her lap. She flipped it over and she gasped. A huge doll stared back at her; a hundred different shades and textures with a pair of bright, brass button eyes. A thatch of silk remnants flopped from the top of its head. Its face was fixed with a permanent, white linen smile.

"Poly!" she cried.

"For her," Jeremy whispered over the head of baby.

Lenore ran her fingers through the silk. She traced the frozen smile with a thumb. She squeezed the chaff-filled body. She sat motionless a long while. The tympani coming from the kitchen tapered to nothing. It became silent within the cottage.

"How is it possible? Where could you have found her?"

"She may not fully match the original," he breathed. "She was irreplaceable, I imagine. I hope she comes close, and perhaps, in time, you'll love her just as well."

"You made her?"

"Yes."

"But how..."

"From your description."

Lenore stared at the doll. She found it difficult to make sense of what her dampened eyes beheld. An apparition. A dear friend from another lifetime. She'd been so sure she would never see Poly again.

"Mrs. Langley," Lenore said finally, "you may go for now. Please return in three hours for her next feeding."

"Ma'am."

Mrs. Langley retrieved her personal effects and left the cottage.

"Abigail, you may also take the rest of the afternoon and evening off. I won't need you again until tomorrow afternoon."

"But Ma'am, what of supper? I've just started a stew."

"I'll manage. Thank you."

Abigail gave a half bow. She removed her apron and straightened her hair. She retrieved her spencer jacket, gloves, and reticule. She stopped at the threshold and looked back at them.

"It's fine," Lenore said again. "Come here a moment."

Abby crossed the room to her, staring at the strange woolen doll. Lenore plucked a shilling from her own reticule and held it out between two fingers.

"For you."

Abby extended her hand, palm facing up. Lenore closed the woman's fingers around the coin and put her own hands around them.

"That will be all for today Abby. Thank you. For everything."

"Ma'am."

Abigail exited the cottage, latching the door behind her as she went.

Lenore listened to the footsteps fade from the porch and the flagstones.

She gazed at Jeremy. He had his head turned, looking down at baby. He touched the tip of his nose to the top of her talc-soft head. Lenore marveled at the serene child, only minutes earlier hungry and cross, so at ease now, so naturally snug within the expanse of Jeremy's chest. A point of light and warmth seemed to concentrate somewhere within the core of her being and expand, radiating outward.

"She's sleeping," he whispered.

With a catch of her breath, Lenore realized she'd never experienced such a moment of immaculate happiness. She rose from her chair, cradling the patchwork doll in her arms. She crossed to Jeremy and stood next to him. Heat from her hip, less than an inch away, warmed his shoulder. She cupped his cheek with her palm.

"I'd made her for you," Jeremy said.

Chapter Thirty-Seven

Jeremy found James O'Neal's sister at the front step.
She had a bird's nest of yarn in her outstretched hand
and, as usual, a strip of damp linen trailing from her
mouth.

He stared at her a moment. The light of the early
summer sun caught the puzzle of her hair and saturated
its blond filaments. It accentuated the delicate features
of her serious face, beneath its streaks of grime.
Outside of the classroom, standing like a figurine in the
refuse of the street, she suggested something precious,
something vulnerable.

James O'Neal's sister shook the bundle of yarn.

"Thank you," Jeremy said, receiving it.

She took the linen from her mouth.

"You're welcome," she said, the first words he'd ever
heard her speak. She replaced the shred and turned. He
watched, amazed, as she bolted down the street.

You could have waited until Monday, he thought.

He returned to the room, put the wool on the table
and spread it out to see what he'd got. A square of
folded paper, no larger than a sixpence, fell to the floor.

"Who was that?"

"Wool."

324

Jeremy retrieved the paper square and unfurled its five folds. Printed in tiny, childish letters, it read:

C. H-man say to master:
I'll kill Gorlay
Today
JO

"Wool? What do you mean wool? Delivered to our door?"

"I need to step out."

"Are you trying to be clever?"

Jeremy crossed the room and kissed his mother on the top of her head.

"Back soon."

∂ ∂ ∂ ∂ ∂

Jeremy and Scriven intercepted Gourlay on his way out of Walker's.

"Castor, Scriven," Gourlay said. "Excellent timing. We all could use a chuckle, I warrant. This Who Wants a Guinea sounds like just the thing."

The Montreal forwarder and the Albany bookseller followed close behind, eagerly discussing the review they'd just read in the Niagara Spectator.

"Mr. Gourlay," Jeremy said in a low tone, "it may be wise for you to remain at Walker's."

Gourlay wheeled on him. His breath, along with its usual fetor, carried smoked herring.

"I think you may be in some danger," Jeremy said. "I think the Hagermans mean to attack you."

"Ha! What information do you have?"

"I received a note today from a student at my school. He'd seen us all at the Gazette the other day. I believe he must have overheard something. "

Gourlay laughed again.

"My dear boy. If I stayed inside at the mention of every rumour and every vague warning, I'd long ago have sprouted an umbrella cap."

Gourlay had already dragged them a block and a half from Walker's.

"Robert," Scriven said, "in this situation discretion might be more appropriate than your usual Scottish valour. More Falstaff, less MacBeth."

"Friends," Gourlay said, "I've been hanged and burned at Cornwall. At Johnstown, I was assaulted by Duncan Fraser, justice of the peace, and protected by those good yeomen that demand the truth. I was put up at the Brockville jail for my limited part in that affair and out again on bail. I've been arrested for seditious behaviour right here in Kingston. Immediately released. I trust to the laws of the land for protection and..."

Christopher Hagerman attacked from behind. The torrent of obscenities and oaths that poured from his mouth as he struck Gourlay with the loaded handle of a horse whip surpassed anything heard in that part of Kingston, before or after. The leather cylinder of the whip handle, packed with lead, clumped Gourlay just above the ear. He lost his balance and nearly fell into the mud. Hagerman continued, without pause, a shouted soliloquy on a theme of perfidy, dishonour and death, as he coiled the lash and tightened his grip. Jeremy and Scriven and the men that had arrived with

Hagerman were joined by onlookers from the street, the curious drawn from their sitting rooms, happy for the distraction in an otherwise dull Saturday afternoon. Hagerman swung the whip handle like he was a blacksmith with a hammer.

Daniel and other associates pulled him away.

"So this is Kingston!" Gourlay cried, regaining his balance. "Not even in the darkest street of London, in meanest Spitalfields, would a blackguard ambush an unarmed man and no bystanders intervene."

Hagerman broke free of his fellows and continued his harangue. Gourlay deflected with raised arms. He managed to catch the larger man by the wrist. They grappled. Hagerman, claret-coloured and frothing, pulled free.

"You would not dare," Gourlay said, "if I was so armed."

"Give him a whip," Hagerman cried.

A postilion drawn by the commotion from his nearby stables stepped forward and handed Gourlay a whip.

"Gentlemen," Scriven said, "this is no way to settle a dispute."

Hagerman jumped, grabbed the lash end of Gourlay's whip, and yanked. He jerked the smaller man around as though he was a marionette. He brought his whip handle down on Gourlay's neck and back. Gourlay staggered. He retreated five steps. Then he swung the heavy end of his own whip at Hagerman and it caught the surprised taller man across the nose.

A magistrate, watching from his front porch, chose that moment to step in.

"That's enough," he said, grabbing Gourlay by the arm. "You will keep the peace."

"Sir," Jeremy cried, "it wasn't him who caused the disturbance."

"Mr. Hagerman is the aggressor, magistrate," Scriven said. "'Twas an unprovoked assault. Mr. Gourlay merely tried to defend himself."

"I know what it was," the magistate said. "I witnessed it all. We'll have peace and good order in my neighbourhood. If he would like to make a deposition, Mr. Gourlay can do so."

Gourlay thought a moment. He shook his head.

"Then, disperse."

The crowd began slowly to recede, buzzing and murmuring. The Hagermans and their supporters collected out front of the magistrate's house. Gourlay, Jeremy, Scriven, the forwarder, and the bookseller found themselves clumped across the street. Christopher Hagerman, dabbed blood from the bottom of a nostril with his handkerchief. He pointed the bloody end at Jeremy and Scriven.

"You've chosen your side," he said, "and poorly."

Jeremy fetched Gourlay's battered top hat from the middle of the street and handed it to him. Gourlay placed it on his head and gave it a quarter turn left, then right, trying unsuccessfully to avoid putting pressure on the rising welts.

"Who Wants a Guinea," he said through clenched teeth. He continued walking in the direction of the theatre, listing to the left. The others followed and none looked back.

Chapter Thirty-Eight
August, 1818

Spafford unlatched the door abruptly. He burst in and snorted.

"I'd hoped," he said, "to find you just stepping from your bath, dewy and dripping."

Amelia, fully clothed and sitting at her desk, looked up from the ledger she studied. Spafford stood just inside the doorway with his back against the jamb. In one hand, he cradled a snifter half-full of applejack. He wore only the late colonel's tatty slippers and the stretched, silk robe hanging loose at his burgeoning waist. Amelia turned her attention snappishly back to the ledger.

"It's just past lunch," she said, without looking up.

"Yes, but surely even you require respite, occasionally."

"From what?"

"Your labours."

"Unlike some," she said, "I have no aversion to employment."

"Woman isn't meant for this. God designed her for another purpose entirely. It's unseemly. And I hope the lodge brothers never learn of it."

Having elicited no reaction, Spafford strolled to the desk. He stood very close, looking idly over Amelia's shoulder. Heat came from under his silk robe, bringing with it traces of ambergris. He raised the snifter and smacked his tongue against its lip, sucking from it. She leant in the other direction.

"How can you mash numbers in this heat," he asked, his enunciation flabby. "So dull!"

"I have my duties, to the staff, to the customers, to the glass factory."

"Wife," he cried, "what of your duty to me?"

"Rupert," she said, shifting further left, her voice rich with sufferance, "I've explained. I've not been well. Pernicious vapours."

"Yes," he said, moving to the window. "But when? When will I share your bed, our bed, again?"

"When I am well."

"You are well enough to jot figures. Surely you are well enough..."

"It's the middle of the day."

"I'm bored!"

Spafford stared past the glassworks and into the woods. He spied the tool shed in which they had sheltered from the rain a year earlier. He looked back at Amelia. She took no notice. He slapped his fingers against the windowsill.

"It is so atrociously tedious up here in this wilderness," he continued. "I had no idea. And, I had no idea that even in the thickest of summer heat, a wife could be so cold."

"I'm sorry that you are so deeply unhappy. Perhaps

you should have examined more carefully the purgatory for which you were volunteering."

"Don't make a pretence of hurt feelings now. I know you have none."

"Rupert?"

Spafford took another noisy sip.

"Yes."

"These remittances here. To Thomson's and Bartlett's. Do you know anything about these?"

"Thomson's?"

"Yes, for silk gloves and a new beaver felt hat."

"A man must dress," Spafford shouted. "I can't waltz naked into St. George's or the officer's mess and say, 'can I talk to you about glass?' I must have accoutrements. Costs money."

"Yes, but it shouldn't be taken out of the glasswork's accounts. And, what of these bills from Walker's, The Black Bull, and Ferguson's?"

"I have to eat! I have to entertain my prospective clients."

"Do you have no income of your own? What of the annuity you spoke of?"

"Yes, yes," Spafford said, now tying his robe at his waist. "Of course."

"You can't draw on the glasswork's accounts, the money is required to pay the staff and our suppliers. What of those five guineas I granted you for monthly expenses."

Spafford drained the rest of his brandy.

"Gone," he said, crossing his arms.

"Already?"

"'Twas a devilish whist game at the Ancient Number

Three. I was ahead by a pound until the last deal. I had the glassworks in mind."

"I will instruct Mr. Thomson at the Upper Canada Bank to suspend withdrawals for the time being."

"You won't," Spafford said, heading for the door.

"Rupert."

He stopped at the threshold.

"The will. You promised you would have it delivered from Montreal so we can have Calhoun draw up a new one, merging our interests."

He turned on his tattered heel and advanced on the stairs.

"Where are you going?" she called after him. "You promised."

"Town."

"Perhaps you could talk to some of those lodge brothers of yours," she said, from the top of the stairs. "Bartlett, Thomson, and the rest, to see if they will allow local glass into town, over the English imports. Get our ad placed in the Gazette."

Spafford waved his hand, without looking back. He entered his dressing room, the Colonel's old room, and slammed the door. He opened the strongbox with the key hidden beneath the loose stone of the mantle in the great room, took ten guineas from the smaller strongbox hidden within, and put them in his purse. He stuffed the advertisement into his pocket. After filling a wineskin with applejack, he strode out the front door. He waved off the postilion when he approached. Spafford would walk. He had steam to release. A room at Walker's. Maybe a visit to the Bottle and Glass, for dinner, refreshment, a little entertainment. Or, maybe, Mother

Cook's. He quickened his step, the bulging wineskin in his fist, cicadas moaning low into his ear.

"Such haste!"

Spafford looked up to see a man in the middle of the track, waving. The traveler wore a square, ill-fitting tunic laced up at the front, tattered breeches, and boots so worn they resembled sandals.

"Carmichael Jones! Ploughman."

Carmichael pointed to his wineskin.

"Water?"

Spafford ignored him and kept walking.

"Too diabolical hot to be rushing anywhere," the man said, strolling up. "You'd best take your time. Ah, isn't water, is it?"

Spafford didn't disabuse him.

"Capital," the man said. "Headed to town? I'll go with."

Carmichael walked alongside Spafford, eying the bulging skin, listening to its sloshing.

"What are you after? Drink? Wagering? Well stuffed petticoat?"

"A little of each," Spafford said, easing his pace.

"I'm of the same mind! I know a place. Headed there now. I've got inside information on a Tartar. He's pipped."

"That so?"

"'Tis. Perhaps you might slow a little and share your bounty. We could drink a toast. I'd be happy to share my information in exchange for a slug or two."

Spafford passed the skin.

Carmichael told him all there was to tell about a Tartar game cock called Castigator.

Chapter Thirty-Nine

Abby skipped toward the alcove where Tim Ghigon had got out his fiddle.

Carmichael hooked her around the waist. He sat her on his lap.

"Buy us a drink," he said, gripping her thigh.

"Go on Carm." She pushed half-heartedly against his chest. "Haven't you had enough?"

"Just started."

"You buy for a change."

"A cruel request. You know how pinched old Carmichael is."

She fenced his hand as it made for her hip.

"Pinchy, I'll grant."

Carmichael wrapped both of his arms around her and clasped his hands, trapping her.

"What have you done with my jolly romper?" he cried. "The generous one."

"She wants to dance. Anyway, it's customary for a gentleman to sponsor a lady."

"Hardly applies to us then."

She cuffed his cheek.

"One round," he said. "Next time - I buy."

"That's what you said last time. And five times before."

Carmichael released his embrace and spread his arms out before her.

"Merciful Abigail, my pocket is as empty as the sepulcher at Easter."

"Blasphemer," Abigail cried and thumped his chest with mock horror. She made to get up and make for the corner of the room where the lame fiddler had started up a rendition of Oyster Nan. Carmichael hauled her back.

"Save your pious horror. A true Christian shares her bounty with those less fortunate."

"It's summer Carm! Why don't you earn balsam the honest way? Why don't you plough?"

"Ploughing," Carmichael said, sliding his hand down and under, "is uppermost on my mind."

She gripped his thumb and a finger in her calloused hands, and she wrenched them upward.

"You must have some work."

"I'm between appointments. Skint as a beggar without a hat."

"What do you do with yourself all day?"

"Ploughing's onerous. 'Twill break poor old Carmichael. Is that what you want?"

When she failed to reply, he squeezed her until she shook her head.

"And you, handmaiden to Lady Stokes. Paid a dapper packet to make tea and plump pillows."

She cuffed him again. He rubbed his reddened cheek.

"A whole hour 'til they beak. Let us elope again to Stoke Cottage. Let's sample us some more of that fine

Amontillado maintained by your mistress and re-evaluate her goose down mattress. We could be back here in time for round one."

"On pain of death, I would not marry you."

"Poor word choice, elope. Let's abscond."

"That era is behind us, Carmichael Jones."

"'Twas a masterful job I done, topping those open bottles with water and turpentine. She'll not notice. And you are a sorceress of the laundry. I know you'll be able to remove that stain from..."

"She's returned."

Abby pried away Carmichael's rising, interlocked fingers and pushed them down, back toward the edge of her hip.

"Damn her eyes! These nobs. To-ing and fro-ing from their estates whenever they please. Not caring a dowser's rod for their underlings."

"Don't say such things. She's a good missus."

"Did she discover the missing sherry?"

"I don't think we have to worry about that. She doesn't touch the stuff now."

"Then it's going to waste."

"She's changed. Not the same missus. I'm not sure what it is. Happier, for a start."

"All that lovely Amontillado, mouldering."

"And then the baby arrived. So many visitors. The wet nurse. The doctor and his assistant, making a house call. That never happens. Missus prefers going out."

"How long does sherry last in the bottle?"

"Here's the strange thing: the doctor didn't examine her. It was the nurse. She spent all the time in the bedroom with missus and the baby. Lilac, I think he called her. I had to keep the doctor entertained, make the tea, and the conversation. He's a rare, pretty bird, that doctor."

"Maybe you could smuggle a bottle out."

"And that bloke that keeps coming around. Ruddy giant. She was so insistent he hold the bairn, even though he wasn't interested and doesn't know a baby from a button. I half expected baby to slip through those big, clumsy hands. Still, she seemed to take to him naturally. Like gosling to gander, truth told."

Carmichael stopped his groping. He faced Abigail.

"What did you say the nurse's name was?"

"It was amusing; the baby has the same colour hair that stands up from its crown in just the same way as this big fellow."

"Giant? What's his name?"

"And the expression on the missus' face. Glowing. I've never seen her look at her own husband that way."

"What are you saying?"

"Oh."

"Is it a Mr. Castor?"

"Oh dear."

"Are you suggesting..."

"Carmichael Jones! I don't want to cause my missus any trouble. She's good to me."

Carmichael began to run his hands up and down Abigail's sides, squeezing and pinching.

"Mr. Jeremy Castor?"

"Stop! Yes!"

"That great Cornish blight. And the doctor?"

"Scriven. Stop! Dr. Scriven!"

Abigail writhed and roiled on the ploughman's lap, thumping his chest, trying to evade the roving hands.

"And the nurse?"

As Abigail twisted, she lost her balance and put her hand down on Carmichael's upper thigh, directly on his pocket. She felt a trio of coins chink beneath her calloused grip.

"Carmichael Jones! What poverty is this?"

"Name the nurse."

"You said you was skint."

"'Tis my fighting stake."

Abigail stared in disbelief.

"I've inside information on McWhorter's entry, the Tartar called Castigator," he continued. "Been snotting and sneezing for weeks. He's a pigeon."

Abigail's brows furrowed further.

"It isn't drinking money! Of that I have none."

Abigail twisted from his lap and headed for the direction of the fiddle music. He caught her by the wrist and wrenched it up to her shoulder blade. He put his other hand on her rib, beneath her breast, and pulled her hard towards him, forcing the air from her lungs. His whiskery, rum-smelling mouth was hot on her ear.

"Ain't funny now," she said, her voice rising. "Hurts."

"The nurse."

Carmichael racheted her arm further.

"Miss Evans, I think he called her. Lilac."

She whimpered.

"That's what I thought you said. The doxy!"

"Why does it matter?"

"Some might like to know."

"I don't want to make trouble for missus."

Carmichael released her arm and spun her toward the corner of the room where the lame fiddler had started up The Hounds Are All Out.

"Dance," he said.

ॐ ॐ ॐ ॐ ॐ

"If you please," Carmichael said as he levered his elbow into Christopher Hagerman. "Ah, Mr. Hagerman, isn't it?"

Christopher Hagerman frowned.

"Carmichael, Carmichael Jones. I like the looks of this one."

Hagerman turned back to the pit.

"Are you laying odds?" Carmichael asked. "Is the Hagerman a wager man?"

Rupert Spafford, his new travelling companion, nudged past Owen Stevens, to his left.

"Rupert Spafford," Carmichael said, by way of introduction. "Inheritor of Willowpath. And the young widow."

"That bigger cock called Nemesis, the Strychnine," Carmichael shouted at Hagerman, laughing, "it looks like you on Store Street the other day Christopher. May I call you Christopher? Look how much bigger he is? If I'm not mistaken, he just hollered: you puckled crowdy swiller."

In the pit, the Strychnine swept his cowl, inflated his chest, and bellowed.

"Chris," Daniel said. "It's true. See! His walk. His squawk! A real cuss. Like you!"

In the other corner, the Tatar puffed the ridge of his white hackles into a continuous arc like it was a shield. He paced low, back and forth in front of his setter, swiveling his black, sloe eyes, muttering an incessant stream of grumbles and peeps, as though berating himself for his predicament.

"And the Tartar resembles Gourlay," Daniel cried, delighted. "Look how he slinks!"

"A shuffler," Carmichael added, pleased at the reaction his observation had made.

"How he rants!"

"Nemesis must have five ounces on him."

"Hardly a fair fight."

"He'll reduce Castigator to tar and feathers."

"Just as you did Gourlay, Chris."

Biscuit and his assistant came around with their purse and slate. Carmichael fished the remaining groats from his pocket.

"On Nemesis," he cried, "Can't lose!"

"Chris," Daniel said, "You have to bet on Nemesis. "

"You must sir," Spafford said, incredulous that a punter would forgo a bet. "Your feathered kin."

Christopher said nothing.

"Gentlemen," Biscuit said. "Last chance for initial wagers."

Daniel put a shilling down on the railing for Nemesis.

"Setters. Set!"

The Strychnine flew at the shuffling Tartar.

Castigator narrowly missed puncture and countered by jabbing his beak into his opponent's breast. Nemesis wheeled and buffeted Castigator, rolling him on his back. The Tartar struggled to his feet and began a retreat, parrying every blow, muttering its strange dialect through every desperate yard, audible even over the frantic shouting of the men.

Already the Tartar appeared to be limping. Was the left leg broken where the scales had been pared and the white bone showed? The Strychnine had a bare patch above his hackle. A flash of crimson beaded his breast, matching the vermilion of his cowl. Otherwise, unscathed.

Castigator hobbled to his corner. Still he chirped.

"One, two, three..." Biscuit began to count.

The men groaned. No denouement. The men chastised the birds, goaded them.

"...eighteen, nineteen, twenty."

Grumbling faded to a low murmur.

Rupert Spafford stood on the other side of Owen Stevens. He lay a silk glove on the railing.

"A side bet," he shouted at Hagerman, leaning over the railing and around Stevens. "Ten crowns to one Gourlay, the Tartar, wins. You must bet on your bird, Nemesis."

"The Tartar is on the run," Daniel said. "The wing is mangled."

"He can hardly see. Look at those feathers over his eyes."

"Spafford's so sodden he doesn't know a cock from a cackler." Carmichael felt around in his pocket hoping a coin might magically materialize. "Easiest crown one could make."

Hagerman put down a guinea. The punters cheered. "Setters re-set."

The setters took their birds and again fed them port-soaked grain. They brought them beak to beak. Reinvigorated, they recommenced pecking. With a spray of feathers, the Strychnine charged straight at the lame bird, knocking him from his feet. He drove his razor beak at the Tartar's neck and face. The Tartar parried and rolled on to his back. With a kick, he launched the Strychnine backwards. Unable to get to his feet because of his broken wing, Castigator rolled further on to his back, to his pure white hackles. Still he nattered. Still he castigated.

Nemesis hopped, spread his vermilion cowl, and soared high above Castigator, enveloping the smaller bird in shadow. A collective intake of breath signaled unanimous anticipation of a death blow. Nemesis descended. Castigator exploded from his crunch, slipping past the onrushing blue stockinged legs. He kicked upward. The needle point of his spur tore through the membrane of the Strychnine's left eye. His upward thrust combined with the downward momentum of Nemesis caused the gaffle to sink into the eye socket up to the ankle bone, puncturing the brain. Nemesis fell, instantly dead.

Silence. The pit erupted again. Punters directly around Spafford shook his hand and slapped his back, congratulating his audacity. Those around Hagerman avoided meeting his dimming eye.

"I'm very glad I couldn't cover it, Christopher," Carmichael said, by way of consolation, "I would have taken that bet in an eighth note."

Castigator, in the middle of the pit, continued his chuntering, trying unsuccessfully to get free of his foe. The Tartar's gaffle had sunk so deep into the Strychnine's eye socket it was caught on the metal edge of the bracket encircling the ankle; bound together in death. The setter snapped Castigator's neck, salvaged both pairs of spurs, and added the birds to the bin.

Spafford shook Hagerman's hand, digging his thumb into his opposing knuckle.

"Chin up, Hagerman," he said. "Come to the bar. Refreshments on me, taken from my recent dividend."

꙰ ꙰ ꙰ ꙰ ꙰

Horatio, the retired red and black Tartar, doddered along the bar between their glasses. His brandy glass empty, he watched expectantly for port-soaked grain.

Spafford collected his winnings and ordered a double round of bittered slings. Biscuit announced the next match, a Strychnine versus a Spangler.

"Another Spangler that looks like Dr. Scriven," Carmichael said. "I heard something amusing about him this evening."

"Scriven," Stevens grumped into his sling. "Rich as a bishop. Stingy with his friend and tailor. Embargo me? The woman is a doxy! Why should I keep her on, jeopardize my business?"

"Scriven!" Spafford cried, as though it was a toast.

"Respectable family. Lord Robert. And the scandal. Disgraceful. The youngest son. Creedence."

"What do you know?" Stevens asked, sullenly. "You keep saying you will share the details. You never do."

"I will send home for the clippings."

"You said," Hagerman said to Carmichael, ignoring Spafford's drunken patter, "you'd heard something amusing."

"Something that could cause him real trouble," Carmichael said.

"Yes?"

"I've just lost my entire stake, Christopher. An anecdote this entertaining requires a measure of compensation."

Hagerman grimaced. He slid a shilling down the bar, past the chalice and Horatio's scarred toes. Carmichael sipped his sling. Hagerman slid another. Carmichael told Spafford about the upcoming match between the Rattler and a Baltimore Top-Knot, a known moper. And, after that, the Derby versus the Sergeant. They made plans that would take them to daybreak. They joined in a drunken chorus of Frisky Sue Welfleet.

Hagerman got up, retrieved his shillings, and made to leave. Carmichael grabbed him by the sleeve.

"Two shillings is a fair price," he said.

He continued his singing.

Chapter Forty
September, 1818

Alice blew steam from the top of her unsipped tea.

"What now?" she cried at the confusion of scuffles, crumpled paper, and stamped boots.

Back soon, she heard, down the hall. The front door slammed.

"I told you not to read the Gazette!" she called.

కా కా కా కా కా

Jeremy arrived at Dr. Scriven's rooms.

"Deacon," Lilac cried. "It's good to see you. I've been alone all morning."

"The doctor isn't in?"

"He left early this morning. In a proper huff too."

"Do you know where he went?"

"Gazette office again. Something set him off. Another letter, no doubt. Against Gourlay. He gets so exercised."

Jeremy looked stricken.

"What?"

He shook his head.

"Don't feel bad for Gourlay," she said. "He gives as good as he gets. A barmy game they play."

"Right Lil'."

"Do you want to stay a while? Scones? I could brew up some chicory?"

Jeremy continued backing out the door.

"All of our morning appointments were cancelled. Mrs. Abernethy sent a trotter with her regrets. Mrs. Wiggins just failed to show up."

Jeremy was now back on the street, paper tucked firmly under his arm.

"Perhaps I'll see you later?"

He nodded and continued in the direction of the offices of the Gazette. Lilac returned to polishing the scales.

❧ ❧ ❧ ❧ ❧

Jeremy walked past the cauldron of simmering linseed. He stepped over the young men lounging around the coffee pot on the front porch. He ignored their knowing smiles.

"It's an outrage Miles," Scriven cried, his voice pitched high, reverberated across the scriptorium's lofty ceiling. "A slander. How could you print it?"

Miles folded his scissor spectacles and placed them on the ledge of the angled table. He rubbed his eyes.

"You must print a retraction," Scriven said. "In the next issue."

Miles sighed. He traced the tabletop with the sharp end of a bodkin, as though carving his name.

"Is it true?"

"'Twill ruin me," Scriven said.

"It won't. We both know you've never depended on your practice. Your annuity will see you through, as always."

"What of her? You must retract."

"Is it true?"

"Ah, Castor, I'm glad you're here." Scriven took Jeremy by the arm. "Have you read it?"

Jeremy nodded. Scriven pulled him up to the table.

"Talk sense to our fair-minded editor."

"Is it true, Creedence?"

Scriven looked at Miles. He looked at Jeremy. He brought his hands to his neck and loosened the Oriental knot, a poppy seed's width.

"You could print a follow up article. Mr. Castor here could write it. An apologia."

"I don't understand why you are so quick to defend a common doxy."

"She's not!" Jeremy said. "She's a victim of circumstance."

"Not to mention a damn fine physician."

"And our friend."

Miles straightened his back. He raised his arms as though they were wings. He yawned.

Scriven drove his fist into his palm.

"What kind of a rag are you printing?"

"I'm selling it."

Scriven and Jeremy watched as Miles climbed down from the high stool. He collated a stack of misprinted paper, carried it across the room, and placed it on another shelf.

"What do you mean?"

"Done. You in here every second day, haranguing me about this or that. Hugh Thomson and the lost boys out front. The Hagermans. Macaulay and Pringle, one over each shoulder, inspecting, correcting, censoring every word. Daily brimstone from the Rector of York. And your friend, the unblinking bedlamite, Robert Gourlay. Have you read what he has written about me? In the Spectator, the Herald, the Mail? Every day a new letter. Every day a fresh insult."

Miles bent at the waist.

"Look!"

With a blue-black hand, scabrous from chemical-induced eczema, he felt his scalp for three red, hairless patches. He stretched his neck and pointed behind his ear at the boil as big as a robin's egg.

"I'm twenty-nine," he cried.

"You should come by my office," Spafford said. "My nurse could take care of that."

Miles' paper-coloured face pinked.

"She's most adept. Surpassed even Dr. Alexander Duncan of Croydon."

"I haven't been outside the chapel for more than ten minutes in a month!"

"But you can't sell the Gazette. You are the Gazette."

"What will you do?" Jeremy asked.

"I hope to one day get ordained and focus on the truth of scripture. Ride the circuit. Get some sunshine."

"Do you already have a buyer?"

"Macaulay and Pringle. They're renaming it. The Chronicle."

Scriven turned and headed for the exit, pulling Jeremy behind him.

"Also," Miles called after them, "Your subscription is in arrears."

He shouted out the door.

"And Macaulay doesn't think there will be room for a fashion column in the new edition."

ૐ ૐ ૐ ૐ ૐ

Scriven and Jeremy found the Gazette on the foyer bureau, neatly folded and open to the offending article:

Public Notice!

Your correspondent begs to inform subscribers of a dreadful charade being played out in the William Street examination rooms of Dr. Creedence Scriven, late of Bournemouth. This isn't meant to be a defamation against the good doctor who, by all accounts, is said to be a loyal gentleman and a member in good standing of the Craft. However, it should be known by all his patients, current and prospective, that his female assistant, Miss Lilac Evans, is a known and convicted felon. Last year, at this time, she spent a month in jail and a half hour in the stocks, punishment for the crime of prostitution. Nor was this her first offence in such foulnesses, as has been confirmed with several local sources. God-fearing and unsullied of Kingston: beware.

Faithfully yours,

Opprobrious

Lilac sat in her bedroom; the small room off the foyer, the servant's quarters. She was putting items into the sack with which she had arrived: her sewing kit, the carefully folded periwinkle dress, her heavy scissors. A small collection of books that Scriven had given her sat in a precarious stack at the end of the bed.

"Miss Evans," Scriven said, "Where is Mrs. Abernethy?"

Lilac looked back at him and Jeremy. Her eyes, no longer hollowed and sunken as they were a year ago when she'd first arrived, were rimmed red.

"Cancelled," she said, without emotion.

"What are you doing?"

"Leaving."

"To where?"

"Returning to the shack by the glebe. My natural profession."

"You most certainly are not!"

Scriven patted the short, inner pocket of his waistcoat.

"I have the key. You shall not have it. You'll not need it as long as you are under my tutelage."

Lilac turned away.

"Besides," Scriven continued. "Who will let the blood?"

She forced her blurring gaze on the clutch of books at the foot of the bed.

"How far along are you with Dr. Buchan?"

"Noxious vapours," she sniffed.

Jeremy slipped past Scriven and stepped sideways into the small antechamber. He stood in front of Lilac.

He put his big hand gently around the neck of the half-full sack, just below her own slender, white-knuckled grip. Gradually, she released. He put the sack on the bed beside her. He extended his hand, palm up. He waited.

"Who will lance the boils?" Scriven asked, from the doorway. "None does it with such enthusiasm. Not in the entire empire, I wager."

"We haven't any patients," she said, petulant.

"They'll return," he said. "They will."

Jeremy remained, palm open. Lilac finally put her hand in his. He helped her up. He hugged her to his chest. She pressed her damp face into the warm folds of his linen shirt.

"Sorry Lil'," he said, absorbing the shuddering of her thin frame. "It isn't fair. And, Mrs. Abernethy's loss too. Let's hope for better news tomorrow."

"Yes, better news," Scriven said, over Jeremy's shoulder, "let's hope we read that Mrs. Abernethy has developed a monstrous, most inconvenient, carbuncle."

Chapter Forty-One
December, 1818

Scriven had his life's work, *Bespoke Bespeaks.* Frayed edges extended in every different direction. They resisted tying off. It needed an ending that would weave together into a majestic tapestry all the divergent threads laid out in the first and second acts; something cathartic; something unanticipated yet inevitable. He stared down blank pages. And yet, he told himself, a dramaturge cannot spend all his waking hours writing and expect his work to have any vitality. He needs diversion. He needs to live. Scriven had the Lodge, the Headstrong Club, the Lancasterian School Board Committee. He had suppers at the Bottle and Glass.

Lilac had none of these. She had Scriven's small library; a handful of tomes and compendiums on topics in medicine. She'd read them all; some twice, some thrice.

Mrs. Abernethy, Mrs. McTaggart, Mrs. Wotherspoon, Mrs. Wiggins, the other clients – none dared to visit. All declined, politely, the offer of a house call.

There were long, empty hours to fill. They were spent reading papers.

ले ले ले ले ले

Jeremy stopped by Scriven's rooms every day after school and before supper, after a look-in on Lenore and Polly at Stoke cottage, and a stop home to bring Alice tea. Scriven always had copies of the latest editions on hand.

One afternoon, James O'Neal and his sister followed Jeremy on his after-school tour. Slipping through the front door behind him, they ran into the embrace of Lilac's outstretched arms.

"Shouldn't they," Scriven asked, pointing his pipe stem over the paper's edge, "be at the tailor's?"

"No work, they claim," Jeremy said. "Besides, James says they prefer it here."

Scriven nodded.

"As long as they're quiet."

His face was back in The Advertiser's dispatches.

Lilac found cushions for the children and a pair of books to read. At the cabinet, she mixed them what she called her magic elixir: cold tea, rosewater, lemon, honey, brandy.

"Lenore is well?" Scriven asked.

"Very well," Jeremy said. "Polly's sprouted a tooth."

"Tell her to visit and to bring the little one. Your mother?"

"She's well."

"You should invite her along too."

"No," Jeremy said, rather too quickly.

"Shouldn't you be at home, with her?"

"I also prefer it here."

"Seems unfortunate for her to spend so much time alone, especially given her condition."

"She's fine. She and our landlady have discovered a mutual love of whist. She made a fourth when Mrs. Edwards passed."

"I thought you said those old spectacles no longer worked."

"They use extra-large cards. Lots of chatter. Suits her well."

Lilac rejoined them.

"Anyone today?" Jeremy asked.

She sat next to Scriven, in the middle armchair. She shook her head.

"Mrs. Forsyth came by," she said as she retrieved a pipe from the side table. She tamped its bowl with a pinch of burley, lit a stick of cedar from the candle, and sparked the tobacco.

"She had no complaints," she continued, between draughts. "None physical, at least. She'd brought pamphlets for me. An unfortunate woman's path to redemption."

Jeremy sat in the third armchair, grimacing sympathetically. Lilac exhaled a cylinder of blue-grey over the children's heads.

"A toxic soot, I thought you told us."

Jeremy pulled his own pipe from his pocket.

"She's reversed her considered opinion," Scriven said

"Haven't," she said. "Still a toxin. One among many. One that gives pleasure."

Jeremy pinched some burley from the canister and

tamped it into the clay bowl. He lit it with the cedar strip.

"'Lil," he said, "I'm sure they'll return."

"I think I've seen your mother only twice in the last year Castor," Scriven said. "Charming woman. Amusing company."

"In small doses."

"Don't be churlish Mr. Castor. Family's important."

"Family," Jeremy repeated. He was going to say something about how they had never met any of Scriven's family. He wanted to remark on how, in fact, he'd never even mentioned them.

"Like ours," James O'Neal's sister said, looking up from the page open before her, the picture of Nice Folks.

Scriven, Lilac, and Jeremy sat in the arc of the three armchairs, puffing pipes, sipping sherry, passing back and forth sections of the Chronicle, Spectator, and Courant, now and then exclaiming at this injustice, and that correspondent's gall. The children sat on cushions at their feet, drinking their elixirs, James reading from Swift and Walter Scott, his sister thumbing a picture book. Each new, fading afternoon unfolded in the same way. Lenore and Polly began to make more visits. Jeremy began to bring Alice along. She delighted in Polly and she sewed and knitted her all manner of toy and doll.

Often, their idylls were interrupted by a knock on the door. James would answer it. He would come back to the parlour and hand Scriven a letter to the editor with a note from Macaulay or Pringle stating, "we regret to inform you that we were unable to print your letter...," sometimes due to "lack of space" or "unfortunate word choice". Sometimes there was no reason at all. Scriven had sent fifteen letters that month. Jeremy had written ten. All rejected. Scriven had submitted three columns on men's attire: a guide to hose, a treatment of cockades, a meditation on cuffs. None had been accepted. There were limitations of space in the Chronicle. There was a paper shortage.

Both Scriven and Jeremy had brought the issue up at several meetings of the Ancient Number Three where Macaulay and Pringle were long time members. Above all, Freemasons were reasonable men. They were brothers. Men who desired nothing so much as bringing light. Before each meeting Scriven had passed his indigo-laden ox horn several extra times through the grey stretches and shaped the sweep with an additional dollop of pomade. He'd ensured maximum starch in the snowy, linen rectangle. He'd required Cranston to adjust the Oriental three times after its initial tying. He'd emptied his gallipots of ambergris and bismuth magistery; the skin of his face gleamed like fine bone china. Through superior eloquence, exceptional bearing, sublime grace, he and Jeremy would persuade them that, despite his querulous way, the gadfly Robert Gourlay often made some interesting points. An agitator, yes. Sweaty-toothed, without doubt. But what he agitated for was worth considering. Scriven would convince them that all voices should be heard. He'd remind them of John 8:7 and how his miraculous assistant had cured McTaggart's infant's colic,

Abernethy's wife's biliousness, Wotherspoon's gout. He'd request from the Chronicle a retraction.

Each time it was the same. Thomson, officious hatter and Worshipful Master, would remind the brothers, with his nasal, schoolteacher's tone, that the Ancient Number Three, any lodge for that matter, is not the venue for political speech. The members would chorus their agreement. Scriven and Jeremy would retake their seats.

Whole weeks elapsed without an appointment. All the implements had been polished and re-arranged. The phials and ampoules had been emptied, rinsed, and re-filled. The scales gleamed.

The tobacco canister needed re-filling more frequently. On days when the children arrived, Lilac would make three magic elixirs. The third she made for herself, salted with drops from the amethyst ampoule. She would sprawl languidly in her chair, one trousered leg hooked over its arm. She would linger over the front page of the Chronicle while Scriven waited for her to finish, having already scoured the Advertiser. Finally, she would let the front-page parachute to the floor, oblivious of his glare. He would retrieve it, smooth it, and begin to read.

Jeremy began attending more meetings of the Headstrong Club. He had brought copies of Robert Gourlay's collected writing. He'd argued that for the province to progress, for the general inhabitants to thrive, for there to be social and economic justice, they needed to start adopting some of Gourlay's recommendations. They needed a universal education policy. The current stratification was systematically unfair. He often got a sympathetic hearing, but he always had the sense he was preaching to the converted.

Jeremy raged when his tenth letter The Chronicle was returned with the note:

> Dear Mr. Castor,
> Your letter is received but we think your remarks too severe for publication.

"We need to establish our own paper," he said to Scriven.

The doctor didn't respond. He was engrossed in The Chronicle's reporting of the July convention, the Upper Canadian Convention of Friends to Enquiry. A petition had been drafted, calling for general provincial elections. They presented it to lieutenant governor Peregrine Maitland. A letter in the paper by the Rector of York claimed that the results of the convention should be thrown out. He claimed that Robert Gourlay had directed the members of the ill-attended convention like children.

"Miss Evans," Scriven said.

Lilac's eyes continued to meander the columns of page three.

"Lilac!"

"Mm?"

"Fetch me some paper, the quill, and the inkpot, will you?" he asked.

Lilac gazed at him.

"My quill!"

"James," she said, softly.

The boy lifted his head from his book.

"Please fetch the doctor his quill."

"And the paper and inkpot," Scriven called after him.

Another letter was scratched out and delivered to the Chronicle.

It was returned by trotter the next day.

Scriven attended a September meeting of the Lancasterian School board. Christopher Hagerman read out a letter from Schoolmaster, declaring his deep reservations about keeping Jeremy on as abecedarian. There was an initial show of hands. Hagerman, Macaulay, and Mr. Stanton were for finding an immediate replacement. Scriven, Lenore, and Mrs. Smith demurred. Scriven asked if he may speak. He began a stirring defense of free inquiry and the unparalleled pedagogical capacity possessed by his friend, Mr. Castor. He was unable to finish. Hagerman, Macaulay, and Stanton had stormed out.

In November, Robert Gourlay was accused of having no fixed place of residence, of being an evil minded and seditious person, and of not taking the oath of allegiance to Upper Canada. He was therefore subject under the Sedition Act of 1804. He was imprisoned at Niagara without bail.

Scriven reached for his quill. Surely, the Chronicle would print his strongly worded letter.

It was returned, the next day, unopened.

At the next meeting of the Headstrong Club, Scriven discussed the matter with Hugh Thomson. The Chronicle hadn't been publishing his letters either.

"What we need," Scriven said, "is a press that is

open to all parties but is under the control of none. It is loyal and patriotic to be a friend of free enquiry. We could combine and found our own. We could call it the Kingston Herald."

"It's an interesting idea Creedence."

"With you editing and publishing and me supplying editorial content we could have the most popular broadsheet in Upper Canada. Knock the Chronicle from its pedestal."

"Yes, but... I don't know how to put this diplomatically, given your situation, I worry that there is a perception of you in the public, not altogether favourable. Something, perhaps, that should be cleared up."

"Et tu? Does no-one in this most righteous Salem believe in redemption? I won't turn that young lady out into the cold. Not ever. She has the makings of a first-rate doctor. Not an apprentice, a doctor."

"It's no use making this case to me Creedence, you need to make it to the citizens, to the papers."

"They won't print my letters!"

Thomson gave Scriven a manuscript: St. Ursula's Convent, or the Nun of Canada, a novel written by Julia Hart, of Kingston. Thomson said he was thinking about printing it if he ever got into the business; the first novel published in Upper Canada, written by an Upper Canadian. Scriven decided he would convince Thomson to print his play first. That night, when he returned from the Headstrong Club, he found Lilac still awake, waiting for him. She again offered to resign and to leave him. He refused her angrily.

Lilac passed Jeremy the front page of the Chronicle. She waited for Scriven to finish with page three. Impatient, she got to her feet and made for the cabinet. She had just measured out the tea and brandy. Scriven emitted a high-pitched keening, a sound you might expect a ghost to make, and it caused her to drop the crystal stopper of the amethyst ampoule. She looked back at the trio of armchairs. Jeremy stared at Scriven. James and his sister looked up at him from their open books. His face had drained of blood. There was no distinction between it and the pallor of his cravat.

"Don't read the letters then," Lilac said. "You get so upset."

"Miss Evans," Scriven said, with unnatural evenness, "since you are up, could you bring me my writing box?"

Lilac huffed. She continued making her elixir.

"James," she said, without looking around.

"Never mind," Scriven said to the boy. "I must step out."

Scriven rose from his chair, clutching the arm for support.

"Cranston!" he called. "My coat."

"Shall I come with you?" Jeremy asked, with concern.

"No!"

Jeremy's face darkened.

"It's fine." Scriven lowered his tone. "You wait here. I'll be right back."

As he waited for Cranston, Scriven began folding page three of the Chronicle.

"I haven't read that section yet," Lilac said, returning.

Scriven didn't answer. He managed seven folds, stuffed the wad of paper into a coat pocket, stepped into his Hessian boots, and left.

ɞ ɞ ɞ ɞ ɞ

Scriven stood in the Chronicle office, before Stephen Miles, hat in hand, his fingers fidgeting the brim.

"It must be retracted!" he cried. "This isn't news. It's fakery."

"I'm just the printer Creedence."

"It's calumny. You wouldn't have published anything so lurid."

"Sells a paper, I suppose."

"Where is Macaulay? I should speak to him."

"Mr. Macaulay and Mr. Pringle aren't here. They don't always come in."

"Surely you can convince them."

"It's no longer my place."

"Who is this Opprobrious? Why does he persecute me?"

Miles looked up from the type case. He looked away quickly. His tight-lipped smile was meant to convey some measure of sympathy.

"I must be allowed to respond."

"Write a letter, by all means. I'll make sure it is delivered to the editors."

"Will it be published?"

"I can't say."

"It's a libel."

"Is it true?"

"An event taken out of context."
"Perhaps. But, is it true?"

❧ ❧ ❧ ❧ ❧

When Scriven returned, he found the letter, clipped from the Chronicle, tacked to his front door:

Public Service

Your humble correspondent begs to inform subscribers of an abomination. A copy of the Bournemouth Examiner, dated July 15th, 1813, has come into our possession. It contains a letter, re-printed below, from one Vindicator, who relates the depravity rife in that apparent Gomorrah. Vigilant readers will note something familiar about the well-dressed man of a distinguished family, found in the attic of a disorderly house, arrested for keeping company with a catamite, suspected of indorsing or playing back gammon, as it is known in Moorfields parlance. This man, if he may be called as such, was spared the pillory, aided by a sizeable donation to the local hospital for foundlings. What of our own Dr. Creedence Scriven, the William St. go-between, of whom nothing is known prior to his arrival in the autumn of 1813?

Watchfully,

Opprobrious

He tore the clipping down and re-entered his rooms. Inside, he found Jeremy and Lilac looking back at him from their armchairs. James and his sister lifted their heads from their books and stared.

"Lenore," he said, seeing her occupying the chaise lounge, Polly in a bassinet at her feet.

She had a copy of the Chronicle folded on her lap.

"You must understand," Scriven started. "It was a house call. That's all. His mother had come to see me. She asked if I would go in to see him, make sure he was well."

Scriven paused. His audience waited. He couldn't discern anything from their blank expressions, neither doubt nor disgust. He continued.

"I examined him. Nothing happened. Constables came. I explained everything."

Still they stared back at him. No-one spoke.

"I was fully acquitted!"

Scriven met Jeremy's eye. Unlike Stephen Miles, Jeremy did not avert his gaze. Lenore got up from her chair and crossed the room. She reached up, kissed Scriven's cheek, and wrapped her arms around him. She led him back to his usual chair. Jeremy poured him a sherry. He guided his fingers around the glass as he did for Alice and her teacup every night. He remained standing beside him, hand on his shoulder. Lilac brought him his pipe and his writing box. She picked up the remainder of the Chronicle.

"Thank you, Miss Evans," he said, "I don't feel much like reading at the moment."

The January 5th edition of the Chronicle was the last Scriven would ever read. He spouted a mouthful of sherry over the notice printed on page three.

Hugh C. Thomson,

OF KINGSTON,

Proposes to Establish

A candid, impartial, independent

NEWS-PAPER, TO BE ENTITLED

The Upper-Canada Herald:

Which will be published weekly, as soon as the necessary arrangements for the purpose can be made, and carried into effect.

The Editor assures his friends and the public, that his Paper shall be loyal and patriotic, open to all parties, but under the control of none; and, as instructive, entertaining and authentic as his best exertions can make it: and he therefore respectfully solicits a share of their support. The Upper Canada Herald will be printed on Paper of good quality and size, with fair, legible Types, and delivered to subscribers at One Pound per Annum, (exclusive of postage) payable half yearly in advance.

Kingston, January 4, 1819

"I suppose," Scriven said, wiping his face with his handkerchief, "I can overlook the plagiarism and the poaching of a good idea. I'd rather hoped that it would be a joint effort. Still, I must see the positive. I'll send a letter so eminently reasonable and fair-minded that it will change everything. Surely, it will find a home in this new Herald."

All work on the play was put on hold. Scriven wrote, edited, and rewrote his multi-page letter five times. While Lilac slept, he read it to Jeremy and incorporated his suggested changes. He and Jeremy brought it to Stoke Cottage and, while Polly slept, read it to Lenore to get her critiques.

Finally, a week later, the letter was ready for delivery to the Herald office.

It was returned a day later.

"Dear Creedence," the note read, "Thank you for your letter. It is well phrased. Unfortunately, it can't be published at this time. In these early days of our press, we aim to attract a wide and temperate audience. We fear jeopardizing this effort by printing anything too iconoclastic. We risk alienating our readership. Also, as I'm sure you're aware, there is a severe shortage of paper and thus, limited space. Please accept this complimentary copy of our first issue as a token of gratitude for your contribution."

"Shortage of paper?" Scriven cried. "Blast him!"

Lilac whimpered at the intrusion into her torpid dreams. She rolled and sank back into the other side of the chaise lounge. Scriven crumpled the page, balled it, and hurled it at James' head. The boy leapt to his feet, startled. He grabbed his sister's hand and they bolted into the next room. Scriven snatched up the Herald. Amid the list of agents, the terms, the advertising rates, the latest statutes, the sale bills; he saw this short announcement:

> ### Notice to Printers.
>
> FOR SALE, on reasonable terms, a Printing Press, constructed on the most approved plan—and which has not been in use for more than four or five weeks, sitting idle in Montreal. Also, a complete assortment of new types and furniture. Application may be made to the Editor of the Herald, who is agent for the proprietor.

"James," Scriven called. "My apologies, son. Bring me the writing box, will you please?"

James fetched the box. Scriven pulled from it a sheet of paper. He picked up the quill, dipped it in the inkpot, and wrote his application. At the bottom, he underlined his postscript twice: *Will match any bid.* He dusted the pounce and, when the ink was dry, he folded it, sealed it, and handed it to James.

"For Mr. Thomson at the Herald."

For once, his letter wasn't rejected.

Chapter Forty-Two

Boxes of scalpels and hammers, mortars and pestles, apothecary's cabinets, barrister's bookcases holding their leather-clad volumes, cupping jars, plasters and crutches, glass jugs free of leeches, a constellation of vials, bottles, and flasks, the stethoscope, the burnished scales; these were packed and stowed in the corner of Scriven's bedroom. They made room for the bed and platen, the inking balls, the slanting bureaux with their upper and lower cases of type, the boxes of quoins and other furniture, the chests containing the sticks, and bodkins, and sheep's feet.

Lilac carried an armful of compresses and gauze into the back room. Scriven hauled a jug of linseed oil in the opposite direction.

"Where will we examine the patients when they visit?"

Scriven looked around the empty waiting room.

"What if?"

"If Mrs. Abernethy ever recovers from her grievous moral strain... we'll deal with it when it happens."

Lilac returned for another armful.

"What will I do?"

"You'll be my printer's devil."

The length of plaster in Lilac's hands unraveled.

"My apprentice," Scriven said. "Just as you are now."

"What does it involve?"

"Boiling linseed, mixing ink, treading beaters, distributing type."

She made a skeptical noise through her nose and headed for the back room shaking her head. She passed Squib carrying an ink pail in each hand. He smelled of ammonia. He poked his blackened tongue at her and winked. Lilac stowed the plasters. She rummaged in another box. She retrieved the amethyst ampoule and put it aside.

"You won't be alone," Scriven called. "I've hired help, to get us started. And Jeremy and Lenore have agreed to pitch in."

Mrs. Moore, when she'd learned of equipment being loaded into her William St. property, had accosted Scriven on the street.

"It shouldn't be done," she'd said. "We can't have a commercial venture. I don't mind a respectable doctor's office. This isn't what we'd agreed."

He'd promised her an extra ten guineas with next month's rent.

Scriven returned to the press. They had to disassemble and reassemble the entire apparatus to get it in through the front door. Scriven ran his hand down the length of the devil's tail. A handsome machine, he thought. How fine it looks here, in my parlour. At first glance, the casual observer might think it resembled a guillotine, with the horizontal plank of the coffin and carriage extending through the middle of the broad-shouldered frame that reached from floor to ceiling. But its function could not be more different. The guillotine is an instrument of destruction; an implement of control and intimidation and state power. The printing press is its antipode. Creation is its essence; it has no other purpose. It disseminates. It liberates.

I didn't want to be a doctor, Scriven thought, with breath-taking suddenness. I wanted to write and print great books.

Scriven guided the frisket down into the tympan. He held the rounce handle and began to ease the coffin back and forth on its carriage. He was foremost, he told himself, notwithstanding his obvious literary potential, a man of science. He was not given to superstition. Still, it seemed a magical mechanism. An immaculate sheet of paper, pure potential, could be inserted into its apparatus and, with the pull of a lever, imbued — with a new identity, with anything, an infinite variety of possibilities, of ideas, of plans, of arguments, of emotional screeds, of recipes, of ledgers, of poetry, of absurdity, of tragedy, of manifestos and constitutions and legal codes, of advertisements for soap powder or beaver hats or paregoric elixirs. An endless sheaf of possibility.

Could it be magic enough to undo the damage that has been done? Can it weave the argument, the defence that will restore us?

For a moment, Scriven imagined he could slide himself into the coffin, have Lilac lower the platen, and he could be transported, to a different place, to an earlier time, before last week's Chronicle, before his exile to cold, muddy Kingston, before his sordid arrest, before his own apprenticeship and the patriarch's order to put away childish things, to a time when he wasn't yet

Dr. Scriven, or even Mr. Scriven, to when he was just a whippet, baby brother Creedence, languidly recumbent in the glades of the estate, recessed beyond the mist-bathed hedges and glowering turrets, away from Lord Scriven and Geoffrey, under the watchful eyes of sisters Agnes and Liz, so worldly, so worthy of trust, reading John Donne out loud, laughing at the insinuations he misunderstood, dressing him in rags, dressing him in gowns, dressing him in buckskins and overlarge boots, an imagined paramour, caressing and cosseting and kissing, dressing him the villain, the emir, the distressed damsel, their captive clothes horse, perpetual understudy in the dramas of their vine-tangled stage — afternoons stretched into ages, evenings into epochs. And Edmund, the gamekeeper's boy, his only friend apart from Bede, the sheepdog, and Chester, Moffat, and Molly, disinterested, near-feral cats, and the caged ferret Mephisto. When Liz and Agnes tired of him, he sought out Edmund, the boy with the unmatched cricket bowl. The boy had taught him everything he'd learned. Edmund, with his uncomplicated, wide-set eyes, his endearing jug ears, his fine brows, aging suddenly in front of Scriven's eyes, an accelerated loss of innocence, now grown haggard, lined, whiskered.

"Creedence."

Stephen Miles stood on the other side of the press, pushing his careworn face toward him. He gripped the coffin with both hands, arresting Scriven's motion.

"Miles!"

"The first thing we learn," the print master said, "the press is not a gimcrack."

"Let me explain," Scriven said. "That gossip..."

Miles waved him off.

"Not so spacious," Miles said. "Ceilings are low. The windows small. Not much light."

"Ours is a lean operation Miles."

Miles ranged his eye around the room, at the stacks of boxes, the piles of jumbled type, the scattered sheets of paper.

"I'm not sure you're justified in terming it an operation, lean or otherwise."

Scriven nodded.

"So."

Miles clapped his hands together. He sent Squib to the street to set the linseed simmering, to prepare the ink. Miles walked around the press. He stopped. He looked Scriven up and down.

"What is it?" Scriven asked.

"Polished calfskin Hessians. Fitted deerskin trousers. Conspicuous ruffles on a white shirt. A pearl cravat."

"Yes."

"You look a damp, fresh sheet. A sponge for ink."

Scriven patted the lapels of his frock coat and looked down his front.

"Rags, Creedence. That's what you want. Smocks. Wooden clogs. Rags, rags, and lots of rags."

As Miles began to examine the press, to test its balance, the resistance of its levers, the friction of its spindles, Scriven and Lilac retired to their rooms to get changed.

Miles took them on a tour. He demonstrated how the sheet of paper was inserted into the tympan and how the frisket was lowered to keep it steady. He showed them where the galleys of type were set on the stone. He indicated the precise mark to which the coffin should be rolled before pulling the devil's tail.

Jeremy arrived mid-afternoon, bringing with him James and his sister, Lenore, Polly, and Mrs. Langley, in case Polly got fussy. Alice too, clutching the crook of his elbow with one hand, a bag of knitting and sewing work in the other. Miles showed them the type cases, the upper ones with the capitalized letters, and how they should be arranged, the vowel openings, the t and s slots, with their larger quantities of metal casts. He explained how to set type onto the stick, putting it in backwards so that it read properly when printed.

"Mind your p's and q's," he said. "They are the mirror image of each other and easy to confuse. If you need a p reach for a q. And vice versa."

Squib demonstrated how to prepare the ink balls. He urinated into a cauldron and invited the others to do as well. When none accepted, he stepped in, grinning, mashing piss and leather between his toes.

"While Squib is softening the beaters," Miles said, "how about we begin a practice page? There is no better way to learn. What should we start with? Something from scripture?"

"Too wordy for beginners, perhaps?" Scriven asked.

"How about a simple advertisement?"

"A playbill."

"*Bespoke Bespeaks!*" cried Lenore. "The first playbill of your professional career, Creedence."

Miles ran a damp sponge over the sheet of paper, to plump it up, to increase the adhesion and bite. He guided them through using the majuscule type for the heading, the quadrats for creating spaces, placing the type on the sticks, and arranging them in columns on the composing stone. They placed quoins on either side of the galleys inside the frame to centre them. By the time the apprentices considered their simple playbill finished, Squib had finished softening the inking balls and he had prepared the ink. He poured out a measure on an inking stone, dabbed the balls into it, and rolled them over each other to even the coverage. He beat the type, deftly tapping the balls over the entire area. Miles placed the sheet in the tympan, closed the frisket, folded them both down on the stone and rolled the coffin in under the platen.

"Who will pull the tail?"

"Creedence," Lenore said, "it should be you."

Scriven stepped up to the press and tugged the lever. The platen screwed down and embraced the paper. He released it.

"Gently," Miles said, as he rolled the coffin back.

With one consistent motion, he lifted the tympan from the stone. It made a kissing sound as it disengaged from the ink-sticky type. Miles raised the frisket and peeled the paper from the tympan. He held it up to show his apprentices:

espeaksB espokeB

"You managed the p's, at least," Miles said.

He flipped the paper over.

"Try again," he said.

They continued for three more hours. Jeremy stepped out with four shillings Scriven had given him. He returned with meat and vegetable pies and a jug of cold ale. They had supper and then they continued setting, proofing, inking, and pressing for another three hours. Lenore and Mrs. Langley took Polly home for putting to bed. Jeremy took Alice home for the evening's final cup of tea. James and his sister left for their lodging at the tailor's. They all returned the following day, mid-afternoon. And the next day. And every day that week. They perfected the playbill. The next week they moved on to a sample broadsheet with its many columns. They ordered four tokens of paper.

"This is boring," Lilac said, as she took a sip from the elixir she kept nearby. She reached for a capital *B*.

"Focus, Miss Evans," Miles said, pointing at the *g* she had on her stick.

She made a noise of disgust. She pushed six of the letters off the stick, removed the *g*, and put it at the end.

"At the Gazette, we used to have someone read to us. To ease the tedium. Something from Paul's epistles, perhaps? Romans? Corinthians?"

"We're all picking at type," Lilac said, "or distributing. Or stamping paper. Who can read?"

"James' sister can do it," Jeremy said, seeing her sitting on a chair in the corner, gnawing linen. "'Twill be good practice for her. Homework," he said, smiling.

They settled on epistles. Letters from Robert Gourlay. And the Rector of York. Nemesis, Castigator, Traveller, Briton, Canadian, and others. They put a stack of Gazettes, Chronicles, and Heralds on a table in front of James' sister. She began to read, quietly at first. None could hear her over the clink of type and the rattle of sticks. Jeremy and James encouraged her to project. She got louder and louder, until her voice rang like a clarion.

Miles took Scriven aside.

"Have you decided on a name?"

"Mirror."

"Let the devils caper. We'll write a notice and design a masthead."

The next issue of the Herald displayed a notice:

Dr. Creedence Scriven,
OF KINGSTON, UPPER CANADA
Hereby announces
The Kingston Mirror

Unbiased and true, just and unafraid

The *Kingston Mirror* to be published weekly, beginning the first week of February, 1819. It will be printed on a modern press with first rate paper and new, clean types. It will be available to subscribers for Eighteen Shillings per Annum (plus postage), paid in advance. The Editor notifies his friends, and the general Public, that his Paper is neither for the Crown, nor against it; he seeks a variety of voices, to inform and entertain, with articles both political and literary. Always, to shed light.

Please note that printing for all occasions: advertisements, playbills, pamphlets, etc. can be achieved at the Mirror at fair prices.

Kingston, January 30, 1819

Scriven opened the two bottles of Perrier-Jouët that he'd been sitting in the window. He poured out ten glasses.

"Creedence," Miles said, clinking Scriven's flute. "It's beginning to look like a printer's chapel."

Creedence looked back at him, searching his expression for a hint of sarcasm. There was none.

"Thank you, Stephen. Because of you. May we now return things to how they were."

Chapter Forty-Three

Each of the last few frigid nights, as Lilac had lain beneath her many wool layers, she'd seen in her mind's eye, inverted letters jammed into dense, backward sentences. They lingered long enough to intrigue. They were gone before they could be made intelligible. She was desperate to unpack them, to grab at some meaningful handhold. They slipped through her fingers the moment she'd touched their fragile chains. She hardly slept.

She stared at her stick. Letters contorted; they bent, they blurred. Latin alphabets masqueraded as Cyrillic. Blinking, she put the stick down and crossed the room to the cabinet. She poured the cold tea and brandy. Plus, several drops of Paregoric. She had to shake the ampoule. They wouldn't be obtaining more. It had been a month since Mrs. Forsyth had visited, toting her armful of pamphlets. There was even less chance of an appointment being made now that the doctor's office had transformed into a print shop. *Why would we purchase more Paregoric,* Scriven would ask, *without patients to administer to?* Lilac couldn't decide what depressed her more; never again practicing her newfound vocation or exhausting the Paregoric.

She took her tumbler to the chaise lounge and sat

lengthwise with her knees pulled to her chest. She looked back at her makeshift family. Scriven and Miles sat in the old examination room, writing and editing copy. James stamped the goose leathers with Squib. His sister sat on a stool boosted by two, fat medical tomes, swinging her legs, distributing type into the proper slots. Mrs. Langley dandled Polly on her foot. Jeremy and Lenore set lines of type on the composing stone, laughing and chatting. Alice had pulled a penny whistle from her knitting bag. She'd begun to puff out a rendition of Greensleeves.

Jeremy and Lenore sang together as they worked.

> *Alas my love you do me wrong*
> *To cast me off discourteously;*
> *And I have loved you oh so long*
> *Delighting in your company.*

They smiled as they caught each other's eyes.

> *I have been ready at your hand*
> *To grant whatever thou would'st crave;*
> *I have waged both life and land*
> *Your love and goodwill for to have.*

His hand covered hers when he noticed she'd put an *n* before a *g*.

> *I brought thee petticoats of the best,*
> *Thy smock of silk, both fair and white,*
> *I gave thee jewels for thy chest,*
> *And from them shines a loving light.*

Scriven poked his head from the office door.

"Ah, Miss Evans," he said, seeing Lilac reclined. "Could you get that?"

None had heard the knocking over the music. Lilac dragged herself from the chaise lounge and crossed the room. She opened the front door. A dirty child with a cleft ear stood in the street. He held out a folded piece of paper.

"Chronicle?" he asked, one foot pointed down the street.

Lilac was confused. She'd got up too quickly. The blood rushed. Behind her they'd moved on to Auld Lang's Syne. What was he asking?

"Newspaper?" the child demanded.

"Oh," she said, taking the paper. "Yes. Newspaper."

She leaned against the door jam. She opened the bundle.

"Wait!" she cried down the street. "This is a paper. Not Chronicle. Mirror."

The boy was already around the corner.

"Another letter," she said, blowing through her teeth.

She tucked the paper into her trouser pocket, and she re-entered the chapel.

The group, including Scriven and Miles now, in full voice, harmonized Sweet Nightingale. With the blood rushing in her ears, it sounded far away.

My sweetheart, come along!
Don't you hear the fond song

Scriven attempted to hook her arm and swing her round. She kept walking.

The sweet notes of the nightingale flow?
Don't you hear the fond tale

"Lilac," Scriven called. "Who was at the door? Paper shipment?"

She looked back. They smiled. They sang. They swayed into one another.

Of the sweet nightingale,
As she sings in those valleys below?

"Wrong door," she said. "Wasn't for us."

So be not afraid
To walk in the shade,

"I'm not feeling well," she said, truthfully, "I think I'll lie down a while."

Nor yet in those valleys below,
Nor yet in those valleys below.

❧ ❧ ❧ ❧ ❧

Subscription orders trickled in. Not as many as Scriven had hoped. Enough. A foundation to build upon. He even allowed himself to imagine that one day the operation might be self-sustaining. He'd produced first-rate copy; a pleasing mix of foreign dispatches, local notices, advertisements, poetic musings, humorous asides. Even Miles had remarked on its potential. "As good as anything we'd printed in the Gazette," he'd said.

And, of course, Scriven had worked long and hard on his editorial centerpiece, a rhetorical tour de force that answered all of his critics in great detail, exonerated himself fully with evidence taken from Examiner court reports, testimony from important persons, and an impassioned proof against false judgments, gossip mongering, and phony news. Above all, he argued for redemption for himself and his apprentice. He proclaimed their truth; so much more layered and chromatic than the single note sung in the pages in the Chronicle. The printing press, that magical contrivance; it would reset the story to the beginning.

Still, paper hadn't arrived. They'd used up most of the initial quarter token that had come with the press in practice runs. The copy was complete. The galleys of the first page had been proofed and set. They awaited paper.

Scriven sent an urgent note to Bartlett.

"Paper shortage," was the reply.

"This is madness," he cried. "Do you mean to tell me there isn't a single supplier of paper in this town? We have subscribers. They await their inaugural issues. How will it look if I have to postpone the very first?"

"Paper is dear," Miles said.

"But how are the Chronicle and the Herald printing?"

"Perhaps they have stored a supply."

"We'll obtain some from outside of Kingston. From another mill."

"There isn't one."

"Not in the entire province?"

Miles shook his head.

"This is ridiculous!"

"I've heard of one operating in Lower Canada."

"New York then," Scriven said. "Just across the lake."

"Illegal to import."

Scriven threw his hands in the air. His face pinked.

"An embargo," he cried. "This is how they do it."

He tugged at his cravat. The linen cut into his throat.

"It's impossible."

He paced. He fidgeted with the knot at his windpipe.

"Creedence...," Miles said

There was a knock at the door.

"Lilac!" he yelled. "Stop mooning about. If you aren't going to set type, you can at least get the door."

Lilac shuffled to the door.

"I'm not sure what's got into her. She's been so out of sorts."

She returned with a sealed letter and handed it to Scriven.

"One second," he said to Miles "This might be from Bartlet."

Scriven looked at the face of the letter. It wasn't hastily folded; sent from cross town. It was in a heavy envelope, well-sealed, postmarked Bournemouth.

He opened it:

Dearest Baby Brother,

Father has instructed me to contact you forthwith. We have lately received, by anonymous post, copies of a broadsheet, the Kingston Chronicle. We have been dismayed to read in those editions, a series of contributions made by Opprobrious, carefully marked out by the sender. You will recall that the generous annuity made to you on your embarkation to the colonies was made on the condition that there would be no further publicity of past transgressions, true or otherwise. It was most certainly contingent on an absence of fresh indignities such as that which appeared in the September issue of the Chronicle. As I'm sure you can understand, it is a great embarrassment to Lord Scriven in the City, and in the House.

I am thereby instructed to inform you that your annuity has been rescinded effective immediately. Given what I understand about the nature of your medical practice and other activities and the monies you must have invested from these many years of largesse... I trust that the annuity won't be missed.

Postage will not be paid on future communication.

With filial affection,

Geoffrey

Scriven plodded to the chaise lounge. He sat where Lilac had sat. He sipped from her drink. The clinking, clattering chapel and its grinning, chanting congregation spun before his eyes.

"Creedence," Miles said a third time. "We can make it."

"Can we?"

"Yes, of course, that's what I'm trying to tell you. If we can get the cabbage. Rags."

"Cabbage," Scriven said. He spoke slowly and looked beyond the press in the direction of the street. "That's the nub of the matter isn't it? Money. Always is. A man without cabbage isn't much of a man at all."

Miles paused.

"If we can get some rags," he said, enunciating each word. "We can make the paper."

The two men regarded each other.

"I suppose we can," Scriven said, uncertainly,

holding out the tumbler. "Miss Evans, could I entreat you to make me another?"

"Squib is a master rag cutter. He will guide us."

"That's good then."

"With enough rags, we can make all that we need."

"Excellent," Scriven said, receiving the fresh elixir from Lilac and drinking half. "I must step out."

Scriven attempted to get up from the chaise lounge. Miles helped by taking him by the elbow.

"You get started," Scriven said, retrieving his frock coat and hat. "We must have some lying around. Miss Evans will be able to help you with that. Back soon."

᷒ ᷒ ᷒ ᷒ ᷒

Scriven straightened and extended his right hand. Thomson clasped it and pressed the top of his thumb hard between the first and second knuckles. They released their grip. Thomson gestured to the cane backed chair across from his desk.

"Thank you for seeing me," Scriven said.

"There is always time to meet with a brother."

Scriven took his seat. He shifted. The unpadded maple was hard and unforgiving. He levered two fingers between his neck and the cravat. He'd had Cranston tie an Oriental just as he had a hundred times before. Why did it suffocate?

He opened his mouth to speak.

"I must admit," Thomson said, "it's such a busy time just now. My duties at St. George's. Administering the monies of the Midland District School Society. The

Upper Canada Bank. And the Lancasterian school.
Managing the store..."

Thomson proceeded with his litany. Scriven
watched, hypnotized by the dance of his full, rose-
petalled lips and the rise and fall of his eager chin. He
no longer heard words. The boy's voice — after all,
decades Scriven's junior, a boy is what he was —
brimmed with enthusiasm and élan. A lifetime of
triumphs and defeats lay ahead of him. Scriven shifted
again, pulling at the top hem of his trousers, where it
imprinted at the arc of his paunch. Unconsciously, he
bent at the waist to relieve the pressure. As always,
Thomson's cravat of exquisite, ivory silk was tied into
an American. His frock coat hung flawlessly from his
straight, athletic shoulders. And, his hair. Thick, swept
ardently forward. Unadulterated. Scriven fantasized he
stared into a looking glass, admiring an earlier,
idealized version of himself.

"And Elizabeth is expecting! We're very hopeful this
time."

"My sincerest congratulations."

"You don't have any children, do you?"

Scriven pictured James O'Neal, massaging the ink
bladders beneath his feet, laughing at the latest
grotesque face Squib had pulled. He could see James'
sister, swinging her legs from that high perch, her
expression so serious, having fully absorbed Miles'
sermon about how the type must be distributed properly
lest they get out of sorts. Good little bantlings. Castor's
doing, undoubtedly. And cherubic Polly, the foundling,
oscillating on Mrs. Langley's knee. Urchins were to be
avoided, or so he'd always thought. It hadn't been

unpleasant to have them in the shop. A swatch of colour amid the newsprint grey. It occurred to him; he'd miss them if they weren't there.

"No," he said.

"We pray we'll be blessed."

"I'm sure you will be," Scriven said. "You already are."

"Thank you. Oh, and I have my committee work at the lodge. We haven't seen you there lately Creedence."

"No."

"I hope that bit of unpleasantness in the Chronicle..."

"Hugh, please let me explain about that. I did nothing. I'd made a house call to see the boy, that is all. I didn't realize..."

Thomson raised his hand.

"Creedence," he said. "I'm a man of God. I'm also a committed liberal. Judge not lest. Whatever you have done is between you and your Creator."

Scriven wanted to weep. He wanted to scream. None wanted to know. Not really.

"Oh!" Thomson cried. "And now the Herald! Most exciting of all. It's no small effort to get a press up off the ground. As you well know. What progress at the... at the... Mirror is it?"

"That's what I've come to speak to you about."

"Please."

"Hugh. You recall the primary lesson of the Entered Apprentice."

Thomson formed a practiced smile.

"If you should ever see a friend," Scriven quoted, "or more especially a brother in a like penniless situation, to contribute as liberally to his relief as his situation may require, and your abilities will admit, without material injury to yourself or family."

"Yes, of course."

"You may know that my annuity, provided by my family back in Bournemouth, has been rescinded. I'm unable to draw upon it through the bank."

"It's true, I'm afraid. Still. You must have built up a decent stockpile from that and your practice."

Scriven adjusted his Oriental.

"Creedence?"

"As you know, since you were the agent, I purchased the printing press at an inflated price."

"Match any bid were your instructions. If memory serves."

"It serves admirably. I had to make up the shortfall on credit, based on my ability to pay back through the annuity."

"Yes. Hmm."

"I've already attracted a number of committed subscribers. Once the Mirror becomes operational and we collect our subscriptions, I'll be able to pay it back."

"Good."

"The thing is, Hugh, I need a bridge loan. Until that time."

"Ah!" Thomson said. He rocked back in his chair, clasping his fingers together into a cage, seemingly relieved that the petition had finally been delivered.

"Hmm," he said, again. Bringing his interlocked fingers up to his nose, he made a long series of similar noises. Scriven began to despair.

"This is a tricky matter," Thomson said finally. "I'm acting agent. I must inform the seller, of course."

"Must you?"

"The bank is young. Positively green. Not overflowing in liquidity just now. I'd have to meet with the directors and discuss it. There are other ventures..."

Thomson continued talking, his lips and tongue and chin resuming their frantic gallopade. Scriven watched their beguiling movements a while longer. In the middle of a laborious sentence emphasizing the notions of calculated risks and highly leveraged assets, Scriven stood. He took his hat and cane from the rack. He shook Thomson's hand and nodded at his robustly cheerful 'awfully glad you came by' and his 'hope to see you again soon at old, ancient number three'.

Scriven arrived back at the front door of the print shop. From within, the penny whistle trilled.

For a' that, an' a' that,

sang the combined voices inside,

Our toils obscure, an' a' that,
The rank is but the guinea's stamp,
The man's a man for a' that.

Scriven entered. Lenore sat with the children next to a mound of rags on one side and a pile of fragments on the other. They sang while they cut rags with scissors. Miles and Squib were busy with wood and hammers, building frames and deckles to hold the paper. Jeremy ground cloth fragments with the same mortar and pestle that a few months earlier had been used to powder benzoin, jalapa, and St. John's wort.

"I told them," Lilac said, "it isn't a prescribed use of the mortar and pestle. I do hope they won't ruin the enamel. Should be kept hygienic."

Scriven nodded.

"Creedence," Miles said when he caught sight of him. "I've started Mr. Castor on the grinding. A big bit of timber."

Scriven nodded.

"It's a good start," Miles said. "I think we probably have enough for another quarter token. But we'll need more. Cotton or linen. Wool's no good, especially if it's dyed. Underthings, ideally. Drawers, bloomers, the like."

"Shabby unmentionables," Alice said, "fitting for a newspaper, wouldn't you say?"

"Could you," Miles continued, "buy some more rags from some nearby tailor?"

No, Scriven said. He hadn't moved from where he stood. He watched Jeremy grind the rags. No, he repeated. He didn't offer further explanation. Miles exchanged glances with Jeremy and Lenore.

"We may not have enough for the first issue," Miles said.

Scriven shuffled into his bedroom.

"Creedence," Lenore called out. "Is everything all right?"

He returned with an armful of shirts, trousers, stockings, scarves, kerchiefs, and nightcaps. He dropped them on top of the mound next to Lenore.

"Excellent," Miles clapped his hands together. "Top notch."

"Creedence," Lenore said, as she ran a fine linen sleeve through her fingers, "are you sure?"

He was already back in his bedroom. He returned with an armful of drawers, leggings, waistcoats, vests, and gloves. He dropped them on the pile. He made four more trips. On the third trip, Cranston had tried to intervene, offended that this eminent wardrobe could be reduced to newsprint. Scriven had given him his last guinea and had informed him that he was terminated, that he no longer needed him.

"Don't worry," Lenore had said to Cranston as he packed his things and prepared to leave. "Take the day off tomorrow. He'll have returned to his old self by Monday."

Scriven changed into his raggedy pressman's uniform and wooden clogs and dropped the clothes he'd worn to the bank in the pile. On his final trip, he returned with a giant bouquet of cravats, all he owned. He dropped them on the pile.

"Are you sure," Lenore asked again.

Scriven nodded.

"'Twill be the finest newsprint in the colonies," Miles said.

"Perhaps we should adjourn for the day," Jeremy said. "It's been a hard shift we've put in. And, it's nearly the Sabbath. We all could use a rest, I warrant."

"Aye, you're correct Castor," Miles said. "Fatigue is error's handmaiden. Creedence, you aren't yet accustomed to a pressman's hours."

Scriven nodded.

"Get thee to bed. Nurse," he said to Lilac, "make sure our patient follows orders."

Lilac regarded him, her own eyes cloudy and heavy-lidded.

"Until Monday?" Miles said.

The makeshift family of printers took their leave and returned to their homes.

Lilac took a few steps toward Scriven. He sat in the chair between the rags and the fragments.

"Another elixir," he said, "if you please, Miss Evans."

She crossed to the cabinet and emptied the last of the Paregoric into a tumbler of tea and brandy and honey. She took a long sip. She topped it with more brandy.

"To bed?" she asked, putting the drink in his hand.

He shook his head. Lilac shuffled to her little room, side stepped the crates of medical equipment, and slid under the woolen blankets. She closed her eyes and awaited the parade of contrary letters.

Scriven sat back in his chair. He surveyed the mound of clothing; a lifetime's sartorial reckoning, each article representing a moment of ecstatic promise, the possibility of a different, more lustrous, Creedence Scriven; none of them quite fulfilled. He picked up Lilac's tailoring scissors from the nearby table. They had surprising heft. He ran his finger over the letters pressed into the grey steel of the blade. He ran his thumb obliquely along its shearing edge. He jabbed its terminal point against his thumb. A crimson bead slowly formed on the whorl. Scriven extended his arm over the mound of clothing. The bead of blood expanded and dropped, marking the end of the pearl cravat with a crimson asterisk. He opened the blades wide. As long and as sharp as any amputation knife. He plucked the speckled cravat from the top of the pile.

He began cutting.

Chapter Forty-Four

When the first rock came through the window Scriven remained slumped in his chair. The second rock flickered the single lamp. Was it a nightmare?

Untrimmed wick. Low oil. Abruptly cold. A devilish racket. From the street? From his head? Harsh voices, shrieking. Catamite! Door pounding. Shouting. Catamite! Catamite!

From his head? To jail, Molly. Utter darkness. And noise. Breathless chill. Rolling rum brume. Shouting. A torch. Movement. Shouting. Gourlay lover. So cold. Catamite!

Rags kicked and thrown. Figures and shades. Darkness. Confusion.

Me know don't you. Words reversed. Like set type.

An extra, terrible limb? A cane. Slashing. He stands. He yawps. His throat scorches.

The press! Wondrous device. Pieces falling. Leave him!

New voice. Shrill. Frightful. The doxy! Cane raised. Protect it.

Horn pipe? Hickory strike. Temple. Chapel. Searing. Brilliant light. Fading. Away. Away.

You... kilt... im.

❧ ❧ ❧ ❧ ❧

Scriven opened his eyes. Still dark. One eye completely blind. The other made out shapes. A square penumbra of light where the window used to be. His legs, extending past the end of the chaise lounge. Miss Evans on the floor, at his shoulder, under a coat, dozing. Beyond her, a pandemonium of paper and rags and jumbled equipment. Cases of type tipped to the floor. Sticks, bodkins, quoins, and other furniture scattered like flotsam post-flood.

He sat up. He groaned. His head pounded. Stars constellated his eyes.

"Doctor," Lilac said, rubbing her face.

He put his hand to his temple. Sore and covered in cloth.

"I couldn't find a single uncut rag," Lilac said. "Had to sew some together. The wound is nicely stitched. Treated with a little honey and brandy."

"So cold," he said.

"I'll stoke the stove. Stay put. You've been concussed. I'll make tea."

Lilac stood, shivered, and wriggled into her coat.

"They put out two windows," she said, as she blew at the embers beneath the fresh kindling. She pulled out a stick, lit two candles with it, and threw it back in. "I papered them up. Jammed the door closed too. We should report them to the bailiff, to the magistrate."

Who?

Scriven, for the first time, noticed tympan and frisket sheared from the press, dangling by a splinter. He made a noise that sounded like a gust whistling through the eaves.

"Doctor?" Lilac said, alarmed.

"Miles?"

"No."

"Castor? Lenore? Children?"

She shook her head. She brought the candles over to the chaise lounge and put them on a side table.

"At church, I suspect. 'Tis Sabbath."

"Of course. Of course. We should get ready."

"I think it unwise, Doctor. We'd be late anyway."

He stood up. He saw, amidst the swirl of debris, a piece of paper bent in an unusual shape. Tied to something. A rock. He picked it up and sat again, spots dancing before his eyes. He untied it. A letter.

> To the editor of the most specious Mirror,
> Who do you think you are?
> Inquiringly,
> Opprobrious

He let the rock and paper fall from his hand, reclaimed by the debris.

Lilac brought him a cup of hot tea. She put the wool blanket back around his shoulders. He held the cup between his two hands like it was a glowing coal.

"Pass me a section of the Chronicle, would you?" Scriven asked.

"I'm not sure it's the best thing to be reading a newspaper, in your condition, in this dim light."

"Miss Evans."

"Rest is best, in this situation, I warrant."

"The paper, if you please, Miss Evans."

Lilac searched; rummaging through the mess of torn rags and crumpled newsprint, until she found a section of the Chronicle. She brought it to him.

"Thank you," he said, without taking the paper.

She stood in front of him, holding it out. Scriven stared up at her. He had never looked at her before, not like this. He met her eyes; he beheld them, as if for the first time. It was though he was reading her like a page of text.

"Miss Evans," he said, "Lilac. You are a revelation."

She blushed and turned away.

"Have I told you that before? Because you are. Absolutely first rate. I'm proud to have you as my colleague. And, I hope, my dear friend. Cut from the same cloth, you and I."

Scriven took the Chronicle and snapped it open.

"Thank you," Lilac said. "I think you may be a bit light-headed. I'll pop out and see if Mrs. Moore is back from sermon. Perhaps, I can scrounge some biscuits."

"You stay here," she added, from the foyer.

Scriven, still shrouded in the Chronicle, said nothing. He didn't move. Lilac stepped out and secured the broken latch of the front door with a piece of rope.

Scriven scanned through the usual advertisements, bank notices, foreign correspondence, and the port report. And then, an article headed in oversized block letters:

THEATRE.

Being for the benefit of Mrs. Williams

Mrs. Williams respectfully informs the Ladies and Gentlemen of Kingston of two much admired comedies performed for her benefit: *Wives as They Were and Maids As They Are!* in five acts. Followed by the farce *A Budget of Blunders.*

"Assuredly," Scriven said.

He threw the Chronicle to the ground and looked across the room. There tacked to the wall was the clipping from the Herald advertising the foundation of the Mirror. Next to it, their first practice run, the poorly set playbill advertising *Bespoke Bespeaks*. He got to his feet, swayed, and crossed to his writing desk. He opened one of the drawers of the bureau, pulled from it his manuscript, and crammed it into a satchel. Quill and ink too, just in case. And the newspaper. He crossed the room, ripped the poster and the clipping from their tacks and folded them into the satchel. He headed for the door. Where were his boots? His Hessians? Not by the door. He returned to his bedroom. He looked under the bed. He looked inside the pilfered wardrobe, its door still gaping. Not there. He slammed the wardrobe door shut. He saw his reflection in the see-sawing looking glass. Printer's rags and smock.

"Cranston," he called.

There was no answer. His own voice echoed the shell of his rooms.

"Cranston!"

He trotted back into the sitting room and stopped halfway. He looked around wildly, expecting to see Cranston shimmer from a closet. Scriven spotted his portrait, the one painted by Mr. Wentworth at the Bottle and Glass, the one he'd paid an entire guinea for, hanging over the mantle. So elegant. So refined. So smugly arrogant. So different from the man he had just witnessed in the looking glass. That mocking smile!

Scriven hurried back to his bedroom. His waistcoat

hung from the back of the door. It was of finest merino wool, useless for paper; thus spared from the cutting. He removed his smock and replaced it with the waistcoat. Boots could not be found. He wrapped his feet in paper and wedged them into wooden printer's clogs. Again, he made for the door. He saw the makeshift rope holding it closed. It summoned a montage of the night's most diabolical scenes. They came from beyond that door. He looked back and surveyed the wreckage of the parlour. He spied the tailor's shears beneath the chair. Knives. He would take them as well.

❧ ❧ ❧ ❧ ❧

When she returned, with a half dozen biscuits in a toque, cooling, Lilac found the door ajar.

"It's frigid! Why is the door open?" she asked. "Mrs. Moore wasn't in. I had to walk all the way to Stuartsville."

The rooms were quiet, dark, and cold. The fire in the stove had smouldered.

"Doctor?"

No reply.

"Doctor!"

There was a knocking at the door. It was the bailiff with a man carrying a stout chain and padlock.

"Repossession," the bailiff said, "due to unpaid debts."

"It can't be," she said, "the Doctor is a wealthy man."

"Then he should settle his bill. In the meantime...say, don't I know you?"

She shook her head.

"You look familiar."

She turned her face.

"Merciful Lord." The bailiff surveyed the wreckage. "'Twas a grand carouse last night."

"Ruffians," she said. "Drunkards broke in and did this."

"Mm-hmm." He lifted the limp frisket with his index finger.

"Where were you last night? Will you be able to apprehend them?"

The bailiff shrugged.

"We'll need to lock it up."

Lilac looked at him, uncomprehending.

"Please take all of your personal effects. None of the printing equipment please."

"The Doctor isn't here."

"No matter. Let him know he can contact the bailiff's office if and when he would like to retrieve his belongings."

"He lives here."

"I'm sorry. Rent in arrears too, it seems. He'll have to take it up with his creditors."

Lilac stared.

"If you don't mind. A bit snappish, Miss? We have another to do today."

"And it's Sunday."

"Quite."

Lilac went into her room and fetched the sack she'd arrived with two years earlier. She stuffed it with the case of scalpels and hammers, the best mortar and pestle, a collection of vials, bottles, and flasks from the apothecary's cabinet, the stethoscope, and Dr. Buchan's Domestic Medicine. She added some minimal articles of clothing, whatever was woolen and warm, and her periwinkle dress. Some candles, a flint and tinderbox, and her sewing kit. She looked for her tailor's scissors but couldn't find them. She put on as much clothing as she could and put her coat back on. She emptied the biscuits from the toque into a handkerchief and put the toque on her head. She patted the purse in the breast pocket holding her life's savings, wages paid by Scriven. She exited past the two waiting men. They applied the chain and then the padlock.

"Will you investigate the break-in," she called after them.

The bailiff tipped his hat. Lilac waited in front of the locked shopfront for fifteen minutes. Scriven did not show. Her toes and fingers became numb with cold. She could no longer feel her nose. She began to feel conspicuous; sidelong glances from passersby made her uncomfortable.

She would go to see Jeremy. He would know what to do.

The boy with the cleft ear came around the corner.

"You daft bat," he shouted, "That ain't the Chronicle. 'Tis the Mirror. I've had to deliver the damn letter again."

He waggled his fingers at her and raced up the street toward the office of the Chronicle.

The letter. She patted her trouser pocket. It was still there.

Her pulse raced. Could it be a timely intervention? A

promise of payment? A pledge of money from a wealthy subscriber?

She read it:

> Dear Editor,
>
> Your humble correspondent begs to inform subscribers of another outrage against common decency threatening the moral fibres of our fair town. For weeks now it has been an open secret, whispered in Kingston's most reputable salons and club lounges; an Illegitimate Child. It is, of course, regrettable when such a state of affairs should hold in some of the poorer quarters among the less educated. But surely elegant extracts should set an example.
>
> It pains me to mention anyone by name for fear of the shame and embarrassment it might cause. The townswoman is a known confederate of Dr. Creedence Scriven, of whom we've written earlier. We fear a cult of degeneracy in our impressionable, young town. It is therefore our duty to ask, out of the shadows and in this public forum, some uncomfortable questions:
>
> Where was this childless townswoman between last Christmas and the first day of summer? How come no-one has come forth to claim the baby that was left on her porch days after her return? Why has she taken this child in, rather than take it to the foundling hospital, as is customary? Why, on the word of her housekeeper, does she spend so much time in the company of a favourite; the newest schoolteacher of the Lancasterian School? What would her husband think, the illustrious Major, heroically fighting for freedom and justice in New Grenada, if he knew his wife had, in his absence, mysteriously procured an infant?
>
> The moral health of our fledgling community depends upon the rectitude of its leading citizens. It behooves someone, the gentlewoman or her putative paramour, to provide satisfactory answers.
>
> Reluctantly,
> Opprobrious

Lilac refolded the letter and she held it to her breast. She turned and looked at the broken, darkened window of the Mirror, remembering how just a day ago it was full of people singing. She started walking toward the Chronicle.

ôô ôô ôô ôô ôô

Scriven knocked hard on the door of Thomson's house. Smethurst answered.

"Mr. Thomson, please," Scriven said, clutching the satchel to his chest. He shook violently.

"Ah..." Smethurst said, nonplussed.

"I must see him!" Scriven cried. "I must!"

"Smethurst," came a voice from inside. "What ruckus?"

"Sir," Smethurst replied, looking back. Thomson's face appeared over his shoulder.

"Scriven!" he cried. "What are you doing there? Thank you Smethurst, I'll take care of this."

"Hugh," Scriven said, peering up at him from the front step. "I need to speak to you. I have something for you."

A female voice called out from the interior of the house.

"Nothing dear," Thomson called back as he stepped outside and shut the door. "Be just a moment."

"I came to you first Hugh," Scriven said, earnestly. "You're a proper entrepreneur. "

"I just got back from church," Thomson said, indicating his own outfit.

Scriven hopped back and forth in paper stuffed clogs, hatless, hastily waist-coated, swaddled in ink-stained rags, a patchwork bandage encircling his head, his ears and nose bright red.

"You'll love this opportunity," he said.

"Come into the drive shed," Thomson said, looking furtively across the street.

Thomson gripped Scriven by the elbow. He led him into the shed, closed the door, and gestured to a bale of hay.

"We have the Wilkinson's coming over for luncheon," Thomson said, his expression pained.

Scriven sat on the bale with the satchel on his knee.

"What is it Creedence?"

"Won't you sit?"

Thomson shook his head.

Scriven noticed the sheen of Thomson's Sunday suit; the immaculately white shirt, the glossy boots, the pressed frock coat of finest wool. Scriven looked down at his satchel. One of his knees poked through the threadbare linen. He opened the satchel and reached in, surprised by the touch of the scissors' icy steel. He raised his wide eyes to meet Thomson's impatience. The younger man's flesh coloured cravat encircled his soft throat superbly, just grazing the threshold of his downy chin. Scriven's finger traced the lettering pressed into the blade's length.

Thomson folded his arms.

"*Bespoke Bespeaks*," Scriven said, before Thomson could ask him to hurry.

"Pardon?"

"*Bespoke Bespeaks*, Or, How Clothing Makes the Man. A play in five acts."

Scriven pulled the manuscript from his satchel.

"A play?"

"Yes, an epic, heart-rending portrait of a young man who must leave, unjustly, the home that he loves and the one he adores, to make a new life in exile, on a foreign shore. Through his own determination, he builds himself back up, redefines himself. Through adversity, he learns the truth about himself, Hugh. He discovers what sort of cloth he's made from. With elements of gentle comedy and high tragedy, it's sure to be a smash hit. It could have its premiere right here in Kingston. And I'm giving you the right of first refusal."

"Me?"

Scriven nodded. He held out the sheaf of paper.

"I'll sell you full rights. You can take ownership of the first part immediately. I'll send you the ending when I'm done."

"The ending? You haven't even completed it?"

"Almost. Endings are difficult. It needs something unanticipated yet inevitable."

"Creedence. I don't know what you're playing at. I'm a merchant. I'm a church warden. I'm a treasurer of a handful of different philanthropic organizations. I'm an investor and a bank officer. I'm a Freemason. And, I'm the editor of a public press. But, one thing I am not is an impresario. What do I know about theatre?"

"What's to know? Get Mr. Kennedy to stage it. Consider yourself a silent investor."

A woman's voice called from the front of Thomson's house.

"No," Thomson said. "It's absurd Creedence. I must go to luncheon now."

"Hugh," Scriven said, shaking the papers at him, "give it some thought."

"No. I must go."

The woman's voice became increasingly frantic. Scriven began to put the manuscript back into the satchel, slowly and sadly.

"Hurry, please."

"Hugh," Scriven said, after fastening the satchel and getting unsteadily to his feet. "Promise me."

"Exit through the back, if you don't mind," Thomson said, leading Scriven again by the elbow towards a side door of the drive shed.

"Promise me Hugh," Scriven bridling under Thomson's grip, trying to turn to face him, "you will stay true to the Herald's motto."

"It's what I intend," Thomson said, giving Scriven a gentle nudge out the door. "Best go home. It's cold. Get yourself a fearnought will you?"

❧ ❧ ❧ ❧ ❧

Scriven arrived back at the Mirror. He regarded the blackened front window, backed by the heavy woolen blanket, admitting no light, in or out. The battered door was now securely fastened with thick iron chain and a doughty padlock. None were inside. Scriven's shoulder sagged; his arm slackened and the satchel plummeted to within inches of the snow. He stood motionless, staring at his paper stuffed clogs. He inhaled deeply, savouring the icy scald. He put a dampened finger on a link of the chain. It froze instantly, tearing at the skin when he pulled it away. He could not stay here. He could not return to Bournemouth. Scriven patted the pocket of his waistcoat. He smiled, feeling inexplicably and incomparably lighter. Lighter than he had since he was a child. He shuffled from the front of the Mirror, with no urge to look back.

Chapter Forty-Five

Scriven stood outside Lilac's old shack by the glebe. There were words carved into the door: bunter Hotel, drab, doxy. An apple sized hole had been punched through it. Otherwise, the shack was as they had left it; a rectangular pine box stood on end. He patted his waistcoat pocket. He pulled from it the key and, with some coaxing, he eased the padlock tumblers through their rust. He poked his head into the doorway. Mouse droppings covered the tops of the crates and the straw mattress like a handful of scattered caraway seed. It smelled of mildew and dry rot, decay suspended only by the cold. Even so, the floor was dry and, except for the evidence of mice, clean. The board walls kept out most of the bitter wind.

He stepped inside, blowing on his hands. He found the beeswax burner and lit it with the tinderbox. Light filled the confines of the shed. Not one of the candles had more than a third of its original wax. Still, with all five burning, they shed heat. It wasn't warm; but the sharpness of the chill had been blunted. Thirsty, he packed a clay cup with snow and put it on the burner. It occurred to him he should also be hungry.

With the back of his hand, Scriven swept the end of

the mattress least perforated by mouse holes. He sat and propped his back against the wall. He took out sheets of blank paper from his satchel, plus his quill and ink pot. He began to write. Freed by his newfound lightness, words flowed from the nib and filled the pages. He knew now how his story would end.

Within an hour, on the final page, he had written his *Finis* with a double line flourish beneath. He shivered as he collated the pages and stacked them on the crate. He'd been so engrossed in writing, he hadn't noticed that cold had penetrated his every fibre.

Scriven pulled the heavy tailor's scissors from the satchel. He turned them over in his hands and tested their action. The length of polished steel caught the light from the candles and for an instant reflected back a grey, indistinct shape. Scriven looked down at himself. He saw dusky, blotted printer's rags beneath a wrinkled waistcoat. He ran a hand over the thin cloth from his shin up over his knee and thigh and torso. He shivered again, violently. Scriven retrieved the needle and thread from the shelf. He took up the scissors in his right hand. With his left he took the first page of *Bespoke Bespeaks*, the dramatis personae. He began to cut.

He cut and sewed. He sewed and cut. One by one, the candles extinguished themselves. One remained lit. His fingers, wrapped in tubes of paper, were frozen into position, clasped into the scissor handles. He cut the playbill and the newspaper until there was no paper left except for a single clipping.

The last candle fluttered and flickered, suffocating in its own melt. He pulled the scissors from his crabbed fingers. He sat back on the bed and unfolded the clipping. *Public Service Notice, it read*:

Your humble correspondent begs to inform subscribers of an abomination.

Scriven re-read Opprobrious' letter. Again. A third time. He couldn't hold the paper any longer. He brushed useless fingers at his head where it throbbed. The flame furled around the wick and the room went dark before it unfurled again, returned to burn its epilogue. He closed his eyes. It had become too exhausting to do otherwise. On the back of his lids he saw a copy of the Bournemouth Examiner, dated July 15th, 1813. With his mind's eye, he re-read the original article.

He remembered the front door of that so-called disorderly house, a shambling Baroque monstrosity. It had a gargoyle-shaped knocker. Not that anyone knocked. They walked straight in. It's what he'd done. A house call.

He'd scaled the many curving stairs, vaulting the gaps, deaf to the creaking. He'd traversed the murk of the landing with its brocade carpets of worn burgundy and the impossibly ornate balusters some, like rotted teeth, missing here and there. Past the smoke-dense lounge, lamps set low, just enough light to see the bodies draped across divans in layers of pastel chiffon and garish georgette, stupefied faces rouged and mascaraed. Up again. Feeling his way, using the bannister as a guide. Another lounge. A closed door. Smells: the decoction of faded flowers, evaporated spirits, dander and dust, mildew and musk. Noises:

grunts and shrieks, murmurs and oaths. Further.
Narrowing staircases. Darker. Third floor. Fourth. A tap
on the stout, final door. Shouldered open.

The gamekeeper's boy stood in a shaft of waning,
pearl-grey light descending from the overhead dormer
window. He wore a cloth neatly wrapped around his
midsection and a turban-like device on the back of his
head. He stood in the middle of the room, poised
perfectly, shoulders square, one leg bent slightly at the
knee. His pale, sculpted arms hung languidly from his
body, palms turned toward Scriven. Fine, downy hair
traced a line from his sternum to the top of his
loincloth. Sandy hair tufted from beneath the brink of
the turban. His eyes, beneath straw-coloured, finely
shaped brows, shone grey-blue. They twinkled
dreamily, emitting a cool, queer light.

"Creedence," he'd said, drawing the letters out and
lilting it, like it was a lullaby.

"Edmund."

"So long."

"Are you unwell?"

"I'm older."

"I can see. Do you need help?"

"I've missed you."

"I came as soon as I could."

Edmund smiled. His eyelids pooled drops of grey-
blue. He stood in that rapidly diminishing shaft of light
as though installed on a plinth, a shadowy miniature
David.

Creedence gazed. He had never seen anything so
beautiful.

ৰ ৰ ৰ ৰ ৰ

So cold.

How long had he stood there? He took a step. Edmund faded.

Was the window open? Sky beyond the dormer turned to slate. Twilight coming on so soon?

He took another step. He could no longer distinguish the angelic features, the wistful smile. He stepped again. Edmund was barely discernible. He put his hand out. He felt the rounded shoulder. Smooth and cold as marble. The delicate slope of his neck. The cheekbone's perfect ellipse. The trembling of his compliant lips.

Creedence retracted his hand. It was damp.

Edmund, he breathed to the fading spectre of the boy, nothing more now than an evanescent outline. My dear one. My only. I'm sorry.

Distant noise. Shouting. Gruff. Harsh. Whistling. Shrill. Hobnails. Clattering. Thumping.

You don't know me, he heard himself screaming, struggling. You don't know who I am.

The fifth candle guttered.

It could not get colder. It could not get darker.

Chapter Forty-Six

Lilac stood in the doorway of the shack. James O'Neal craned his neck around her.

The growing light of the February morning poured in around them, illuminating Scriven in an attitude of serene repose, his fine, undyed hair made silver and feathery, dressed head to toe in immaculate white. The pages of his script had been reversed and layered, wrapped and stitched together to form the articles of his wardrobe: a pair of slippers in the shape of Hessians, form-fitting britches, classic shirt complete with paper ruffles waving from the chest, abbreviated frock coat. At his neck: the inverted playbill, folded and fastened, stiff and sharp. Glowing as he did in the mid-morning sun, surrounded by the squalor of the dissipated mattress and the verminous debris, he suggested something celestial, fallen to earth.

They heard a distant rumble, like the shudder of a vast underground cable; the sound of the lake ice contracting. Lilac entered the shack. She touched Scriven's lips, now faintly grey-blue. She kissed his frozen cheek. She closed his eyes.

Lilac picked up Scriven's inkpot, cupped it in her hands, and sat next to him on the mattress, hunched over. She motioned to James to join her. He didn't budge; half in, and half out of the doorway. After a while, when she didn't move, he entered, cautiously. He poked her shoulder, worried that she too had become frozen. He jumped when she moved suddenly, tearing a corner from the Chronicle clipping. She took up Scriven's quill from the crate and stirred the thawing ink with it. She scrawled out a note on the paper fragment.

James put his hand on Scriven's papered knee. A kindly man; eyes full of light.

Lilac folded her note and gave it to James. She got to her feet and embraced him tightly. She whispered in his ear.

Lilac hoisted the sack over her shoulder. She headed for the thunder coming from the lake.

Chapter Forty-Seven

Amelia shifted. She rolled. She pulled the blankets higher and tamped them down over her ears. That baying. The deep, drunken slur. Wet murder prowling the fields. The presence she flew from but could never quite elude.

She looked for the moon. It waxed on the other side of the house. Pale, pearly light rebounded from the clouds through the window. Daybreak was hours away.

The hooting came from within. Downstairs.

Amelia sat up. She wrapped a robe around her shoulders and cinched it tight at her waist. She opened the door. She walked to the landing.

"Darling! I won!"

Spafford stood in the middle of the great room. In one hand he held up a jangling leather pouch. He gripped a pewter mug in the other. A medley of bottles and glass covered the low table adjacent to the armchairs, lit by three blazing oil lamps. He wore an empire topper festooned with pinecones and cedar twigs. His knee length Hessians traced a trail of muck and melting snow from the threshold to the centre of the room. Around his neck, he wore a garland of red and black tail feathers.

"We have a guest," he said, slushily. "Miss Amelia Spafford, my darling wife, may I introduce..."

Amelia shrieked.

"We've met," Carmichael said. His tongue tracing his top lip. He removed his straw sennit and bowed.

"Get him out," she said, her voice low. "He's forbidden in this house."

"Shocking," Spafford said. "Shocking hospitality."

"'Tis," Carmichael said.

"Mr. Jones here has offered to take me fishing. Turns out it isn't entirely deathly boring here. Apparently, one can fish through the ice. We'll go tomorrow."

"Can be boring too," Carmichael said, philosophically, "unless offset with a decent quantity of brandy."

"You said you'd meet with Reverend Ainsworth," Amelia said.

"Change of plan. Nothing will keep me from fishing," Spafford shouted. "Where is the applejack, darling?"

"We haven't any. Get him out."

"Ah, Mrs. Simkins," Spafford said, as she and Nat appeared from the shadows, holding a lamp. "Mr. Nathaniel. We have a guest. I can't find the applejack."

"There isn't any," Amelia cried from the landing. "You drank it all. An entire year's supply."

"Impossible," Spafford said, gesturing at the array of nearly finished bottles on the table. "That's hardly a cellar. We must make more next year. Make a note Simkins."

"Sir," Simkins said, looking up at Amelia, inquiringly.

"It's the middle of the night," Amelia said. "He must leave. Nat, please."

Nat moved to escort Carmichael toward the front door.

"Ah. Ah," Spafford said, holding up his white-gloved hand. "This gentlemen is my guest."

Nat stopped. He looked up at Amelia.

"Look at me God damn you!" Spafford cried. "I am the master of this house. And this man is my guest. Treat him with deference."

A shadow flickered from the lamps, darkening the green of Spafford's eyes. He stared up at Amelia, his thumbing rubbing up and down the etching of the mug's handle.

"No matter," he said, finally, a cookied grin softening his face. He rifled the bottles assembled upon the table until he found one half full. He uncorked it and smelled.

"Port," he said. "'Twill do."

Amelia made an exasperated bleat, turned on her heel, retreated to her room, and latched the door.

"Put another log on the fire Nat, we'll be up a while. Thank you Simkins," Spafford called after them, "I'll bellow."

Nat did as he asked. He and Mrs. Simkins returned to their rooms.

"You're the lucky man, Mr. Spafford," Carmichael said, still gazing up at the landing.

"Aye," Spafford said, without conviction, as he distributed the remainder of the port. He, too, followed Carmichael's gaze, back up to the landing.

"So frothy and fair."

"Aye."

"Like melted butter."

"Aye."

"Imagine. Every icy night...," Carmichael paused, noticing Spafford's expression. "Pardon."

Spafford made a surreptitious glance toward the room where he slept, the Colonel's old room.

"It's fine," he clinked his glass against Carmichael's. "Perhaps you should scale those stairs, not me."

"Gladly!"

Spafford gulped at his mug.

"After me," Spafford said.

"Whatever you desire," Carmichael said. "Lord of the manor. You are the lucky man, tonight."

"You wait here," Spafford said, putting the mug down on the table.

At the first stair, he gripped the bannister tightly.

"Your turn next," he said.

Carmichael nodded, grinning.

ক ক ক ক ক

The lock was flimsy; still, Spafford had to shoulder the door twice to force it. Amelia sat up, brought the blanket up to her chin, scowled, and burrowed back into the pillow.

"Darling," Spafford said, stepping inside and pushing it to. He jangled the leather pouch. "I thought you'd be happier about my very good luck. Wilkinson pounded the Tartar. Won it all back and then some."

"Go away."

"So cold," he said, as he advanced on the bed, shedding clothes. "Not at all in accord with the fine opinion of you held downstairs by Carmichael Jones."

"Go away!" she cried, folding the pillow over her ears.

"But darling. I have more good news. More good luck, for you and I. Don't you want to hear my good news?"

"No."

"I have something to show you."

"Leave me alone."

Spafford's hand, white and bloodless, burrowed under the blanket. It nudged below the hem of her cotton shift. Amelia jumped when he grasped her bare calf. She attempted to writhe away, to the furthest point of the bed. He held her fast, his one hand leaving its frostbitten mark above her knee, the other taking her arm and wrenching it behind her back. He got into the bed and put all his weight on her wrist, flat against the small of her back.

"I want to show you something."

"It hurts," she said into the pillow.

"I found it," he whispered into her ear, his breath cool and syrupy.

Spafford hiked up her shift and knelt on the top of her thigh. He took the back of the shift with both hands and tore it from neck to skirt. He pressed his chilled, turgid body against hers. He pushed her face deeper into the pillow.

"My will," he breathed into her ear. "I've found it."

Amelia whimpered.

"I continue to misread you. I thought you'd be pleased," he said. "You've asked for it for so long. I said I would show you. I'm a man of my word. Here it is. A Spafford always consummates."

ɔ̃ ɔ̃ ɔ̃ ɔ̃ ɔ̃

Amelia sat in a chair next to the bed, clothed in a heavy flannel nightgown. She stared at Spafford's head on her pillow, the spill of dark hair lank and greasy. She listened to his stertorous breathing, the fumes in and out. In her lap: one of the Colonel's Henry Nock dueling pistols, packed and primed. This one was no antique. She sat for five minutes, cocking and uncocking the hammer.

Finally, she stood up and went to her bureau. She leaned the pistol against the copy of Plutarch's Lives lying there. She retrieved a key from an inner compartment and used it to open a small box hidden within one of the drawers. She placed Spafford's pouch of guineas into it. She took an amethyst ampoule from out of the box. She held it to the window where the waxing crescent was now just a watermark against the brightening sky. Half full. She tucked the ampoule into her pocket.

She took up the pistol and descended the stairs. She loomed over Carmichael, sleeping hard in front of the decayed fire, beneath a scrounged blanket. She kicked a toppled pewter at his head.

He said something unintelligible, half a-dream, staring into the black hole of the pistol's muzzle.

"Leave," she said.

"Now, Missus," Carmichael said, sitting up, raising his hand. "Mind your beard splitter."

"I'll hole you," she said, cocking the hammer above the priming pan, "and call you intruder."

"Ma'am?" Nat appeared at the corner of the room.

"Nat'll vouch," Amelia said. Nat didn't contradict.

"The ploughman is leaving," Amelia said, as Carmichael got gingerly to his feet. She kept the pistol trained on his chest as he retrieved his coat, hat, and boots.

"He's never to be admitted to this house again, do you understand?"

"Yes ma'am?"

"My regards," Carmichael said, as he slipped out the door, "to your most hospitable husband."

Amelia eased the hammer back down so it would not spark. She barred the door. She turned to Nat and Mrs. Simkins who had now joined him.

"Mr. Spafford overreached last night," she said. "He'll sleep late."

They nodded. She started back up the stairs, still clutching the loaded pistol.

"When he rises," she added, "I'll bring him tea."

℘ ℘ ℘ ℘ ℘

It sounded like a gun shot.

Rupert bolted upright. He pulled the blankets into a bunch around his midsection as if for protection. His nostrils filled with what smelled like burnt powder.

Was he dying?

He scanned the room. Amelia sat nearby, in a wicker chair. She looked back at him, smiling sweetly.

"You were having a dream," she said, with nonchalance.

His head pounded.

"Was I?"

There was an anxious knocking at the door. Mrs. Simkins called from the other side.

"Ma'am?"

"Everything is fine," Amelia shouted back. "Just a bad dream. Thank you, Mrs. Simkins."

Rupert groaned.

"I brought you tea."

Amelia poured from the pot into a waiting cup. Steam rose immediately from the delicate porcelain.

"I dreamt," he said, "I dreamt..."

"Yes. A proper nightmare."

Rupert craned his neck to try to look out the window.

"Is someone...?" he began to ask.

"I thought it best to wake you."

"Is there shooting?"

Amelia's expression of forbearance changed to one of surprise. She turned toward the window.

"I didn't notice."

He sniffed.

"Is that powder?"

"Mr. Jones, perhaps?" she said. "Hunting pigeon?"

Twisting to look out the window had caused the blood to rush and pulse behind his eyes. He winced.

Amelia handed him the cup of tea.

"Part of the nightmare, I reckon," she said, her tone serene. "After all, you were thoroughly refreshed last night."

He sipped from the tea, savouring its restorative

power, effective even from the first. As he did, he regarded Amelia. She returned his gaze, her fond smile undiminished. He slurped a longer draught. Details of the previous night flooded back. He felt an initial flush of pleasure recalling the climactic moment, the gratifying release after months of frustration. He remembered the thrill and satisfaction of the eventual conquest. He drank again. He'd have preferred that it was offered freely. But he'd been left no choice. A moment of passion. He hadn't had time to consider the aftermath. How the weather might change. Now, here she was.

Amelia stood from her chair. She picked up the tea pot and leant across the bed. She aimed the spout above his midsection. She topped the cup, pouring carefully. Before she retook her chair, she met his eyes and smiled again.

"It revives," she said.

He marveled as he took another long draught. He couldn't remember her ever being this pleasant. Not since the early part of that first meeting in the tool shed during the thunderstorm and even that didn't last the moment. A thought occurred: she's one of those that requires bridling. Like the breaking of a spirited filly. She couldn't be happy until she'd been dominated and been made to acknowledge a master. He'd been withholding that from her. The night before had been a gift.

"Also," she said, taking the half empty cup from his hand, "I didn't want you to be late."

Rupert frowned.

"Your appointment with Mr. Jones."

"Ice fishing," she added, when he still didn't understand.

Rupert groaned, lay back, and pulled the blanket up to his chin.

"Tell him never mind."

"He's waiting, as we speak," she said, pulling the blankets back, "at the hut on the lake."

"Another day."

"You arranged it, last night."

"Yes, but I'm feeling a bit..."

"Mr. Jones has it all prepared. I expect he's been there for hours."

He studied her face a moment.

"Why this eagerness?" he asked. "Fishing didn't impress you much last night."

"I look differently at it today. It would be a handsome thing for you to catch us supper."

The way she said it caused a slight stirring.

"I do love to angle," he said. "I'd like to try it through the ice."

"I could come with you."

"Fishing?

"I'd stay in the sleigh and watch."

He measured the metronomic throbbing in his head. It seemed like it might be deadening the pain.

"More tea?" she asked, as if reading his thoughts. "It will stiffen you."

She had fairly purred it. He took the offered cup.

❧ ❧ ❧ ❧ ❧

Rupert descended from the footplate and stepped into the slush. Shivering, he pulled the collar of his fearnought closer around the gooseflesh of his neck. Already he could feel the meltwater seep through the stitching of his boots into his woolen stockings. He walked several paces toward the rime-encrusted beach before he stopped and turned. A pulsing, flickering orb of amber radiated from the middle of the sleigh, pushing back against the dinge of the late winter dawn. Inside, Amelia sat under a buffalo robe, warmed and illuminated, three argand lamps arrayed around her. She stabbed her finger toward the hut standing fifty yards out on the lake.

Why was he outside? Why was he not still in bed, nursing this most vengeful hangover? Rupert took a step back. Amelia rapped the edge of the sleigh with a knitting needle and pointed it across the lake. He sighed. He set out again, stepping gingerly, avoiding the pockets of water skinned with ice. Carmichael waited for him out at that hut, she'd said, kitted out with all the necessary tackle. The pot-bellied stove inside had been stoked, making the shack cozy. See there, she'd said, the wisp of smoke rising from the chimney. He screwed up his bloodshot eyes. He saw only a dirty haze of drizzle and mist, obscuring the structure, coating the trees along the shoreline. I sent Mr. Jones, she'd said, with a picnic lunch and a full bottle of fine, warming brandy. Rupert's stomach wobbled at the thought.

At first, the tea had a miraculous effect. The pain had dissipated. He'd felt resurrected. Now a mild nausea came in waves. Deadening fog replaced the ache in his head. As he peered through the freezing vapour he could no longer distinguish between water and sky, lake and shore. His gait became unsteady. Twice he lurched, losing his footing on the slick stones.

He would have preferred to return to the carriage and be brought back to Willowpath. He would have liked to spend the rest of the day in bed. But it seemed somehow embarrassing and unmanly to do so, after making such a big show of wanting to go fishing the night before, to leave Carmichael waiting, to acknowledge his failure to hold his liquor.

He kept walking. He'd get to the hut and get under a buffalo robe next to the stove. He'd snooze. Let Carmichael tend the fire and mind the lines.

He was on the lake. The flat, wind-swept ice made it easier going. Which was just as well because strength continued to drain from his limbs. His field of vision had narrowed so that he could make out the silhouette of the hut in the gloaming but not much else. Looking back at the carriage he could still make out Amelia glowing in the sleigh. She'd returned to her knitting.

Midway between the shore and hut, he paused. He felt so weak and lightheaded he considered sitting down. He'd sit for just a few minutes. Until the sap returned. But what if it didn't? He couldn't stay there. He'd freeze solid. The hut, shrouded in freezing mist, seemed no closer than it was twenty paces ago. He turned. The carriage stood even further away. Forward or back? He had to make one destination or the other.

It sounded like a gun shot.

He'd dropped to ice level. His lungs emptied. Had he

been hit? He felt no pain. He felt nothing. Numbness to every extremity. What he could see was blurred at the edges. Dream-like. Was he dying? He peered down. His legs had disappeared. His torso had disappeared. Only parts of his arms and hands were visible, intermittently, flailing and thrashing at panels of ice. He was up to his neck.

Frigid air returned to his lungs in great, gulping rasps. He opened his mouth. He couldn't hear his own shrieking. He forced the air back through his vocal cords, hoping the screaming grew louder. Nothing. All was mute.

Rupert pitched shoreward. The yellow light coming from the sleigh remained conspicuous, like a beacon in the fog. Even from that distance, he could see Amelia's face looking back at him. He couldn't discern her expression.

He dug his fingernails into the brittle layer of snow. With waning strength, he hauled himself up onto the ice sheet and out of the gathering lake. The edge gave way.

He clawed again. The ice disintegrated.

His mouth gaped.

Help, he screamed, soundlessly. Save me.

The face looking back watched a moment. Then, returned to a dropped stitch.

Chapter Forty-Eight

Jeremy took his seat and opened the latest edition of the Herald.

"Shouldn't you be at school," Alice asked.

The moment Scriven had been discovered, frozen to death in Lilac's old shack by the glebe, Christopher Hagerman had convened a meeting of the Lancasterian School board. Over Lenore's strenuous objections, his brother had been added to the board. They had voted four to two to dismiss Jeremy from his post for the reason of radicalism. He had been declared unfit to instruct the young, impressionable minds of the district's working and indigent class. Lenore had subsequently resigned her own position on the board.

"Closed," Jeremy said.

"Why?"

"Out of respect."

"For what?"

"Dr. Scriven's death."

Alice murmured her sorrow and approval.

"A lovely man," she said, "such a pity."

She resumed sewing her seam.

Lenore had paid to have Scriven's body removed from the shack and carted to Stoke Cottage. The paper had been carefully pared from his body and preserved. Jeremy had collected some items that had been given to him by Scriven. Lenore found some clothes in her husband's wardrobe that he wouldn't miss. Between them, they were able to dress Scriven from head to toe in an ensemble he would have accepted. Lenore had paid for a burial plot and a simple pine coffin. Stephen Miles, in the capacity of his Methodist ordination, presided over a tasteful ceremony and Scriven was put to rest in the company of his friends and his many lodge brothers, regardless of political or aesthetic allegiance. Even past patients such as Mrs. Abernethy had attended the service. Later, at the Bottle and Glass, Jeremy had made a toast to absent friends, and they all raised their glasses to Dr. Scriven. He'd also toasted Lilac Evans who had first alerted him to Scriven's location and had promptly disappeared.

Lenore had paid for the following notice in the next week's Herald.

In Memoriam

Dr. Creedence Scriven, of Bourne-mouth, died accidentally, on the night of February 24th, from exposure to cold. Dr. Scriven was a kind and generous man who gave liberally to our community and served on many charitable boards. He was a talented man of medicine helping to cure the afflicted of our fellow citizens on many occasions. In addition, he was one of the town's leading literary lights, an inspired playwright, sadly struck down before he could complete his life's work. Not least, he was widely considered to be the best dressed man in Kingston. He was a friend and a patron. We will be at a disadvantage without him and he will be sorely missed.

Jeremy scanned the rest of the Herald, looking for situations advertised. In paying for next month's rent and food for the next week, he had begun to dip into their meagre savings.

Another notice caught his attention.

 **NOTICE**

It has been communicated to this office the identity of the mother of the foundling deposited on the front step of Stoke Cottage last summer. The mother of the infant, now known as Polly, is a Miss Lilac Evans, of no known address. This is the same unfortunate Lilac Evans who spent a month in jail and a half hour in the pillory for the crime of prostitution, two years previous. Miss Evans has herself claimed to be the mother of baby Polly, voluntarily taking responsibility. She has moved from Kingston, vowing to redeem her life in the eyes of her friends and the face of the Lord. Having paid her awful penalty, we wish her every success.

There was a knock at the door. A trotter with a letter.

"Is this the postmaster's office?" Alice asked Jeremy, when he'd returned.

He didn't reply.

"Another from the widow Spafford? Calling you back?"

"Alice. She's re-married."
He opened the letter.

Dearest Jem,

Jeremy looked across at his mother. For once, she'd guessed correctly. He continued reading.

I read the news about your Dr. Scriven in the Herald. Terrible news. My condolences. I did not know him overly well, but he seemed a kind and decent man. I know that you had developed a friendship. He always struck me as somewhat ill-suited, if I may use the phrase, to life in Kingston. Nonetheless, he certainly didn't deserve such a fate.

I understand that you and Dr. Scriven had lately been planning the establishment of a new press; a liberal, nonpartisan broadsheet encouraging local commerce and free trade. I must admit; I have not written only to express my condolences. I have experienced an unexpected windfall. And, as such, I would like to invest it in your venture as a silent backer, to resuscitate your moribund press. I have sent a parallel letter to Mr. Thomson at the Upper Canada Bank instructing him to authorize a bank draught on your behalf to remove any liens from the printing equipment and to pay initial wages of any staff you might need. There is a growing hunger for truth and a diversity of voices in this province, Jeremy. I think it is an excellent opportunity and necessary for progress. I have a name in mind.

Will you be my editor?

I hope we will meet again soon. I've missed you.

I await your answer with hope and expectation. I've enclosed two articles to include in our first edition.

Yours, in commiseration,
Amelia

❧ ❧ ❧ ❧ ❧

Mr. Jeremy Castor,

OF KINGSTON, UPPER CANADA

Hereby announces

The Kingston Guardian

Unbiased and true, just and unafraid

The Kingston Guardian to be published weekly, beginning the first week of March, 1819. It will be printed on a modern press with first rate paper and new, clean types. It will be available to subscribers for One Pound per Annum (plus postage), paid in advance.
The Editor notifies his friends, and the general Public, that his Paper is neither for the Crown, nor against it; he seeks a variety of voices, to inform and entertain, with articles both political, and literary. Always, to shed light.
Please note that printing for all occasions: advertisements, playbills, pamphlets, etc. can be achieved at the Guardian at fair prices.

Kingston, February 28th, 1819

The next week's Herald carried this notice:

Jeremy managed to lure Squib and another type setter away from the Chronicle. Stephen Miles declined. "You don't need me anymore," he'd said. Jeremy also hired James O'Neal and his sister on full time as printer's devils. They each arrived at Scriven's old rooms, the new office of the Guardian, bearing two bulging sacks of clean, white rags, and undergarments.

"Where did you get these," Jeremy asked, amazed.

James didn't answer. He put the sacks in the corner with the rest of the rags. He looked at his shoes.

"Did you come straight from the tailor's?"

Gabby nodded, grinning. She no longer chewed a linen fragment.

"Never mind," Jeremy said, "I don't want to know."

Jeremy watched as Gabby pulled a fresh sheet of paper from the stack next to the press and a pencil from the jar. She sat cross-legged on the floor by the window. She began to doodle, singing to herself as she did:

> *So be not afraid*
> *To walk in the shade,*
> *Nor yet in those valleys below,*
> *Nor yet in those valleys below.*

Jeremy peeked over her shoulder. It was a collection of stick figures, arranged in a room. A family.

He recalled the last few months, the long winter evenings, before Dr. Scriven had been maligned in the press, before he'd lost his annuity. They were a patchwork quilt: Jeremy, Creedence, Lilac, Alice,

Lenore and Polly, James and his sister. They would spend many hours together there, reading, arguing, joking, complaining, laughing. It hadn't been entirely happy. But there had been moments of true contentment. Of connection. Of love.

Aside from Gabby's soft humming, the parlour was quiet. Jeremy looked out the south-facing window above her head. Creedence had left them. He gazed in the direction of the lake. He imagined his cousin Merit, hidden somewhere across this same water, among the log cabins and hunter's lodges. Would they ever see each other again? And where had Lilac gone? He struggled to banish the recurring notion that the spring thaw would reveal her body, slight and bird-like, broken against the shore. The notice that would appear in the Guardian continued to get written in his mind and then struck out.

He looked down at Gabby bent over her sketch. Two smaller stick figures had been added, one with a cap and another with hedgerow hair. Both were smiling. He resolved to make a different life for her.

The first issue of the Kingston Guardian was delivered to subscribers a week later. On the front page, three articles featured prominently:

GONE, BUT NOT FORGOTTEN

Miss Lilac Evans, previous resident of Kingston, has moved on. We hope she finds greener pastures. Some citizens will know that Miss Evans is a keen student of medicine and with her departure our town has lost its most able physician. Those of you who's infant has been cured of colic, or saved from puerpal fever, those of you who can walk again, free of gout; you will understand Kingston's loss. Driven away for a single transgression long past, judged harshly by those among us who consider themselves sinless, she will be keenly missed. We hope she might one day forgive our failings and return to us.

Remember John 8:7.

Friends of Miss Lilac Evans

And,

Willowpath Glass Factory

The subscribers beg leave to acquaint their friends and the public at large that Upper Canada's first glassworks now has in stock a wide ranging inventory, which they offer wholesale and retail, at their Willowpath warehouse located up the Montreal Road on the Spafford grant, on as good a terms as can be had at any manufactory west of Montreal, with a liberal discount made for cash. Country merchants and others are requested to call.

Flutes, tumblers, vases, carafes, window glass, 6x8, 7x9, 7x8 , 8x10, putty and frames, at the most reasonable prices. Please inquire of this office, care of Mr. Jeremy Castor.

March 1819.

And the third:

Tragic News

March 1, 1819

Mr. Rupert Spafford, of Meath, Ireland, found dead, trapped under reformed ice at the southern end of Loughborough Lake, victim of an ill-fated ice fishing expedition. Let this serve as a warning to other would be ice fishers: beware of rotten ice. After a small service, Mr. Spafford was buried in the King's Mill Methodist cemetery. He is survived by his widow, Mrs. Amelia Spafford. He left no will.

Chapter Forty-Nine

Early in July 1821, the Kingston Guardian printed another unfortunate report.

Sad News

Major Peregrine Stokes, occasional resident of Kingston, has been declared missing and presumed dead, a casualty of the heroic attack on Royalist forces during the battle of Carabobo; the decisive victory which observers believe will lead to an independent Venezuelan state and the establishing of Gran Colombia republic. Major Stokes has been posthumously awarded the Order of the Liberator. He is survived by his wife, Lenore Stokes. Mrs. Stokes has organized a memorial service in the Major's honour this Saturday at 1:30 PM at St. George's church. Officers, family, friends, and the public at large may attend to pay their respects.

By July 1822, Lenore had cast off the black veils and gowns of mourning. She had replaced them with white. She looked eagerly for this item on the front page of the early July issue of the Kingston Guardian:

☞ NOTICE

Mr. Jeremy Castor, of Kingston, Upper Canada, begs leave of subscribers to announce his intended marriage to Mrs. Lenore Stokes, widow of the late Major Peregrine Stokes, at St. George's Church, the fifteenth day of July 1822, Stephen Miles presiding. Mr. Castor and Mrs. Stokes hope all friends and family will be able to join them on this joyous day.

Epilogue

By 1824, Hugh Thomson's Herald had the greatest circulation in Upper Canada. He had hired Stephen Miles, now his brother-in-law, away from the Chronicle. It was in that year that he published the country's first novel: St. Ursula's Convent, or the Nun of Canada written by Julia Hart née Beckwith. Mrs. Hart was born in New Brunswick, but later moved to Kingston with her husband, stationer and bookbinder, G.H. Hart. The novel appeared anonymously in two volumes. It garnered a two-page review in the Canadian Magazine, published in Montreal, one of the first literary journals in the Canadas.

These two little volumes, the reviewer wrote, *the one containing 101 pages, and the other 132, printed in large type, upon coarse paper, and charged inordinately high, contain a mass of incidents, all borrowed from other works of imagination, greater than we ever remember to have met with in so small a compass.*

Later that year, the Free and Accepted Masons of Ancient Number Three placed a bottle containing items for posterity in the cavity behind the cornerstone of the newly built County Courthouse and Jail. Hugh Thomson made sure that it included a copy of Mrs. Hart's novel, the first printed in Upper Canada. When no-one was looking, Jeremy Castor slipped in a copy of *Bespoke Bespeaks*, the first dramatic script published in Upper Canada, printed with Caslon's English Roman, in fourteen point, on the finest, linen-sourced paper to be found in the province, designed to last another five hundred years. Close examination would reveal fragments of the best ruffles, kerchiefs, and cravats.

A Short Bio Note:

Morgan Wade's first novel, **The Last Stoic,** edited by Helen Humphreys, was long-listed for the ReLit Prize. His second novel, **Bottle and Glass,** also edited by Helen Humphreys, was featured in the Kingston Writers Fest 2016. In conjunction with Theatre Kingston, Morgan adapted the novel into a site-specific, immersive play that ran through five sold out shows in October 2016. Audience members followed the story through the streets and pubs of Kingston, walking and drinking along with the characters. In the spring of 2017 he collaborated with the Thousand Islands Playhouse in Gananoque to develop a new script for the Sunset Ceremonies at Fort Henry. His short stories and poems have been published in Canadian literary journals and anthologies, including, *The New Quarterly*and *The Nashwaak Review*. Morgan attended the Humber School of Writing and worked with mentor Michael Helm. He lives in Kingston, Ontario.

Acknowledgements:

Many thanks to Richard Grove/Tai of Hidden Brook Press; to Catharine, Ian, Cameron, Patty, and John of the Inkstons for their excellent feedback over the last several years and, in particular, to Art and Corina of the Inkstons for their close readings of the manuscript and helpful comments; to Bruce Geddes for, yet again, being an early reader and providing insightful critiques; to Frank Streicher for reading and discussing an early version; to the Queen's University Archives, the W.D. Jordan Rare Books and Special Collections (especially Kimberley Bell), the Ontario Archives, the National Archives, and the Kingston Public Library for their research support; And to Nancy, love and gratitude for your patience, encouragement, and for continuing to be my first and last reader.